GOOD THING THEY HADN'T
ANNOYED PLUTO OR ZEUS!

"Ah, Doc, is this stuff supposed to be hallucinogenic?"

"Not that I had heard. Why?"

"Because there's a guy made of gold and about twenty feet high standing over there."

Slowly, Chalmers turned to look. The figure strode toward them; when he was near, their chins were level with his kneecaps, and they had to squint their eyes against his brightness. His beautiful, terrible face glared down at them. He was not happy.

"Mortal fools! Know you who I am?"

"We—" Chalmers began.

"I am Phoebus Apollo, Silverbow, Shootafar, Apollo of the Golden Locks, solar deity extraordinaire!" The god bent low and hissed. . . . "You know what happened to mortals who mess with me? Ever hear of Niobe? My sister Diana and I killed her six daughters. Shot them dead! I guess you've heard of Marsyas, the satyr who said he was a better musician than Apollo?"

"I'm not sure," Shea said weakly.

"I skinned *that* bastard alive!" Apollo chuckled sadistically. "I'm going to have to think up something *really* bad for you two!"

"But, but we didn't . . ."

"Oh, shut up, you little worm! And while I'm thinking this over, I want *you* to think it over. I'll be seeing you, mortals, just when you least expect it!" There was a sudden gusting whirlwind and Apollo was gone. . . .

"Well," Chalmers said weakly, "it might have been worse."

"How?"

"How? My dear [. . .] nicer gods. . . ."

THE ENCHANTER REBORN

L. SPRAGUE de CAMP   CHRISTOPHER STASHEFF

BAEN FANTASY

THE ENCHANTER REBORN

Acknowledgements—A few of Don Quixote's statements in *Knight and the Enemy* have been quoted from *Don Quixote* by Miguel de Cervantes Saavedra, translated by J.M. Cohen, Penguin Books' Penguin Design Classics Edition, Viking Penguin, NY, copyright 1950.

—Quotations from the *Te Tao Ching* are from a translation by Robert G. Henricks, Ballantine Books.

A Baen Books Original

Baen Publishing Enterprises
P.O. Box 1403
Riverdale, N.Y. 10471

ISBN: 0-671-72134-8

Cover art by Dean Morrissey

First printing, September 1992

Distributed by
SIMON & SCHUSTER
1230 Avenue of the Americas
New York, N.Y. 10020

Printed in the United States of America

CONTENTS

**Knight and the Enemy* and *Arms and the Enchanter* were developed from outlines by L. Sprague de Camp and Christopher Stasheff.

INTRODUCTION

Christopher Stasheff

I grew up reading a bit of everything, as most of us do—a few biographies, a few mysteries, the occasional Western, some historical novels, the usual run of juvenile books, and, now and then, a science fiction book. SF was only part of my literary diet then. You see, I would finish my current book, but I wouldn't be able to get to the library until Monday night, and there were science fiction books and magazines here and there around the house. My father had been a steady reader of SF since before Hugo Gernsback—the only reason he didn't qualify for First Fandom was because they hadn't invented fandom yet. Mind you, he never read SF exclusively—he insisted on taking time out to read James Joyce, or James Michener, or Henry James, or . . .

No, now, wait a minute. It is not true that Dad only read books by people whose names were "James." In fact, he and Mom had both been English teachers officially, and remained so unofficially all their lives—

still are, in fact; he can't help himself, has to read my manuscripts with a red pencil—so there were great works of literature in the bookcase downstairs, in the bookcase upstairs, on the end table ... I think my mother began her weekly trips to the library just to cut down on the clutter. Anyway, a bored boy could always find a book to read, but there was just as good a chance of finding a Heinlein as a Costain. So I read my merry way through childhood and adolescence. For a while there, I celebrated Christmas every year by rereading Jules Verne's *Journey to the Center of the Earth*. But I was scarcely an avid science fiction fan.

Then, one bored and rainy Tuesday during Easter vacation, I ran out of books to read. As usual, I started looking through the shelves in the living room—and I found a modest-looking volume with the title, *The Incompleat Enchanter*. Well, that looked interesting— especially since someone had apparently made a spelling mistake on "incomplete"—so I took it off to my room, lay down, and opened the first page.

Well. This was interesting. An eccentric psychologist, and a boss who had an idea about traveling to parallel universes.

Parallel universes?

Universes besides ours, where magic might really work? Hey, that was fascinating! And the idea that magic might work according to rules? Hypnotizing!!

Then Harold Shea hit the world of the Norse myths, and I was lost in the Fimbulwinter. It seemed only a short while later that the sound of Heimdall's horn was filling my ears, Ragnarok had begun, and Shea was back in his own universe.

I was hooked. From that time on, I've been a die-hard SF reader.

Oh, mind you, I do still read the occasional non-SF book. I try to read a little bit of everything—Louis

L'Amour, Thomas Pynchon, some Regency romances, Umberto Eco, John D. MacDonald—but ninety percent of what I read is science fiction and fantasy. All because of *The Incompleat Enchanter*.

"Dad!" I said. "This is really great!"

"Like that, do you?" he said, and pulled another book off the shelf. With a proud smile, he opened it to the title page, displayed it before my eyes—and there, to my amazment and incredulity, was a signature that definitely spelled out "L. Sprague de Camp."

"Dad! You got it autographed!"

"That I did." And my father went on to explain, with great delight, that he had actually talked with L. Sprague de Camp. His pedestal instantly grew three inches higher.

Maybe that was part of the magic—finding out that my own parents had actually talked with the fabled greatness of the author of so splendid a story. In the terms de Camp explained in the book, maybe it was the Law of Contagion—or maybe it was just that it suddenly made the author real to me. Up until that time, of course, I had thought of authors as being remote and mythical, sort of like Arthur and his knights. That autograph, and my parents' telling me about their acquaintanceship (yes, it turned out Mom had known L. Sprague and Catherine Crook de Camp, too), were my first hints that authors were human beings, and lived not on Olympus, but in Pennsylvania.

So I became a devout reader of science fiction— and of course, I read everything by de Camp that I could get my hands on.

Of all my reading, I enjoy science fantasy most, even though some eminent authorities in the field assure me that mixing science fiction and fantasy is almost impossible to do well. One of these authorities has written several science fantasies himself (which have influenced me almost as much as *The Incompleat*

Enchanter), so I suppose he knows what he is talking about. I agree that it's hard to do well, so I've built my own writing career trying to do just that.

Of course, any time I start having difficulty, I just remember *The Incompleat Enchanter*.

As Dorothy Parker has assured us, when you learn to read, you'll want to write, and so I did. Of course, I didn't try to write science fiction—to do that, you had to know something about science, and not being a chemistry major or a physics major, I was sure I didn't.

Then, a year out of college, bored and lonely in a new town, I saw an ad for a contest in a science fiction magazine, and decided, Why not? All I had to lose was time, and I had too much of that hanging heavy on my hands, anyway. So what if it didn't work? Nobody but me would ever know.

But it did work, because I'd learned more than I knew.

I'd learned from L. Sprague de Camp, and Lester del Rey, and Robert Heinlein. I had learned from Hal Clement and Theodore Sturgeon and Fritz Leiber. I had learned from Frederik Pohl and Poul Anderson and Isaac Asimov. I had never met any of these illustrious gentlemen, of course—but I had read their books.

And it was *The Incompleat Enchanter* that had set me on the road to this fabled kingdom, that had opened the door to the magical realm.

So my new novel turned into science fantasy very quickly.

That was what I had the most fun with, you see— coming up with scientific explanations for magic, or trying to make science seem magical (which, for me, has never needed much trying, frankly). So I wrote a novel about a secret agent for democracy, who landed on a planet in our own universe, but on which magic seemed to work. The locals assumed his high-tech gadgets were magical, and decided he was a warlock, which he adamantly denied.

Of course, looking back on *The Warlock In Spite of Himself* now, I can see the resemblances between Harold Shea and my own Rod Gallowglass very easily—the young man who doesn't fit in, has a lower self-image than he deserves, and goes looking for a world in which he does fit. Both of them are also emissaries from our mundane universe to magical worlds, and both of them have to learn about magic on the job, and fast. *The Incompleat Enchanter* blended adventure, humor, and romance. I tried to do the same.

The resemblances are even stronger in *Her Majesty's Wizard*, where my hero, Matt Mantrell, has to learn how to work magic under fire, and gets it wrong as often as he gets it right.

An English professor once told me (and the rest of the class) that, in one sense, all modern American authors have been trying to rewrite *Moby Dick*. I suppose I've spent my whole career trying to rewrite *The Incompleat Enchanter*.

But I'm not alone.

There are at least half a dozen authors who have written variations on the magician who has to try to learn magic on the job, and whose spells misfire. This self-taught magus almost always works in a world in which magic operates according to clear, consistent rules that can be learned by anyone who is willing to work at it.

Pratt and de Camp started something—not just an anomalous book, not just a rare hybrid, but a new idea that has grown into a whole sub-genre. New writers keep joining it, new variations keep shooting off. It's alive and very healthy, and produces some of the most delightful, most whimsical, stories of our time.

But the one thing that very few of us manage to do, is to teach as we amuse—at least, not as well as Pratt and de Camp did. Harold Shea goes where no SF hero has gone before, and few have gone since—into the myriad worlds of classical literature. It was from the Harold Shea stories that I first learned of Spenser's *Faerie Queene*; it was "The Roaring Trumpet" that first made the world of Norse myth come alive for me. "Castle of Iron" introduced me to the *Orlando Furioso*, and "The Green Magician" showed me the wondrous world of Irish mythology.

We have tried to do the same, in this book. Each of the stories takes place in the universe of a famous epic, each a part of our cultural heritage. I have read them with delight, learning as I was entertained all over again.

Because, you see, when I found out there was a new Harold Shea project in the works, I just had to be part of it. The opportunity of actually *writing* a story about Harold Shea, is the stuff of dreams.

The dream has come true, for me, and Mr. de Camp has been gracious enough to allow me to write a story within his universe. I have enjoyed it immensely. I hope you will, too.

PROFESSOR HAROLD AND THE TRUSTEES
Christopher Stasheff

They were meeting in the conference room just off the President's office. It was a stalwart old room, panelled in walnut and lighted by tall lamps in the corners. Beneath them were low bookcases and one tall one, filled with leather-bound volumes that looked as though they'd never been opened. The chairs were upholstered in burgundy plush, and the Trustees were upholstered in pin-striped suits.

"It's rather difficult for me to answer any of your questions, gentlemen," Shea temporized. "I'm only a junior member of the staff."

"Yes, we're aware of that," said Trustee Incise. He was the lean, ferret-faced publisher of the local newspaper, and wrote editorials that were carried by papers in St. Louis, Chicago, and Cincinnati.

"Since three of the four members of the Institute's professional staff have taken leave of absence, you can understand our concern," said Archangle, the Chairman of the Board of Trustees. He was in his sixties, still affecting a pince-nez with a long black ribbon connecting it to his lapel. He had bulldog jowls and a few strands of hair arrowing back from the center of his forehead to the grizzled fringe, neatly trimmed, looking very much the banker that he was.

Trustee Windholm rumbled agreement. He was tall and wide, with pale skin and paler eyes, a wisp of a mouth, and wispy hair. He rarely spoke, but often made meaningful sounds.

Athanael pressed on, undeterred. "Being part of Curling Stone University, the Institute is supposed to serve not only as a mental hospital, but also as a teaching laboratory; we do have graduate students studying the patients as advanced work in psychology. But the Institute's founders and patrons were also hoping for some fame accruing to the University, through the research efforts of its staff." He turned to Shea. "If your colleagues are developing results that will be publishable, Dr. Shea, we would scarcely want to discourage them. A revolutionary idea in psychology, soundly buttressed by valid data, would definitely enhance the reputation of the college."

"Well, perhaps if it's genuinely earth-shaking," Trustee Lockjaw said impatiently. He was a square-chinned, hard-eyed lawyer with a Roman nose.

Athanael turned to Shea. "Precisely what is the nature of the research that has required all three of them to leave campus for the year?"

Shea took a deep breath. This was going to require some fancy footwork, since the plain truth of the matter was that he and Chalmers had both gone a-wandering to escape the suffocating life of academia, not to augment it—and though Bayard and Polacek had gone off as much out of curiosity as anything else, that curiosity had scarcely been academic.

Anyway, plain truth was not what college trustees wanted to hear.

"We began by studying the logic patterns of Garaden patients," Shea said, "then moved farther afield to engage in other case studies. We discovered that delusional patients seem to be living half in worlds of their own invention, and half in the world that is real. Dr. Chalmers, Dr. Bayard, Mr. Polacek, and myself, are hoping that, by charting the principles underlying such delusional worlds, we'll be able to find ways to bring the patients into correspondence with the principles of the real world, then into identity with it, thus curing them."

"A fascinating notion, and it does clarify the rather lengthy explanation in your briefing," Archangle harrumphed. "I can understand why some of you needed to continue the field work—but why send *you* back? Why didn't you stay?"

Because I brought back what really mattered—Belphebe. Shea couldn't say that aloud, of course; instead, he merely shrugged. "I'm the youngest member with a doctorate."

"And you're sure that there really is a need for further field studies?" Incise snapped.

"Oh, I think that's quite clear." Turning back to Incise, Athanael said, "I think you can see, though, that if the project is successful, it could produce a revolution in therapy, and redound greatly to the credit of the University."

"Oh, yes, no question about it." Windholm's rumbling finally turned into words. "If they can make it work, it might even give us a counter-argument for the notion that movies and radio plays are leading people into fantasy lives."

Shea remembered that Windholm owned three radio stations, and that one of them had started a Western that had become so popular, a national network had picked it up.

"It could offer a valuable yardstick in legal insanity cases," Lockjaw said thoughtfully.

"Then we're agreed." Archangle didn't sound happy about it. "We'll let the current situation continue through the spring semester—but by midsummer, Dr. Shea, we really do need to see some preliminary results."

"We should stipulate, however, that the research of Doctors Chalmers and Bayard be published under the Institute's auspices," Lockjaw pointed out, "and frankly, gentlemen, I must question whether Dr. Shea has enough experience to coördinate such a group effort by himself. No offense intended, of course, Doctor."

"None taken," Shea ground out.

"Yes, there is need for more experienced direction," President Athanael said easily. "Dr. Shea, we really must insist that you do your best to persuade Dr. Chalmers to oversee the effort, at least in the capacity of a consultant."

"It would also help if you could persuade Dr. Bayard to resume correspondence," Incise advised.

Shea sighed. "I'll try my best, gentlemen—but it may be very difficult to contact Dr. Chalmers."

"Can't you reach him by telephone?"

"No," Shea said. "I'm afraid there aren't any, where he's gone. You might say it's a rather remote location."

"So that's all I'm supposed to do," he told Belphebe over a predinner martini, in tones of exasperation. "As though all I had to do were to mail a letter or send a telegram!"

"Naetheless," she said, smiling proudly, "you have triumphed, Harold."

"Triumphed?" Shea did a double take. "How do you figure that?"

"Why, because your Institute will continue, and the University will not even insist on hiring new men to replace our friends," Belphebe answered. "That is what you had said you did dread, is it not?"

"Why yes, now that you mention it," Shea said slowly, with a thoughtful look. "I did, didn't I?"

"Then surely you have triumphed in averting both catastrophes." She squeezed his hand, eyes glowing.

Shea squeezed back, with a very fond smile. "I'm awfully lucky I met you." She was tall and slim, with red-gold hair trimmed in a long bob. It went splendidly with the green dress she was wearing, somehow suggesting the forest that was her natural home. Shea reflected once again on his amazing good luck in finding her, and the unbelievable phenomenon that she had actually fallen in love with him. "Maybe we can't begin to plan for the future yet, but at least the present is safe—for a little while."

Belphebe frowned. "Odd words, for a knight-errant."

"This knight-errant has suddenly begun to be more interested in security than in adventure," Shea said sourly, "and his native universe is certainly higher in the former, than any of the others he had visited."

Belphebe smiled, touching his hand, her face glowing. "Wherefore so huge a transformation?"

"It has something to do with having a wife at home," Shea admitted. "I tell you, dear, when Archangle hinted that the "project" might be eliminated, it sent a chill through me. He implied that the Institute might need an overall replacement of personnel, myself included. I never would have thought the hint of losing my job would send me into such a panic."

Belphebe frowned. "That is not good."

"No, because there are always more jobs, right? But it's comfortable here, and Garaden is a good town for . . ." He caught himself; child-rearing was a topic they had not discussed. Much. ". . . a good town for a young couple. I'd just as soon not have to move."

"If you must, we shall," she said simply, with a squeeze of his hand.

"Thanks, sweetheart." He smiled into the sun-dazzle of her eyes, then frowned. "But what am I supposed to do about contacting Doc and Walter?"

"Well," she responded quite reasonably, "since you cannot write to them, and cannot call them on this magical far-speaker of yours ..." She gestured to the telephone, "... then you have no recourse but to visit them, and present to them the Board's request."

Shea felt a stab of apprehension. "No, I don't suppose I have, have I?"

"Oh, be not so troubled!" Belphebe reached forward to take his hand in both of hers. "At worst, they'll give you definite answers that you can present to the Board; at best, they might decide to return to visit a while."

Shea smiled back, returning the handclasp, heartened by her support. "True. You always see things so clearly." Then he frowned. "But there's no telling how long it might take, dear, and I don't like the idea of leaving you for so long."

"Oh, as to the first, once you are arrived in a universe in which magic operates, you can easily cast a spell that will take you to him whom you seek—and as to the last, fear not! I shall come with you."

Shea stared. "You ... ?"

"Of course." Belphebe rose, smiling, and pulling him up with her. "Have you forgot wherefrom I came? Or are you foolish enough to be concerned for my safety?"

"Well, uh, now that you mention it ..."

"Foolish man! Have you forgot my skill with the bow, or who 'twas saved you from the Losels?" Belphebe gave him a sidelong, roguish glance. "Nay, if you were to leave me behind, I would be every bit as concerned for you! Come, Harold, let us sup and sleep, then rise and go!"

So the next morning, Shea made a quick trip back

to the Institute, to rifle his colleagues' desks. Then he came home, to find Belphebe dressed in the short-skirted tunic and feathered hat of her home world, with her bow in her hand and quiver on her back. He dressed in tunic and hose with sword and dagger at his side. Then he stepped into the middle of the living room, left hand holding the papers filled with the arcane characters of symbolic logic, right reaching out for Belphebe. Smiling, she came to stand beside him and clasped hands. He gave her one of the sheets of paper and grinned at her, feeling more lighthearted than he had for months. "Ready?"

"Ready, Harold!" She answered his grin with one of her own. "Sing hey, for ancient Eriu!"

Then, holding each other's hands and reading from the sheets of paper, they began to read, reciting the sorites in unison, over and over, again and again, until the gray mists gathered about them, thickening and swirling until they seemed to be all the world there was, then shredding and dissipating to show them a countryside that was so green as to seem unbelievable.

Shea looked about him and breathed deeply of clean, fresh air. He felt the weight of patients, students, and administrators roll off his shoulders. He turned to Belphebe, and saw her looking about her with the same deep breath, then turning to him with sparkling eyes. " 'Tis not home, Harold—but 'tis a delightful place to sojourn."

"I know what you mean—I wouldn't want to live here either," Harold agreed.

"Nay, sir." A shadow crossed her face. "If we should chance to meet that brute Cuchulainn . . ."

"Not likely." Shea rummaged in his wallet and brought out a stub of pencil. "We're just going to meet Walter, then on to the *Ariosto's universe*."

Belphebe stared. "With naught but a bit of lead in wood? How shall that aid?"

"Because it's something that Walter used very often. It should have enough of his personality impressed on it to respond according to the Law of Contagion."

"Ah!" Belphebe's frown vanished. "Aye, then, chant!"

Harold reached out for her hand again, and held up the pencil stub, concentrating on it as hard as he could and reciting,

> "Inscriber of letters and numbered sums,
> Take us where your owner comes.
> Graphite rod and bit of tree,
> Take us where he soon will be!"

There was a moment's disorientation—the trees seemed to tilt and slew, blurring into a mass of green. But that mass slowed and separated into trees again. . . .

Trees all around. Shea looked about him, startled, then turned back to Belphebe, alarmed. But she was standing right beside him, looking only a trifle green, though she was clinging to his hand even more tightly than when they'd left. " 'Twas . . . odd, Harold."

"Yes, it certainly was," Harold agreed. "We must not have had to travel terribly far—but far enough so that we definitely noticed the discontinuity." He looked about him again. "Forest, huh?"

" 'Tis most indeed like to home." Belphebe brightened at the sight of her native habitat. "Trees, wood, no doubt creatures great and small. . . ."

"But no Walter."

"Aye, there is that." Belphebe frowned.

Shea sighed. "What did I do wrong this time?"

"Naught, I should think." Belphebe eyed the shadows with a hunter's accustomed wariness. "You told the pencil stub to take us where he comes, so if we are not by him, we should surely see him."

"Or will!" Shea slapped his forehead. "I got the words in that last line out of order! I meant to say,

'Take us soon where he will be,' but instead I said, 'Take us where he *soon* will be!' I shouldn't have used the future tense! I should have paid more attention to my teacher in grammar school!"

Belphebe looked up, startled. "Could that be why magic is termed 'gramarye'?"

"What?" Shea stared at her, taken aback, then recovered, shaking his head. "No, no, can't be! Must be a false cognate, just a common linguistic root, maybe, a . . ."

Shouting broke out around a bend in the trail, out of sight, underscored by the ring of steel.

Shea and Belphebe stared at one another for a moment, startled. Then Belphebe cried, "Walter!" and they both turned and ran.

They skidded around the curve and saw half a dozen scruffy men in patched tunics, flailing with rusty swords at a prosperous-looking group. Shea whipped out his own blade, and Belphebe stepped back to string her bow, then dropped to one knee, nocking an arrow and waiting for a clear shot.

Harold did not help; he grabbed the nearest rough-neck by the shoulder, yanked hard, spinning him around—and blocking him from Belphebe's view. The man roared with anger and swung down with a huge axe. Shea skipped back, then lunged, stabbing in. His blade scored an arm, and the man dropped his axe, clutching at the wound and howling. But he managed to stumble forward, barreling into Shea and knocking him down. His stench almost paralyzed Shea, but he forced himself to move, heaving the man away. The scruffneck rolled up to his knees, drawing a rude-looking dagger, but Shea was in too much of a hurry to oblige. He slapped with the flat of the blade, and the grubby one howled, the dagger spinning from his fingers. Shea shoved him aside and clambered to his feet, looking about for the next victim—just in time to see an arrow sprout from the buttock of another robber. The man howled and leaped back, hand clapped to his posterior, hopping away. Shea cast an anxious glance at Belphebe, saw she had another arrow nocked, and turned back to the melee. . . .

Just in time to see a huge flower of flame explode all about the travellers. The remaining bandits howled, tumbling away, their clothes smoking—but they could not have been hurt too badly, because they scrambled to their feet and took off running toward the forest. Shea's victim went staggering after them, still holding a bleeding forearm, and Belphebe's target came hopping after, bellowing in pain.

Belphebe leaped to her feet, but a mellow voice called, "Let them go. They are but bullies, and will not trouble us again."

Shea looked back, startled by the authority in the tone, and saw a tall, white-haired man in a long robe, with two younger men beside him, similarly clad.

And one of them looked familiar—big, brunet, and calming into his usual sleepy-looking state—though Shea was not used to seeing him with a beard.

"Hello, Harold," Bayard said. "Thank you for your assistance."

It turned out he had not really needed it, of course—all three of the travellers were druids. The bandits had known they had to cripple them instantly, before they could cast a defensive spell, or they were done for.

"They were fools to try it, of course," Bayard said as they marched along, the other two druids in front. "Bora and I held them off long enough for Ordrain to work up a spell—though you two certainly helped."

But had not really been necessary, Shea thought wryly. "So you've decided to take up magic as a profession?"

"I am considering it quite seriously," Bayard said.

"The life can be quite rewarding, in a universe in which magic really works."

"But are not the druids also priests?" Belphebe asked.

"That is the rub," Bayard admitted. He glanced at his companions ahead, and lowered his voice. "As you know, I have never been terribly religious, and I find myself unable to take a pagan mythos seriously, as anything more than literature."

"But in this universe," Shea objected, "the Celtic gods could be quite real."

Bayard cleared his throat and said, "Yes, there is that possibility—in which case, I am even less eager to put myself in a position that would attract their attention. I am well aware, of course, that none of them could be a true deity—only a sort of superbeing, brought into existence by collective belief, or a Jungian archetype, expressing racial memory. . . ."

"But for all practical purposes," Shea said, "they could have the same effects."

"Yes, there is that," Bayard said, "so you can see that I have a bit more thinking to do before I declare my profession."

"But you *have* a profession," Shea reminded him. "You're a psychologist, and a professor."

Bayard gazed off into space, reminiscing. "Ah, yes! The fascinating speculations of Freud and Jung, as useful here as they were there! The ivy-covered towers, the scent of chalk on a warm summer's afternoon, the rows of bored faces yearning to be anywhere but in my classroom, the academic infighting, the tormented patients pouring out their agonies into my ear. . . ." He shuddered, coming back to the here and now. "No, now that you remind me of it, this world does have its advantages. It is rough and brutal, of course, and certainly has few enough amenities— wouldn't I love a few days with indoor plumbing! But all its detractions aside, it is still a far more enjoyable milieu for me. Not for you, apparently, Harold. . . ."

"Oh, I enjoy the visits well enough," Shea said. "It's just that after a while it gets to be . . . well, boring."

"Boring?" Bayard turned to him in surprise. "I could think of many disadvantages to ancient Eriu, but boredom is certainly not one of them! With bandits likely to lurk behind every bend in the road, clan fights every year, spells to learn, women to . . ." He broke off into a cough, glancing uneasily at Belphebe. She just smiled, looking interested.

"Yes, well, everything considered," Bayard said, "I would not term it 'boring.'"

"Ask one of the peasants," Shea countered, "the ones for whom those battles you spoke of are about the only variation in the routine."

"Well, no," Bayard said judiciously. "They have seasonal festivals, and there are fairs . . . but by and large, yes, I'd have to agree that their lives are monotonous and grinding. You, however, are not of their class."

"No, but I'm one of those crazy idealists who feels he has to be doing something to help other people— and I don't think I have to tell you what the noblemen here would think of it, if I tried to help the peasants too much. At least, back in Ohio, they're more than glad to let me help everybody I'm fool enough to pity."

"Then praise folly," Belphebe said, slipping her hand into his and squeezing it.

"Yes, I see your point," Bayard conceded. "Felt that way myself not too long ago, until I began to realize that there were few enough who really improved, and I was gaining very little for myself."

"But you were associate professor," Shea objected, "earning a good salary—and you could probably be full professor in a few years."

"Yes? And then what?" Bayard asked with feigned interest.

"Well ... then you ... could become director," Shea said. "Maybe even president of the University."

"All very pleasant, except that I dislike the drudgery of administration," Bayard said. "Therefore I would reach the pinnacle of my career, with no place further to go, by the time I was forty. After that, financial increases would be few and small, and there would be very little accretion of status."

"There's always more to learn," Shea objected.

"True, but there's a great deal to learn here, and as a druid, I would be already in the top ranks of Irish society. The more I learn, the greater my status would become—and my wealth with it; the druids find no special virtue in poverty. No, Harold, I am delighted to see you again, and the company of your lady is always a joy. ..." He gave Belphebe his most charming smile. She returned it, amused, and Bayard sighed, shaking his head. "Yes, your company is quite pleasant, but I am afraid I should not feel the same way about Ohio. I have been studying Irish magic, of course, and am quite excited about the spells I have been learning, but even more, with the natural laws that underlie them."

"I didn't know you were interested in physics," Shea murmured.

"Oh, but that is the joy of it! In this universe, physics and psychology are so thoroughly intertwined that it is virtually impossible to study the one without the other! Why, their heroes are virtual Ur-figures, and half their spells are rooted in inherited responses to symbols! No, Harold, I find the study fascinating, even compelling, and the developments in contemporary psychology definitely pall in comparison. The movement toward attempting to analyze human behavior with statistics strikes me as particularly exasperating, with its underlying implication that the norm is the only valid standard of human behavior. Really, there is very little intellectual stimulation remaining to me in Ohio, but a great deal of it here!"

"This may start boring you some day, too, Walter," Shea cautioned.

Bayard shrugged. "If it does, I can always visit Ohio, and if that does not reawaken my appreciation of Eriu, I am certain that a trip to New York will."

"But you won't have a job there," Shea pointed out. "If you don't come back from your leave of absence on time, you won't be given tenure. In fact, you'll be unemployed."

Bayard looked up with interest. "I wasn't aware that I'd put in for leave of absence."

"Oh, yes," Shea assured him. "It was a sudden, last-minute thing, but you did send me a note telling me that you wouldn't be able to teach this fall, because your research had reached a very crucial stage."

Bayard laughed. "Well, that's true enough. Very resourceful of you, Harold. But really, I've no desire to return to my position at the Garaden Institute."

"I'm sorry to hear that," Shea said, "but if you're sure, could you give me a letter of resignation, so that I can hire another full-time professor?"

"Yes, certainly! Really quite thoughtless of me; I had not considered it. How have you stalled President Athanael into keeping my position open even this long?"

"By concocting a research project that we're all involved in," Shea explained, "you, Chalmers, Polacek, and myself."

"Indeed!" Bayard smiled. "And may I know what study it is in which I'm engaged?"

"The application of symbolic logic to the analysis of delusional universes," Shea said, "with the end goal of discovering ways to reconcile delusional universes with the real one."

"Meaning twentieth-century Ohio, of course." Nonetheless, Bayard nodded, interested. "You did not even have to lie—only slanted the issue a bit. Excellent, Harold! In fact, the study may even yield positive results. Very well, then, I'll proceed to analyze this fantasy universe to the best of my ability. I am afraid it will be rather difficult to apprise you of my results, though."

"Once a year would be enough," Shea said. "An end-of-the-year summary, as it were."

"Well, yes, I believe I could manage that—visit Ohio for a few days, once a year. Perhaps I might even work out a way of sending the report in without me. . . ." Bayard gazed off into space again, then gave himself a shake. "No, we'll deal with that issue at a later time. So, then, once a year it will be."

"Thanks a lot, Walter," Shea said fervently. "It will help me a lot. I'll tell you what, though—for the first year-end, I'll come visit you, okay?"

"That would be convenient," Bayard conceded, "and in return for the favor, I shall make a copy of my notes to date, detailing the magical system of Eriu."

"Not much written yet, eh?"

But there was—fifty pages of cryptic, telegraphic statements that took three hours of explanation. Bayard had the time, though, sitting by the campfire and chatting with Shea and Belphebe till almost midnight. He had not said that he would copy the notes— he had said that he would make a copy, and he did: by magic.

They parted company the next morning, as dawn was lightening the forest. Shea and Belphebe stood by the campfire, shaking Bayard's hand; his fellow druids waited impatiently at the edge of the clearing.

"Do not forget to drop by at the end of the year," Bayard admonished.

"Oh, you can be sure I will," Shea assured him.

"I shall look forward to it. And, Harold . . ." A trace of anxiety crossed Bayard's face. ". . . if New Year's Day passes some year, and I do not arrive . . . look in on me again, will you?"

"You're afraid of something?" Shea tensed. "Enemies already?"

"Oh no, nothing like that," Bayard said quickly. "Well . . . perhaps a jealous husband or two. But nothing beyond my capabilities. No, it is merely that I suspect that I may tire of this universe someday, but will have become so accustomed to it that I may lack the will to leave it. It is, after all, a very pleasant milieu for me, so I may require assistance in summoning the resolution to leave."

"I'll make sure to check," Shea assured him.

"I should appreciate it." Bayard clapped him on the shoulder with a nostalgic smile. "So good to have seen you again, old friend! And you, my dear." He stole a quick kiss, then turned away before Belphebe could do anything more than look amazed. He strode quickly over to his companions, then away down the path. But he turned just before they went in under the leaves, to wave; then he was gone.

"Well, it was good to see him again," Shea sighed. "Never thought I'd say that, but it was. Ready to go, dear?"

"Yea, assuredly, Harold." But Belphebe was gazing off after Bayard with a very thoughtful look. "Those spells he explained last night, and the principles beneath them . . ."

"Lets not try them just now," Shea said quickly. "After all, we still need to catch up with Doc and Florimel." He caught her hand, taking out his copy of the sorites. "Ready, dear?"

"Um? Oh, certainly!" Belphebe took out her own copy. Together, they began to recite the sorites for the universe of the *Orlando Furioso*. The world seemed to dim about them as their concentration deepened—but no, it wasn't an optical illusion, the world really was dimming, its colors swirling and fading into mist and smoke, gray nebulosity that thinned and stabilized and blew away, to reveal a hillside covered with heather and wildflowers.

Belphebe gasped and leaned against him. Shea clasped her to him, holding her upright, though he was leaning as much on her as she on him. Finally, they caught their breath and looked about them.

"There's no assurance that we've come to the right universe," Shea cautioned.

"Oh, but there is." Belphebe looked about her with sparkling eyes, breathing deeply of the scented air. "'Tis within me. This is very similar to mine own world, Harold, that gave me birth and nurtured me. 'Tis not quite mine own place, but nearly."

Harold stared, then looked away, wondering why he did not feel that way about Ohio.

"Enough!" Belphebe turned to catch both his hands, her eyes bright, vitality fully restored. "How shall we seek out Reed?"

"The usual way, I suppose." Shea reached into his wallet and took out a small black notebook. "I rifled his desk, too."

This time he was a little more careful with the spell.

Chalmers was just coming out the door to breathe in the scents of the new day when a flicker of movement caught his eye. He turned, and his jaw dropped. "Harold!" He stood frozen for about a second, long enough for Shea to derive a great deal of satisfaction from seeing his former boss staring at him in total amazement. However, there was no small amount of amazement on his own side—Dr. Reed Chalmers' rejuvenation spells had worked very well. His bushy hair was glossy black and covered his whole head, showing not the slightest trace of gray, and the only lines on his face showed when he smiled.

Then Reed recovered and hurried over to them, seizing his hand and pumping it. "My dear fellow, so good to see you! And Belphebe, how charming! How wonderful, how wonderful! He released her hand and turned back toward the house, a hand on each one, ushering them inside. "Florimel will be delighted—we have so little company these days. The disadvantage of being a magician, you see—very few wish to take a chance on your friendship; only neighbors, and they are few, here in the forest. Oh, this is a genuine delight!"

"I regret that we could not inform you of our coming," Belphebe apologized.

"Of course not, my dear! Why, I haven't even perfected the spell for projecting objects into another universe, myself! No, how could you have sent word? Florimel will be so pleased!"

She was.

Unlike Reed, she did not seem to feel there was any shortage of social life. "In truth," she confided to Belphebe, "I am quite relieved to be free of the incessant maneuvering for favor of the Court, and the constant seeking to discover whom one could snub, and upon whom one must needs fawn."

Belphebe smiled. "I could not agree more. I have ever preferred the solitude and directness of the forest to the intrigues and deceptions of the castle."

"Sounds as though a quiet cottage in the forest would be very welcome indeed," Shea commented.

"Another glass?" Chalmers held up a flask of ruby liquid.

They were sitting in hourglass chairs, sipping wine and nibbling little cakes, in Florimel's solar—a spacious, high-ceilinged room with tall clerestory windows facing the morning sun. The walls were hung with tapestries, and a rich Oriental carpet covered the floor.

"I thank you, but I've scarcely tasted the first," Belphebe said, dimpling prettily.

"I'm still nursing mine." Shea looked around at the decor. "You've done very well for yourselves, Doc."

"Why, thank you." Chalmers nodded, looking around. "My experiments have been progressing quite nicely."

"Experiments?" Shea swung back to him, staring. "You mean you *made* all this?"

"Oh no, certainly not! But furnishings like these are not available for purchase this far into the interior of France, quite yet; I have had to work out spells for transporting myself to Flanders, for the tapestries, and to Persia, for the carpets." Chalmers frowned. "Though the inhabitants are quite insistent that I not call them 'Persians'; apparently, their ancestors drove out the people of Xerxes long ago, and they were the only ones who could properly be referred to by the name. . . ."

Shea saw a need to steer the conversation back onto the tracks. "But once you were there, what did you pay with?"

"Oh, money is no problem," Chalmers assured him. "I mastered the spell for transforming pebbles into gems very early in my sojourn here, though lead into gold still eludes me. . . ."

"Probably be radioactive if you could bring it off," Shea agreed. "It's about those experiments that I wanted to talk to you, Doc."

"Surely you can have no need for them in Ohio! . . . You are still living in Ohio, are you not?"

"Yes, and I'm the only full-time psychologist at the Garaden Institute—which means I'm also half of the teaching staff in psychology."

"Really!" Chalmers frowned. "I hadn't realized I was leaving you in quite so hard a bind."

" 'Fraid so, and I can't even hire new people unless Polacek and Bayard resign."

"Not to mention myself," Chalmers said, with chagrin. "As to Bayard, of course, I can't say—but in reference to Polacek, I have only the most irresponsible conduct to report."

"What else could we expect, from Polacek?" Shea asked. "The exuberant enthusiasms of youth and all that, Doc. What's he been doing?"

Chalmers sighed. "He has gone off with a peasant wench, and only contacts me every few months, so I can not say where he is just at the moment. I am always aware of where he has been, though—I have only to listen for rumors of bizarre happenings."

"So the Rubber Czech is still bouncing, eh?" Shea smiled. "And if I know him, he's working magic with the delight and abandon of a kid with a new toy."

"Yes, and with no greater sense of responsibility," Chalmers said, disapproving. "If he restricted his efforts to established spells, there really would not be terribly much of a problem. But . . ."

"He insists on doing research, huh?" Shea shook his head. "Poor Votsy! Has he managed to conjure up a demon that carried him off, yet?"

"No, but I have heard reports of a dragon with a rather large pair of jaws. Apparently Polacek acquired an excellent opportunity to study reptilian anatomy from the inside. Piecing together reports, I gather that he managed to project himself outside the beast in the nick of time, then banish it back to whatever realm it had come from." Chalmers shook his head. "I fear that magic, Polacek, and the spirit of free inquiry, are a very volatile combination."

"A recipe for disaster," Shea agreed.

"Yes, though so far, he has not quite managed to

follow the recipe accurately, thank Heaven," Chalmers sighed. "I have urged Polacek to restrict his studies to the investigation of theory, and to refrain from experiments unless he is in my company, but from the tales I hear of very singular events, I do not believe he has paid much heed to my exhortations."

"It is really quite foolish of him," Florimel said indignantly. "Can he not see that you are the senior magician?"

"I'm afraid Votsy never did pay too much attention to seniority and respect for experience," Shea sighed. "Well, I think I can forget about his coming back, anyway." He said it with a certain amount of relief.

"I can understand his point of view on that matter, at least," Chalmers said. "There is no real chance of my wishing to return to Ohio for any considerable amount of time, Harold, so I shall surely write you a letter of resignation."

"Uh, let's not be hasty, Doc." Shea held up a palm. "There's another dimension to the problem. Besides, I already checked in with Walter."

"Really! And how is he getting on?"

"Just fine. He's studying Celtic magic, and thinking of becoming a druid."

"Oh, my." Chalmers sat back down. "How odd a course, for a man who did not take religion sufficiently seriously to even become a confirmed agnostic."

"That's why he's still considering. But he did give me a letter of resignation—and a promise of year-end reports."

"Year-end reports?" Chalmers frowned. "Whatever for?"

"Well, I had to come up with some excuse for all three of you being gone." Shea took a deep breath. "So I concocted a research project that we're all engaged in, and promised Athanael that it might yield publishable results."

Chalmers only smiled, amused. "Ingenious! And not far from the truth, though we would scarcely dare publish the matters we are truly researching. What aspect of it have you said you could make public?"

"The relationship of alternate universes to reality. You remember, that's how you first got the idea for the syllogismobile—by realizing that some of our delusional patients were living only half in our own universe, and half in some other one that had an entirely different logic, and a different set of natural laws."

"Yes, of course I remember." Chalmers frowned. "Surely you don't think you could make the profession take the idea seriously?" But before Shea could answer, his eyes widened. "Of course! If the patient's delusional universe can be described in symbolic logic, you can work out intermediate steps to gradually bring his personal universe back into coincidence with the real one! . . . Well, real in terms of twentieth-century Ohio."

Shea's heart sank. "Pardon me for feeling dumb."

"Eh? Oh no, my boy, quite the opposite! You saw it much sooner than I did, and without the slightest hint from anyone else, such as the push you just gave me! What a stroke of genius, to create a polite fiction that will allow our colleagues to treat the whole matter as though it were not real at all, but still make use of the concept! Really, Harold, a master-stroke!"

Shea smiled, pleased, reflecting that this universe was having a wonderful mellowing effect on Chalmers; he never would have been so fulsome in his praise, back in Ohio. This universe, or Florimel.

"But I take it that the project would require my more or less active participation?"

"Well, yes." Shea glanced at him uneasily. "Fact is, the Board of Trustees isn't too happy about having a mere assistant professor in charge of the project, and one who hasn't even published his first article, at that."

Chalmers stared. "They're not thinking of bringing in a new man to coördinate it!"

"They're definitely thinking of bringing in a new man—but we might be able to keep him away from the project, if we can convince Athanael that you're officially coördinating it. In a consultant's capacity, of course, not back in Ohio physically. At least, not full time."

Chalmers smiled. "Harold, is this a delicate way of asking me to pay a small visit to my erstwhile precincts?"

Shea heaved a sigh that ended in a grin. "That's right, Doc. I'm putting the touch on you. Just a week or so, until we have the project set up formally, to the satisfaction of the Trustees. Then we can hire new psychologists without cutting them in on the project."

"Because to be included, they would have to ask me, and I shall unfortunately be unavailable." Chalmers nodded. "Yes, I believe that will work—and certainly I should have no objection to a brief visit to my former home. It should be pleasant for variety, if for nothing else—if you would not find that objectionable, my dear?"

"Of course not, my husband." Florimel smiled, amused. "Though by your leave, I shall remain while you journey."

"Are you sure?" Chalmers was instantly concerned. "It will be quite lonely here, by yourself."

"We do have neighbors," she reminded him gently. "I shall dine with them twice a week, instead of once. And fear not for my safety, for you have warded this house well with puissant spells, as you know."

"That is true, yes." Chalmers frowned. "But I had rather looked forward to showing you the admittedly prosaic sights of my homeland. Are you certain my absence will not pain you?"

"I shall miss you sorely," Florimel assured him, "though not so sorely as to bar your leaving. Yet 'twill be sorely enough to give me great joy at your home-coming, I warrant you."

Chalmers' eyes glinted at the suggestion of a joyful reunion. "Ah, but to return, I must first depart, eh? Well enough, my sweet! I shall leave you—but not for long."

Belphebe was hiding a smile, Shea realized—no doubt in admiration of Florimel's adroit handling of the situation. Shea gave her a hundred points for tact, himself. In fact, he thought she seemed almost relieved, and Shea found himself wondering if married people did benefit from occasional vacations from one another. He wasn't particularly anxious to find out per-sonally, but he found the thought reassuring, just in case.

"Before you depart, though," Florimel reminded Chalmers, "there is a matter that really must be resolved."

"Hmm, yes." Chalmers frowned. "We have had a bit of an upset recently, Harold."

"An upset? What kind?" Shea saw a cloud on the horizon of his hopes.

"Just a niggling little matter," Chalmers said, "but one with which I should appreciate your help."

"Help? Sure!" Shea knew it was illogical, but he felt a glow of pride that Reed had asked him. "What is it? An evil baron? A flock of bandits? A plague of bats?"

"A hydra," Chalmers said. "It has been terrorizing the countryside for the last fortnight or so, and a mes-senger brought word of it just this morning, beseech-ing my assistance."

"Of course," said Florimel, "he could not refuse."

But she glanced at Chalmers anxiously, then back at her guests. "I am so glad that you have come!"

She included Belphebe in her gaze of gratitude. Shea could understand that—he was awfully glad for the company of his archer/wife, himself.

"Let us step into my workroom and pack such items as we may need, eh?" Chalmers rose.

"Sure!" Shea rose, too. "If you'll excuse us, ladies?"

"Certes, Sir Harold," Florimel said, and Belphebe looked up, amused. "Shall we wait dinner for you?"

"Oh, come on! We won't be that long!"

"If you say so," Belphebe rejoined. "Naetheless, I have seen you 'talk shop,' as you put it, and waited whilst you did so."

Not entirely patiently, as Shea remembered it—but that was the hazard of going to faculty parties. "I won't be, this time," he promised. "See you soon, dear."

Fortunately, Belphebe and Florimel enjoyed each other's company. They did not wait dinner, but they did insist the men join them for a late supper.

"Oh, well," Shea sighed as the door of the guest room closed behind them, "we needed a good night's sleep before we tackle that monster, anyway. Sorry, dear."

"You may make it up to me," Belphebe said, looking up at him through long lashes.

As they rode through the forest toward the terrorized parish, Shea had plenty of time to regret his willingness, and to get a bit more information about the situation. "What's a hydra doing in medieval Europe, Doc?"

"I do not really know," Chalmers answered. "There are only rumors of its sudden appearance—but there is also mention of a sorcerer seen in its company."

"Oh." Shea frowned. "So an evil magician imported it from the universe of Greek mythology, eh?"

"That would be my conjecture," Chalmers agreed, "though as I say, I do not truly *know*."

The peasants were more than willing to direct them toward the hydra's lair, though they made it clear that they thought the two magicians were out of their minds.

"You, at least, should stay, lady," one brawny peasant objected.

"I have fought vile monsters, good man, and lived to tell the tale," Belphebe assured him. "But I thank you for your concern." She might have thanked him for the glint in his eye, too—but she certainly would not have welcomed his "protection."

They followed one set of directions after another, through an outcrop of woodland, up the slope to the top of a ridge—and found themselves looking down on a little meadow around a rocky outcrop. At the base of the rock was a cave, large enough for a small congregation.

Shea reined in, surveying the bones that lay about in front of the cave—deer, pig, and quite a few cattle. "I think we've found it."

"Then I shall prepare." Chalmers started to dismount.

"Wait," Belphebe suggested, stringing her bow. "Let us first knock, to see who is home." She drew an arrow from her quiver.

"I don't think that's the world's best ..." Shea began.

Belphebe drew the feathers back to her ear, and loosed.

The arrow shot into the cave mouth, struck against rock and ricocheted, then struck rock again, and again. A huge roar came out.

"Yes, it is home." She paled a little.

The hydra surged out of its cave—a snake as thick as a cask, three of its nine heads roaring fire, the other

PROFESSOR HAROLD AND THE TRUSTEES   29

six coursing close to the ground in search of dinner, jaws gaping wide.

Shea reined in, face paling. "We've got to fight *that*?"

"Only with magic, of course." Chalmers dismounted and drew a small brazier, a tripod, and a miniature cauldron out of his saddlebag. "I have several new spells I'm rather anxious to test under field conditions. They will take some time to set up and activate, though, so if you could manage some defensive enchantments, Harold, I should very much appreciate it."

"We cannot wait," Belphebe said as she dismounted. "It has our scent."

Shea looked up, alarmed. Sure enough, the monster was moving toward them, one of its heads low and glaring at them.

Belphebe's bow thrummed, and a clothyard shaft sprouted in the cavernous nostril. The head fell to the ground, eyes glazing, but the other eight screamed in pain and rage, and the beast charged.

"The poor thing, to know such pain!" Belphebe nocked another shaft. "Quickly, husband! We must put it out of its misery!"

"How about ours?" Shea drew his sword. "But I'll agree we have to be quick!"

Belphebe's bow thrummed again, and another arrow stabbed in at the base of one of the necks. The hydra shrieked in pain, but kept on coming.

"Around us a circle as round as a moon!" Shea shouted:

"Till that we have done what we must do soon,
    Within this circumference lot none but us tread!
    If aught else should come there,
    Let it lose its head!"

The hydra smacked into something unseen, a few yards from Shea and Belphebe—and Chalmers, who had a little fire going in the brazier, heating some sort of mixture in the little cauldron. The breeze wafted it toward the hydra, five of whose heads recoiled, offended.

A sixth reached over the unseen wall and down inside the circle, jaws gaping wide for Belphebe.

Shea shouted, leaped, and caromed into his wife, knocking her aside. The huge head slammed down into the ground right where she had been.

"Darling!" Shea cried, scrambling to his feet. "Are you . . ."

The hydra roared with frustration, and the head hooked up toward him, jaws gaping.

Shea sprang back, anger at the monster surging—Belphebe might be lying injured! He had to get rid of that head! He lunged up as it went past him, stabbing just below the jaw. Blood spurted, and the head screamed, whipping up and away, splashing the side of Shea's face. He shouted and leaped back, wiping frantically at the fluid; it burned! He wiped it clear with his sleeve, feeling a tingling in his forearm, but there was no time to worry about that now. The head gone, he could see Belphebe climbing to her feet, and relief shot through him, followed by blood-lust—he had to kill the creature before it had a chance to hurt Belphebe again!

It gave him the opportunity, for though the wounded head hung back, thrashing, its neighbor struck down at Shea, jaws wide. He leaped aside, stabbing up with his sword. He missed the nose; the head swerved, tracking him, and the huge mouth came down all about him; his head filled with a charnel reek, but he managed to riposte and stab again, at the soft palate.

A shriek like that of a dozen steam engines filled his whole head, and the gaping maw lifted away from him abruptly, wrenching the sword-grip from his hand. Shea staggered back, senses reeling, and Belphebe's bowstring thrummed. The monster howled again, and Belphebe was beside Shea, her arm beneath his shoulders steadying him, while she cried, "Harold, are you hurt?"

"B-bow," he managed to gasp, pointing frantically at her weapon. "Sword . . . gone . . ."

Belphebe understood, and also understood that he had not suffered any vital injury. She leaped to catch up her bow—but just then, a huge cloud of fragrant smoke blew past them, and Chalmers' voice rose.

> "Heads, all rise; necks turn to wood!
> Monster, stop, as any should!
> Living yet, immobile be;
> Reptilian fable, turn to tree!"

The monster's six remaining heads whipped up, noses pointing straight at the sky. The whole form of the beast began to change color, starting at the tail and sweeping quickly over the body, turning brown, then roughening with the texture of oak bark. The heads quivered as the cellulose tide swept over them; then they were all frozen, rooted to the spot, transformed into a living tree. The tendrils at the tops of the heads sprouted leaves; the legs and drooping, dead heads dug into the earth, turning into roots.

Shea relaxed with a very shaky sigh. "Amazing, Doc. Why didn't you change him into stone, though?"

"Too much danger of radioactivity," Chalmers snapped.

Shea turned, surprised at the tension in his voice; but Chalmers threw a handful of powder into his little fire and called out,

"Come forth, and seek some greater room!
Conjurer, come to meet your doom!
Smoke, fill this cave from west to east!
Drive forth the man who raised this beast!"

Shea stared, then leaped to yank his sword out of
one of the fallen wooden mouths. If he was going to
have an evil enchanter to face, he wanted to be armed.

Belphebe nocked another arrow.

A gust of wind blew the smoke's powder in with
the fumes from the cauldron, and the whole swirled
toward the cave, churning in as though being sucked
into a vacuum. Coughing and spluttering came from
the darkness, and a tubby figure in a midnight-blue
robe came running out, rubbing at its eyes and crying,
"Gas attack! Unfair! Unethical!"

"Votsy!" Shea cried.

Chalmers rose to his feet with a weary sigh. "I
might have known."

Polacek wiped at his streaming eyes. "Don't get me
wrong, I really appreciate the help—but did you have
to be so caustic about smoking me out?"

"My apologies," Chalmers said, making it sound like
an accusation. "Rumor said the monster was animated
by an evil magician."

"Evil! Careless, maybe—possibly even not completely a master. But, evil? You know me better than
that, Doc!"

"Yes, but I didn't know it was you who had raised
the hydra. I take it the beast went out of control?"

"You can say that again! It was barely there before
it was trying to eat me! The only thing that saved me
was a handy hole in the ground, a tiny passageway
between two caves that the monster couldn't worm its
way through! I've been hiding out there for weeks,
living on a trickle of water and whatever food I could
conjure up."

"Could be worse," Shea said. "Czech cooking is good."

"Yeah, but I don't know the recipes. All I could order up was whatever I'd heard singing commercials for."

Shea winced, thinking of two weeks on patent breakfast cereal—without even milk!

"Whatever possessed you to conjure up a hydra?" Chalmers demanded.

"You did, Doc."

"*Me?*"

"Yeah. I mean, you told me I should play it careful, try my experiments on a very small scale . . . you remember, that was right after that blizzard. . . ."

"On Midsummer's Night, yes," Chalmers said grimly.

"Right. So I was trying to conjure up a pond-water hydra—you know, one of those microscopic creatures from freshman zoology? As small as you can get and have all the characteristics of animal life, including sexual reproduction—the ideal subject for a limited-scope experiment. . . ."

"And you messed up the spell," Shea inferred.

"Right."

"Just a matter of scale," Chalmers said witheringly.

"No, I think I got the context wrong. You see, the only way I could think up a verse, was to base it on Greek mythology, and . . ."

". . . you finished with the original rather than its namesake," Chalmers sighed. "Mr. Polacek, perhaps you should restrict your experimentation to more controlled conditions."

Which meant, of course, with Chalmers standing by.

Polacek frowned. "What do you mean? That I'm not qualified to practice on my own? I finished my course work, you know!"

"Yes, but the research for a dissertation should

always be supervised. Besides," said Chalmers, "I do not believe your coursework was in the area of magic."

"Well . . . related." Polacek looked sulky. "Jung and mythology, you know."

"Quite so—but that brings it all the more within my province, too," Chalmers pointed out.

Shea took his opportunities where he could find them. "That's kind of what I wanted to talk to you about, Votsy."

"Wanted to talk to me?" The incongruity of Shea's presence finally penetrated Polacek's indignation. "Yeah, come to think of it! What're you doing here, Harold? You're supposed to be back in Ohio! Along with your lovely lady, I might add." He caught Belphebe's hand and kissed it. She smiled, pleased, and dropped a half-curtsy.

"I *was* trying to find *you*," Shea said, trying to hide his annoyance—all right, jealousy. "I had to cover for all three of you being gone. . . ."

"All three?" Polacek frowned.

Shea sighed, striving for patience. "Bayard went, too," he reminded Polacek. "You're not the only one who's universe-jaunting, you know."

"Oh, yeah! Come to think of it, that did kind of leave you in a bind, didn't it?"

"So nice of you to think of it," Shea said, with sarcasm. "I explained your communal absence by inventing a research project that you're all supposedly studying on-site."

"Nice trick." Polacek grinned. "How'd you manage it? This isn't archaeology, you know."

"Don't I ever," Shea sighed. "I explained it to President Athanael as a study in delusional universes, describing a patient's delusions with symbolic logic, then working out the intermediate steps that would allow us to bring him back into contact with the real world, a little at a time."

"Hey, nice idea!" Polacek said, intrigued. "Suppose you could really get it to work?"

"We might," Shea hedged, "especially if you guys keep me informed as to what you're learning about the natural laws of the universes you're in."

Polacek nodded. "Be glad to."

"But the Trustees were hoping I'd be able to persuade Doc, here, to come back and set up the project, at least," Shea added.

Polacek kept on nodding. "Makes sense—he's had the experience. Not that I don't think you could do a good job, Harold, but it might be nice to have somebody else to take the responsibility."

"It would also be nice it I could bring back more than just Doc, at least for a visit," Shea said. "I don't suppose you'd be interested in a little Ohio scenery for a week or so, would you?"

To his surprise, Polacek turned thoughtful. "After a few weeks penned in a cave by a hydra, the idea isn't exactly repulsive. Tell you what—let's stop by my place for a few drinks, and we'll talk it over, okay?"

"Uh . . . yeah!" Shea said, startled and pleased.

" 'Twill be a pleasure," Belphebe assured him.

"Yes, certainly," Chalmers said, but he had that resigned look that went with gritted teeth.

Shea would have wondered why, but he was too busy squeezing Belphebe's hand as they followed Polacek down the trail. She looked up, surprised and pleased. "What troubles you, Harold?"

"The hydra pouncing on you," Shea answered. "Now that it's over, I've just realized how close I came to losing you."

Belphebe turned and slipped into his arms.

After a few minutes, Chalmers coughed delicately.

Polacek looked back, saw how far behind his guests had fallen, and called out, "Hey, come on, you guys! Some things can wait, you know?"

"Not this one." Shea held Belphebe away, just far enough so that he could looked straight into her eyes. "I nearly thought I'd lost you. It definitely makes me begin to think twice about doing any more adventuring."

"Oh, be not so rash," Belphebe said carelessly. Still holding his hand, she turned away to follow Polacek. "The life of the knight-errant stirs the blood, and makes life vivid."

"True, but it also makes it short," Shea returned. "I'm beginning to see distinct advantages to Ohio."

Polacek lived in a large house, for the time—it had two stories, and must have had all of six rooms. It also had a thick coating of dust on every horizontal surface, papers strewn all about, and dessicated snacks left sitting on tables and chairs.

"Sorry—it's been a few weeks since I've been home." Polacek started gathering up the detritus. "I can make tea, at least. It will take a little while, though, so make yourselves comfortable."

Belphebe looked around her, dazed, and Shea could tell she was fighting the impulse to wrinkle her nose. He wandered over to the hearth, gathered up kindling, and recited a small spark-spell. By the time Polacek came back in with a kettle of water, Shea had a nice fire going.

Polacek grunted as he hefted the little cauldron onto the swing-arm and pushed it over the flames. "Thanks, Harold. Not used to doing for myself, you see."

"Have you meal?" Belphebe asked.

"Yeah, sure, in the bin over there." Polacek pointed. "Cassie was keeping the place tidy, see, but when I said I was going to conjure up a hydra, and told her what it was, she walked out."

"Ran, I should think," Chalmers put in.

"Don't blame her," Polacek agreed. "Maybe now that it's dead, I can get her to come back."

"You have not married, then?" Belphebe brought over a pan with a meal-cake and set it on the hearth.

"We haven't formalized the arrangement, no. She was hinting at it at first, but she hasn't said much about it lately."

"I think that I can understand that," Belphebe murmured.

Polacek looked surprised, but had the good sense to let it pass.

Shea tried to clarify it. "Do all your experiments backfire the way that hydra did?"

Polacek frowned. "You think maybe that's why she hasn't been pushing for anything permanent?"

"It's a possibility," Shea said, and Belphebe just stared at her meal-cake. "Do they all turn into qualified disasters?"

"Not always qualified," Polacek said, with chagrin, "but not always disasters, either. Some of them work right the first time."

"How many?" Chalmers demanded.

Polacek shrugged. "Oh, twenty percent."

Shea automatically revised that down to ten. "Let me guess at a standard distribution curve. What's the center like?"

Polacek shrugged. "Most of them have been—well, I suppose you could say amusing. . . ."

"If you have a morbid sense of humor," Chalmers muttered.

"Okay, so maybe some of them turn out scary—but they aren't exactly lethal, either!"

Chalmers said, "Perhaps your efforts would meet with greater success if your motives were less personal."

"What's so bad trying to work out the magic-cum-physics of this universe in detail?"

"Nothing," said Chalmers, "if it were only from

motives of pure, disinterested academic interest, or of attempting to cure mentally-ill people who are caught between universes. I suspect, however, that you are far more concerned with gaining greater magical power for yourself."

"Well—what's the matter with trying to get ahead in the world?" Polacek's jaw jutted in stubbornness. "Or several worlds, for that matter?"

"Nothing, so long as you do it by improving the lot of other people, or at least not injuring them. Your experiments, however, seem to be characterized by a total disregard of your neighbors' welfare. Certainly they have resulted in calamities that have damaged the property of a good number of people."

"But no lives," Polacek pointed out. "I haven't caused any accidents that have killed anybody—or even injured them. . . . Well, not much."

Chalmers threw up his hands and turned away.

Shea decided it was time for a politic change of subject. "Maybe you need a rest," he suggested, "a sojourn in a universe where magic doesn't work."

"Like our home one, eh?" Polacek's grin returned. "Not a bad idea, Harold. Settle down for a few months and collate all my results, look for correlations, make sense out of it all—and then come back here for more experimenting."

"Had your fill of magic for a while, eh?"

"Well—let's say it'll be a relief to go someplace where I don't have to worry about the moon turning blue if I sing the wrong song. Besides, I kinda miss some of the little stuff. I could really go for a dozen White Castle hamburgers and some cola. Moorish Spain is great in its way, but modern comforts would be nice for a while."

Shea breathed a sigh of relief—and, all things considered, he and Belphebe were very glad to be joining hands with Chalmers and Polacek, and reciting the sorites for Garaden, Ohio.

The mist boiled up around them, churned, cooled, thinned, dissipated—and they found themselves standing in the Sheas' living room. They released hands with a collective sigh, and Polacek crowed: "Home! A fireplace with a chimney! A broadloom carpet! An indoor bathroom!"

"A kitchen," Belphebe prompted.

"A liquor cabinet," Shea added.

"Hey, good idea! Wouldn't have any ice in the freezer, would you?"

"There should be a tray," Belphebe said.

"Scotch on the rocks! No, don't bother, Harold—I can find it!" And Polacek swirled into the kitchen in his wizard's robes, looking for a refrigerator.

"It almost seems alien, somehow," Chalmers looked about him with a fond smile. "But quite comforting, to see familiar artifacts."

"Good to have you back, Doc." Shea grinned. "Only, now I need *your* help with another many-headed monster."

"The Board of Trustees?" Chalmers smiled, amused. "An unkind metaphor, Harold, though perhaps an apt one. Well, give me a night's rest to re-acclimatize myself, and I shall be at your disposal."

"Harold will fetch clothes from your house tomorrow," Belphebe said. "For this night, though, will you not grace our new guest room?"

"I shall be delighted." Reed said, with a little bow to her. "However, Harold, might I trouble you for a shirt and slacks tonight? I find that I, too, would welcome a hamburger."

The Board was relieved to see Chalmers return, and Shea was very relieved, too—at first. Chalmers fielded the Board's questions with an easy grace, responding to their reservations about the project with improvisations that sounded as though they were the result of long study.

But after a while, his skill and persuasion began to seem too good, and Shea thought that Chalmers was enjoying the central role a little too much.

"You will oversee the organization of the project, then, Dr. Chalmers, and will establish the methodology?" Archangle asked.

"Certainly," Chalmers said, without an instant's hesitation. "I was present at the inception of the study, of course—Dr. Shea brought his findings to me as soon as he had some validation for the hypothesis, and we embarked on a pilot project together."

Shea managed to contain a smile; the Board certainly had no idea just how literally he and Chalmers had "embarked."

"Dr. Shea and I proceeded to work out the basic methodology as we prepared a second project," Chalmers went on, "and brought Dr. Bayard and Mr. Polacek into the study; so as you can see, gentlemen, I have overseen the organization of the project from its inception, and have already approved the methodology."

Shea was startled to realize how much of the truth there was in what Doc was saying, though the motives had been entirely different. However, he found himself irritated by Chalmers' bland assumption of authority, and his presenting himself in the central role in the study.

"However," Chalmers went on, "I must stress that the initial empirical confirmation was Dr. Shea's, and that he has himself conducted the bulk of the research." That was true enough; Shea had filled Chalmers in on his adventures in ancient Finland and mythological Ireland. Shea relaxed a little, gratified by Chalmers' credit.

"Commendable, certainly." Athanael looked as though he wished it weren't. "It is vital, of course—but with so much of his time expended on this study, the University cannot help but be concerned about the impact on Dr. Shea's progress toward publication."

Shea looked up, startled, then quickly masked his expression. He had not even thought of working up something publishable on his own—he had been way too busy lately.

But of course, he was going to have to—if he really intended to stay in this universe, supporting a wife and, hopefully, children. The rule was "Publish or Perish." If he did not start publishing a string of erudite articles, he would never be promoted to full professor.

While he was still adjusting to the notion, Chalmers was saying, with bland confidence: "This project will provide Dr. Shea with an excellent topic for at least two articles, and he will certainly glean his fair share of the credit from the publication of the study as a whole. Perhaps of even greater importance, it will provide direction throughout the remainder of his scholarly career."

Well, that settled that—Shea was going to have to start writing. But where was he going to get the time? He began to think Belphebe's home universe of Faerie might have its advantages.

There wasn't really much more Athanael or the Board could say, and they did seem much relieved. The project that had sounded very questionable when presented by a mere assistant professor, sounded quite respectable when presented by a full professor with an impressive bibliography of published articles—and with Chalmers' bland confidence and total self-assurance.

Nonetheless, Shea found himself nettled, and a little resentful, by Chalmers' having so very clearly assumed the authority of Director of the Garaden Institute again, even though he was now supposedly only a consultant.

Chalmers noticed Shea's discomfiture right away, of course, and confronted the problem as soon as they were outside, picking their careful way over the icy walks, between snowdrifts left by the crew of shovelers. "I know that sounded as though I were trying to usurp the position you have established in my absence, Harold, but I really have no such intention."

Shea felt a lot better just hearing that. "Thanks, Doc. I know you had to present it that way, just to pacify the Board—but you're right, it did make me uncomfortable."

"My regrets," Chalmers murmured. "Please be assured, dear boy, that I have absolutely no intention of reclaiming my former position."

"That's good to hear," Shea said, "I think. Trouble is, if you resign, I'm going to find myself lumbered with a new boss—and he might not be as sympathetic as you are."

Chalmers nodded. "Moreover, he will undoubtedly wish access to your records of this project, and will demand to know all the pertinent facts."

Shea shuddered. "We can't have that. Just imagine some career academic trying to horn in on our universe-hopping!"

"Yes, quite," Chalmers said drily, and Shea realized, with a start, that he had just described Doc himself—or himself as he had been, before their trip to the universe of Spenser's *Faerie Queene*. "Assuming, of course, that a new Director would not immediately declare the whole project to be stuff and nonsense or, worse, a mammoth hoax, and fire you."

Shea shuddered. "Uh, do you mind officially staying on leave of absence, Doc? If you're technically still Director, then I can still be Acting Director. If I don't want a new boss—and I don't—it has to stay that way."

"I am quite willing, of course," Chalmers said, "but the Board can be stalled in that fashion only so long, Harold. You have two or three years at most. How shall you manage when that time is up?"

"I hadn't thought about that," Shea admitted, and they plodded through the gray January day, Shea sunk in gloom.

Chalmers broke the silence. "You shall have to assume the directorship yourself—and that means that you shall have to acquire the necessary credentials. You absolutely must publish a few articles."

Shea was amazed to discover that he actually had been more or less assuming that he would eventually become Director of the Garaden Institute. Forced to confront the matter, he realized how ridiculous it was, without a publication record. With a shock, he realized that he had become more interested in the directorship than in kiting off on swashbuckling adventures; he found the prospect of the security and status oddly appealing. "Doc! *I* didn't even know I was thinking along those lines—how did *you*?"

"It is a natural consequence of finding the right woman," Chalmers explained, "which usually results in a desire to settle down, especially if the two of you are considering having children."

That was true, Shea reflected—but he said nothing, surprised that such insight could come from a middle-aged man who had never had a family, nor even married until he had met Florimel just a year ago—in another universe. But he was a psychologist, after all, and knew the mind of man. "The possibility has occured to us," Shea admitted.

"How wonderful!" Chalmers beamed. "I could not be more pleased for you, my boy! But you do realize, I trust, that you will be shouldering a very heavy burden—and no small part of the bearing will be the publication of your findings."

"If I can find any to publish," Shea said, with irony.

"Oh, never fear, the inter-universal project will provide the material for that," Chalmers assured him. "Your original notion of using its principles to cure delusions, may prove accurate—who knows? Even if it does not, the simple notion of describing delusions in symbolic logic could be publishable in itself, since it will offer a new and more efficient avenue to analysis."

"Maybe we could collaborate. . . ." But even as he said it, Shea knew he was shying away from the responsibility.

"Desirable." Chalmers smiled. "But it would be too difficult for me to communicate on the steady basis collaboration would require. I do not plan any great stay in Ohio, Harold—only enough to supervise the organization of the experiment as a unified whole. Oh, yes, I am taking this very seriously, now! You will not, of course, publish the vital datum—the 'syllogismobile,' as you have dubbed it, the ability to travel between universes—but in all other respects, the project is quite viable. Once the overall structure is in place, with methods established and research underway, I shall gladly return to the universe of the *Orlando*, and to Florimel."

"Thanks, Doc," Shea said, with feeling. "Not just for bailing me out—but for straightening me out as concerns my goals."

"My pleasure," Chalmers said. "I believe the technical term for the process is 'maturation.' Tell me, though, Harold—who, in your opinion, should be on the research team, other than ourselves, Polacek, and, by correspondence, Bayard?"

Shea thought for a moment. "I suppose we really should bring in Pete Brodsky as an auxiliary investigator, so that we can have everyone who knows about inter-universe travel under the same roof."

Chalmers nodded. "That will have the additional advantage of keeping the knowledge contained until we have determined how to publish it safely, without causing a wholesale migration to other worlds."

"I'd like to make Belphebe an auxiliary, too," Shea said slowly.

"There, I am afraid the Board might raise its collective eyebrow," Chalmers said regretfully. "The implication of nepotism is too strong to be ignored, especially since she has no academic credentials in this universe. Besides, I am afraid American universities are not yet ready to have both husband and wife employed at the same institution. I shall feel rather guilty accepting the good lady's hospitality, now."

"Oh, she probably would have said 'no,' anyway," Shea sighed. "I suppose it doesn't matter—we know she's on our side."

With Chalmers ensconced in the guest room, Shea and Belphebe sat down to evaluate the situation.

"I was really amazed," Shea told her after summarizing the afternoon's events. "I never thought I'd begin to see the advantages of the settled life."

Belphebe smiled, and snuggled a little closer. "I, too, am amazed to find that my hunger for the chase has become only a fleeting notion. Yet in its place has grown a yearning for children."

"If I can support them." Shea nodded. "But Doc has me thinking that, if I succeed in setting up the experiment with his help, it will give me enough credit so that I just might stand a chance at the directorship, and a full professorship."

Belphebe looked up at him with glowing eyes. "Surely the professorship, even without being director!

And would you not then earn enough to feed and clothe children?"

"I guess so," Shea said slowly, marvelling. "I never particularly liked the little blighters before. Of course, I didn't *dis*like them, either—but since I married you, I've begun to think babies look downright cute."

Belphebe smiled. "I have always had a fondness for infants, myself."

She smiled up at him, her eyelids heavy, her lips close, so close. Shea couldn't resist a temptation like that, nor had she intended him to.

That night, as they were drifting off to sleep, Shea suddenly found himself wondering just why Florimel had been so willing to have Chalmers visit his home world, and the Sheas. But he dismissed the thought as unworthy, kissed the red hair in glorious disarray on the pillow beside him, and fell asleep.

SIR HAROLD AND
THE GNOME KING
L. Sprague de Camp

"Darling," said Belphebe, "will you *please* stop worrying! The doctors all confirm that it be nought but a normal, healthy pregnancy."

"I know," said Harold Shea. "But I just can't help—"

"And you really must go off on your syllogismobile to fetch back Walter. If you do it not soon, he'll lose his tenure; the committee meets next month."

"What sort of husband goes off on some goofy quest when his wife's time is getting near?"

"Oh, cease your fussing and get along with you! Marry, I shall be just as pleased if, when you return, the babe's born and I have my wonted shape. Besides, the police are prey to ever-waxing suspicions—"

"Oh, all right," grumbled Shea. "But if anything goes wrong, I'll never forgive myself. . . ."

Thus it came to pass that Harold Shea, incomplete enchanter, sat on the floor of his study arrayed in boots and breeches for his journey through other space-time dimensions, with a feathered hat on his head and a saber by his side.

He had decided that the épée, which he had used on other journeys to mythological worlds, was too specialized a weapon. It had served him well against opponents afoot and unarmored; but even so, it was more by luck than by management that the slender blade had not been snapped in parrying the ferocious cuts of edge-men, nor bent to breaking against stout armor.

His present weapon was a nineteenth-century officer's saber, with the blade shortened by a few inches. The original thirty-six-inch blade, suitable for a horseman, was too unwieldy for combat on foot. The swordsman who swung it might swing himself right off his feet.

As a backup weapon, Shea wore a bowie knife in a sheath at his belt. Moreover, whereas he had formerly scorned protective devices, he now wore beneath his outer garments a shirt of fine mesh-mail.

The last he had seen of Walter Bayard before his recent brief visit to mythical Ireland, his fellow psychologist at the Garaden Institute, was in the hut wherein he, Bayard, Belphebe, and Detective Peter Brodsky had been imprisoned by the chiefs of the world of the Finnish *Kalevala*. Shea's spell, with help from Belphebe and the cop, transferred them all to the world of mythical Ireland, with Cuchulainn and Queen Maeve. But Bayard, if indeed he came through the dimensions, was nowhere to be seen. Shea thought that he had probably been dumped somewhere else in the same world of myth.

But should Shea go back to Cuchulainn's Eriu to look for his colleague? The search might take years, with no end in sight. Moreover, these quasi-Irishmen showed a disturbing fondness for collecting people's heads as trophies.

There was, however, a plausible shortcut: the Land of Oz, as chronicled by L. Frank Baum and later by Ruth Plumly Thompson. In Oz, a major magical artifact was the Gnome King's Magic Belt, confiscated by Dorothy Gale of Kansas after the King had treacherously tried to imprison her. The Belt was effective as a teletransporter. If Shea could enlist the help of the Belt's present custodians, he could fetch Bayard from mythical Eriu to Oz, whence the custodians could send the two of them back to Ohio.

Shea launched into the sorites that, he hoped, would bring him to the world of Oz: "If P equals not-Q, then Q implies not-P, which is the same as saying either P and Q or neither, but not both. But the counter-implicative form of the proposition . . ."

On went the sorites, adjusting Shea's senses to the stimuli of the other world he sought.

At length the study around him dissolved into a whirl of spots of color. He seemed suspended in nothing, as if in free fall. Then things solidified.

Shea found himself standing on a pavement of onyx squares among several small buildings of boxy shape. Behind these structures rose towering crags, in which yawned large black openings. Paved paths led up to these aperatures. Up and down the paths walked figures in ankle-length gowns, with hoods drawn over their heads.

Shea stood still, trying to orient himself. Wherever he was, he did not think that this was the land of Oz—at least, not any section of it in the books by Baum and Thompson. Of course it had been years since . . .

He began to sort out the pedestrians. Some were of normal human stature and aspect, in hooded gowns of various colors, running strongly to somber purple. Others, inhumanly tall and lean, wore black; these had a single horn emerging from each hood. A closer view showed that those in black walked on hooves instead of human feet.

Looking around, Shea saw, rearing against the

surrounding cliffs, a single lofty spire. Overhead the sky was overcast and so dark as to imply a dawn or a sunset. Flames of cressets and torchères mitigated the gloom. The orange light flickered, making it hard to be sure of anything.

Pedestrians walked past Shea without evincing interest. The hooves of the horned ones went clop-clop on the sable flagstones. Some of the walkers passed in pairs, conversing in quiet tones.

A shriek from the direction of the slender tower brought Shea about. He turned in time to see a gown-clad figure falling, doubtless from high in the tower. The garment fluttered with the body's rising speed, and the arms and legs thrashed the air. The figure landed with a sound that reminded Shea of hitting a melon with a mallet.

The hooded pedestrians continued their ways without even looking around. Soon a pair of horned, black-gowned beings picked up the corpse and bore it off.

Unable longer to stand the suspense, Shea touched a passerby on the arm. "Excuse me, sir."

The passerby, in a purple gown and holding a walking stick, turned and threw back his hood. "Eh? What is it?" He was a tall, handsome, swarthy, black-haired young man.

At least, thought Shea, the sorites had worked to give him fluency in the local language, whatever that was. From its wealth of gutturals, Shea suspected Arabic. He said:

"Could you please tell me where I am?"

The tall youth stared. "Do you mean you don't know?"

"No, I don't. A magical journey just dropped me here, but I don't think it's where I wanted to go. Could you set me right?"

"All right. You are on the campus of the University of the Unholy Names, in Death Valley."

"But what world?"

"You mean you don't even know *that*? You must be a little touched here...." The youth tapped his forehead.

"Maybe so, but I really must know. Please!"

"Well," said the tall youth, "this is the world called sometimes Dej, an acronym of Dâl Ay Jím—or, as the infidels say, Delta Epsilon Gamma."

"And you, sir?"

The youth ducked a little bow. "Bilsa at-Tâlib, an undergraduate at good old UUN, at your service. And you? You must be a pretty good magician, to go flitting from world to world."

Shea smiled warily. "Oh, I know a trick or two. My name's Shea, Harold Shea."

Shea almost put out a hand before realizing where he was. Recovering, he touched his fingertips to his heart, lips, and forehead. Bilsa, he was relieved to see, did likewise.

"What about that fellow who just fell from the tower?"

"Failed his exams and was dropped." Bilsa shrugged, then continued with an eager rush of words: "Say, you see this stick? I was on my way to show it to the dean. When I throw it down, it turns into a snake, which gets bigger and bigger until I hit it with this little wand, and it shrinks back into a walking stick again. I've got a swell idea! I'll turn this stick into a snake, see, and you conjure up your own monster; and we'll see which one of 'em wins!"

The youth was evidently of the kind that, in a college chemistry laboratory, starts mixing chemicals at random to see which mixture will go *boom*. Before Shea could protest, Bilsa threw down the stick, which instantly turned into a snake of the python kind. It grew and grew, soon reaching a size beyond that of any earthly serpent. It reared up and swung its tapering head, now as big as that of a horse, toward Shea. It opened fangsome jaws and hissed like the safety valve of a steam boiler.

Shea had no monster-conjuring spell to hand and did not wish any such contest. He must, he thought, have substituted a Q for a non-Q in the sorites. Against such a foe, his sword was of little avail. Frantically he again began the series:

"If P equals not-Q, then Q implies . . ."

The monstrous head, now of tyrannosauric size, swooped. The jaws came down upon his head and snapped shut like the door of a bank vault, cutting off the meager light. Shea felt himself snatched off his feet as the jaws clamped on his midriff. The mailshirt kept the teeth, now spikes the size of fence palings, from piercing his body, but the pressure of the jaws blew the wind out of him. By a mighty feat of concentration, he continued the spell:

". . . which sets down Harold Shea near the abode of Dorothy Gale in the Land of Oz!"

The agonizing pressure on Shea's midsection let up. Again he seemed to be suspended in nothing and surrounded by a galaxy of whirling colored dots.

Then he landed on solid earth, rolling over and over as if he had fallen at a slant from a height. The scabbarded saber banged and poked him.

He sat up, wincing at the pain of the places bruised by the pressure of the reptile's jaws. Every movement of his trunk was painful. Around him rose a forest of green-leaved cornstalks, several of which he had broken in his fall. They were just coming into ear.

Battered, bruised, and sore, Shea gathered his legs and rose. His head and the upper part of his torso were covered with gooey serpent saliva, to which the brown dirt clung in patches. He must, he thought, look like nothing on Earth. He was bareheaded; his hat must have gone down the sorcerous serpent's gullet. Had he not finished the correct sorites, he would surely have followed the hat. He was thankful that, more by luck than by management, the spell had translocated him alone and not both him and the super-snake.

He had begun to thread his way out from the cornfield when a man shouted: "Hey, you there! What are you doing in my field?"

"Trying to get out without damaging anything," said Shea, picking his way among the cornstalks.

"The blazes you ain't! You mean without doing any *more* damage. You've knocked over a dozen stalks already!"

"I'm very sorry. In going from world to world, one can't always count on a soft landing."

"Jeepers Cripus, what world do you claim to come from?"

The speaker was a man of medium size, with work-roughened hands and a sun-wrinkled neck. He wore yellow knee breeches and a yellow shirt, both faded and patched, and a broad-brimmed straw hat. He gripped a cultivator like a weapon.

"From Ohio, in the United States of America," said Shea.

"Oh, the mundane world," said the man. "Well, now, that's interesting. . . ."

"Is Dorothy Gale's house near here?" asked Shea.

"Huh? Oh, you must mean my wife! She was Dorothy Gale before she became Mrs. Stidoth. Well, now . . ."

"Stidoth!" came a woman's voice.

"Yeah, honey? Hey, come on over here! We got a visitor from your world!"

A woman approached—a blonde of middle years, well-featured and a little plump.

"Says he's lookin' for Miss Dorothy Gale," said Stidoth.

"Okay, mister, you found her," said the woman. "Where in my world did you come from?"

"Ohio. Shea's the name."

"Back east, eh? Well, another real American's always welcome. We don't see 'em around all that often, since we moved out from the Emerald City. Come on in the house. You look like you could do with a bit of a cleanup."

"If you'd been half swallowed by a giant snake— well, you know what I mean. Lucky for all of us I didn't bring the super-serpent with me. A magician conjured it up and sicked it on me."

"Come along; you can wash up in the house and tell us all about it. We got running water and everything."

Cleaned up, Shea had finished the tale of his adventure, saying: "Things look different from what I expected."

"How different?" said Stidoth, who without his straw hat proved somewhat balding.

"I thought people in Oz stayed the same age forever, until some accident took them."

Stidoth explained: "That's how it was, more or less, before the big change."

"Big change?"

"Yeah. Seems there was this kid, Dranol Drabbo, who couldn't wait to grow up. The way things were, he'd have growed up, all right, in a couple of hundred years; but he was one of these here flibbertigibbets who can't wait five minutes for anything they happen to want.

"Well, now, this here Dranol Drabbo went to Wogglebug College and majored in magic. And one of his experiments canceled the spell that some queen of the fairies laid on Oz centuries ago. People say that there spell got rid of death, but it ain't really so. All it did was to slow down the normal business of aging to a crawl, like a snail walking. Aging was already a lot slower for us Ozians than for you mundanes. You seem to us like them there bugs that flit around for a day and then die."

"Must have been a tragedy for the Ozites."

Stidoth shrugged. "Got advantages and disadvantages both ways, like most things in life. As 'twas, the population was getting out of hand, with the old folks hangin' on forever.

"Anyway, I was Dot's age at the time. So when we growed up we got hitched, and here we are. I didn't much like the idea of our boys going to Wogglebug, on account of what happened with Dranol Drabbo. Besides, too much book-learning can spoil a good farmer. But they sold Dot on the idea, and—well, you a married man, Mr. Shea?"

"Yes," said Shea. "Quite happily—but I know what you mean."

Stidoth chuckled. "The older boy'll be out in a couple of months, looking for a way to earn his three squares. Claims he's invented some sort of calculating machine." Stidoth's eyes narrowed. "All right, Mr. Shea, now tell us just what you came here for, and in particular why you wanted to see Dot."

Shea told of Walter Bayard's predicament. ". . . so I thought that, if I could persuade whoever's in charge of the Gnome King's Belt to fetch Bayard here and then send us both back to what you call the mundane world . . ."

Stidoth sat in silence for several seconds, then said: "Mr. Shea, if you owned one of them there atomic bombs we hear about, would you keep it in the cellar, where some kid might set it off accidental-like?"

"Of course not!"

"Same way here. That there belt could be just as dangerous, in the hands of some amateur piddler in magic like Dranol Drabbo, as one of them bombs. So it's kept locked up in the palace in the Emerald City."

"What happened to Dranol Drabbo?"

Stidoth sniffed. "Queen Ozma's a fine woman, and don't let nobody tell you different. But when she was a girl, she was full of airy-fairy impractical ideas. One was you shouldn't hurt nobody or nothing, even to save your own life. She almost let Oz be conquered several times, because she wouldn't believe anyone was so wicked as to plot agin her. Even when she was warned, she wouldn't fight, because that meant hurting or killing people. Each time she was saved by some lucky, last-minute magical trick; but you can't count on that kind of luck forever.

"So the question was, what to do with young Dranol Drabbo? I'd have called in Nick Chopper and had him operate with his ax on Dranol's neck. But no, the Queen decided the worst punishment she'd allow was to send him to exile in Ev.

"Well, you know the gnomes live under the ground where Ev is, and it didn't take long for Dranol to get in cahoots with the Gnome King, Kaliko—the one who followed Ruggedo. They say Kaliko fired his chancellor, Shoofenwaller, and gave his job to Dranol. Don't rightly know what sort of devilment they're cooking up; but I'm sure it's something.

"Course, when Ozma growed up and married King Evardo, it steadied her down. He's got plenty of hard common sense."

Shea thought. "This king—is he of the royal family of Ev?"

"Sure; he's King of Ev. But he lives here in Oz and lets his brother Evring run the kingdom as regent. That way, Evardo gets the fun of being king without the headaches."

Shea grinned. "Reminds me of a song from a show back in my world:

"Oh, philosophers may sing
Of the troubles of a king;
Yet the duties are delightful and the privileges
    great . . ."

Stidoth chuckled and slapped his thigh. "Hey, that's
good! Wouldn't mind seeing that there show. Anyway,
Evardo also got the duty of providing the most beautiful woman in Oz with heirs to the throne. Boy, that's
one job plenty of men—"

"Stidoth!" said Dorothy sternly.

"Sorry. Anyway, they've only got two kids so far.
The older's a boy—young man, almost—and I hear
he's away visiting kinfolks in Ev. The other's a girl,
just starting school. But a royal family needs a whole
raft of heirs, in case something happens to the older
ones. So I guess Evardo has lots of fun trying—"

"Stidoth!"

"Anyway, reckon you'll have to get to the Emerald
City and hand a petition to some flunkey at the
palace."

Shea shook his head. "It just doesn't seem like Oz
somehow, those young fairyland girls growing up and
having children of their own."

"Well, that's what they do in your mundane world,
ain't it?"

"Yes; I'm an expectant father myself. It's just—well,
it somehow spoils the magic." How logical, Shea
thought, that Dorothy, though here ranked as a princess, should wed a man of background like her own!

"Don't you believe it, Mr. Shea. We got plenty of
magic left. It's a matter of this here now mental attitude. When you was a kid, didn't your mundane world
seem like a kind of fairyland to you, full of exciting
things you later found out didn't exist? But when you
growed up, you had to trade in those exciting things

for the exciting things of the real world, even if they wa'n't so pretty.

"As for Ozma's getting spliced, I mind me some years ago, before Dranol worked his spell, some little princeling named—let me think—Pomp-something. Anyway, he asked Ozma to marry him. Course, he got turned down flat. Lucky young fella found another princess, who took him on.

"Then there was that there Baron Mogodore, who captured the capital by surprise and said he was going to marry Ozma whether she liked it or not. Since the law says a marriage has got to be with the free will of both parties to be legal, there ain't really no such thing as a 'forced marriage,' leastaways in Oz. It's just a fancy name for plain old—"

"Stidoth!"

"Oh, all right, Dot honey, if you won't call things by their right names. I'll say he was going to 'subject her to an indecent personal assault.' That fancy enough for you?"

Shea reflected that the Stidoths had a very normal marriage, solid but not without occasional rifts and irritations. He changed the subject: "If I have to go to the capital, how do I get there?"

"You can walk, but it's quite a piece. Don't have no magic carpets or broomsticks or nothing here."

Dorothy spoke: "Dear, why don't we lend him Alis? He can ride her to the city, turn her loose, and tell her to go home. She knows the way well enough."

"Reckon that's a good idea. How about it, Mr. Shea?"

"Who is Alis?"

"One of our mules. I forget; you mundanes ain't used to animals that talk and understand like people do. But it's too late to start now. You better stay overnight with us and set out at sun-up."

"You're much too kind, really—"

"Think nothin' of it, Mr. Shea! Anybody that's got legitimate business with the Queen, it's only right to give him a hand to get him there."

From what he recalled of the Oz books, Shea believed that Ozma's court did not go in for elaborate formalities, such as requiring presentees to prostrate themselves or knock their heads upon the floor. But his travels through alternative universes had given him a fair command of protocol. The flunkey announced:

"I present to Your Majesty Doctor Sir Harold Shea, a mundane with a petition."

She put his hand over his heart and bowed to the horizontal, flourishing an imaginary hat with a sweeping gesture. When he straightened up, he faced Queen Ozma on her throne. She must have been about Dorothy's age in terms of mundane maturity; but she was still one of the most beautiful women Shea had ever seen. A circlet of gold, to each side of which was fastened a large red blossom, confined her midnight hair. After scrutiny, Shea decided that the blossoms were artificial.

"Master Shea," said Ozma. "Your pardon, Doctor Sir Harold Shea. Do not, pray, take offense at our curiosity; but we should like to know whence you obtained those appellations of rank, 'Doctor' and 'Sir'?"

Shea smiled easily. "Your Majesty, the 'Doctor' was awarded in consequence of my studies at the Garaden Institute in the mundane world, and I was dubbed a knight by the warrior lady Britomart in the world of *The Faerie Queene*."

"Of what sort were these studies whereof you speak?"

"In the workings of the human mind, Madam."

"Perhaps we should keep you with us, to unravel the mystery of why people, living secure and comfortable lives, persist natheless in acts of mischief, dishonesty, and violence. But now tell us what you would of us, pray."

When Shea had again told the story of Walter Bayard's stranding in mythological Ireland, Ozma sat quietly for some time. Twice she leaned forward and seemed about to speak but then sank back on her throne. At last she spoke, not to Shea but to a flunkey:

"Where is our consort?"

"My last knowledge, Your Majesty, is that he was on the tennis courts."

"Kindly request him to join us in the Audience Room." She turned back to Shea. "Sir Harold, you appear to have led a lively career, leaping from world to world. Whilst we wait, will you tell us of one of your adventures?"

"Gladly, Your Majesty," said Shea. "When I sojourned in the iron castle of the enchanter Atlantès, in the world of the *Orlando Furioso* . . ."

Shea was telling how he and Polacek had bribed the goblin Odoro to fetch them a bottle of liquor in the nonalcoholic Muslimoid environment, when the consort entered, carrying a tennis racquet. King Evardo was a tall, lean, well-muscled man, with blond hair streaked with gray. He wore shorts and a T-shirt, and sweat beaded his features.

The flunkey made introductions, and Shea repeated his bow. To his surprise, Evardo thrust out a large hand. Shea shook it and got the impression of a crushing grip, deliberately held back from its full power.

"A pleasure, Sir Harold!" boomed the consort, wiping his face with the towel a flunkey handed him. He turned to Ozma. "What's the problem this time, darling?"

On request, Shea repeated the tale of Bayard's stranding. He ended: ". . . So I thought that if Your

Majesties would use the Belt to fetch Bayard here and then send us both home . . ."

"I see," said King Evardo, looking through narrowed lids.

Ozma spoke: "It sounds like a praiseworthy enterprise—"

She broke off as Evardo raised a hand. The consort said: "My darling is sometimes a trifle impulsive, perhaps a bit over-accommodating. This is a lovable quality in a spouse but unrealistic in a ruler. Assuming that we can, with the Belt, accomplish these feats, wherein lies the benefit to the Kingdom of Oz?" After a pause, he added: "To put it in the mundane vernacular, what's in it for us?"

"I—I hadn't thought," said Shea. "What could I possibly do for Your Majesties?"

"One task stares us in the face, namely: the rescue of our son Oznev from captivity by the Gnome King."

"Huh? Do you mean old Ruggedo? I thought you had turned him into a potted cactus!"

Evardo gave a grim chuckle. "So we had; or to be exact, so our friend the elf Himself had. But Ruggedo's former chancellor, Kaliko, succeeded him. Kaliko's a less contrary, cantankerous character than old Rug, but you trust either at your own risk.

"Anyhow, we sent Oznev off to visit his cousins in Ev, during his summer vacation from Wogglebug U. Then, when we looked in Ozma's magic picture to see how he was getting on, it showed us poor Oznev chained in an underground cell. Next we got a note from Kaliko, delivered by messenger bat, saying he would trade the boy for the Belt. If we didn't agree, he would send Oznev home—but a piece at a time."

"So, what do you expect me to do?" asked Shea.

"We'll transport you to Ev by the Belt, dropping you off near the Gnome King's western palace, which is actually a glorified cave. We'll give you a chart, showing how to find the entrance to the Kingdom of Gnomicia. Once inside, you're on your own."

"If you know where Oznev is, why can't you fetch him home by the Belt?"

"Because the Gnome Kingdom is so well protected by magical barriers and counter-spells that no device like our Belt can get through into it. We can just barely bring it into focus in our magic picture. The Royal Wizard of Gnomicia, Doctor Potaroo, set them up and keeps adding new ones. Other wizards call Potaroo a fifth-rater, but there's nothing fifth-rate about his magical defenses."

Shea said: "I understand that Gnomicia is a labyrinth of caves and tunnels, in which an outsider could easily get lost."

"Right you are!" said Evardo.

"Then how do you expect me to find my way around it? Wandering through miles of tunnels wouldn't do your son a bit of good. Do you know a trustworthy guide?"

Ozma spoke: "The only person in Oz who knows the tunnels is Ruggedo—"

"What!" exploded Evardo. "We mustn't even think of turning that villainous old scundermuch loose on an innocent world!"

"Perhaps, if he promised to reform—" began Ozma.

"Darling! He's promised that before, more than once, and each time he backslid. It's out of the question, Sir Harold."

"Then," said Shea, "I'm sorry, but I really don't see how I can help you in this matter. Of course, Your Majesties and several of Her Majesty's subjects, like Princess Dorothy, have been in the caverns and come out again; but I don't suppose—"

"You don't suppose correctly," snapped Evardo. "It's true that the Queen and some of our friends have visited Gnomicia, but only briefly, seeing but a small fraction of the complex. Your chances of finding Oznev were as good if you went in cold as they would be with, say, the Scarecrow or Tik-Tok as guide . . ."

The argument growled on and on, Shea refusing to agree without a sure guide, living or documentary; the royal couple refusing to help recover Bayard unless Shea undertook the mission. At last Shea suggested:

"Maybe Ruggedo would be so pleased by a chance to oust Kaliko and get his throne back that he'd be glad not only to show me around but also to stay there, without further conditions. I believe he did once recover his kingdom but wasn't allowed to keep it."

Evardo sighed. "I still wouldn't trust him any farther than I could throw a chimney by the smoke. Sometimes you mundanes are too sharp for us poor, simple fairylanders. Let's drop the subject and take it up again tomorrow, when the Queen and I have discussed it. You are welcome to dine and pass the night in the palace."

The audience resumed at ten the next morning. Evardo said: "Sir Harold, the Queen and I have decided to take you up on your proposal to give Ruggedo back his gnomish form. Then we shall see if he'll fall in with our scheme. Pray come with us to the conservatory, good my sir!"

Following the royal couple and a brace of guards, Shea ducked right and left to avoid masses of greenery. The air was steamy. Evardo and Ozma stopped at a long bench on which were lined up flowerpots containing spiny and prickly plants, such as cacti, agaves, and thistles.

"Here they are," said Evardo, indicating two pots at the end, in which stood prickly-pear cacti of the genus *Opuntia.* "Are you sure you know which is which, my dear?"

"Certainly," said Ozma. "The tall one is the King

of Silver Mountain, and the short is Ruggedo. He used to be fat and tubby, but all his efforts to best the Ozites wore him down."

"All right, my dear," said Evardo. "Just a minute while I fetch some more guards to grab Ruggedo in case he tries something. . . ."

Evardo was gone for several minutes. During this time, Ozma showed Shea the rare plants in the conservatory, explaining the provenience and properties of each. Evardo returned with another pair of stalwart, sword-armed guards in palace livery. He handed Ozma a wand and a small phial, saying:

"Number three-forty; isn't that the one you wanted?"

"Yes. Everybody quiet, now."

The Queen made passes with the wand, speaking words of power in an undertone. At last she poured the contents of the phial over one of the cacti, crying:

"Awaken!"

The flowerpot burst into fragments, spilling dirt across the bench and on the floor, as the cactus changed into an aged gnome, sitting on the bench amid potsherds and the dirt in which he had been planted. His first word was:

"Ouch!"

Ruggedo pulled a large, jagged potsherd out from beneath him and threw it away. Then he slid down from the bench and ducked a bow to the royal couple, saying in a creaky voice:

"Well, well! Queen Ozma, or I'll be egged! But how you've grown! I should hardly know you but for that fancy fillet you always wore. What in Oz has been happening? Have centuries passed while I was under that villainous leprechaun's spell?"

"No," said Ozma. "A few years after Himself enchanted you and the King of Silver Mountain, a youth studying magic accidentally canceled the aging-stasis spell."

"So now Ozites die of old age as other folk do, without waiting for an accident to get them?" Ruggedo gave a sneering laugh.

"That is right. It makes less difference than one might think, because our natural lives are longer than those of mundanes to begin with."

"And what befell the King of Silver Mountain? Did he become a plant, too?"

Ozma pointed her wand. "Your fellow cactus."

"Well, strike my topsails! You will have to give me some time to gather my wits. And who are these other people?"

Shea remembered that Ruggedo had led a brief career as a pirate captain; the locutions of that milieu had evidently remained with him. Ozma said:

"My beloved husband, King Evardo of Ev, and Doctor Sir Harold Shea, a mundane."

Ruggedo chuckled. "Well, well, little Evardo! You've grown even more than she has!"

"And you've lost a lot of weight," said King Evardo, "since the time you turned me into a piece of bric-à-brac on a shelf in your palace." He added: "As you have already guessed, Sir Harold, you behold the former Gnome King, Ruggedo the Rough, a.k.a. Roquat the Red, a.k.a. the Metal Monarch. He used to be as round as a grapefruit."

Ruggedo sighed. "Life has been hard, especially that five-year stretch as a mute peddler. You have no idea how difficult it is to give customers a hard sell without a voice. No wonder I was starved down to a skinny old swabbie! The things that have befallen me in trying to recover my just rights!"

"You look better skinny," said Evardo. "You used to resemble a grape or an olive with toothpicks stuck to it."

Ruggedo put his fists on his hips. "Very funny, ha-ha. Now then, don't tell me you've revived me just out of the goodness of your hearts. Ozma just might, but I judge you, fellow monarch, to be a tougher character. You were as a boy. So what do you want of me?"

The gnome glared defiantly. Evardo said: "Just to act as a guide to Sir Harold into Gnomicia, that's all. And to help him to rescue our son—Ozma's and mine—from captivity by your successor Kaliko."

"So Kaliko worked a snatch on royalty?" Ruggedo snickered. "As chancellor, he was always warning me against overreaching; and here he's done the same fool thing himself! The last thing I said to him, when he threw me out of my kingdom the second time, was not to mess with the Ozites. I had tried every way I could think of and come a cropper each time. But some people don't learn from others' experience."

"And power corrupts," added Evardo. "Well, how about it? Will you undertake this quest?"

Ruggedo looked sly. "Yes, if you will give me back my Belt."

"Out of the question! We'll use it to send you and Sir Harold to your western entrance."

"No Belt, no guide," snapped Ruggedo, crossing his arms on his chest.

"Of course," said Ozma casually, "I can always turn you back into a cactus."

"Go ahead! At least it's painless, though life as a potted plant is pretty dull. Almost as tedious as being a walnut or a crockery jug, both of which I know from experience."

Shea spoke: "King Ruggedo, this trip would give you a chance to oust Kaliko and resume your kingship."

"Hmm. I'll think it over. If you offered the Belt along with this rescue mission, I'd say 'yes' like a shot."

"Forget the Belt!" roared Evardo. "Guide and help

Sir Harold, and you shall have a chance at your former kingdom. Otherwise, not."

Ruggedo's normally gray complexion flushed an angry red. "You mean," he shouted, "that even if I do you a vital service, you still won't return my own hard-earned property?" The gnome began to hop about, and his voice rose to a scream. "You're all just a band of bandits, thieves, robbers! You pretend to be so noble and virtuous, but it's all a sham! Hypocrites! Plunderers!"

The gnome seized a small flowerpot holding a plant, raised it high, and hurled it to the floor with a mighty smash, sending dirt and potsherds flying.

"Grab him!" said Evardo to the guards. Two stalwarts seized Ruggedo's arms and held him fast despite his yells and struggles.

"Oh, my poor Ragbadian daffodil!" cried Ozma, stooping to pick up the remains of the plant.

"You two," said Evardo to the remaining guards, "find another flowerpot, put the dirt back in—as much as you can—and replant the bulb. We may save it."

Shea said: "In the mundane world, back when monarchs really ruled, anyone who spoke that way to a king or queen would soon find himself shorter by a head."

Ozma smiled. "We know old Rug." Then to the gnome: "You might as well calm down, Rug. You make much of your property rights in the Belt. But, you see, we know the story of how you obtained it in the first place."

"That was entirely different!" said Ruggedo. "You haven't heard my side of the tale—"

Evardo interrupted. "Later; some other time. We're getting off the subject. Do you accept our deal or not? Don't hope that, once in Gnomicia, you can hatch another plot against us. We shall watch you."

Ruggedo looked hurt. "What, me plot against Your

Majesties? Perish the thought! I tried that several times without success and hope I have learned a few things in my centuries. Since I have this time really resolved to reform, I will agree to your terms, unfair though I deem them."

"Very well," said Evardo. "When shall we send you off? Tomorrow?"

"Just a minute, Your Majesty!" said Shea. "You haven't fetched Bayard yet."

"After you have released Prince Oznev," said Evardo. "Not before."

"But Bayard is a big, strong fellow, and very smart. I'll need his help, especially if it comes to a fight."

"No."

"Then no rescue mission. You can turn Ruggedo back into a cactus."

"Dear," said Ozma, "we had better consult on this. Will you gentlemen excuse us?"

She swept out, followed by Evardo and two guards. The other two guards remained, glowering uneasily at Ruggedo. The gnome said to Shea:

"Who is this Bayard? What's this all about? Since I've been a dumb plant for I don't know how long, you can't expect me to sound very intelligent."

Shea repeated the tale of Bayard's stranding in Eriu. Answering Ruggedo's questions, he was in the midst of a summary of twentieth-century mundane history when the royal couple returned. Evardo said:

"How is this, Sir Harold? We will get out the Belt and fetch Bayard from that barbarous world wherein he dwells. But we will not send him to Gnomicia with you. On such a mission, two is fine but three is a crowd, more likely to be discovered.

"Instead, Bayard shall remain here until you return from your quest. If you perish in the attempt or, despite valiant efforts, fail from circumstances beyond your control, we will send him—or the twain of you, as the case may be—back to your mundane world. Fair enough?"

"In other words," said Shea, "you'll hold Bayard as a hostage."

"That's a crude way of putting it; he'll be very well treated. And I would not insult a dubbèd knight by implying that he might slip away and run out on his obligations."

"I'll buy it," said Shea, "provided you equip me with enough magical gadgets to enable me to succeed."

"The Queen and I shall consider the matter and outfit you in the morning."

On a small table before Ozma's throne lay two round, woollen, peakless caps. When Shea picked one up, he found it so much like the common Mediterranean beret that, when he looked inside, he expected to read *Fabriqué en France* or *Producto de España*.

"Don't put it on yet," said Evardo, standing beside the throne. "They are the best we could find in the magical arsenal. Most of our magical devices will not work in Gnomicia because of Potaroo's counter-spells. These tarncaps will, I am sure. They are set for full charge, so they will render your clothes as well as your body invisible."

Shea: "The lesser charge, which would affect only my physical person, wouldn't be very practical, would it?"

Evardo smiled. "We wouldn't ask you to strip naked before invading the Gnome Kingdom. I can think of base uses to which persons of low morals might put a tarncap—

"Evardo!" said Ozma sternly.

Evardo sighed. "My dear! I was only thinking of the loot an invisible thief could garner, and that therefore we must keep these headpieces under strict control. What had you in mind?"

"Never mind!"

She suppressed a grin. Ozites, he thought, had some remarkable Victorian attitudes. Ozma and Dorothy Gale, close friends as girls, had evidently matured with similar ideas on the management of husbands. He said:

"Your Majesties! We'll need three caps, one for Oznev when and if we release him and are on our way out. You said yourselves you couldn't use the Belt to snatch us away until we're free of the caves. Hadn't we better take a look in your magic picture to see what we'll need?"

"Right on both counts, Sir Harold," said Evardo. "Let's take a look, my dear."

Looking at the magic picture, Shea said: "We mundanes have a thing somewhat like this, called a television screen. But we can't always see what we wish, and much of what is shown gets pretty tedious."

Ozma, facing the picture, placed her fingers against her temples and whispered. Presently the scene in the picture, a conventional landscape with trees and a waterfall, faded. Instead, the picture darkened, showing an adolescent youth on a bench in some sort of crypt or dungeon. Stout chains joined the gyves on his wrists and ankles to massive staples set in the masonry.

"Is the cell barred?" asked Shea.

Ozma whispered some more, and the view moved back from the prisoner. There was indeed a set of bars with a door closing the front of the cell, but the door stood ajar.

"Shiver my strakes!" growled Ruggedo. "Kaliko's a careless sort of king. When I ruled, any jailer who left cell doors open would be fed to the slicing machine!"

"Next," said Shea, "assuming we gain entrance to the cell, how do we dispose of the chains and handcuffs?

Picking locks is not one of my skills. Haven't you a wand or something I could zap the chains with?"

"I fear not," said Evardo. "If we had, it probably wouldn't work in Gnomicia."

"Is there a bolt cutter in Oz?"

"I know not, but I shall find out."

The next day saw Shea at the royal smithy, trying to explain to the royal smith, with the help of a diagram, the principles of a bolt cutter.

Back in the informal reception room of the palace Shea told the royal couple: "I think I got the idea over, but his first try at a bolt cutter may not work. The last I saw, he was muttering spells over a piece of bar stock. Are you going to fetch Bayard now?"

"Yes; we were waiting for you," said Ozma. She wore a wide belt that reminded Shea of the belts favored by motorcycle gangsters. She leaned forward, closed her eyes, waved a wand in an intricate pattern, and whispered. With a *floomp* of displaced air, something bulky landed with a bang on the carpet. Blinking in surprise, Shea realized that the object was a large bed of primitive construction, with a rough-hewn wooden frame and a network of rope in lieu of a mattress.

Moreover, the bed was occupied by two persons, who thrust up heads beyond the end of the blanket. One was that of a big man with a bushy brown beard; the other, that of a red-haired, pale-skinned young woman. As they sat up, the blanket fell down to reveal that both were naked, at least to the waist. The woman snatched up the edge of the blanket to cover herself, emitting a shriek:

"Fomorians! 'Tis a pair of dead corps that we are!"

The bearded man blinked, stared around, and finally said: "Hi, Harold! I thought you'd get me out sooner or later. But where did you get us out *to*?"

"The Land of Oz," replied Shea. "These are Queen

Ozma and her consort, King Evardo of Ev. This is
Ruggedo, the former Gnome King. Doctor Walter
Bayard, Your Majesties. Sorry to have snatched you at
an inconvenient time, Walter."

Bayard bowed as best he could sitting up in bed.
"Pleased to meet Your Majesties. Excuse my not getting up, but as you see I don't have on my court dress.
This—" (he indicated the red-haired girl) "—is my
caile dhonn, otherwise Mistress Boann Ni Colum. Tell
me, Harold, are the people here as fussy about expo-
sure as those of mythical Ireland?"

"We observe the normal decencies," said Ozma.

"Then," continued Bayard imperturbably, "may
we borrow some clothes? Had we but known in
advance . . ."

Ozma gave orders to a bodyguard, who departed.
Shea said: "I didn't know you with the whiskers,
Walter."

"A druid without a beard is no druid at all."

"You're a druid now?"

Bayard smiled. "I got to the third degree in the
order of Vates or wise men. A little modern psychology, tactfully applied, put me so far ahead of the competition that it was no contest."

The guard came back with four muscular flunkeys,
who carried out the bed. Ozma explained:

"I'm putting them in the fourteenth guest room,
with clothes to don. Do they wear clothes in this mythological Ireland, Sir Harold?"

"Indeed they do! In that climate, without them
everyone would die of pneumonia."

Bayard appeared in green knee breeches, shirt, and
vest; Mistress Boann, in a gauzy gown that Shea suspected of being one of Ozma's castoffs. Bayard bowed
ceremoniously saying:

"I thank Your Majesties with profound gratitude."
After a gracious royal dismissal, Bayard asked:

"Harold, where's Belphebe? I'd have expected to see her with you."

"Home having a baby," said Shea.

"Congratulations. I'm surprised she let you go, even to spring me from the land of poetical headhunters."

Shea frowned. "On the contrary, it was she who insisted I go. I think she feels somehow guilty over the fact that it's to be a girl. She comes of a culture that rates sons far and away above daughters. I explained about Y chromosomes and told her over and over the gender didn't matter, and I'd be delighted whichever it was; but she feels she's somehow failed me. So she practically bullied me into going before the kid was due. Silly, but there it is."

Later that day, King Evardo said: "Sir Harold, may I speak with you privily, whilst the Queen shows our new guests around the palace? In my cabinet, pray. This way."

"Okay, Your Majesty," said Shea. "Spill it."

Seated behind a big desk, Evardo twiddled his fingers uncertainly. "This subject is a trifle awkward, but the Queen insists. Your comrade Bayard and his—ah—Mistress Ni Colum are plainly on intimate terms. But—ah—is their union legitimate?"

"You mean, are they married?"

"Precisely, Sir Harold. You see, the Queen insists on the strictest standards, at least in the palace. Our new arrivals seem to expect assignment to the same quarters, but our rules cannot be stretched to cover—ah—irregular unions. Which is it in this case?"

Shea suppressed a snigger. "I don't know how they do it in the world of Irish myth. From what I recall of the legends—which may or may not accurately describe conditions in Eriu—they were pretty free and easy about sex, although puritanical about nudity. A chief could demand that a subject lend him his wife for a few nights."

"Galloping Growleywogs!" cried Evardo in horrified tones. "We can't have that sort of thing here!"

"Of course not," said Shea soothingly. "Eriu's a pretty barbarous world; I've been there. But my impression is that if a man and a woman set up house together, they were married by definition. You could say Walter and Boann were married by the local laws and customs of the place where they met."

Evardo frowned. "I know not how far that tale will go to convince the Queen, but I'll try. I was a little surprised when Doctor Bayard made no objection to being left here, as a kind of polite hostage, whilst you and Ruggedo set forth on your adventure."

Shea shrugged. "Walter's an easygoing fellow who takes things as they come, and he's seen enough adventure not to feel a need to seek it for its own sake. I'm sure he'd have come if he'd been asked. And he'll have certain—ah—amenities here that I shall lack."

Evardo smiled. "I take it you mean Mistress Ni Colum. I deem myself broad-minded, but pray do not speak thus lightly on such matters to the Queen. She might take offense."

"As you say, sir. I, too, have a strong-minded wife."

"How goes your bolt cutter?"

"The first one worked badly. The smith says he has trouble spacing the pivot pins correctly. He's familiar with scissors and pincers with a single pivot, but five in one tool baffle him. He's working on another model now."

"If I remember aright," said Ruggedo's creaky old voice, "the entrance ought to be just over yonder ridge."

"That's what the chart shows," said Shea.

Shea finished his lunch, while Ruggedo put away the concertina on which he had been playing a melancholy tune.

"Then let's go," said Shea, with a pack on his back and his saber at his side. "You lead, since you know the country."

The somber crags of western Ev rose all around them, occluding the cloudy sky to right and left and before and behind. Ruggedo tramped ahead, seeming to gather strength from contact with his native soil. He briskly poled along with a bill from the royal armory of Oz, well stocked by King Evardo after he became Royal Consort.

This was the weapon Ruggedo had chosen over an assortment of swords, axes, maces, pikes, halberds, crossbows, and arquebuses. (When Shea saw these primitive firearms, he regretted not having brought a pistol with him, since it might work in this milieu.) When Shea had questioned the choice of the bill, Ruggedo, drawing himself up to his full four and a half feet, challenged him to a practice bout, quarterstaff against wooden sword.

Padded and masked, the two squared off. In no time, Ruggedo poked Shea in the belly with the end of the quarterstaff. Shea demanded two out of three. On the second bout, he managed to drag out the match until Ruggedo began to pant and weaken, when Shea got him in the chest with a lunge.

Shea thought he had the third bout in the bag. But it had hardly begun when he received a crack over the head, which made him see stars despite the padding.

"You see, my boy," grinned Ruggedo, "it's not the particular kind of weapon so much as knowing how to use it."

Ruggedo's bill was a six-foot spear with a head that included, besides the foot-long steel blade, a hook on one side and a point on the other. It was shod with a pointed bronzen butt, which could be thrust with. Shea was girt with his saber. Ruggedo, marching ahead, snarled:

"Klumping Kaloogas, Sir Harold, hold that thing so it doesn't clank! The Long-Eared Hearer could hear us a mile away."

Shea grasped the scabbard in his left hand. This silenced the clank but also made his footing less certain. He stumbled over a rock and cursed beneath his breath, wishing he had something he could use as a walking stick. He could have drawn his sword, but the thought of marring the needle point and razor edge he had painstakingly given it dissuaded him.

"Clumsy clodpate!" muttered Ruggedo.

They plodded along a winding trail, which led zigzag up one side of the ridge and down the other. Something flew overhead with harsh screams. It was neither a bird, a bat, nor a pterosaur but combined a little of all three.

The distance was greater than Shea had thought. After a time they stopped for a respite.

"Sir Harold," grated Ruggedo, "isn't 'Shea' an Irish name in the mundane world?"

"I believe it is. But my people have been American so long it doesn't matter."

"Humph! That's what Himself the elf used to say. Claimed he was an American leprechaun from New Jersey. I'll never trust any being more than one-sixty-fourth Irish, after what that treacherous elf did to me. What did you do for a living in the mundane world?"

"Psychologist," panted Shea.

"What's that? And don't try to confuse me with fancy words!"

"A man who studies the workings of the human mind."

"Humph! If you be so learned and all, then tell me: Why does everybody hate me so?"

"That's a hell of a question to spring on a poor innocent foreigner!"

"Well? Do you mean that, with all your studies, you still can't answer a simple question?" Ruggedo snorted contempt.

"Well, now," drawled Shea, gathering his mental forces, "let's look into the matter. From all I've heard about you, you are two things that, together, account for the phenomenon. One: You're an unscrupulous, treacherous, selfish, greedy, lying, thieving scoundrel."

"You've been reading what those mundanes wrote!" cried Ruggedo, beginning to dance with rage. "They got half the story wrong and the rest distorted. That writer couldn't even spell 'gnome' right. A farrago of half-truths, errors, and outright lies—"

"Hold on!" said Shea, raising his voice. "You haven't heard the rest, yet. If you want my answer, then shut up until I finish!"

Ruggedo, grumbling, subsided. Shea continued: "In the mundane world, we'd call you a paranoid sociopath. At the same time you're an irascible, ornery, cantankerous, ill-mannered, bad-tempered old grouch. Now one—"

"Lies! Vile calumnies!" yelled Ruggedo.

"Do you want the rest of my answer or don't you? All right, then, hold your tongue until you hear it! I was saying that some scoundrels are successful, provided they are also polite, affable, obliging, winsome charmers. In the mundane world we had a charming scoundrel of that kind, who knew something of the world I accidentally touched down in on my way to Oz. He became enormously rich despite being an even bigger villain than you've ever been.

"On the other hand, even a cantankerous grouch can be admired if he also practices honesty, kindness, generosity, and unselfishness long and hard enough. Why, do you wish no longer to be hated?"

Ruggedo grunted a vague assent. "Suppose so."

"Then you must either stop being a treacherous etcetera scoundrel or stop being an irascible etcetera grouch. If you managed to cure both, you might become as beloved as Queen Ozma."

"Humph!" growled Ruggedo. "You give me one Hades of a choice. It's not easy to change at my age; but I'll think it over. I tried to reform before, several times; but my good resolutions never seemed to stick. Still, it would be nice, just once, to be known as a good king. Come on!"

Off went the gnome, poling himself along with his bill. They crossed the crest and picked their way down the other side of the ridge. Ruggedo halted in front of a recess in the rocks, which looked like the entrance to a tunnel blocked by a granite door.

"Sure you remember the way?" asked Shea.

"Of course, nitwit! I once got my throne back from Kaliko, and I'd have had it yet but for that sanctimonious little meddler Ozma." Ruggedo flourished his beret. "Time to put 'em on," he whispered, donning the tarncap.

At once the gnome disappeared, save that by staring hard in the gloom, Shea could just make out a pair of disembodied eyeballs hanging in space. Shea put on his own cap, saying:

"How shall we keep together?"

"I'll raise this pike high enough so the point shows," said Ruggedo. "Keep your eye on it!"

The gnome then rapped the door with his knuckles in a peculiar pattern and uttered a warbling whistle. The door groaned open.

"Come on, stupid!" whispered Ruggedo. "Hurry!"

Shea started after the gnome but, trying to keep his eyes on the barely visible spearhead, tripped and fell full-length, tearing a hole in his breeches' right knee. The scabbarded sword struck the ground with a clank.

"Awkward ass!" groaned Ruggedo. "If that doesn't alert them, an earthquake wouldn't!"

Shea felt stringy but powerful arms invisibly helping him up. In they went.

The tunnel was not so dark as Shea had feared. Along the walls, enormous faceted gems—or at least prismatic glassy objects that looked like enormous gems—were set in the rock and shed soft lights: ruby, emerald, and other hues. The footing became more even, but Shea still had to look down with every limping step to avoid another fall.

Rasping voices wafted from ahead. As the invaders approached, Shea saw a pair of gnomish sentries, each standing in a recess in the sides of the tunnel. They held halberds somewhat like Ruggedo's bill, slantwise so that their shafts intersected at about man-height. The gnomes complained in growls:

". . . that cursed sergeant has it in for me. Nothing I do pleases him."

"Trouble with you, Ungo, is that nothing pleases you. If you were told you had no duties at all, you'd crab about that . . ."

"How shall we get past?" whispered Shea.

"Crawl, idiot!" The eyeballs sank down to within two feet of the tunnel floor.

Shea got down to hands and knees, wincing at the pain in his injured knee. He would, he thought, leave a trail of blood wherever the knee touched ground.

Silently Ruggedo and Shea crept beneath the halberds and past the sentries, one of whom said: "I feel something's going on, Ungo. We both heard that clank."

"Too much imagination," rasped the other. "You'll get ulcers, worrying over every little sound."

Past the sentries, Ruggedo and Shea arose and resumed their way. For an hour they stole through tunnels, now and then choosing among alternative branches. Shea tried to remember the choices, since he depended for guidance on Ruggedo. He kept repeating to himself: right once, left twice, past three side tunnels ... But soon the number of forks and branches surpassed his ability to remember which was which. A few times, groups of gnomes approached them from the tunnel ahead, and they had to slip into side passages until the parties had gone past.

They passed chambers in which gnomes were noisily at work: mending weapons, polishing gems, and other gnomish tasks. A smell of cooking came from one cavern, in which female gnomes, no prettier than the males, bustled about.

They passed a huge assembly room, lined with doors of gleaming metal and commanded by an overhanging balcony. The hall was empty save for a few gnomes polishing panels of gold and silver in the doors.

At last they turned into a downward-sloping, foul-smelling corridor. A few steps brought them to a spacious chamber, against the far wall of which yawned a row of cells. At the entrance, a gnome sat on a high chair and smoked a long-stemmed pipe.

Ruggedo walked briskly to within reach of the seated gnome and smote him over the head with the shaft of his bill. The pipe fell clattering, and the gnome slumped and fell after it.

"Come on!" hissed Ruggedo. "There's the cell we want, Number Six! The lazy bastards have left 'em all open, to save the trouble of locking and unlocking."

On the bench at the back of the cell sat the stripling whom Shea had seen in the magic picture. As the rescuers entered the cell, Shea spoke:

"Prince Oznev, can you hear me?"

The youth sat up with a start. "Who—what—where are you?"

"In your cell, invisible. We've come to get you out. Don't shout or do anything foolish!"

Shea reached into his pack and pulled out the bolt cutter. If it had worked on small-gage bar stock in the smithy in Oz, it ought to function here. He snipped off the chains near the cuffs on Oznev's wrists and ankles.

"But who *are* you?" said the youth. "All I see is two pairs of eyes floating around."

"I'm Sir Harold Shea, and this is ex-king Ruggedo," snapped Shea, snipping the final link. "Now come along, son; no time to lose. Here, put this on your head!"

"What is it?"

"A tarncap, to make you invisible like us."

"It seems a cowardly sort of trick. A prince should face his enemies in plain sight!"

"Oh, lord!" said Shea. "Rug, we've got a terminal case of chivalrous scruples."

"Leave the brat if he won't come sensibly," growled the gnome.

"Can't." Shea stepped close to Oznev and, with a quick motion, jammed the third beret down on the head of the young prince, who disappeared. "There, Your Highness. I put it on you, so it's not your fault you're wearing it."

"I'll take it off!" muttered the invisible Oznev.

"You do, and I'll knock your royal block off!" snarled Shea. "Now come along like a good princeling!" Shea felt around and caught Oznev's wrist.

"Sir Harold!" rasped Ruggedo. "The sentry's gone!"

"Must have come to and gone to spread the alarm," said Shea. "Better run for it. Pick up your feet, Your Highness, if you don't want a tumble!"

From another cell came a rattle of chains and a cry: "Hey, get me out, too!" Similar cries and chainy sounds came from other cells.

Ignoring these appeals, the three dashed up the sloping passage and then along the labyrinth of tunnels, turning right and left at forks. The ex-king, trotting ahead, made the turns without hesitation. Shea hoped Ruggedo's memory of his kingly days did not play him false.

They passed more work rooms, all of which, earlier full of gnomes, now yawned empty.

"Where have they all gone?" Shea called, as loudly as he dared.

"Kaliko's probably making a speech," panted Ruggedo. "From what—I hear, he's gotten pompous. You know—how it is with us kings, surrounded by flunkeys—and flatterers. Flattery—rots the brain."

"Better save your breath, Rug," said Shea.

On and on they went. Shea heard a buzz ahead, indicating a crowd of gnomes. The light grew, and the fugitives came in sight of the hall of assembly.

They glanced inside, where thousands of gnomes now crowded the floor. On the balcony, picked out by spotlights, stood a beardless gnome in glittering regalia. Gnomes in gleaming armor, holding spears and swords, flanked the central figure.

"Wait!" said Ruggedo. "I want to hear him."

The robed and crowned gnome, evidently King Kaliko, had just launched into a speech. To Shea it sounded like a thousand other soporific political speeches that he had heard or read:

". . . We must seize the moment. . . . Productivity must rise. . . . Family discipline should be tightened. . . . We must be alert against foreign influences, especially of the subversive plots of the skulking Ruggedo . . . We must rid ourselves of bureaucratic waste. . . . Beware those who plot against us. . . . My reign has brought prosperity, despite the damage by my foolish predecessor and the grumbles of malcontents. . . ."

Another gnome, in gnomish working clothes,

pushed through the attendants on the balcony. "Your Majesty! I have news of moment!"

The newcomer looked like the jailer whom Ruggedo had stunned, although Shea did not know gnomes well enough to tell one clearly from another. Kaliko turned upon the newcomer, shouting:

"What mean you, knave, interrupting my speech?"

"But, sire, this is important! Surfacers have invaded—"

Kaliko roared: "Here, *I* decide what is important! Take him away!"

Shea glanced at Ruggedo, or at least at what he thought were Ruggedo's eyeballs. Ruggedo was muttering and, from the jiggle of the eyeballs, dancing about in a rising paroxysm of rage. Then Ruggedo's beret came off in the gnome's hand.

Before Shea could interfere, Ruggedo hurled the tarncap to the floor and dashed into the chamber. He ran a few steps along the wall, past some of the golden and silver doors, until he came to a plinth, on which stood a statue of a gnome in combat with a monster. With a muscle-cracking effort, Ruggedo tipped over the statue, which crashed to the floor. The old gnome vaulted atop the plinth, waved his bill above his head, and screamed:

"Gnomes! I am Ruggedo the Rough, your rightful king! Rally to me against that pompous fool of a usurper!"

For a few seconds, silence fell. A stout gnome dashed to the plinth and knelt, crying:

"Hail, King Ruggedo! It is I, former chancellor Shoofenwaller! Hail to our true and rightful king!"

The audience burst into a roar of talk, questions, and argument. Kaliko yelled from the balcony and Ruggedo shouted from his plinth, but their words were lost in the din. Calls to arms resounded.

More and more gnomes clustered round Ruggedo's

plinth. The gnomes had at first been unarmed, but now weapons began to gleam. Steel clanged and wounded gnomes screamed.

"Come on, Oznev," said Shea, pulling the prince after him. The hall of assembly, he thought, was near enough to the western entrance to enable them to find their way out without Ruggedo.

"Wait!" said Oznev's voice. "A prince should stand by his comrades! I must help Ruggedo in his fight for the throne!"

The prince wrenched loose and pulled off his tarncap. As he raised his arm to throw it away as Ruggedo had done, Shea, who had half drawn his sword, whipped out the weapon and smote Oznev on the head with the pommel.

The prince collapsed. Shea sheathed his blade, snatched up the discarded tarncap, and jammed it down on Oznev's head. Then he picked up the stripling and slung him over one shoulder. This took all of Shea's strength, because Shea was of no more than average size. He could not have done it if Oznev had been as big as, say, Walter Bayard.

Inside the chamber, partisans of Kaliko and Ruggedo coalesced into discrete masses. Other gnomes passed among them, handing out weapons. A roar of combat drowned all other sounds. Shea stumbled over a gnome's head, which rolled, trickling blood, out of the hall of assembly and into the corridor.

Shea limped and staggered along the tunnel, away from the hall. His battered knee hurt like blazes.

Then a figure popped out of a side tunnel. As it neared, Shea saw, by the light of the luminous gems, a human being in gnomish costume.

"Halt!" shouted this one. "I see your eyeballs! You cannot escape!"

The man advanced, swinging a sword right and left, high and low, to keep anyone from slipping past him.

He was a huge man with long arms, so that he covered the entire tunnel with his sweeps. Closer he came.

"One of Ozma's tricks!" roared the man. "Well, she can't fool Dranol Drabbo! Have at you, spook!"

Another step would bring the man within sword's length of Shea, who let the limp Prince Oznev slide to the floor. He had not completely drawn his own sword when Drabbo aimed a slash that, had it gotten home, would have sent Shea's head rolling like that of the gnome.

Shea did a quick squat. The sword whistled over his head, sending his tarncap flying.

"I knew it!" yelled Dranol Drabbo, making a running attack. Shea parried and backed, backed and parried. Dranol Drabbo was a stout fighter and a skilled cut-and-thrust swordsman, who wielded a long, heavy blade as easily as if it had been a flyswatter. In parrying one mighty downward cut, Shea's sword, on which he had lavished such care, broke off a hand's breadth from the hilt.

Dranol Drabbo threw himself forward in a lunge. His point struck Shea's chest, and the force of the blow knocked Shea off his feet. His mailshirt, however, kept the point from piercing his skin.

Shea scrambled up, reaching for his bowie knife. But Dranol Drabbo was hopping about, clawing at something invisible that clung to his back.

Shea sprang forward and whacked Dranol Drabbo's skull thrice with the flat of his oversized, machete-like knife. Dranol Drabbo sank to a sitting position, not completely unconscious.

"Good!" cried Oznev's voice as the prince untangled himself from Dranol Drabbo. "I couldn't desert you in a fight, either. Here's your cap."

"Just a second," said Shea. Reaching down Dranol Drabbo's back, he sawed through the man's belt with his knife.

"Okay," he said. "Now run for it!"

Soon they reached the western entrance, with Shea limping heavily. A glance back showed Dranol Drabbo, small in the distance, staggering to his feet. When the man started in pursuit, his breeches fell down, and Drabbo went to hands and knees. His roars of frustration echoed down the tunnel.

"My head aches like fury," said Oznev. "What hit me?"

"The force of destiny," said Shea.

"Why didn't you kill him?"

"Wasn't necessary, and experience teaches that today's friend may be tomorrow's foe and vice versa. Waste not, want not."

Shea hobbled along the trail. They had not gone a hundred paces outside the caves when Shea felt the now familiar symptoms of magical teleportation—the fading of the scene, the misty whirl of colored dots. . . .

"Well!" said Queen Ozma when she and King Evardo had embraced their son. "You, Sir Harold, appear to have had a time of it!"

"Your Majesty is a mistress of understatement," said Shea, handing over the two surviving berets. "Hi, Walter! Who won?"

"Ruggedo," said Bayard. "At least, just after the Queen actuated her Belt to fetch you, we saw Kaliko and his chancellor pop out the western entrance, in flight with a few followers."

"Demonstrating," said Shea, "that gnomes show no more wisdom in picking leaders than we mundanes."

"Oh, dear!" said Ozma. "I'm sure old Rug will start plotting to conquer us again."

"He told me," said Shea, "that this time he was really determined to reform. Whether he'll succeed, your guess is as good as mine. But permit me to suggest that Your Majesties hire someone to keep him under constant surveillance in your magical picture."

Evardo: "Sir Harold, we are greatly in your debt. We should like to honor you with a fine banquet in celebration. Oz is renowned for its parties."

Shea gave his courtliest bow. "I appreciate the courtesy, Your Majesty. But back home my wife is about to give birth. So, if you will forgive me . . ."

"I see," said Evardo. "In other words, you would prefer to be sent home forthwith, as soon as your hurts have been mended. It shall be as you wish. Do you also speak for Doctor Bayard and his—ah—wife?"

"No, sir. If they wish to remain, that's fine by me."

Shea lay stretched out in the bathtub. Bayard came in and sat on the toilet lid, saying: "Just been watching Ruggedo in Ozma's picture. We hear from our spies he's telling the gnomes that monarchy is obsolete. So he's proclaimed himself Lifetime President and Founding Father of the Gnomic Republic."

Shea replied: "Like one of those pipsqueak dictators we have in the Third World, eh? What are your plans?"

"The Queen will send us home after you as soon as the party is over. It promises to be a real blowout, with all the famous characters, such as Ozma's father, ex-king Pastoria, hauled in from his elegant tailoring establishment. Boann will play the harp and sing sad songs. Now give me the blow-by-blow."

Shea narrated his adventures. Bayard said: "Of course we watched you in the magic picture. But it's not wired for sound, and we couldn't watch every minute. When Kaliko's chancellor—that fellow with a name like a drain-cleaning compound—got you with his lunge, we thought you were a goner. What saved you?"

"How do you suppose I got this big purple bruise

on my chest? If you look yonder, you'll see a mailshirt of alloy-steel mesh."

"You, wearing armor? You used to brag you never touched the stuff."

"Circumstances alter cases," said Shea. "Do you know a verse by Kipling, called *The Married Man* or something? It begins—I won't try to imitate the cockney dialect Kipling used—but it goes something like this:

"The bachelor, he fights for one
    As joyful as can be;
But the married man don't call it fun,
    Because *he* fights for three.

"If you ever get married, you'll find out what Kipling meant. Speaking of which, how's it with you and Miss Ni Colum?"

Bayard pondered. "I suppose I could fare further and do worse. Guess we probably are married in the sight of Crom Cruach, or whomever these bloodthirsty quasi-Celts worship. Good thing you didn't fetch us to Oz in the midst of our quasi-nuptials; might have been downright embarrassing.

"When I explained that she might either be sent back to Eriu or go to America with me, as he liked, she threw a shoe at me and burst into tears. Thought I was trying politely to 'cast her off,' as she expressed it. So I guess Boann is Mrs. Bayard henceforth. It gets us all sooner or later, I suppose."

"Your enthusiasm overwhelms me," said Shea, rising from the water. "If you do it right—and I speak from experience—it's the very best thing around. Hand me that big towel, will you?"

SIR HAROLD AND
THE MONKEY KING
Christopher Stasheff

Harold Shea loved to have friends drop in, but he did like a little warning first, especially if he was going to have to catch them.

He was working late at night in his study, taking a break from his usual toil—that of transcribing interviews with delusional patients into symbolic logic, looking for keys to the universes they were perceiving. For variety, he had started trying to transcribe the *Tao Te Ching*, *The Book of the Way*, by the legendary sage Lao Tzu. The book was the foundation of the Chinese religion of Taoism, and Taoist priests had the reputation of being magicians, so Shea was looking for clues to their magical principles—when he heard a sigh behind him.

He glanced up, thinking that perhaps Belphebe had wakened and come out, needing talk—the demands of a newborn left her craving adult conversation—but all he saw was an amorphous, translucent white mass writhing in the dark of the study.

His hair tried to stand on end; he froze for an instant, then reached into the desk drawer and touched his dirk. Then he looked over his shoulder, hoping he wouldn't have to trust his safety to its two-hundred year-old design.

The amorphous mass became more and more opaque as it churned, pulling itself into a human form—and Dr. Reed Chalmers stood there, drawn and pale, in a medieval robe.

"Doc!" Shea cried, leaping out of his chair—and virtually caught Chalmers as he sagged. Shea turned, stepped, and lowered him into the desk chair. "Hold on just a minute—I'll get some brandy." He stepped out into the dining room, took a glass and a bottle from the liquor cabinet, poured, and took the snifter back to Chalmers.

Chalmers accepted it with both hands, drinking it off in a single swallow. His color began to return even as he lowered it. "Yes. Much better now. Thank you, Harold."

"Don't mention it," Shea said. "Travel by syllo-gismobile does have that effect, sometimes." Actually, it never had with him, but it sounded like a good face-saver.

"No, it wasn't really that." Chalmers frowned. "But how did you guess, Harold?"

"Something to do with the medieval robe, proba-bly—and the fact that you didn't bother with the front door. What happened, Doc? Thought you talked us into a ban on inter-universe travel."

"Yes, but that was only for those who already know how. I never thought it would be necessary to tell someone who had never made a journey before."

"Florimel?" Harold stared. "Don't tell me your wife decided to try it on her own!" But his sinking stomach told him the truth; he remembered how Chalmers' wife had seemed relieved to have Reed take a "vaca-tion" to his native universe.

"Well, of course, there was no good reason to deny teaching her how," Chalmers protested. "Unfortunately, she didn't bother learning symbolic logic completely before she tried. . . ."

"And with only a medieval education to back it up, she wouldn't be able to figure out the right referents anyway!" Shea stared in horror. "My lord, Doc! How can you tell where she went?"

"By this." Chalmers drew a parchment out of his robe. "Apparently she didn't keep too tight a hold on it when she travelled—I found it on the living room floor."

"But that means she doesn't know how to get home, either!" Shea snatched the sheet and frowned down at the symbols. "Nothing I can recognize, Doc—oh, a chain here and there, and a paradox-loop or two, but nothing coherent."

"So I feared," Chalmers sighed. "I tried it myself, but the terrain was so unusual, I thought . . ." His voice trailed off.

"That you'd better come back for reinforcements?" Shea nodded and turned away. "Help yourself to the brandy, Doc. I'll just be a few minutes getting into my travelling outfit—and telling Belphebe."

The travelling outfit was quick and easy—Shea always kept a general, all-purpose tunic and tights handy, along with his sword and quarterstaff—and his revolver, and a wallet filled with hardtack and pemmican. Saying goodbye to Belphebe, though, took a bit longer, especially since he didn't really want to.

He waked her with a feather-light kiss, but she came awake on the instant anyway, like the huntress she was. She smiled up at him with pleasure, then saw his outfit, and her eyes went wide. "Harold! What alarm calls you out?"

A surge of affection moved him, gratitude that she had seen the nature of the situation so quickly, and knew him well enough to know that only an emergency could take him from her and their six-month-old baby. "It's Florimel, dear. She has disappeared, leaving only a sheet full of equations behind."

"Florimel? Attempted the syllogismobile by herself? But Reed must be distraught!"

"Very much so, especially since he just got back from the universe she went to. It was so odd that he decided he needed somebody to back him up."

"Of course you must!" She caught his hand, knowing his misgivings. "Fear not for the babe and myself—we shall be quite well in your absence. Only return safe and sound!"

"I'll do my best," Shea promised, and took her in his arms for a kiss that was the best pledge he could make.

A few minutes later, he came back into the study. "Okay, Doc. Let's go." He opened the desk drawer and took out a box of cartridges, slipping it into his wallet.

"But why the revolver, Harold?" Chalmers frowned. "It won't work, in an alien universe where magic is physics."

"Maybe not—but if we don't know where we're going, we might wind up in a universe where the rules are hybrid, and gunpowder *does* explode. I brought matches, too. If they don't work, I can always throw them away—but if they do, I'm going to be sore as hell that I didn't bring them. Shall we, Doc?"

"By all means." Chalmers took his hand and held up the sheet of equations. They began to chant the symbolic-logic statements in unison, as the study began to grow dim about them.

Suddenly, there was light.

Light all about them, and grass of an amazingly rich green, covering the slope beneath their feet—a steep hillside that broke out into rocky shelves here and there, and that was adorned with trees and shrubs everywhere.

Everywhere, and every tree bore fruit, every shrub was burdened with blossoms. The air was perfumed, and all the colors were bright.

"Doc," Harold said slowly, "I don't think we're in any universe I've ever seen before."

"Nor I," Chalmers said evenly—but his hands trembled.

Shea knelt to run a hand over the grass. "It's real. It looked so perfect, I thought it might have been a carpet."

Chalmers nodded. "And isn't that a pagoda, over there? Though it's very tiny with distance."

Shea stood up, looked, and nodded. "All the colors are so bright! It's as though the air were super-clear!"

"Perhaps it's just that we've come to a place where the internal combustion engine hasn't been invented," Chalmers offered half-heartedly, "or that we're in the mountains. But do you notice, Harold—no chiaroscuro?"

"Shading?" Shea looked about, realizing that everything was either full-color, or shadow, with nothing in between. "You're right, Doc. In fact, it looks almost . . . like a . . ."

"Chinese scroll," Chalmers finished for him. "I think we can assume we've left the Western hemisphere behind—especially since I see we're about to be visited by a band of local fauna."

Shea looked where he pointed, startled, and saw small brown and gray shapes flitting through the trees. Then he heard a whirling, racheting, burbling sound— the noise of a whole tribe of monkeys, shooting toward them.

In an instant, the animals were all about them, hooting and chattering. One large, grizzled old animal called down, "Who are you, strangers, and what do you here, on our Mountain of Flowers and Fruit?"

Shea did a double take—he wasn't used to having the local wildlife speak English. Then he remembered that he probably was not speaking English at all, but the language of this universe, instead. That helped— but not much. He still was not used to talking monkeys.

Chalmers recovered first. "We are travellers . . ." Then he ran out of gas, and Shea snapped out of his stupefaction in time to take up where he'd left off.

"We're looking for a friend of ours," Shea called back. "Have you seen her, maybe? A pretty, slender woman—no, Doc, let me do the describing, you can't be objective! She would have appeared all of a sudden, the way we did!"

"Aye, such a one did appear yesterday, and we told her what we will tell you—that you trespass in the land of the Monkey King, and he will be wroth if he finds you here! She, at least, had the good sense to turn her footsteps down the slope. You had best do likewise, before our king comes!"

"Foolish, foolish people!" a younger monkey chattered. "You dare to trespass on his lands, believing that he has been imprisoned by Buddha!"

"Be still!" the older monkey snapped.

"Wherefore? Since our lord has just been released from his jail, after five hundred years of waiting! Surely the foolish mortals should flee, and not trouble us to beat them away."

"Beat?" Chalmers cried, dismayed, but Shea assured him, "They said Florimel had the good sense to go on her own, Doc. But we need a little background information, and we're in a good situation to get it." Then, back to the monkeys, "You mentioned Buddha. Is this China?"

"China? What is that? You are on the Mountain of Flowers and Fruit, behind the great Water Curtain, in Zhung-Guo—the Middle Kingdom!"

"Middle Earth? The center of all the universes?"

"What is a universe? Foolish mortal, Zhung-Guo is

the Land Between the Four Seas, the country at the center of the world, which must therefore be an example and a source of governance to all other countries!"

Yes, that was China—at least, as seen by the Chinese. "Why was your king imprisoned?"

"Buddha clapped him in jail for five hundred years, to punish him for his mischief!" The monkey bared his teeth. "How unjust is this! As well punish a bird for flying, or a dog for barking!"

"I suspect it depends on the magnitude of the mischief. . . ."

A loud chattering went up at the fringe of the monkey band, and several of the little apes turned, then pointed to the sky.

"Yonder he comes!" The grizzled monkey pointed, too. "Flee, foolish barbarians! Or you will suffer greatly, for trespassing in the domain of the Monkey King!"

"What do you think, Doc?" Shea muttered.

"They may speak wisely," Chalmers answered, "but I confess my curiosity has the better of me. Besides, we couldn't be off this hillside by the time he arrived."

That was true enough. The monkeys were pointing at a little cloud that was growing larger and larger. As it came closer, they could see a speck on top of it, a speck that rapidly grew into the form of a gray monkey, a little larger than most, holding a two-foot stick.

Shea stared. "It's just mist! How does he keep from falling through?"

"Magic," Chalmers said tersely. "I think I'd better work up a few spells."

The cloud slanted downwards, diving toward them. As it touched down, the monkeys set up a glad chattering: "Monkey! Monkey! Our Monkey King!"

Monkey jumped off his cloud with a grin, flourishing his staff in triumph—until he saw the two humans. Then the grin disappeared, and the staff was flourishing for an entirely different reason.

He ran at Shea and Chalmers with a howl. Shea did not want to hurt the little guy, so he did not pull out his sword, just held out his staff to block. . . .

Monkey's two-foot cudgel cracked through Shea's staff as though it had been a spaghetti noodle.

Shea leaped back, staring at the two half-staves in his hands, then lifted them to block. Monkey howled and swung, and his staff grew even as it whirled, extending to six feet, with a dull sheen. Shea saw it coming and tried to roll with it, but it cracked into his shoulder anyway. He fell, pain flaring through his joint—but rolled up right next to Monkey and, still not wanting to really hurt him, slapped at the little creature's head as he stood up.

Pain shot through his whole hand.

"Yeow!" he yelled, leaping back. "What're you made of—granite?"

"Exactly!" Monkey snapped, and swung again.

This time Shea just dodged. With his left shoulder throbbing and his right hand a web of agony, he could not do much of anything else. But he did notice that behind Monkey, Chalmers was on his knees, frantically jabbing short sticks into the ground. That gave Shea hope—if he could just stay away from Small and Deadly long enough, maybe Doc could get him out of this.

But staying away from Monkey was easier said than done. Leaping, swinging from tree branches, bounding down at Shea, bounding up, and always howling, howling, the little monster swung again and again with that lethal staff. Shea dodged and dodged, but he was beginning to tire, and the staff tagged him on the shin, on the hip, and left burning pain wherever it touched.

Then suddenly, iron bars seemed to fall out of the

sky and land straight up. An iron roof slammed down on top of them, and Shea fell, rolling on an iron floor.

Monkey hit the bars of the cage with a horrendous scream, trying to reach through at Shea. When he found he could not, he leaped back and assaulted the cage with a dozen blows. Shea shrank into a little ball in the center as bars bent and the roof dented—but they held. Finally, the Monkey King ran out of gas and leaned on his staff, glaring at Shea through the bars and panting. Then he began to scream. "Round-eyed barbarian! Foul dungheap! Bag of offal!" He went on like that for a little while.

Shea waited it out, remembering Cyrano's comeback. When the little blighter finally shut up, he said, "You are? Well, I'm Harold Shea." He held out a hand.

Monkey nearly came through the bars, screaming again. "Foul, mannerless thief! I am the Monkey King, as you well know, and I shall tear this cage apart and rip you limb from limb!"

At a guess, he had not had a good day. Shea tried to remember that he was a psychologist and asked, "Why?"

Monkey stared, at a loss for a few seconds. Then he snapped: "Because you have trespassed on my mountain, and insulted me to boot!"

Shea did not feel it was tactful to point out that the only insults Monkey had received were the ones he had given, coming back at him. "I'm sorry about that—but we were looking for a friend of ours, who became lost."

Monkey frowned. "Why would you think he was on my mountain?"

"She, actually—and we just followed her trail, in a manner of speaking."

"A magical trail?" Monkey looked sharply at him. "You are a sorcerer, then."

"Just a general all-purpose magician."

"What is the woman to you?"

"My wife," Chalmers said behind him.

Monkey spun about, his cudgel coming up, but he only glowered at the older man and asked: "What was her appearance?"

"About this tall." Chalmers held up his hand. "Slender, with brown hair."

"And pale skin, and round eyes, like yourself?" Monkey nodded. "I came upon her on my way here."

"Really?" Chalmers leaped on it. "Where was she going?"

"Nowhere; she was beset by bandits. I was angry at bandits, for six of them had just tried to kill Tripitaka, the monk whom Buddha bade me accompany, and I slew them for it. Then the foolish bonze had the audacity to rebuke me! Rebuke me! For saving his life!"

Chalmers was in an agony of impatience to learn about Florimel, but Shea realized he was going to have to bring Monkey back to the topic gradually. "Maybe he had a good reason."

"Good reason! No, nothing more than that I could have spared those outlaws, could have disabled them as easily as slaying them! As though you should spare the life of someone who attacks you, simply because it is not necessary to kill him!"

"That does make sense," Shea said, "provided you think human life is something worthwhile in its own right."

Monkey's teeth writhed back, jeering. "I should expect your kind to think so."

"Well, yes, we do have a certain vested interest in human life. But maybe that's why Buddha assigned you to this monk."

Monkey frowned. "Why, how is that?"

"To learn Buddha's morality." Shea realized that he

must be crazy, talking about Buddha as though the sage were still alive, and were something more than a myth—but maybe he was, in this universe. After all, his first trip by syllogismobile had taken him to a universe where the Norse gods were real. Anyway, he had to talk to Monkey on the beast's own terms. "Didn't he say anything about why you were supposed to go with the monk?"

Monkey glowered. "Something, aye."

"Was it Buddha who turned you into stone, too?" Mind you, Shea did not believe for an instant that something so alive as Monkey could really be made out of stone . . .

. . . or maybe he could. After all, each universe had its own physics, its own principles. Why could not a living creature be made of stone? Maybe, to Monkey, Shea seemed odd, being made of soft tissue.

"Nay," Monkey said. "I was born so—if 'born' is the word for it."

" 'Hatched,' maybe?"

Monkey stared. "How did you know?"

Now Shea stared. "You don't mean you came out of an egg!"

"Aye." Monkey sat down on his heels, grinning. "When the world was made, O Foolish Barbarian, there was made with it a huge egg of stone. For eons it stood, alone and waiting; then finally, when men had appeared upon the Earth, that egg broke open, and out tumbled myself—the Stone Monkey."

Shea tried to keep the look of disbelief off his face. After all, if monkeys could talk here, why couldn't one have hatched out of a stone egg? "How did you become king of the monkeys?"

"Shortly after I wakened, a band of them came tumbling along, playing as they went. They told me I was one of them, and brought me to look in a still pool. I saw that I was a monkey, too, and went with them a while—but I learned how sore beset they were, by tiger and by wolf, and began to wonder how to make them safe. Then, one day, we came to play near a Water Curtain . . ."

"A water curtain?"

"A sheet of water that fell from a great height, fool! I wondered what lay behind that veil, and plucked up my courage to leap through it. I find myself here, on this mountain of eternal spring, then leaped back through the veil, to find them mourning me. They rejoiced to see me still alive, and followed me through the Water Curtain—with some trepidation, it must be admitted, but with willingness to follow. When they saw how rich and safe a place I had provided for them, they made me their king."

"Sounds great." Shea frowned. "But so far, I don't see anything Buddha should have punished you for."

"Nay. That came later, after some years, when I had begun to chafe at my life here, and to find it growing tedious. I wished to learn more of the world, and I wished to learn how to keep my monkeys safe from the occasional bear that stumbled through the Curtain. I heard of a sage in the south, the Patriarch Subodhi, who could teach me magic, so I departed from my little monkeys and went to him."

"Studying magic?" Shea frowned. "I begin to see possibilities for mischief."

"I assure you, I was the best-mannered of monkeys! The Patriarch took me as his disciple, and I studied as hard as, or harder than, any of the others. At last I came to so much knowledge of the Way of Virtue that he gave me a name-in-religion—I am the disciple Aware-of-Vacuity."

"Vacuity?" Shea frowned. "Why is it important to become aware of emptiness?"

"Because until you know that you are empty, you cannot begin to be filled. But I, having reached this

stage, desired to demonstrate for my fellow disciples
how much I had learned—so I displayed all the
marvels that I could now work, as a result of the Patriarch's teaching."

A show-off, Shea realized. "I take it the Patriarch
didn't like that too much?"

"Nay, he cast me out from his presence." Monkey
grinned again. "Why should I care? I had learned the
magic I sought. I came back to my mountains, and
found my little monkeys sorely beset. I chased away
the wild beasts and taught them Mock Combat, so
that they would be able to practice Real Combat, if it
ever became necessary—as it has, many times since."

"I take it you were planning to go on your travels again."

"Aye, for it is the way of monkeys to become easily
bored. I flew to beset the Dragon of the Southern
Ocean, defeated him, and exacted tribute from him. . . ."
Monkey brandished his cudgel. " . . . this iron staff,
that can grow amazingly when I wish it."

"Correct me if I am wrong," Chalmers said slowly,
trying to hide his impatience, "but I thought dragons
were heavenly creatures, in Chi . . . in this country."

"They are." Monkey's grin grew savage. "The Jade
Emperor of Heaven therefore invited me to take a
place in his realm, so that I would cease to bedevil
his subjects."

"The direct route to heaven?" Shea stared. "And
you didn't stay?"

"Nay, for I found that the 'place' he had for me was
that of a groom in the Heavenly Stables! In revenge, I
invaded the workroom of Lao-Tzu, the founder of the
Way, and stole from him a flask of the Elixir of Life.
It was for this that Buddha imprisoned me—but even
He had to make my jail the top of a mountain! There
He bade me dwell for five long centuries, until a monk
should come who could teach me patience and humility. Now that monk has appeared—a prince who has

forsworn all the vanities of this world, and who has been sent by the Emperor of Tang to go to India, and bring back three baskets of Buddhist scrolls. For this he has taken the name 'Tripitaka,' which means, O Ignorant Barbarian, 'Three Baskets.' And he has the gall to chastize me for having saved his life!" Monkey leaped to his feet again, reminded of his grievance. "I screamed imprecations at him for his ingratitude; I rushed off in anger. What need I with such a fool for a master? No, I have come back to my Mountain of Flowers and Fruit, and here I shall stay, whether Buddha wills it or not!" But there was a look of trepidation in his eyes as he said it.

Shea did not want that club to start whirling again—but he did want to be able to get out of that cage without becoming the Target for Today. "Sounds as though he was trying to teach you what Buddha wanted."

"What?" Monkey stared at him.

Shea shrugged. "If Buddha told you to become this monk's disciple, he must have wanted you to learn whatever he had to teach."

"To let murdering bandits live!?! How could this be holy?"

"Sometimes you just have to take it on faith," Shea explained. "We have an archetypal story about that, back where I come from—about a man who is famous for patience, but who really ought to be famous for holding on to his ideals."

"Ideals?" Monkey scowled at him. "Whatever are you talking about?"

"Job." Shea settled himself for a long session. "His name was Job, and he was a very religious man who had everything he could want—a beautiful, loving wife, well-mannered children, a fine house, and lots of money. But a, um, demon, tried to tell the, uh, King of Heaven, that the only reason he was religious, was because he had everything he wanted. Take all of that away, the demon said, and Job would lose his faith and curse the King."

"Surely the Jade Emperor would not listen to such foolish speech!" Monkey frowned. "Or is it so foolish?"

"That's what the demon said—and the King of Heaven figured it was necessary to prove that it was foolish. So He gave the demon permission to take away everything that Job held dear—house, money, children, wife. One by one, the demon did just that. First the children were killed by accidents and disease . . ."

"Why, what goodness can there be in letting children die?" Monkey demanded.

"Presumably, they went straight to Heaven." Shea shrugged away the objection. "Anyway, it's just a story, to make a concept clear. Then a depression hit, and Job lost all his money. A fire burned down his house. Still, all he would do was to cry out to God to tell him what he had done to deserve all this. Finally, his wife began to despise him, because not only hadn't he kept all these things from happening, he wasn't even complaining about the King of Heaven being cruel."

"So she left him."

"Seen it happen before, have you? Yes, she left him, but Job still wouldn't cry out against the King of Heaven—and the demon acknowledged defeat. He had to admit that human ideals have something more to them than just reward and punishment."

"But what of this Job? Did he learn why he had been so accursed?"

"He didn't need to; the King of Heaven just sent an angel to tell him that sometimes He does things for reasons that people don't understand."

"And that was enough for Job?" Monkey stared.

"That was enough," Shea confirmed. "Once he was reassured that the King of Heaven was there, he had

faith that there was a reason. All he really needed was
to be reassured."

Monkey frowned at him, then bowed his head so
that his chin rested on his chest, and was silent. Chalmers fidgeted in an agony of impatience, but kept his
peace.

Finally, Monkey looked up. "There is merit in what
you say—and I, who know personally that Buddha
does exist, am a blind fool to doubt Him, am I not?"

"There is that possibility," Shea agreed.

Monkey gazed at him, brooding.

Then, suddenly, he leaped to his feet, slapping his
thigh. "Come! I will return to the monk; I shall make
my apologies. Perhaps, in time, he will convince me
of the merits of humility. I doubt there are any, but
I will give him his chance to teach me. Let us go!"
He whirled about and struck the collection of twigs
with his staff; the result was instant toothpicks, and
the iron cage disappeared from around Shea.

Chalmers stared, horrified.

So did Shea, feeling suddenly very vulnerable. "You
could have done that any time!"

"Why, so I could have," Monkey agreed, "but I was
too angry to think of it. Let us go!" He beckoned, and
suddenly a cloud swooped down from a clear blue sky.

"Wait a minute, now!" Shea backed away. "What
do you mean, 'we'?"

"Why, the two of you as well!" Monkey gestured,
and the cloud shot in against Shea's legs, and Chalmers'. They both yelped with surprise as they tumbled
onto its surface. Monkey grinned and leaped aboard.
"It is you who have inspired me—so you must come
to see the fulfillment of your plan!" He looked back
over his shoulder, and his grin turned menacing. "If
it ends in disaster, so shall you."

"But my wife!" Chalmers cried. "What happened to
Florimel?"

"Oh, the barbarian woman?" Monkey shrugged. "I sent her further on her travels. This world was not the one she had intended to visit, so I bade her tell me of the one she sought—a world ruled by a queen without a king—and sent her there. But enough! Come now, away!"

Chalmers moaned.

"Travel by cloud isn't all that bad, really, Doc," Shea said bravely, "once you get used to the idea that it's a magic cloud, and a lot more like an innerspring mattress than a patch of fog."

"Perhaps," Chalmers groaned, "but I didn't think to bring my Dramamine."

Then they were both crying out in alarm, as the cloud tilted down sharply. A few seconds later, Monkey hopped off, crying: "Master! Forgive me!" and the cloud disappeared completely, dropping Shea and Chalmers with a very unceremonious thump. Shea pushed himself upright, massaging an aching sacroiliac, and saw a young man in a saffron robe sitting cross-legged—no, in the lotus positon, without the slightest sign of discomfort! He looked a little nervous, and he had a robe of a rich red in his lap, with a matching hat that had a band of gold around its rim.

Monkey was bowing deeply before the monk. "I have erred, Master, in presuming to refute your teaching! If this is the Way of the Buddha, I shall learn it! Only forgive, and be patient with me!"

The young man nodded gravely. "You are forgiven easily, Monkey, for Buddha's mercies are manifold. In recognition of your spiritual progress, I give you this robe and hat, as signs of your advancement."

Shea frowned—how had Tripitaka known Monkey was going to be coming back? He was about to raise the issue, but Monkey caught up the red robe with a glad cry and pulled it on, strutting to and fro. "How well it looks on me! And just the right length, not quite to my knees! Master, you are a genius of observation!" He grabbed the hat and clapped it on. "Now! Do I not look like a king?"

"Like a jester!" Tripitaka's tone was suddenly stern. "You prance and caper with vanity! Really, Monkey, if I had known you would behave so ..."

That was as far as he got before Monkey turned on him with a roar, charging with his cudgel held high.

Tripitaka shouted out some words that Shea could not catch at all.

Monkey stopped dead in his tracks, howling in agony. He fell on the ground, tugging at the cap. "Take it off! Take it off! It binds about my temples like a clamp! It sends agonies through my brain! It will break my head!" The cloth ripped away, but the headband remained and would not budge.

Tripitaka only waited, face impassive.

"It was enchanted!" Shea gasped.

Chalmers nodded. "A trap!"

"Forgive me, Master!" Monkey cried. "I was wrong to lose my temper, to turn against you! I apologize!"

"Will you swear to do whatever I tell you?" Tripitaka demanded.

"I swear, I swear!" Monkey cried. "I will obey you in all things! I will never lift my hand against you! Only make the agony stop, Master, make the agony stop!"

Tripitaka gestured, reciting another short verse which somehow eluded Shea completely.

Monkey sagged with relief. "Thank you, Master! Oh, thank you! Where did you get that wondrous hat?"

"From the Bodhissatva Kuan-Yin," Tripitaka answered.

"From Kuan-Yin! But she is the Goddess of Mercy!"

"Of mercy, certainly—but the Taoists are mistaken in thinking she is a goddess. She is a Bodhissatva, a person who has attained Enlightenment but postponed passing to Nirvana so that she may guide and instruct those of us here on Earth."

"Oh yes, Master! A Bodhissatva, not a goddess! Of course, Master!"

"But she is, as you say, the patron of mercy," Tripitaka rejoined, "so you can be sure that she must have a merciful reason, for so binding you to my authority."

Monkey stilled, half-risen. Then he lifted his head. "Perhaps it is even as you say, Master. In any event, I have sworn to obey you, and I will."

"It is well." Tripitaka looked massively relieved.

"Why, he was as loath to hurt Monkey, as he was afraid of him," Chalmers hissed to Shea.

Shea nodded. "Exceptional young man, here. Maybe one of the ones who justified monasticism."

Tripitaka looked up, alert. "Who are these you have brought to join us, Monkey?"

Monkey looked up at Shea with blood in his eye. No, not blood—the little monster's orbs were actually beginning to glow with fire! "These? Why, they are the barbarian sorcerers who persuaded me to return to you, Master! This one is Xei, and that one is Chao-mar-zi."

Shea did a double take, but Chalmers only opened his eyes a little wider, then bowed politely. He had become accustomed to hearing his name mispronounced.

"They have a strange appearance." Tripitaka frowned. "But they must be wise, even magical, if they could have persuaded you. What did you tell him, barbarians?"

The "barbarians" was beginning to chafe on Shea, but he tried to ignore it. "Just a parable showing him the virtues of patience and respect for authority, Your Highness."

"I am only a monk now," Tripitaka protested. "I

have forsworn worldly titles with all other vanities. If
you are so wise and patient as that, I doubt not that
you would be a great help on our quest. Do you wish
to learn the Way of Buddha?"

"Well, actually, we were just visiting," Shea said.
"We're trying to track down Dr. Chalmers' wife, you
see, and Monkey tells us he found her and sent her
further on her way. So if you'll just send us to the
same place, Monkey. . . ."

"Nay." Monkey bared his teeth, but Shea could not
have said whether it was a snarl or a grin. "I find I
have taken a liking to your company."

"But my wife!" Chalmers cried.

"If you aid us in coming to India," Monkey said, "I
will gladly send you to the place where she is—when
we have found the stupa that holds the Three
Baskets."

"But the time!" Chalmers cried. "Months may have
elapsed!"

"Years," Monkey corrected, enjoying his discomfiture.

"Years! But any number of things could have happened to her in that much time! She could have fallen
prey to bandits, been enslaved, or . . ." Chalmers swallowed heavily. " . . . fallen in love with another man!"

"Monkey!" Tripitaka intoned severely.

"Oh, all right!" Monkey said, disgusted. "When we
have attained our goal, I will send you not only to the
land where she is, but to the time at which she arrived
there! Will that suit you?"

Shea goggled. "How can you do that?"

"Magic," Monkey said, all teeth. "Will it satisfy
you?"

Shea looked at Chalmers, who gave him a frantic
nod, then turned to Monkey with a sigh. "Why, sure,
Monkey—anything you say. Which way is India?"

India was south and west, of course, and they did
take a long time on the road. It seemed considerably

longer because, though Tripitaka had a horse to ride, the rest of them were expected to walk, in spite of Monkey's knack with magical clouds. Shea kept trying to console himself, and Chalmers, with the spectacular scenery they were seeing, but their enthusiasm was somewhat dampened by the encounters they had along the way. For example, fairly early on, they started to cross a river, but wound up running away from the dragon that surged out of the waters. Everybody got to safety except Tripitaka's horse, which the dragon gobbled up as an hors d'oeuvre, then turned his attention to the rest of the band, intent on a five-course banquet. Monkey killed his appetite with a running fight, but had to go to Kuan-Yin for help. She changed the dragon into the spit and image of the horse he had gobbled up, and commanded him to go with the expedition, to help protect Tripitaka. Monkey almost forgave the Goddess for that.

Kuan-Yin had been foresighted, it seemed—she had sent ahead two spirits who had sinned against the Jade Emperor of Heaven, commanding them to wait for the Pilgrim Monk, then to accompany him, protect him, and learn the Way of the Buddha from him. The first had been locked into the form of a humanoid pig for his sins; his favorite weapon was an iron muckrake, and he and Monkey had an epic running battle before Monkey finally thought to mention whom he was protecting, whereupon Pigsy surrendered and joined up for the duration.

The other monster was an even harder case. They met him at the River of Flowing Sands, where he was accustomed to collect travellers trying to cross the river and having them for lunch. He was an Expressionistic monster who wore the skulls of his nine victims around his neck. Even with Chalmers' and Shea's magic assisting Monkey and Pigsy, they could barely fight the monster to a draw. Shea volunteered to keep the monster preoccupied while Monkey went for help.

Shea managed to get the monster involved in a philosophical discussion about whether or not he was a cannibal. Shea's case was that eating human beings made him a cannibal, but the monster replied that since he was not strictly human, the people he had been eating were not his own kind, so he was only a carnivore.

Meanwhile, Monkey went to ask help of Kuan-Yin. She came and converted the monster, who was a fallen spirit like Pigsy. He repented, swore off eating people, and joined the expedition, transforming himself into the likeness of a human being. Since he was the Monster of the River of Flowing Sands, they nicknamed him Sandy. He became a pious monk and a vicious infighter.

Meanwhile, they had been travelling farther and farther south, and though they were not near the foothills of the Himalayas yet, they had travelled much farther west. Shea could tell how far south they had gone by the heat and the size of the mosquitoes.

"You can tell the physics of this universe are magical," he grumbled as he lay down on a straw pallet in the guest room of the monastery at which they had just arrived. "Something that big could never fly, where we come from."

"Come, now, Harold," Chalmers sighed. "They're not nearly as bad as some of the nurses who take blood samples at the Institute."

"Bad! Doc, have you *looked* at these critters? Ever since we crossed the border into this Kingdom of Crow-Cock, they've been like Dracula in insect form! The last one that buzzed my ear was the size of a B-29!"

"Then if we need to fly," Chalmers sighed, "we can just borrow their wings. Do go to sleep, Harold."

"Why? So they don't have to deal with a moving target?"

"Oh, be still, Xei," said Monkey. "Be glad you have the roof and walls of the Treasure Wood Temple about you tonight, rather than the grasses of a riverbank."

"It's all right for you to say," Shea growled. "They can't get their needles into your granite hide."

"If the Master can bear it, so can you."

"Tripitaka? I don't see him in here. He's a full-fledged monk, after all—he gets better quarters."

"You think the Zen Room is more comfortable? You forget that he is sitting in meditation all night."

"Oh, is that what he's doing?"

"Yes—just sitting," Monkey sighed. "Good *night*, Xei."

"Oh, good night," Shea griped. He cast a last accusing glare at the snoring bulk of Pigsy and Sandy, mere outlines in the gloom, then closed his eyes and tried for sleep.

"Wizard Xei!"

Shea sat bolt upright, his heart hammering. "Who the hell . . . ?"

"Closer than you think," the visitor snapped.

He was tall, severe, and drenched from head to toe. In fact, the water was running off him and pooling on the teak floor.

Shea reached for his sword and dagger and came slowly to his feet with both on guard. "Monkey! Pigsy! Sandy! Doc! We've got company!"

But the forms of his companions lay still in the moonlight, except for the slow rise and fall of breathing. Shea realized that he could not even hear Pigsy's snores.

"They will not hear you," the wet man said impatiently. "Now tell me—where is your master?"

"I have no master—I'm a free man."

"Do not bandy words with me, slave!" the man shouted. "Tell me the whereabouts of your master, and that quickly!" The apparition stepped closer.

Shea brandished his sword. "Hold it! Cold steel, remember?" He hoped that what worked on European elves might work for Chinese haunts.

Apparently not. Contemptuously, the man stepped right up to let the tip of Shea's sword disappear inside him. "Now tell me—where is the monk!"

Shea felt a chill pass over him—he knew which monk the man meant, but was not about to give any clues. "We're in a monastery. There are a lot of monks—just take your pick."

"Fool!" the man shouted, and swung a back-handed blow at Shea's head. Shea ducked and lunged—and stumbled straight into the apparition. There was a gust of icy wind; then he straightened up, to find himself facing the man's glowing back.

Slowly, the apparition turned, glaring. "What manner of monk are you, who bears a sword?"

"Not a monk at all," Shea said bravely, "just a traveller who has decided to join a holy man and his disciples for mutual protection."

"Yes! That is he—the Pilgrim Monk!" The apparition's eyes lit, glowing in the dark. "That is whom I spoke of! Where is he?"

Shea's eyes narrowed. "Why do you want to know?"

"Insolent cur!" the man shouted. "Vile peasant!

"That really makes me want to help you," Shea said slowly.

"Fool!" the spirit raged, and swung a back-handed blow at him. Shea knew it would not hurt, but by sheer reflex, he fell back out of the way and rolled—and heard Monkey saying: "Xei! What troubles you!"

"Him!" Shea pushed himself up on one elbow, jabbing out a forefinger—and found he was pointing at empty space. He blinked, stupefied. "He was there, I tell you! He was there!" Then he sagged. "It must have been a dream."

"Why, then, tell it to me, and I will tell you the meaning of it." Monkey sat down beside him, looking grave.

Shea looked up with a weak smile. "I thought that was supposed to be my line."

"As you will. But who was it whom you saw in this dream?"

"A wet man! Sopping wet, from head to toe! He wanted to know where Tripitaka was, but I wouldn't tell him!"

"Sopping wet?" Monkey raised his head, eyes glowing. "How was he dressed?"

"In silken robes, and he had a funny sort of hat on his head."

"A king, then," Monkey said. "Did he strike you when you would not tell him?"

"Yeah. And he stepped right onto my sword, too—it went into his chest by a foot, at least, but he just kept on threatening me."

"A ghost," Monkey said with conviction, "the ghost of a king who died by drowning. And he wanted the Master, you say?"

A hoarse scream echoed down the hall.

Monkey was out the door like a shot. Shea followed, yelling: "Pigsy! Sandy! Doc! It's Tripitaka!"

Pigsy and Sandy passed him halfway down the hall.

He swerved in through the door of the Zen Room, to find Tripitaka seated in lotus with his face in his hands, his shoulders shaking. Monkey knelt by him, Pigsy and Sandy a little farther off. "He was wet through," Tripitaka was moaning.

"Yes, but he is gone now, Master," Monkey soothed. "Lift your head and look about you, so that you may see there are none here but your disciples and friends."

"I know, I know," Tripitaka moaned, lifting his head. "I saw him leave, I saw him go!"

"Then you know there is no further cause for alarm," Monkey assured him. "Tell us the tale from its beginning, then—it will purge it from your mind and heart."

"There is truth in that." Tripitaka composed himself, sitting up ramrod straight again. "I meditated long, but about the middle of the night, I must have lapsed into a doze—for I saw a man come in through the door. Thinking him to be one of the monks, I kept silent, and he came to me and demanded, 'Are you the Pilgrim Monk?' Now I began to be afraid, for I could see the night-lamp through him, and saw that his garments were soaked—indeed, that water ran off him to pool on the floor, and I knew I was in the presence of a ghost of one who had died by drowning. Still, I took courage from the thought of Buddha's serenity and replied, 'I am. Who are you?'

" 'I am the rightful King of Crow-Cock,' he answered, 'and he who sits on my throne now is a usurper, and my murderer.'

" 'That is surely a grievous crime,' I answered, though I was far more shaken than I would let him see. 'How could he have done this to you?'

" 'Because he was my Prime Minister,' the ghost answered. 'One day, as we were walking in the garden near the well, he suddenly pushed me in, then changed himself into my exact duplicate—and thus did I discover that he was a sorcerer. When he was sure I had drowned, he took my throne, commanded that the well be covered and hidden, and took over the rule of my kingdom.'

"What a horrible tale!" Pigsy cried. "Out upon this sorcerer! We must revenge the rightful king!"

"We do not speak of revenge, disciple, we who follow

the Noble Eight-fold Path," Tripitaka said sternly, and Pigsy shrank back. "Even as you say, Master."

But Tripitaka was looking troubled again. "There is the worst part of it, though, Monkey—for the ghost of the King implored to help him in his revenge!"

"Asked a monk to help in *revenge*?"

"Yes. He asked me to tell his son the truth of his father's death. Once convinced, the prince will be sure to revenge him." Tripitaka buried his face in his hands. "Revenge! How can I, a priest of Buddha, condone revenge?"

"Be easy in your heart, Master," Monkey soothed again. "Did you not perform a similar deed, in righting the wrong of your own father's death?"

Tripitaka stilled, then lifted his head slowly. "There was justice in that, not revenge—the punishment of a murderer and regicide. But you speak truly, Monkey—here too we find a situation that cries out for justice, does it not?"

"With the voice of the poor and the starving," Monkey agreed.

"Yes, even as in my own country. The usurper, of course, did not have the Mandate of Heaven, and so the land suffered under his rule. The fields would not bear crops; the woods were filled with bandits. The people starved."

"But this usurper has been enthroned for only three years," Monkey protested, "and already, as what came into Crow-Cock, we have seen one deserted village and several barren fields! We traversed a wild forest, which lies only half a league from this very temple—and as we passed through it, we were attacked by bandits and had to fight them off—which is much more difficult when we must try not to kill them, I can tell you! Truly, Master, the land has begun to suffer under the usurper! If you do not wish that suffering to extend to the people, if you aspire to justice

in any way, you must help this poor drowned ghost—
the more so since all he asks of you is to tell his story
to his son!"

"Not as easy as it sounds," Shea put in. "What
would you say if somebody told you the man on the
throne was an imposter? He looks the same, he sounds
the same, but he isn't the real thing. If you believe
that, let me tell you about a piece of land you might
want to buy. . . ."

Tripitaka looked up, frowning, but Monkey said:
"The point is well taken. How shall you prove the
truth of what you say?"

"The King left that behind." Tripitaka pointed.

They all turned to look and saw something white
on the floor by the wall in a puddle of water. Gingerly,
Sandy picked it up by thumb and forefinger, and
brought it to lay at Tripitaka's feet, shuddering. "There
is the feel of death about it."

It was a white jade tablet, inscribed with columns
of Chinese characters.

"This was his, and his alone," Tripitaka told them,
"and he was never without it. He assured me that if
his son can see it, he will know that whoever bears it,
speaks truth."

"That should be convincing," Shea said, though he
had his doubts. "How do we get to the prince,
though?"

"The drowned king told me that tomorrow, his son
will go hunting in the forest," Tripitaka said.

"And it is only half a league away." Monkey gazed
off into space, musing.

"I hope you're not thinking of taking Tripitaka into
the woods to try to ambush the prince," Shea said.

"Truly?" Monkey looked interested. "Wherefore
not, Xei?"

"Credibility," Shea answered. "Would you pay any
attention to some nut who jumped out of a bush and

cried, 'Your father's really dead—that guy who's sitting on the throne is just a delusion!' Would you, really?"

Tripitaka nodded slowly. "But how else am I to speak with him?"

"Let us bring him to you. If he comes in this door and sees you sitting here, calm and cool, he's going to be thinking of you as a sage, not a wild-eyed hermit."

"But it is not fitting!" Tripitaka protested. "It is a violation of protocol!"

"Why? You're a prince, too, you know."

"Yes, but I have forsworn such worldly vanities, Xei, as I keep telling you!"

"Those worldly vanities, unfortunately, can be rather necessary when you're dealing with worldly people," Shea said.

"Even so! Even if I were to tell him my rank—I am the visitor in his kingdom, not he in mine! It is fitting that I come to him, not him to me!"

"Fitting, but totally impractical. He'll have a dozen retainers around him, and you can be sure every single one of them will be loyal to the current king, and eager to ingratiate himself by reporting every word the prince says."

"The barbarian speaks truth, Master," Pigsy said. "Let us bring the prince to you."

Tripitaka glanced at his brutish face, and his eyes widened in alarm, but Monkey only grinned. "Not all of us, Master—only me."

"Now, how did Monkey say he was going to do this again?" Chalmers asked nervously, eyeing the monastery gate, where Pigsy and Sandy lounged, one at either side against the wall, their weapons ready to hand.

"He said he's going to change himself into a rabbit," Shea muttered back, "a white rabbit. Apparently, they're pretty special here, and Monkey seemed pretty certain the prince would drop everything to come chasing him."

"But what about his entourage?"

"Monkey seemed pretty sure he could lose them." Shea eyed Pigsy and Sandy. "Just in case he can't, though, Pigsy and Sandy are supposed to surround them and keep them here."

"Surround them? How few does Monkey think there are going to be?"

"It doesn't seem to matter. Would *you* want to go up against our worthy travelling companions, no matter how many people you had at your back?"

Chalmers took another look at Pigsy's face, and shuddered.

Shea stiffened, laying a hand on Chalmers' arm. "I hear dogs."

"Do you?" Chalmers lifted his head. "Why, yes, so do I!"

The belling of the hounds came closer. Suddenly, a small white blob came dashing across the meadow, straight toward the monastery gates. As it dashed through, the riders came into sight—four of them, with a young man in embroidered silk robes at their head. He rode yelling with excitement and dashed through the gate just as the white rabbit dodged in through the temple door. "Curse it!" the young man cried, dismounting. He threw his reins at Shea, crying, "Hold him, fellow!" and ran into the temple.

Shea stared at the reins in indignation, then looked up at Chalmers, who was trying to hide a smile—but a racket at the gate distracted them. They turned to see the four other riders come plowing up a cloud of dust as they halted—then looked up in alarm as the gates slammed shut, and Pigsy and Sandy stepped out from the wall.

"Keep your seats," Pigsy grunted, levelling his muck-rake.

The hunters pulled together in sudden fear, but one of them tried to bluster. "Who do you think you are, fellow? Hold our horses and stand aside! We must follow our master!"

"This is a holy precinct." Sandy grinned, showing pointed teeth—not filed, naturally grown, the only vestige of his monstrous past. "This is a holy precinct, and men of violence are not allowed inside."

The man eyed Sandy's halberd, no doubt noticing the glint of sharpness along the edge, and tried one more weak protest. "What kind of monks are you, who hold weapons?"

"Very strong ones," Pigsy answered. "I have repented my violent ways—but alas! My temper keeps getting the better of me!"

"Be at ease," Sandy invited, though his blade did not waver. "Your master will rejoin you soon enough."

The hunters eyed the two erstwhile monsters, and held their peace.

Shea wrapped the reins around the nearest post and beckoned to Chalmers. "Come on! This is one interview I really want to hear!"

They got to the door of the Zen Room just in time to hear the prince rage: "Why do you not bow to me, foolish bonze? I arrest you for your impudence in failing to bow to a prince!" He looked behind him to gesture to his men—and suddenly realized he was all alone.

"The white rabbit, too, has disappeared," Monkey said. "Why not your men?"

"How dare you talk, audacious rascal! Know you not that monkeys only chatter?"

"I am the Stone Monkey," the simian answered, "and my master, Tripitaka, is as much a prince as yourself."

"So I was born," Tripitaka admitted, "but I have forsworn all worldly titles. I am only a Pilgrim Monk,

Your Highness." His back was as straight as ever, though.

The prince was not all that dense; he was beginning to get the drift that something unusual was going on. He frowned at Tripitaka and said: "I do not seek wisdom yet."

"Every prince should seek wisdom," Tripitaka returned, "the more so when he shall one day rule—as you shall have to do, and very soon, too."

The prince's sword flashed out. "Do you speak of slaying my father, fool?"

Monkey calmly reached up and took hold of the prince's wrist; the young man's eyes bulged, and he dropped the sword with a tiny mew of pain.

"Your father is already dead," Tripitaka said gently. "He has been dead for three years, and he who sits on his throne is an imposter." Then, to Monkey, "Release him."

Monkey let go, and the prince held his wrist, massaging it and staring wildly at Tripitaka. "What nonsense is this you speak! I saw my father only yesterday, and he was as hale and as hearty as ever!"

"You saw a sorcerer who had stolen his appearance," Tripitaka answered, then began to tell him the whole tale from the beginning. The prince stood listening, his eyes growing wider and wider.

Finally, when Tripitaka was done, the prince bowed his head, chin resting on his breast, scowling at the floor, his face somber.

The companions waited, watching him closely, holding their breath.

Finally, the young man lifted his face. "It may be as you say," he said, "but I cannot believe something of such magnitude on your word alone, even though you are a holy man. What proof can you give?"

Silently, Tripitaka reached into the folds of his robe and drew out the white jade tablet.

The prince seized it with a heart-rending cry. "This never left my father's side! How have you stolen it? When?" Without waiting for an answer, he ran for the door, crying, "Guards! Courtiers! Arrest these thieves!"

Pigsy leaped between him and the door, but the look on his face was grave. "Please do not, Your Highness. We are no thieves."

"You must be, for that tablet is a family heirloom!" The prince whirled, pointing at Tripitaka with a trembling hand. "It has been the property of the Kings of Crow-Cock ever since our dynasty began! My father had it from his father, and will give it to me in his turn!"

Silently, Tripitaka held his gaze.

Trembling, the prince caressed the tablet, but his eyes were on Tripitaka's. "You did not steal it?"

"I did not," Tripitaka returned. "The ghost of whom I spoke, he gave it to me."

The prince faltered, but regained his composure bravely. "I cannot be certain! You may have stolen it from his pocket as he passed through a crowd—he may have given it to the temple on some foolish impulse!"

Tripitaka sighed with exasperation, but Shea said, "Why not ask your mother?"

The last vestiges of color drained from the prince's face. He stared at Shea in outrage. "What is your meaning?"

"Why, only this." Shea spread his hands. "No one knows him as well as his wife. If there has been any change in him, wouldn't she be the one most apt to notice it?"

The prince still eyed him dangerously. "In what way?"

Shea sighed; the kid was determined to be obtuse. "Ask her if the King still loves her as much as ever."

The prince still stared at Shea, but his color came back; indeed, his face began to darken. But he gave a curt nod and said: "It is well advised. I shall attempt it. If she says he has turned cold to her, I shall return and seek your assistance in my revenge." He spun on his heel and stalked toward the door.

Tripitaka caught Pigsy's eye and nodded. The pig-headed creature reluctantly stepped aside.

On the threshold, the prince spun about, his finger stabbing at them. "But if she says he is as much in love with her as ever, I shall return with an army to slay you all!" He whirled about, and was gone.

They stared at one another, listening to his footsteps receding down the hall. Then Monkey said: "I note that he waited till he was at the door before he threatened us."

"He's not totally rash," Shea agreed.

"It was well thought, Xei," Tripitaka said. "How did you come by such an idea?"

Shea shrugged. "Just an incurable romantic, I guess. I have this notion that everybody only has one true love, so that if the current King of Crow-Cock is a fake, he couldn't possibly be really in love with the Queen. Of course, I'm assuming they were really in love with one another in the first place, which I understand isn't always the case here."

"Marriages are arranged," Monkey agreed. "What has love to do with it?"

"Apparently it did, in this case," Shea said. "At least, our prince seems to think so, or he wouldn't be going to question his mother. Wouldn't it be great to be a fly on the wall during that interview!"

"Why, what a charming idea!" Monkey cried. "Would you truly like it, Xei? Then come, let us fly!" He made a magic pass, and Shea felt some very sudden and very odd sensations. The room swam before his eyes, and he felt panic; then it steadied, and he could see more of it—he had a 270-degree field of view, though it was broken up into dozens of fragments, a sort of living mosaic. He turned to Chalmers, but Doc towered above him like a mountain, looking appalled. With a shock of horror, Shea realized he was now a fly!

Then another fly buzzed over to him—a huge fly, as big as he was, and with Monkey's face! "Are you ready, then?" asked the simian sorcerer. "Then come, away!" His face changed back into a fly's head, and he turned away, darting up off the floor, wings a blur.

Shea followed him, then realized he had not even thought about doing so. With a sinking heart, he wondered if he could have resisted, if Monkey had not cast a compulsion of some sort over him.

They flew out the window, over the forest, and found the river. Upstream they went, till they saw the walls and towers of a city before them. It was not terribly big, by Shea's standards—he doubted if it held more than twenty thousand people—but it was very pretty from this height, with little white houses and a tall stone palace.

The Monkey-fly arrowed down toward that palace. Shea followed.

Monkey buzzed from window to window, then ducked in through an ornate carved screen. Shea came right behind him, just barely beginning to worry about fly swatters.

He really had no need; Monkey spiralled up and up to alight on the top of a tapestry, fifteen feet above the floor—though from Shea's new perspective, it looked as though he were gazing down from the side of Mount Rushmore. He perched beside Monkey, feeling like Teddy Roosevelt's image, and scouted the surroundings.

They were in a high-roofed, light, airy chamber, hung with silks and tapestries and floored with a rich carpet. The furnishings were luxurious, but uncluttered—a rich, wide bed, a table with two chairs, a chest or two. By the window sat a woman painting a scroll, which was an amazing feat of dexterity, considering how long her fingernails were. She was richly dressed in an embroidered silken gown, black hair elaborately coiffed. She was in her forties, but still strikingly beautiful. But in spite of her luxurious surroundings, she seemed listless, unhappy. Her brush strokes were few and labored, and her gaze kept drifting off through the window.

There was a scrabbling from that window, and she sat up in alarm.

"Mother!" came the prince's voice. "Admit me, please!"

"My son!" She rose in a single, fluid motion that contrasted oddly with her tottering walk as she hurried to open the screen. Shea saw why—her feet were so small that they might have been those of a child. He suppressed a surge of nausea and focused on the events below him.

The Queen was clasping her son to her breast, weeping openly, then stood away, as though remembering the proprieties. "My son, it is so good to see you! It has been three years since your father forebade us to meet! I have heard tales of your deeds, but have longed to see you with my own eyes!"

"And I you, Mother." The prince knelt, bowing. "But I must speak briefly, for I come in secret."

"In secret?" The Queen glanced at the screen and quickly pulled it closed. "Yes, of course. It will go hard with you if your father learns of this, will it not? Oh, how foolish of you, to take such a risk!"

"It is necessary—because of that same king." The prince looked up at her, his face intent. "And because of my father."

"Why . . . why do you speak of them as though they were two separate people?" she asked, her voice faltering.

"It is for you to answer that," the prince returned. "I was led today by a magician, led to a holy man who told me of a dream, and because of that I must ask you a question. . . ." He blushed and turned away. "Oh, but it is too personal!"

The Queen began to see where the conversation was going. She drew herself up, composing her face. "If it touches on your father's welfare, my son, you must ask it."

"I have no right. . . ."

"But you have a duty. He is your king. Ask what you will."

Neatly done, Shea decided—the prince had warned her of what was coming, but had managed to phrase it in such a way that she could not object. He bowed his head now, and asked, "Forgive me, Mother, but I must ask—has my father become less fervent in his love for you these three years past?"

She stared, stricken, then burst into tears. The prince was on his feet beside her in an instant, arms open to console, but she shrugged him off and tottered over to sit by the window again. She mastered her sobs, nodding. "It is even as you have guessed, my son. Your father suddenly turned very cold toward me, and has remained so to this day. He avoids me as much as he can, and when he cannot, he treats me with cold civility. Oh, he is never cruel or infuriated— but I could wish that he were!"

"The monk's dream was true, then," the prince said, his face grave. "Forgive me for having saddened you, Mother." He bowed and started to turn away, but she caught his sleeve and cried: "Wait! Surely now you must tell me this dream the monk spoke of!"

The young man hesitated. "It might imperil you to know of it. . . ."

"I think I do already! For know, my son, that I, too, have had a dream, only this night past—a dream in which your father appeared to me, and he was soaking wet from head to toe. I cried out, asking him what was the matter, for I had seen him hale and hearty only a few hours before. He told me that the Prime Minister, he who disappeared so suddenly and with so little explanation three years ago, had actually drowned your father in a well, then taken on his face and form—and throne!"

The prince bowed his head. "It is even this that the monk told me."

"Then there must be more, for your father's ghost told me that he had asked the Pilgrim Monk to avenge him! Oh, son, is this true? Is there any proof?"

"The monk showed me the white jade tablet that Father always carried with him, and that the King has not shown to anyone these three years past."

The Queen turned away with a wail of grief.

"Mother . . ." The prince stepped forward, reaching out to the Queen.

"No, no, I will endure, I will endure!" she said between her sobs, mastering the emotion and wiping her eyes. "There will be a time for grief, there will be a time! For now, son, you must seek out proof that all the ministers of the kingdom will acknowledge, and aid the monk in avenging your father's death!"

"I must, and I shall." The prince knelt before her, bowing his head. "Courage, mother. Soon we shall talk more freely, and the kingdom will share our grief."

She clasped him in one more brief, impulsive hug, then pushed him away. "Go, and be quick, and careful! For if I should lose you, too, I should wish to lose my life!"

The prince bowed and turned to the window.

Monkey dropped off his perch and buzzed away toward the carved screen.

Shea stayed only a moment longer, for one last look at the Queen, who was quietly weeping, then leaped into flight and followed Monkey.

The freedom of flight was glorious, without an airplane or a broom between him and the elements. Shea resolved to get Monkey to teach him the spell, then remembered that it probably would not work in any other universe—and he was not sure he would want to try, if he did not have guaranteed results. He resolved to enjoy it while he could, and found himself almost sad to be soaring in through the door of the Treasure Wood Temple and settling on the floor. It was a real wrench to feel himself growing so huge and leaden, becoming human once more.

By the time he had readjusted, Monkey was already finished with his report, and Tripitaka was asking, "So he is bound back here to us, then?"

"He is," Monkey confirmed.

"And he's in such a stew that he probably isn't going to think to be careful," Shea added. "He'll probably have five spies following him before he's out the city gates."

"Well, they will not manage to follow him all the way through the wood," Monkey answered, and turned to Pigsy. "Will they?"

Pigsy grinned and said, "Of course they shall not, Monkey." He turned away to the door.

"Remember, no killing!" Tripitaka called, alarmed.

"No killing," Pigsy agreed, with real regret. "I will not even give them one more blow than is necessary— but I assure you, Master, they will not follow the prince here."

"Even if they did, what matter?" Monkey shrugged. "Who could fault a prince for visiting a temple?"

"That is so," Tripitaka allowed. "But what are we to tell him when he has come?"

Boots sounded in the hall.

Monkey looked up, alert. "Sandy! Make sure Pigsy succeeded!"

The reformed cannibal gave him a sharp-toothed grin and turned to the door. He bowed as the prince strode in, then slipped out.

The prince had not even noticed him. In fact, he did not even seem to notice Monkey, Shea, and Chalmers. "Reverend prince! Holy sage! I apologize most abjectly for my rudeness and my skepticism!" And he bowed low.

"I am honored by your apology." Tripitaka inclined his head. "But I must caution you, prince, to seek only justice, not revenge."

"Justice will have to satisfy me, then," the prince sighed, "though I will not deny that I had rather see the usurper suffer the Death of the Thousand Cuts. Still, if justice it must be, I shall be content. How, then, are we to go about it?"

Tripitaka sat very still. Shea hid a smile; the monk had been about to ask the same question.

"It would seem to me," Monkey said, with deference, "that before we can speak of justice against this sorcerer, we must capture and hold him. Then may we judge him."

"True." The prince frowned. "Yet if we do not kill him outright, how are we to convince his ministers and generals that he is a false king?"

"How are we to prove it even if we *were* to kill him outright?" Monkey countered.

Chalmers cleared his throat and stepped forward.

Both princes looked up, surprised.

"Pardon my intrusion into so lofty a discussion," Chalmers said, "but it is written that the sage seeks wisdom from the East and from the West."

"It is?" Shea stared.

"By W.S. Gilbert, Harold," Chalmers hissed.

"How is it written?" Monkey demanded.

Chalmers recited,

"I've wisdom from the East and from the West
That is subject to no academic rule.
You may find it in the jeering of a jest,
Or distill it from the folly of a fool."

"And you are from the West." Tripitaka smiled. "Though, I hope, you are not a fool. Well, then, Magician Chao-mar-zi, what wisdom have you to offer, to aid us in our plight?"

"An instance from the law of my country, Reverend Sir. There, if a man is imprisoned and not released after three days, his counselor can demand that the jailers present the body, to prove that the man is alive and well."

"Or beaten and dead," Monkey said darkly. "Drowned, in this case—but I take your meaning, Chao-mar-zi." He looked up at Tripitaka.

The monk nodded. "Surely presenting the dead body of the king would be most convincing proof of the usurper's falseness. Do you not agree, Your Highness?"

"Why, of course," the prince said, astonished. "But how are we to retrieve it?"

"That, I think we may leave to the wizard who recommended the course of action," Tripitaka said slowly. "May we not, Wizard Chao-mar-zi?"

Chalmers stared, totally taken aback.

Shea stepped forward. "Why, of course, Reverend Sir." Frantically, he was trying to figure out what sort of spell could raise a dead body from a well.

He still had not figured out the answer by the time the prince left to start plotting, and Monkey turned to him with a grin. "Excellently thought, Xei! And how *shall* you raise the dead king's body?"

Shea stalled. "It'd be kind of chancey. It would need a brand-new spell, and I don't need to tell you how many things could go wrong with that."

Chalmers blanched—he knew very well how much could go wrong.

Monkey nodded, satisfied. "Truly said. Indeed, there are some puzzles that are best solved by the use of brute force."

Pigsy strolled in, grinning. "It is done, Master. The prince had passed by on his homeward course before the spies who followed him began to regain their senses."

"But there was no killing?" Tripitaka asked anxiously.

"Not even by accident," Pigsy said regretfully. "In fact, I'm sure none of them even saw me."

"Pigsy," said Monkey, "would you like to find a buried treasure?"

Pigsy's little eyes expanded amazingly. "A treasure! Gold and gems, all for myself? Where is it, Monkey? Tell me, tell me!"

"I'll do better than that," Monkey said. "I'll show you." He turned to Shea. "Would you care to accompany us, Wizard?"

Shea knew better than to decline.

The moon was high when the three bats landed near the grassy mound with the mulberry sapling on top, in the center of the palace gardens. They crouched on the ground, then expanded amazingly into Monkey, Pigsy, and Shea. Shea was almost regretful about it—he had enjoyed the bat's soaring even more than the housefly's buzzing. On the other hand, that was definitely the kind of spell that could get him into trouble in other universes, including his own.

"It is under here," Monkey told Pigsy.

"Stand back, then." The pig-face grinned, showing tusks. "We shall uncover it quickly." He yanked the sapling out by the roots and tossed it over his shoulder. Shea jumped back in alarm, and so did Monkey. Good thing, too—Pigsy got busy with the muck-rake, and the dirt flew out in a continuous stream. Quickly, the whole of the mound disappeared. Then the muck-rake thudded on wood, and Pigsy frowned. "Wooden boards? What is this?"

"A well cover." Monkey stepped up and, with one titanic heave, flipped the cover off the well.

Shea glanced up at the walls nervously. How could the sentries help but notice?

Foolish question. With a magician like Monkey beside him? Why did he bother asking?

"Down there?" Pigsy looked down, frowning. "You did not tell me anything about a swim, little brother!"

"Why should it bother you?" Monkey asked. "You've done your share of diving in your time. Down with you, Pigsy! The treasure is at the bottom of the well!"

"If you say so," Pigsy grunted, and dove in with a splash that Shea could have sworn must have waked the sorcerer-king—but there was no reaction, no cry of alarm, no gongs sounding. In fact, he heard nothing. Nothing but night-birds—and no sound from the well. When he was sure five minutes had passed, he said, "Has he drowned?"

"He can hold his breath far longer than this," Monkey assured him. "Do not fear for our brutish companion, Xei—and do not worry; it is a deep well."

Very deep; another five minutes must have passed before a bloated body suddenly shot from the surface of the well with a huge splash. Shea flinched back in sheer reflex, then realized that the body was hanging from the prongs of a muck-rake. Pigsy's head was right behind it. "This was all I found! Where is the treasure, Monkey?"

"Why, this is it." Monkey pulled the dead body onto the well-curb.

"What! Nothing but this? Monkey, you lied to me!"

"It is for the best," Monkey assured him. "What would you have done with gold and jewels, anyhow? We could not take time to spend them."

"You tricked me! You bamboozled me!"

"We had to have this body," Monkey explained, laying out the dead king on the ground, "and you are a far better swimmer than I."

"I'll get even," Pigsy growled. "You see if I don't!"

Shea looked at the drowned body, then looked away again, shuddering. It was swollen, bloated, and the color of a fish's belly. Still . . . "It's in strangely good shape for a three-year-old corpse, Monkey."

"It is." The stone simian frowned. "Almost as though a magician had cast a spell of preservation over it—or as though Yama, King of the Dead, had not yet taken his due." He looked up at Shea, brooding. "Perhaps he knows something that we do not."

"Maybe," Shea agreed, feeling a prickling of dread envelop his back and neck. "Let's get the stiff out of here, Monkey, okay?"

For some reason, the sentries were all looking the other way as Shea and Monkey hoisted the dead king over the garden wall and off into the night. They must have been selectively deaf, too, for Pigsy was not worrying about how loud he was grumbling.

"It is he, even as he appeared in my dream!" Tripitaka shuddered, staring at the dead body before him. "In truth, his body does not appear anywhere nearly as ravaged as I dreaded. What could have caused this, Monkey? Why would Yama not have taken his due of it?"

Monkey shrugged, for once without an answer.

But Chalmers was not. "Could it be," he said slowly, "that the King is only in some sort of coma?"

Shea looked up, frowning. "No, impossible, Doc! Even a body in coma has to breathe! Besides, he's bloated."

Tripitaka looked from one to the other, frowning. "What is a 'coma'?"

"A state of unconciousness," Chalmers explained, "much deeper than sleep, but still just barely living. It usually ends in death, though the body may linger for years. Sometimes, though, occasionally, very rarely, a person will come out of a coma, and regain full use of his faculties."

"A deathlike sleep?" Tripitaka frowned. "How could the dead return to life?"

Pigsy saw his chance. "Why, just ask Monkey, master! He can bring the dead to life! Just ask him!"

"Be still, lump of lard!" Monkey frowned. "I can do no such thing!"

"Oh, aye, he will deny it!" Pigsy jibed. "But he has been in Heaven, and even in the laboratory of Lao-Tzu! If anyone can bring the dead back to life, he can!"

"What nonsense are you speaking, fool!" Monkey barked. "Only Yama can bring the dead back to life!"

"Oh, of course he will deny it!" Pigsy cried. "But only say the magic words, Master! Invoke the spell of the golden headband! Make it tighten about his temples, and he will admit the truth!"

Tripitaka, looking very stern, began to recite the rhyme.

"Master, no!" Monkey cried in a panic. "He speaks only in spite, he seeks revenge because I tricked him into . . . Aieeee!" He fell on the ground, clutching his temples and shrieking. Pigsy laughed, enjoying the sight immensely.

"Speak truth, Monkey," Tripitaka said sternly. "If you can raise the dead, it is needful that you do so!"

"I can, I can!" Monkey cried. "I will find a way! I will bring the dead king back to life, if I have to go to Yama himself to demand it! Only make the pain stop, Master!"

With a curt nod, Tripitaka recited the counterspell. Monkey went limp with relief.

"Remember your promise now, Monkey," Pigsy jeered. "Raise the dead king to life!"

Monkey leaped to his feet, eyes glowing fiery red, and ran at Pigsy with a bellow.

"Disciple!" Tripitaka snapped, and Monkey came to an instant halt, shouting, "I will be revenged on you, Pigsy!"

"Did you speak of revenge?" Tripitaka demanded in dire tones, and Monkey froze. Then, slowly, he turned and bowed to Tripitaka. "I shall do your bidding, Master."

Behind him, Pigsy snickered.

Tripitaka eyed him coldly. "I shall deal with you later."

Pigsy blanched.

Tripitaka turned back to his smallest disciple. "How shall you do this thing, Monkey?"

"There are only two ways," Monkey sighed. "The one is to go into the Abode of the Dead, and beg Yama to restore the soul to the body—but Yama has no reason to grant our request, and is very stingy with the souls he has gathered."

"Agreed," Tripitaka said slowly.

"The only other way," Monkey said, "is to force my way into Heaven and beg a grain of Life-Restoring Elixir from Lao-Tzu—and that is what I must do. I know the way, for I have been in Heaven before."

Tripitaka said severely, "Yes, I know you were, and I have heard the tale of the havoc you caused there, five hundred years ago. Do as you did when you were a groom to the Jade Emperor's horses, and every deity in Heaven will seek to punish us." He turned to Shea. "Do you go along with him, Magician Xei, for I have found that you have an understanding of people that may enable you to restrain Monkey from his wildest excesses. And, too, your diplomacy may gain more help than all Monkey's bullying could ever do. Will you go?"

Shea swallowed, hard, and glanced at Chalmers, who shrugged almost imperceptibly, then gave him the slightest of nods.

Shea turned back to Tripitaka. "Of course, Reverend Sir, if that is what you ask." Inside, he asked himself frantically if Heaven could really be real.

The Chinese Heaven? Why not? As real as the Norsemen's Asgard, anyway—and Shea had been there already. Why not, indeed?

Seconds later, they were on a cloud and rising fast. Shea had to gulp air to quiet a queasy stomach, and tried to remember a spell for Dramamine. He decided that he definitely preferred a broomstick, under his own control—or better yet, a reclining seat with a seatbelt and a stewardess.

Then they rose above the floor of a cloudbank, and Shea found himself facing a huge Chinese gate in a wall that towered up and up. Both were of gold, and the gate was inlaid with mother-of-pearl and jade.

Monkey hopped off his cloud and swung up his cudgel; it lengthened into a six-foot iron staff.

"No, hold it a minute!" Shea grabbed the tip of the staff—and almost got another free ride, but Monkey halted in the nick of time and grunted, "Wherefore?"

"Because breaking down somebody's front door isn't the best way to get them to like you."

"Why should we want them to like us?"

"Because if they do, they're more likely to grant us a favor."

Monkey bared his teeth in a grin. "I assure you, Xei, none here has cause to like me—and they all have long, long memories."

"Still, we might try another way."

"Why?"

"Humor me."

Monkey sighed. "You western barbarians are so unreasonable! Well enough, Xei—how would you gain entrance to Heaven? We are neither of us ghosts, you know—and, if truth be told, neither one pure enough for Heaven!"

"There's some truth in that, I suppose," Shea sighed, "but Heaven is common to both our cultures, so maybe I can impose a little of my own on this image of it." He frowned at the gate, concentrating very hard on his own private image of the Pearly Gates—and a small metal rectangle with two buttons appeared on the right-hand jamb. "There, see?" he said triumphantly, and stepped forward to press the button. The two gates slid apart with a slight hiss, to show a richly appointed little room, painted with red laquer and gold leaf, and hung with silken tapestries.

Monkey stared, the white showing all around his irises.

Shea stepped in quickly, pressing one hand against the edge of the door. "Come on in, quick, before it closes!"

Monkey snapped out of his trance and jumped aboard.

"Where are we going?" Shea was inspecting the panel, trying to decipher the buttons—they were in Arabic numerals, and he was currently geared to Chinese characters.

"The Thirty-third Heaven." Monkey eyed his surroundings like a caged animal.

"Thirty-third it is." Shea managed to figure out what those two backward-facing fat characters were, and pressed the button.

The car began to thrum about them.

"It is alive!" Monkey cried, and leaped so high he crashed into the ceiling, brandishing his staff. He fell with a thud, and Shea helped him up, trying to sound reassuring. "It's no more alive than one of your clouds. They move too, don't they?"

"True enough," Monkey said, but he crouched in the corner and brandished his staff, eyes flicking from side to side and top to bottom, trembling the whole time the elevator was moving.

"Yes, but my stomach does not sink when it flies," Monkey moaned.

"Mine does." Shea felt the pressure inside ease up. "Besides, the car's slowing—it must have been an express. What should we be expecting to see, Monkey?"

The doors slid back.

"That," Monkey whispered.

Shea stepped out and found himself facing a vista of cotton-candy hills bedecked with pagodas and palaces.

Monkey stepped out behind him, looking about him in awe. "That is far faster than I came here last time, and with much less adventure."

"Sorry to miss that last part," Shea sighed, "but we don't really have time for it right now. Which way is Lao-Tzu's laboratory?"

"Yonder." Monkey pointed.

Following his gesture, Shea saw a plain and simple hut—that glittered. "I thought he advocated austerity."

"He does, but the Jade Emperor insisted." Monkey gestured, and a cloud detached itself from the nearest cotton-candy mountain. "Your turn to suffer my mode of transport again, Xei."

The cloud barrelled into them, knocking Shea off

his feet. Monkey, of course, sprang lithely up onto it, and caroled with delight. Shea was just managing to get his feet under him again when the cloud stopped, and he pitched headlong into its softness again. He extricated himself, grumbling: "For such a short distance, we could have walked."

"Believe me, Xei, it would have taken half a day, in this clinging stuff." Monkey stepped up to the door and knocked with his staff.

Shea looked up, amazed. Yes, a plain, simple hut— the size of a palace! And made of mother-of-pearl and white jade, too!

The door opened, to show a young man shaved bald, with a saffron robe. He saw Monkey and stared, horrified.

"Let us in," the little ape blustered, "or I will bring your door down around your ears!"

"Monkey . . . !" Shea moaned, but the young man's expression firmed into stony impassivity. He cried, "Master! It is that horrible little monster again!"

"Horrible little monster yourself!" Monkey shouted, raising his cudgel. "I'll teach you to insult your betters!"

But the young man stepped aside, and a little old man in a plain tunic stepped into the doorway. He was bald except for a fringe of white hair, and wore a long white moustache and goatee. When he saw Monkey, he scowled. "Why do you trouble my disciple? And why have you come back, you thief and brigand?"

"Thief and brigand!" Monkey exclaimed indignantly, but Shea decided it was time he took a hand. He stepped up beside his companion, just incidentally getting between the simian and the sage, and bowed. "Have I the honor of addressing the reverend sage, Lao-Tzu?"

"You have, though I am only a man," the sage

answered. "And you are Harold Xei. I have watched your skipping through universes with some interest. Do you truly think there is anything to be gained thereby?"

"Knowledge," said Shea, totally dumbfounded that the sage had noticed him.

"Knowledge?" Lao-Tzu shrugged. "What use is that?"

"Discovering new knowledge is a source of great joy," Shea answered slowly.

"Beware of such joy, young man. It will seduce you away from contemplation of the Way."

"So does all of human life," Shea sighed, "but I'm not quite ready to give up on it yet. Which is why we've come to speak with you, Reverend Sir—to ask your help in bringing a king back to life."

"We ask one grain! Only one grain! Of the Life-Restoring Elixir!" Monkey cried.

"One grain? Was not one whole flask enough for you?" Lao-Tzu scowled.

"That was five hundred years ago," Monkey protested, "and Buddha took it away from me!"

"As well he should have," Lao-Tzu said. "They who have eternal life but have not won it through virtue— it is they who fear death most; and they who fear death can be most easily intimidated. What would have happened to the world if the Elixir of Life had been spread far and wide?"

Shea forbore the temptation to mention overpopulation, and tried to remember a few of Lao Tzu's own verses instead. "But the King of Crow-Cock has been replaced by a usurper—and if the rightful king does not rule, will not the people suffer?"

"They must learn to want less, so that they will suffer less," Lao-Tzu returned.

"But," said Shea:

"The reason why people starve,
Is because they take so much in tax-grain.
Therefore they starve.
The reason why the common people cannot be
    ruled,
Is because their superiors act for private reasons.
Therefore they cannot be ruled."

Lao-Tzu frowned, recognizing his own words. He answered:

"The reason why people take death lightly,
Is because they so avidly seek after life.
Therefore they take death lightly.
Only those who do not act for the purpose of
    living—
Only these are superior to those who value
    life."

"Yet who would be less likely to act for the purpose of living," said Shea, "than one who has already been dead?

"When people are born, they're supple and soft;
When they die, they end up stretched out firm
and rigid."

Lao-Tzu smiled. "You forget the end of the verse:

"Rigidity and power occupy the inferior position;
Suppleness, softness, weakness, and delicateness
occupy the superior position."

"True," Shea admitted, "but who would know that better than a king who has already been dead, yet is now restored to life?"

Lao-Tzu frowned. "This is true. But would he there-

fore live as a sage, that his people might follow him
into virtue?"

Shea spread his hands. "What man can, who has
taken up the responsibilities of living among other
people? Surely you don't think he should try to deny
those commitments!"

Monkey stared up at him, frowning, puzzled.

By way of explanation, Shea added:

"The Way gives birth to them, nourishes them,
 matures them, completes them, rests them,
 rears them, supports them, and protects
 them.

"Should not a king emulate the Way?"

Lao-Tzu smiled. "Will a king who has been saved
from death, from the penalty of his own mistakes,
emulate the Way?"

"I should think so," Shea replied, "for if he has
been brought back to life, wouldn't he be like a newborn babe? And:

"One who embraces the fullness of Virtue,
 Can be compared to a newborn babe.

"So wouldn't someone who is like a newborn babe,
embrace the fullness of Virtue?"

It was lousy logic, and he knew it, but it might
work.

But Lao-Tzu knew it, too. His eyes twinkled with
amusement, and he said, "His chances, at least, are
greater than those rulers who have never experienced the Afterlife—and there is a reason why I
should wish to see this king live again, which you
may not know."

Shea frowned; he did not like secrets, unless they
were his own.

Lao-Tzu clapped his hands, and a disciple appeared beside him, holding a little box. The sage took it and handed it to Shea, saying, "Herein is a tiny flask, containing one drop of the Life-Restoring Elixir. See that it is used only for the King of Crow-Cock—and do not let this truant touch it." He nodded at Monkey.

All the way back to Earth, Monkey was muttering: "Truant! What does he think he is, the old fool! Thirty-third Heaven! Jade palace! Who preached the virtues of simplicity, anyway?"

It was a very bumpy ride.

Monkey pried open the jaws of the corpse, and Shea upended the tiny bottle over the gaping mouth. A single shimmering drop fell in. Monkey shoved the jaws closed and wiped off his hands in disgust.

The bloating began to diminish, and the blueness faded.

"It's working!" Shea stared.

"Unbelievable," Chalmers was muttering beside him. "Absolutely unbelievable."

"Is it really?"

"Oh, I believe it! Here, at least!"

The pallid flesh began to turn tan again. The bloating was completely gone now; the body before them lay gaunt. The cheeks gained a flush, the nostrils quivered. . . .

With one convulsive shudder, the King of Crow-Cock sat bolt upright.

"Father!" his son cried, and threw his arms around the older man. Chalmers reached down to pry him loose, saying: "Give him air," and the prince let go and leaped back with alacrity.

The King put out a hand to prop himself up and sat panting and looking about him, wild-eyed. "Never was air so sweet!"

"Have you learned Virtue, then?" Tripitaka asked.

"Virtue, and humility!" The King turned to bow to the monk. "Let me carry your baggage, Holy One! That I may learn the ordering of the state for the good of my people, through submission to the Way!"

The prince stared, amazed, but Monkey stepped up and said, "Just as well. How else are we to smuggle you back into Crow-Cock, eh?"

So they came into the palace, with the prince marching smartly at their head to open doors. Sentries sprang out of his way and bowed, and the whole entourage followed—especially the middle-aged man in the center of the procession, who was bowed under a load of bundles.

Pigsy was grinning from ear to ear—carrying the baggage was usually *his* job.

But at the doors to the throne room, the guards crashed their halberds together. "The King sits in judgment!"

"I must speak with him instantly!" The prince did not slacken his pace for a moment. "Step aside!"

They hesitated only a fraction of a second; after all, who was going to be their boss when the old man died? They yanked their halberds back and pushed the door open.

The prince strode into the throne room.

The King looked up, then waved away the petitioners and jumped to his feet, scowling. Shea shuddered—it was eerie, seeing the same face that he had just restored to life. "What is the meaning of this?" the King thundered.

The porter straightened up, dropping his bags. It means that I have come to reclaim my throne, and you are unmasked!"

Time stood still while the two kings stared at one another.

The hesitation was all Monkey needed. He sprang at the false king with a howl of rage, swinging his cudgel.

The imposter whirled to him, gesturing, and Monkey's cudgel cracked against something unseen with a shower of sparks. The sorcerer sprang into the air and soared out the window, his form blurring as he went.

The prince cheered, with Pigsy and Sandy backing him up.

But Tripitaka was shouting, "He must not escape! Or he will brew unparalled mischief!"

"I go, Master!" Monkey cried, and a cloud appeared right next to him. He sprang upon it and shot out the window.

Shea ran to the opening to watch. Chalmers, Pigsy, and Sandy were right behind him.

They saw the cloud whirl up to head off the fleeing sorcerer. Lightning flashed from him toward Monkey, but the simian deflected it somehow, making it rebound toward its source. Before it could reach him, however, the sorcerer had changed into an eagle, and was soaring higher on an updraft. Monkey changed into a dragon, beat up higher than the eagle, and pounced.

The eagle dropped like a stone, changing as it went. By the time Monkey's claws closed around it, it was a sparrow that darted between the dragon's talons and went arrowing right back toward the window it had come from.

"Back!" Shea shouted. Everybody jumped aside, and the sparrow shot through the window with a monster right behind it, half dragon and half Monkey.

The bird arrowed straight for Tripitaka.

Sandy shouted and jumped after it—but before he could get there, the sparrow was growing and grasping Tripitaka, whirling him around in a circle, around and around as it turned into something tall and yellow. . . .

Then two Tripitakas stood there, side by side, both in saffron robes, identical to the last detail.

They all stared.

Then Monkey howled: "Master! Speak and tell us which one you are!"

"I am here!" answered both Tripitakas. "I am the true Tripitaka!" Then they both turned to each other and snapped in unison, "Be still, imposter! You know that I am the true Tripitaka!"

"How are we to tell?" Pigsy moaned.

But Chalmers pursed his lips in thought. "Monkey . . . insult your Master."

Monkey's eyes lit with glee; then his face filled with apprehension, but he mastered it and sprang at the two monks, crying: "Fraud! You have told me that Virtue would make me immune to sorcery! You dared to tell me to spare the life of a villain, when it would be easier to kill him! You have lied to me, false sage!" And he swung the cudgel.

Both of the Tripitakas looked up in anger, but one of them chanted a quick rhyming couplet, and Monkey fell to the floor, howling in agony and clutching at the gold headband.

Pigsy roared in rage and fell on the other Tripitaka. Sandy was only one beat behind him.

Tripitaka looked up, astounded, then realized what had happened, and recited the counterspell. Monkey leaped to his feet with a cry of relief, then whirled toward the sorcerer.

Pigsy and Sandy had him pinned down. Monkey jumped up on his chest, swinging his cudgel up; it stetched out to its full six-foot length and began to descend. . . .

"Stop!"

Everyone froze. Then Monkey looked up, staring in disbelief, staff still held high.

There was a glow in midair above him, almost too bright to look at, and within it was a human form—but Shea could not make out anything else, the light was so bright.

"Manjusri," Monkey whispered. "It is the god Manjusri!"

Everyone else in the room fell to their knees, bowing low.

Chalmers and Shea exchanged a quick glance, then began backing away toward the walls.

"There is more to this semblance than you know, Monkey," the god intoned with a voice like a gong. "This King of Crow-Cock was originally so good a monarch that, some years ago, Buddha sent me in the form of a man, to bring the King to the Western Paradise. The King, however, loved his wife, son, and people too much, and was not yet ready to leave his earthly life. For this reason, he had me bound and cast into the river, where I stayed for three days and nights before spirits from Heaven fetched me out. As punishment, Buddha sent my mount to assume the form of the enchanter and win his way to office as the King's Prime Minister! Now the pose is unmasked! Let my mount return to his true form!"

The body under Pigsy's and Sandy's hands shimmered and flowed like hot wax. They cried out and leaped back, staring.

The hot wax pulled itself together in a new form—and a blue lion stood before them, roaring.

"Of course!" Monkey breathed. "Manjusri's blue

lion is gelded! No wonder he showed no interest in the Queen!"

The King stood, pale and trembling. "Then it was at Buddha's mandate that the enchanter threw me into the well?"

"Even so," Manjusri confirmed. "This was your punishment for seeking to drown me, Buddha's messenger. No one else has really suffered much; the Queen and the concubines have been ignored, and have had cause to complain only of his disinterest. As to the people, they have had a lean year, but none has died of starvation, and adversity has strengthened them."

The former enchanter turned and sprang into the dazzle of light, and they could all see the form of the god seated on the silhouette of the blue lion.

The King knelt, his head low. "Forgive me, Manjusri! I knew not whom I mistreated—and I was too proud to submit to the judgment of Buddha! I shall atone in asceticism and good works for the rest of my life!"

"See that you do," rang the voice of the god, "for you must now spend many years regaining the Virtue that you had when first I met you. And as for *you*!" A finger speared out toward Shea and Chalmers. "Barbarian wizards! You have completed the task for which Buddha kept you here! Go now where you will—go to the world to which the errant wife has fled!"

Fire shot from that finger and enveloped Shea and Chalmers, roaring all about them. They cried out in surprise and fear, but there was no pain, only a dazzle that blinded them. . . .

KNIGHT AND THE ENEMY
Holly Lisle

Dedication

To L. Sprague de Camp and in memory of the late Fletcher Pratt, whose Compleat Enchanter stories were the first fantasy for grown-ups I ever read—and still some of my favorites. Without, them, I would never have considered writing fantasy.

And to Toni Weisskopf, my fairy godmother (and editor), who gave me the chance to write a Harold Shea story.

Harold Shea, tired of walking along the unchanging road, thumped down solidly on the nearest rock. He sighed and stared at the bleak landscape around him. On one side, low hills rolled to the horizon, rounded and grimly browned, dotted with clumps of dead grass and stunted trees. On the other, a flat plain sprawled, equally sere and rocky but dotted in the distance with windmills that spun slowly in the hot, sluggish breeze, as if any movement were an effort. The sun lay near the horizon, but it was obviously rising; the day could only get hotter. A steady breeze blew past, but it was already stifling and heavy with dust. Sweat trickled down the back of his neck, and the heavy woolen tunics from the world of Aeneid, stuck to his skin wherever they touched.

Behind him, Reed Chalmers groaned and muttered, "I don't suppose you have any idea where we might be now, do you, Harold?"

"I'd considered asking you the same question." Shea watched the dusty two-rut road that bisected the parched hills. A shimmer and a pillar of dust crept along the road out of the hills, moving closer. He felt at his side for the reassuring presence of the saber, and curled his fingers around the wire-wrapped grip inside the basket hilt. It was a good saber—a better travelling weapon even than the épée that had served him so well in previous jaunts. When forms materialized inside the nearing dust cloud, he merely smiled. After all, a man who had fought giants side by side with the god Heimdall, and bested foul enchanters in the world of the *Faerie Queen*, had little to fear.

"Someone's coming," he told his associate.

Chalmers, who had been watching the listless performance of the windmills, looked where Shea pointed. "Quite so," he agreed. The psychologist ducked behind a boulder. "I hope they aren't hostile. Why don't we stay out of sight—at least until we get some idea what universe we're in?"

Shea remained standing and used his hand to shade his eyes while he tried to make out details of the approaching figures. All he could make out was that there were two of them. "I hope they can tell us where to find something to eat. I'm starving."

"While I value you as a travelling companion, Harold," Chalmers huffed, "I find you lacking in prudence. Get out of sight! May I remind you that dead men have very little need for food?"

"I'd rather you didn't," Shea said, and kept his eyes on the approaching travellers. "I'll just watch from here, thanks."

"I wish you wouldn't take this attitude toward adventures," Chalmers fumed. "You refuse to consider that I am not a young man anymore, and that my contributions to this campaign must be mental, not physical."

Shea chuckled. "You're saying that you're a theoretician, not a fighter?" He glanced over his shoulder at the psychologist and raised an eyebrow. "I already knew that, Reed." Shea looked back down the road. "I can finally make them out. One of them is a knight—and I'd guess the little round fellow riding beside him is his squire."

Chalmers, from behind his rock, asked, "Can you make out the device on the shield? Remember, I'm not unfamiliar with heraldry."

"As clear as day," Shea said. He refused to elucidate.

Chalmers' exasperated snort carried clearly to his fellow psychologist. "Well?"

"There isn't one."

There was long silence from behind the rock. "Suit yourself. Have your amusement at my expense. Get skewered by some strange knight out in the middle of God-only-knows where. I'll make sure I get your body back to Belphebe somehow—if I ever get home again without your help."

Harold Shea climbed up on top of his rock and stood on it. "We look harmless, Doc. A stalwart knight and his loyal squire won't gain any glory by running us through—Halloo!" Shea bellowed, as the pair came into range. He waved vigorously from his perch atop the rock. "Halloo! Over here!"

"I wish you hadn't done that," Chalmers muttered.

The unknown knight stopped and looked at Shea waiting on the rock. Shea watched him turn to his squire and say something—then the knight called out, "Stranger—confess that in the whole world there is no more beauteous creature than the Empress of la Mancha, the glorious Dulcinea del Toboso—or arm yourself and stand against me." The knight couched his lance and waited atop his horse, still as the statue he resembled.

"I'll bet your girl doesn't hold a candle to Belphebe," Shea growled under his breath. "Besides, I bested Sir Hardimore and a pack of loesels with an épée, fella. I can take you on." He rested his hand on the hilt of his saber.

"Harold," Chalmers squeaked from behind his rock.

"He said *this* world. Belphebe isn't on this world. Be agreeable."

Shea heard the squeak, and took his hand off his saber. Chalmers was right. There was not much point in being difficult, he thought. He did not want to fight. He wanted to get something to eat—and soon. "I confess," he shouted. "—That—" He turned to his associate. "What did he say her name was?"

Chalmers had a funny look on his face. "He said her name was Dulcinea del Toboso. The Empress of la Mancha."

"Yeah? That sounds familiar, doesn't it?" Shea frowned, then called back, "—That the Lady Dulcinea is the fairest lady in this world." He watched the unknown knight return his lance to its carrier and cover it. "I mean," he added to his associate, "that sounds *very* familiar."

"Then well met," the knight called back. He began to trot down the road toward Shea and Chalmers. "Who acknowledges my lady fair may sup with me."

"The name ought to sound familiar," Chalmers sniffed. "It belonged to Don Quixote's imaginary lady."

"You're right," Shea agreed. "Quite a coincidence that this fellow and Don Quixote should claim the same girl. I wonder if they know."

Chalmers stood up. "Did it occur to you that this knight might be Don Quixote."

Shea looked at him and smiled blandly. "No," he said.

Chalmers started to say something else. But when he came out from behind his rock and saw the approaching knight and squire, the only sound to come out of his mouth was a slightly breathless "Oh!"

The knight who approached was glorious—no—radiant would be a better word, Shea thought. His plate armor shone in the dull yellow light, bright as quicksilver. His helm was golden—perhaps even gold, with outward flaring peaks of some eastern design. The knight lifted his faceplate, and Shea thought he had never seen a more regal visage—which was saying something, considering Shea had been keeping company with gods recently. The man looked wise and noble, with thoughtful brown eyes and a majestic expression Shea envied. The knight's steed was purest white, unsullied by the dust that roiled around him, massive and muscled. Even burdened with a knight in a full suit of armor, the beast pranced with spirited grace—Shea thought that no creature so huge or so burdened should have been able to manage that.

The squire's bearing also spoke volumes about the success of his master, the unknown knight. The man was well-fed to the point of roundness and dressed in beautifully embroidered robes in his master's colors. He rode a mare that Shea thought was clearly of Arab descent and extraordinary lineage.

The knight studied the two of them silently for a long moment. "I would have taken you for Moors by your outlander garb," the knight finally said, "but you have not a Moorish countenance. From whence came you, O gallant and courteous strangers?"

Shea noticed that Chalmers was staring at the knight with hypnotized fascination. "Sir Knight," the older man said, "I am Reed Chalmers. My lady, the fair and chaste Florimel, was kidnaped away from me by an evil enchanter, the vile Malambroso. My servant, Harold Shea, and I have sojourned from world to world in the hope of rescuing her. The gods of a distant and incredible land sent us to seek her here— they said Malambroso had brought her hither."

Harold glared at Chalmers. His *servant*, indeed! However, the older man paid no attention to his associate.

"A sad tale, and worthy of the might and justice of

my arm and honor," the knight said. He drew himself even straighter in the saddle and rested his mailed fist on his chest over his heart. *"Hear me, Lord in Heaven,"* he intoned, and his voice took on a ringing, amplified quality that seemed to fill the whole barren plain. *"I swear that I will give my aid and my arm to assist in this just cause for the glory of my own fair Dulcinea, though it cost me my life, my estates, and even my own good name. Nor will I eat, nor sleep, nor partake of wine or song or other battle until his lady is recovered unto him, for—"*

The hair on the back of Harold's neck prickled in recognition. Magic. The knight's oath was magic—a form of binding spell.

The plump squire interrupted. "Good Sir Knight and master, we did offer these gentlemen dinner with us."

The knight halted in mid-speech, and stared at the little round man. "Indeed, we did, good Sancho," he said, and his voice lost its unearthly quality. "Then you must spread a repast for them at once—one worthy of travellers from the outer spheres. I, having given my word, shall not dine." And so saying, the knight dismounted and knelt, still fully armored, in an attitude of prayer. "Attend me, Rosinante," he commanded his horse. Then he fell silent.

The squire, Sancho, set forth a cloth and began removing provender from an apparently bottomless supply bag. Meanwhile, Chalmers edged up to Shea and whispered, "That *has* to be Don Quixote! His lady is named Dulcinea del Toboso, his squire is Sancho, and his horse is Rosinante."

Shea whispered back, "Doc, Don Quixote was a run-down, flea bitten, moth-eaten old schizophrenic with a glue-factory horse and delusions of grandeur."

"And this knight obviously isn't." Chalmers scowled at his associate. "Even I have noted the disparities,

Harold. But perhaps Cervantes got it wrong. Perhaps he bore some grudge against this knight, so that when he wrote his chronicle, he made the knight a laughing-stock instead of the hero he obviously is."

Harold Shea sat down on one of the cushions the squire provided and waited until Chalmers took one of the other two. "How could he have gotten it wrong, Doc?" he asked when the psychologist was settled. "Cervantes made the whole thing up."

Chalmers stared at Shea and opened and closed his mouth a few times. His face reddened. Without another word, he began eat.

Shea helped himself to a chunk of black bread and several slabs of hard white cheese, a handful of olives and some grapes. The fat squire brought out several wineskins as well, took a long draught from one, and passed it to Harold.

Shea took a bite of the bread and cheese, washed it down with the wine, and sighed. The bread was slightly bitter, the cheese strong and rich, and the wine some of the best he had ever tasted. "Delicious, friend squire," he said. "My thanks to you and your master."

The fat squire spread his hands palms up and shrugged. Through a mouthful of food, he said: "It is nothing, Geraldo de Shea. All that we have is yours." He said that in a flat tone that told Shea it was a formula response, and not one to be taken literally. "Sir Chalmero," the squire added, "do you need anything?"

"Only to know the identity of our host, that I may thank him adequately."

Sancho puffed himself up, threw back his shoulders, pointed at the kneeling knight, and declared, "*That* is the famous and wonderful knight, Don Quixote de la Mancha, the greatest knight who ever lived."

Chalmers threw Shea a gleeful look. He smiled

broadly around a mouthful of dry bread and cheese, and after a swig of wine, he remarked, "I told you so."

Shea did not envy the knight his tin-can suit; he was amazed by the man's resilience. Quixote took the broiling sun without complaint, and responded to his squire's ceaseless diatribe against the weather with tolerant amusement. The two famous Spaniards rode ahead, while the psychologists plodded along on foot behind them. The foursome travelled away from the hills and toward the field of windmills. Reed Chalmers, sweat-soaked and dusty, had rolled up the sleeves of his ankle-length tunic and pulled the garment up through its belt until it ended. Shea thought the rotund psychologist looked ridiculous. In spite of the heat, he left his own garb alone.

Chalmers had been regaling Shea with a running commentary on Don Quixote and the world in which they found themselves—Shea had tuned the monologue out several miles back. Suddenly his ears picked up an interesting comment, however, and he began to pay attention again.

"It is extraordinary," Chalmers was saying, "how Cervantes got the small details right, yet completely missed the bigger picture here." He flapped the bottom of his tunic up and down while he walked, apparently trying to cool off.

Shea spat out another mouthful of the dust that gritted between his teeth and tried flapping his own garment to see if it helped. It did not. "What did he get right?" he asked.

"Quixote was given to the grand oath," the older psychologist said, "and to the grand gesture. We have seen that today. I recall a point in Cervantes' narrative where Quixote told Sancho Panza it was a point of honor with knights errant not to eat once in a month—"

Sancho Panza must have been listening to their conversation, for he dropped back to ride beside them. "Even so," he agreed. He tipped his head to one side, studying the psychologist. "His worship told me that except for banquets and such, knights lived off the flowers of the field. And so his worship does. When we're short on daisies, as we are hereabouts, he'll take some sup of mine—but now he's made this oath to help you find your lady, so there'll be no more of that for a while."

Chalmers rubbed his hands together. "Yes, that is it exactly. Quixote was convinced that since his books never mentioned knights eating and sleeping, such things weren't important. I recall places in the tale where the old knight ate nothing, and made a point of staying awake all night, lying on the ground and thinking of his mistress Dulcinea."

Sancho Panza's brows furrowed in worry. "There's not a word of what you say that isn't so," he said, "but send me to the Devil if I can see how you knew it— you who never saw us before today. I'd say you were more enchanters sent to plague the master, but you don't look it." He cast a dark scowl at the two of them. "Still, what things *look* like don't much matter." He kicked his mare once sharply and caught back up with the knight.

Shea bit his lip and, "Nice move, Doc. Now they're bound to think we're evil enchanters and the next thing you know, we'll be speared like shish kebab on the good knight's lance."

But Chalmers was suddenly beaming. He shook his head and grinned at his associate. "Sancho Panza was wrong," he said, ignoring Shea's prophecy. "What things look like do matter—to us, anyway. Think, Harold—when your delusional patients describe themselves to you, what do they describe?"

Shea was watching the squire in earnest conversation

with his master. Something about their attitudes made him nervous. When he answered Chalmers at last, his reply was abrupt. "Gods, mostly. And great heroes. Fiction. What's your point?"

Chalmers appeared oblivious to the little drama up ahead. His round, ruddy face glowed with internal delight. "When Don Quixote described himself, did he describe himself as a crazy old man astride a pitiful swaybacked hack? No. Of course not. He described himself as the greatest knight who had ever lived."

Shea did not see Chalmers' point. He said, "And—?"

Chalmers spread his hands in front of him, palms up. "And what do you see up there? A crazy old man or the greatest knight who ever lived?"

The duo on horseback had finished talking, and were looking over their shoulders at Shea and Chalmers. Harold Shea did not like their expressions. "Unfortunately," he said, carefully loosing his saber in its scabbard, "I see the greatest knight who ever lived."

"Precisely," Chalmers gloated. "We're not in Cervantes' Spain. We're in Don Quixote's delusion. This world is the old Spaniard's psychosis."

"Does that mean we won't die if we get killed here?" Shea asked. Watching the knight on the road ahead, his Adam's apple suddenly felt like a baseball lodged in his throat, and his stomach squirmed and flipped as if it had ridden a roller coaster without him.

"I don't see how we could," Reed Chalmers said, still not noticing the impending doom ahead.

"I hope you're right," Shea muttered, as Quixote, in the echoing magical voice Shea had heard earlier, demanded, "*I shall have truth. Are you foul and evil wizards and enchanters, come to ensnare me? Speak, cravens!*"

"Fabulous. Perfect paranoia," Chalmers whispered. "Fits beautifully with the delusions."

Harold Shea's thoughts regarding Chalmers' delight were unprintable, but he was unable to share them with his boss. Instead, words were coming from his mouth that he had no control over. "*We are enchanters,*" he heard himself saying in a voice that boomed as loudly and weirdly as the knight's, "*but neither foul nor evil. We have come to rescue Reed Chalmers' kidnaped lady, and we mean you no harm.*"

The Don's sound effects switched off, and Shea found he could control his vocal cords again.

"You are enchanters, yet not evil?" Quixote asked. His eyes were as round and puzzled as a confused spaniel's. "I would have thought all enchanters were evil—that it were the very nature of the beast, so to speak."

"Master!" Sancho interrupted, rapping on Quixote's armor. "Sir Knight, we need to be going!" He was bouncing a bit in his saddle, and his eyes darted nervously—Shea had seen the same body language displayed by patients who were trying to hide important information. "We need to head back to the village; we forgot something," the fat squire added.

He's lying, Shea thought, and at the same moment noticed that the windmills seemed to be closer than they had been a moment before. In the next instant, he realized that they did not look as much like windmills as they had. And in the next instant, he realized that about thirty giants, some with four arms, some with six or even eight, were marching across the plain towards him, waving clubs the size of telephone poles.

"Doc, let's get out of here," Shea said, grabbing Chalmers by the sleeve and pulling him back down the road they had just covered.

Chalmers was watching the giants without concern. He resisted Shea's desperate tugs. "Harold, what's gotten into you?"

"The giants, Doc."

Quixote had finally spotted them, too. "Hah, Freston!" he snarled. "Vile wizard—no doubt these monsters are your doing." He uncovered his lance and couched it. His visor clanged down over his face, and he dug his spurs into Rosinante's sides. He roared, "Do not fly, cowards, vile creatures, for it is one knight alone who assails you!" and charged across the plain toward the approaching giants.

Chalmers might as well have been a tree, rooted in the middle of the road. "Those aren't giants, Harold. They're windmills," he said, crossing his arms in front of his chest.

They looked like giants to Shea. However, niggling doubt rose in the back of his mind. He stopped trying to pull his boss back up the road for a moment, and stared at the approaching monsters. The giants swung their warclubs and roared and shrieked. "Do you see windmills?" he asked, suddenly uncertain.

Chalmers sighed, the brilliant lecturer faced with an especially slow pupil. "No, I don't," he said, and his voice dripped with strained patience. "I see giants. But I know they're windmills. And so do you."

The hot breeze, however, reeked with the stench of never-washed bodies, with fetid breath and sweat and filth—and Harold, without another word, ran for the hills. Sancho Panza, on his fine Arab mare, passed him almost instantly, his beast galloping flat out. The ground shook. The air rang with Quixote's battle cries and oaths and the screams of wounded giants. Over the noise, Harold clearly heard Chalmers' bellow— "Harold, wait for me!"

Harold glanced over his shoulder. Chalmers was racing, face red, away from the mayhem on the plain. Behind him, Quixote, astride Rosinante, challenged the monsters. They surrounded him and towered over him, paying no attention to the easier prey that fled down the road. When he saw that, Harold ran behind a rock and crouched there to watch from a point of relative safety. Chalmers joined him, panting and dripping sweat.

Don Quixote's shattered lance stuck out of the side of one fallen giant. He wielded his sword, which blazed with a pure white light that made the sun dim by comparison. Astride his great horse, he darted among the forest of swinging clubs, slashing and stabbing. Already, giants' severed hands and massive warclubs littered the plain. Quixote fought well—but the giants outnumbered him dreadfully.

Then Chalmers gasped. "Look, Harold, the giants' arms are growing back!"

Shea realized that his associate was right. The only giant who was not still in the fight was the one Quixote had killed with the lance. "We've got to help him, Doc," he said. He unsheathed his saber and got ready to charge into the fray.

"Wait!" Chalmers wrung his hands. "Surely if we intervened magically from a distance—"

"We don't know the rules of magic here," Shea objected.

Chalmers shrugged. "The Laws of Contagion and Similarity should hold. They have everywhere else we've been."

"Fine. Then do something helpful—watch your decimals, though. We don't want a hundred pacifist giant-killers instead of one that will do the job." Shea looked over the top of the rock, and noticed that the tide of battle was going against the Knight of the Woeful Countenance. "If we don't do something quick, though, he's going to look like a Buick that collided with a brick wall." Shea ran back down the road. Behind him, he could hear Chalmers beginning an incantation that sounded suspiciously like "The number of things in a given class is the class of all classes—" Shea grinned in spite of everything. Good incantations needed rhyme and meter. Doc's incantations never had much of either. He was a great magician—but a lousy poet.

Harold Shea's smile died quickly. As he raced closer, the appalling stench of giant assailed him, and the monsters—big as the windmills they had once been—shook the very earth over which he ran. Shea realized his saber would reach no higher than mid-calf on the monsters. Thus, his assistance to Don Quixote would be limited to acting as a distraction and stabbing the nightmare in the legs—provided his saber would penetrate giant flesh.

Suddenly Sancho Panza was at his side, sliding out of his saddle and pressing the Arab mare's reins into Shea's hands. "Sir Geraldo," the squire said, "since you go to help my master, ride Dapple. And Godspeed."

Shea nodded and mounted. He cantered toward the battle, saber drawn. The nearest of the giants sniffed the air, then turned from watching Quixote and stared straight at him. The monster glared with milky-white, slit-pupilled eyes, and loosed a gape-mouthed roar which revealed green, dagger-pointed teeth that angled back in rows—like shark's teeth. Shea gulped.

"*Oh, God—*" he whispered—

—And his whisper took on the same odd, echoey character Don Quixote's oaths had.

Magic. Don Quixote had used it—had compelled Shea to tell the truth by an oath sworn to God and the old knight's lady. Could Harold Shea use the same formula?

"*God,*" he said louder, and was rewarded with an increase in the volume of the echoes. "*On my honor, let me—uh, smite— these giants with my sword that, um, blazes—for the ah, glory of my own fair lady, Belphebe of Ohio.*"

His saber burst into oily blue flames that licked

along the blade. Good enough, Shea thought. If the
sword blazed, it probably smote serviceably, too. He
galloped to one side of the nearest giant, darted
around behind him, and stabbed the monster through
the back of the knee. The wound smoked, then ignited
with a vigorous "whoosh," and the giant went down
like a condemned skyscraper.

Shea, keeping out from underfoot, bellowed "*For
Belphebe!*" and galloped behind the next nearest giant.
His blazing saber burned brighter. Clubs whizzed past
his ears, and the Arab mare pranced and started, but
Shea avoided contact, delivered his stroke to the back
of the next monster's knee, and got out again.

The giants paid him more attention after that, and
he found eluding their massive clubs more difficult.
He did the best he could—he was not able to hit fast
or often, but he counted six giants down to his credit
at one point.

Don Quixote attacked head on, lopping off arms;
Shea brought the stinking, club-swinging titans down
from behind. The only problem was that the hands
regenerated, the knee wounds healed, and the giants
got back up, evidently refreshed from their little rests.

Time passed and stretched; the battle became sur-
real, an inescapable nightmare. Dapple wore a thick
coat of lather, her nostrils flared, and her sides heaved.
Rosinante, moving the armored knight around, was in
the same state. Quixote's sword strokes were still
fierce, but they looked a bit less well-aimed to Shea—
and he wasn't surprised. His own muscles ached from
swinging and thrusting. The giants' blows struck closer
as the knight and the psychologist tired. Death
became personal to Shea, and felt very near.

What was taking Chalmers so long? The older magician should have figured out something—if he did not
come up with a spell quick, he would not need to
bother. "*God knows,*" Shea muttered, darting out of

range of an eight-armed monster that plodded after him, swinging, *"I wish these troglodytes would turn back into windmills."*

Abruptly, they did.

Shea hung in his saddle and gasped for air and stared. All around him sat windmills and the toppled, battered remains of windmills. Most lacked an arm or two or three; a few burned steadily. In each of them, he recognized details transmuted from giant to giant structure. Perhaps he anthropomorphized the buildings—but he did not think so.

It occurred to Shea that his wish had echoed loudly in his ears when he made it. Somehow, his statement fitted in with the structure of magic in Quixote's world. Either that, Shea reflected, or Chalmers hit on a solution just as he made his wish. He could check on that later, he decided. Don Quixote, surveying the wreckage with evident surprise, trotted across the battlefield to join the psychologist.

"Nice work, Sir Knight," Shea panted. "I didn't think we were going to make it out of that mess."

"Indeed," Don Quixote replied, watching Shea closely, "we nearly did not. I mind me to tell you, Don Geraldo, that those strokes to the back of the caitiff blackguards' knees were unchivalrous, and not meet for a gentleman. Nevertheless, I thank you for your brave assist—unknightly though it was."

Shea managed an exhausted grin. "That's the advantage of not being a knight and a gentleman. There aren't so many rules."

Quixote spared Harold a smile as he wiped the blood from his sword. "You speak nothing but truth, good man," the knight agreed. "And now, to discover by what means and manner these veritable fiends have been ensorcelled into windmills—I suspect that coward Freston had his hand in these doings from the very start. He ever seeks to unmake me." The knight reined Rosinante around, and trotted back the way he had come, head swinging suspiciously from side to side.

Harold Shea prudently kept his mouth shut.

The four travellers lay on the ground, Quixote and his squire on one side of their cookfire and Chalmers and Shea on the other. Sancho Panza snored like an enraged swarm of bees; Quixote, still dressed in full armor, lay flat on the hard ground staring at the stars that wheeled overhead and maintained his silence.

Harold Shea, hardened to outdoor living, still found the rocky plain an incredibly uncomfortable place to sleep. He rolled from side to side, trying to find one position that did not hurt *somewhere*. Finally, with a gloomy sigh, he gave up. He glanced over at his fellow psychologist and discovered Chalmers engaged in the same futile search for comfort.

"Doc?" he said, keeping his voice low.

Chalmers rolled over to face him. "Hmmm?"

"What went wrong with the magic today? I kept waiting for you to fix the giants, but you never did."

The expressions that ran across Reed Chalmers' face reflected frustration and bewilderment. "The Laws of Similarity and Contagion don't work here," the older man said.

Shea rolled on his side and propped himself up on one elbow. "They don't *work*? I thought they were the magical equivalent of the laws of physics." His voice rose in volume.

Chalmers waved a hand to quiet his associate. "I'll remind you that the laws of physics don't exactly work here either. No. I was doing everything I could think of, from blowing on little makeshift cloth sails to drawing pictures of windmills in the dirt over pictures of giants—and nothing happened. When the giants turned back into windmills again, I had nothing to do with it."

Shea said, "Oh, then I think I did that. I got my sword to flame a little, which helped with the giants—"

The small psychologist propped himself up on both elbows and whispered, "You *did*? I was so busy working on spells to stop the giants I didn't have time to watch you."

"I did. And then I sort of accidentally turned the giants back into windmills." Shea shrugged.

"How?"

Shea glanced over at Sancho Panza and Don Quixote. Quixote hadn't moved; his eyes were still open and fixed at some point in the distant heavens. Panza had rolled over on his side and was not snoring so loudly anymore, but still looked as if he were asleep. Shea scooted closer to Chalmers and confided, "I'm not completely certain, but I think I have the basic principles of the spells I used worked into a feasible law. Tentatively, I'm thinking of calling it the Law of Heroic Namedropping."

Chalmers gave his associate a disgusted look. "That's a ludicrous name."

Shea grinned, delighted to get a rise out of the stuffy psychologist. "Not really," he insisted. "It fits. The spell is cast by swearing a binding oath while calling on God and one's lady. I'm guessing that the more important people you drag into the oath, the more powerful the spell will be. Sincerely planning on fulfilling the terms of the oath makes a difference, too, I imagine."

Chalmers hissed suddenly and began burrowing in the dirt under his bedroll. "Hah! There you are!" he muttered finally, and came up with a large, irregular rock. "I'll have bruises from that tomorrow." He flung the rock into the darkness and returned his attention to Harold Shea. "All right, if what you say is so, then why wasn't *Quixote* successful in transforming the giants back into windmills?"

The younger psychologist shook his head. "He never tried, Doc. He was too busy fighting them for the glory of his lady to think about the bigger picture."

"You're saying he could have—that in this world, he is truly an enchanter?"

"That's what I'm saying, but I'm not saying it too loudly."

Harold Shea began to feel the effects of his arduous day. He nestled back into his bedroll, marveling that the ground had somehow grown much softer and smoother. "You saw how he compelled me to tell him what we're doing in this world. Still, I don't think Don Quixote would be too happy imagining himself occupying the same role as his archenemy Freston," he added.

Chalmers harrumphed. "There's a problem with your theory, of course, Harold."

Shea yawned. "Really? What's that?"

Chalmers' voice sounded pendantic, and very far away. "Evil enchanters," he was saying, "aren't too likely to use the name of God in binding oaths to cast spells. That sort of thing could backfire. And Malambroso, if he is here, will be using this world's version of black magic. I believe what we must do is determine how Don Quixote's delusions affect the operation of magic. Perhaps by curing him of his delusions, we can alter the rules of magic, thus rendering Malambroso powerless and—"

Shea, however, never heard the rest. With a gentle snore, he rolled on his back.

Knights liked their mornings early and busy, Shea noted unhappily. He lay inside his bedroll, listening to the activities going on around him. Quixote had already fed and was currently brushing Rosinante and it was not even dawn yet. Chalmers stood next to the knight, handing him things and holding things, all the while talking earnestly. Sancho Panza snored on, oblivious to the activity.

Shea wished he could get back to sleep, but it did not feel likely. The ground had turned to brick during the night. He also wished he had not run out of toothpaste. It was a minor point, really, but waking up after drinking so much wine with his meals the day before—and realizing that nobody in the world had any toothpaste to lend him—made it very hard to face the new day.

He closed his eyes and feigned sleep until he was certain the rocks in the dirt had taken root and started growing beneath him. Then, with a resigned sigh, he heaved himself up and wandered over to see what was available for breakfast.

He found Chalmers and Quixote in the midst of heated argument.

Chalmers glared at the knight and crossed his arms tightly over his chest. "Sir, your name is not Don Quixote. It is Señor Quixiana, or perhaps Señor Quesada—my sources weren't entirely clear on that. But you are not a knight. You are a well-born villager who suffers from delusions—"

"Good sir, it is not I who insists this helmet of mine is a washbasin, when anyone can plainly see it is nothing more nor less than the enchanted helmet of Mambrino, which I won in honorable battle from another knight." Don Quixote put down the last of Rosinante's hooves and straightened up. He towered over the stout psychologist. "It is not I who looks at my fine steed and sees a knock-kneed, sway-backed, thin-tailed nag, and not I who claims the giants his own servant and I fought yesterday were windmills, and never anything but windmills." He stomped over to his saddlebags with his curry-brush and hoofpick, and shoved them angrily inside. "Señor Chalmero, when you go looking for delusions, look first in your own mind."

Chalmers growled, "The insane always insist they're sane."

Quixote nodded solemnly. "On that point, good sir, we are agreed. Now, you will please excuse me. I must attend to my morning devotions and ask God's grace in finding your lady." He walked past Chalmers and out to the edge of the camp. There he drew his sword and planted it point down on the ground. He knelt beside it, and became still.

"Right now, his case *is* stronger than yours," Shea said from behind Chalmers.

His boss jumped and turned. "I do wish you would refrain from making jokes at times like these." The senior psychologist tried to jam his hands into nonexistent pockets, and ended up crossing his arms. "Why don't you go talk to him, Harold? Present him with reality—don't coddle his delusions."

"Ah—" Shea grinned. "Not right now, thanks." He jerked a thumb in the direction of the kneeling knight. "I don't really want to tell him he isn't a knight while he has his sword out. Besides, those giants yesterday might actually have been windmills all the time—" He looked at his partner and sighed. "But they didn't fight like windmills."

Once the sun came up, the weather, to Shea's regret, was a repeat of the previous day's. The scenery, however, was briefly more interesting when the two Spaniards and their quaintly garbed followers paraded through a tiny village. The village sported the usual chickens scurrying in and out of doorways; barefoot, dirty urchins running wild; and run-down whitewashed houses with red-tile roofs sagging precariously in places. Its smell was the usual smell of dirt and dust and poor sanitation. But the people, black-clad peasant men in wide-brimmed hats and black-skirted, broad-hipped peasant women with their babies in tow, were not at all what Harold Shea had expected. When the knight rode into town, they raced out of their houses, shouting, "Don Quixote! Señor Sir Knight!" They lined the streets, beaming at their armor-clad hero, nudging each other and saying, "Look, Rosa, is he not the handsomest knight in the world?" and "Ah, Miguel, are we not fortunate that Don Quixote is our protector?" Men and women pressed gifts and food on the knight and his squire—and when Quixote and Sancho Panza were unable to accept anymore, the peasants forced their largess on Chalmers and Shea.

Harold found himself in the possession of a massive loaf of bread still hot from the oven and a live, trussed chicken who eyed him with deep suspicion and clucked its fowl obscenities at him. Chalmers carried a smoked rump of something, several bunches of grapes, and a basket that proved to be filled to the top with fresh panecillos.

"That was not what it seemed to be at all," Chalmers noted as they left the village behind. "In reality, the villagers mocked Quixote, heaping scorn and trash on him. I dread to think what these foods they've shoved at us must truly be. Hog-slops, no doubt." His expression darkened. "Or worse."

"It looks good and smells good to me." Shea admired the loaf of bread he held, which was a deep golden brown, rolled in the shape of a sheaf of wheat, and still hot and aromatic. He could not feel so charitable toward the chicken.

"You've been pulled in by the mad knight's delusion." Chalmers scrutinized the things he carried with distaste. "None of this is edible."

Shea sighed. "Then what are we supposed to eat, Doc? I'm sure most of what Quixote is carrying he got from villages just like that last one."

The plump psychologist thought. "I'll develop a spell that will turn all this food into what it appears to be. Then we'll know what we're eating is safe."

Ahead of them, Don Quixote turned off the road, and began winding his way along a narrow track that led into the dusty hills. Chalmers put his arm out to stop Shea from following and watched the knight and his squire riding away. "I don't like the idea of wandering around in those hills," Reed Chalmers said under his breath. He looked at Shea, and raised one bushy, graying eyebrow. "In this time period, I suspect the hills of Spain harbor as many bandits as they do shepherds."

"I would think travelling with the greatest knight in the world should be some protection," Shea noted.

Sancho Panza looked back and realized Chalmers and Shea were stopped. Shea saw the fat squire rap on Quixote's armor until the knight reined in Rosinante and turned him around. Knight and squire conferred; then Panza trotted back to the main road.

"Good sirs, you must follow us now," the squire said. He sat straight in his saddle, face gleaming with sweat, fat palms gripped around the reins. He looked down at the two men standing on the dusty road, then glanced nervously toward the hills. "My master says your lady is ahead, held prisoner by your enemy, the evil enchanter. He says we must hurry, though, to catch the wizard unaware."

Shea nodded and started onto the side path, but Chalmers stopped him. "Nonsense, Harold—Quixote has no way of knowing where Florimel is. And I won't follow some delusional old man into bandit-infested hills on a wild goose chase."

Shea gritted his teeth. Chalmers could have chosen a better time to get stubborn. On the path, the knight waited as a boulder would wait—silent and impassive . . . and immovable. Sancho Panza threw anxious glances behind him, and wrung his hands. Shadows lengthened across the parched, desolate land.

Silence stretched like the shadows, until Shea blurted out, "How does your master know Malambroso has Florimel there?"

Sancho looked flummoxed. "Why—by his oath, of course!" He stared as Shea, his expression suggesting Shea had lost his mind.

Harold shrugged and spread his arms in front of him, palms up.

"His oath," Sancho repeated, and when neither of the two men made any response, he sighed and said, "He swore he would help you find your lady, Señor Chalmero. He cannot do otherwise. That was his oath."

Chalmers opened his mouth to protest, but Shea cut him off. "Doc," he whispered urgently, "think of this as an opportunity to prove him wrong. If Florimel isn't there, this will give you a perfect opening to help him differentiate between his delusions and reality."

Chalmers' mouth snapped shut, and he eyed his colleague doubtfully. "I believe you're rationalizing, Harold," he said finally. "I believe you have fallen under the spell of Quixote's delusions, and you are only saying that to manipulate me. However—" he took a deep breath and fixed Shea with a fishy stare, "it also happens that your suggestion is basically sound. Therefore, we shall follow the knight." He took off at a brisk pace, leaving Shea and Panza staring after him.

The squire turned to Harold Shea, and shook his head slowly. "Geraldo de Shea," he said, "please do not take offense—but your master is very crazy."

Shea's mouth twitched into a grin he couldn't suppress. "Occupational hazard of psychologists," he agreed. "It happens to the best of them, sooner or later."

* * *

They rode until well after dark and set up a wretched, fireless campsite. Quixote insisted that a fire so near Malambroso's lair would alert the enchanter, who would then rain down curses upon them. Shea satisfied his hunger with some of the wonderful loaf of bread and a slab of the smoked meat Chalmers had carried all day, ignoring his partner's expressions of disgust and comments about the actual provenance of the food. He gladly handed over the chicken to Chalmers when his partner took a sudden interest in it. And then he went to sleep.

A searing flash of light, the crack of thunder, a sudden sub-bass "cluck" and screaming wind woke Shea from uncomfortable sleep. Dust scoured his face; clogged in his nose and mouth; gritted in his eyes. Another flash of lightning briefly silhouetted both a slight human form and a huge, twisted shape of feathered ghastliness against the craggy outline of the hill— then shuddered away into whale-belly blackness. The crash of thunder almost, but not quite, obliterated another gargantuan "cluck." The earth bucked like a goaded horse and threw Shea from his bedroll, down the rock-strewn hill.

"Attend me, God!" Chalmers bellowed. "And by the grace of the Lady Florimel and all the saints, let this chicken be as it was!"

Chicken? Shea thought. *That's what he did to a* chicken? *I told him to watch his decimals.*

By the lightning flashes, Shea could see the chicken, which remained the size of a bull elephant, chasing after Sancho Panza with dinner in his eye. Don Quixote, still in full armor, lunged in front of the hungry bird and said, "*On my honor, bird, be what you were.*" The softly spoken words reverberated through the hills.

Shea heard another squawk, but this one was far

less impressive. As he climbed back up the hill, cautiously feeling his way, the thunder and lightning subsided, and the wind died down, and the hills stood still again. Shea assumed the chicken-monster also returned to its original form, though there were no helpful thunderbolts to shed a bit of light on the matter.

The camp was in an uproar.

"What is the meaning of this?" Quixote demanded of Chalmers. "For what reason have I pledged my arm and my honor in the aid of an enchanter who seeks to destroy us as we sleep?"

Meanwhile, Sancho Panza milled his arms wildly, shrieking, "Did you see that? The giant chicken tried to eat me like a bug. Did you see it, Sir Knight?"

Chalmers bellowed, "I was demonstrating the true form of the chicken, or rather, the monster that you, in your delusion, insist on calling a chicken. I'm going to make you see this world the way it really is, and you way you really are."

How out of character of Chalmers, Shea thought. *Doc isn't taking the misfiring of his magic well at all.* He noticed that Panza was tying the now-normal chicken's legs together with an almost insane vigor. He tried not to laugh. *I ought to say something to defuse the situation,* he thought; unfortunately, the voices of his three fellow travellers kept getting louder, and he did not feel up to shouting all of them down simultaneously.

From behind him, Shea heard a loud "pop." Without warning, the stench of sulfur and brimstone washed over him. He whirled, and by the sudden glare of a wall of hellish red flames, saw Malambroso appear. The sorcerer's billowing velvet robes were picked out with gold threads that glittered in the hellfire. His hair whipped and tossed in a nonexistent wind.

"Doctor Chalmers!" Malambroso waved a hand in a delicate gesture and the wall of flames vanished. His robes quit billowing and his hair settled into place. The rotten egg stink, however, hung in the air. "My sincerest thanks for alerting me to your presence." The sorcerer bowed, and snapped his fingers, "Give me back my wife," Chalmers yelled.

Malambroso smiled.

"Not possible, dear sir. I've decided I want to keep her. Incidentally—" His smile grew broader. "I challenge you here and now to magical battle. I noted your little fiasco with the chicken—I don't imagine you will do very well against me. *I*, after all, have learned to use this world's magic."

That whiff of sulfur and brimstone gave Shea a clue about how Malambroso's half of the magical world worked. The religious alignments probably went both ways, he thought. The good could call upon God, the evil on Satan. Except that Chalmers was not having any luck with magic, and he was a good man. He wondered if, in Quixote's world, only the truly pious and the truly evil could be great enchanters. There was a flaw in that theory, too, though. Shea was no more pious than Chalmers, but he was having a great deal more success with his magic.

Was there no rhyme or reason to the magical system in Quixote's world? If that were the case, things looked bad—not just for the moment, but for even getting back home.

Chalmers puffed and glowered at the evil sorcerer. "I'll accept—" he started to answer, and was interrupted by the booming voice of Don Quixote, amplified by God.

Shea had forgotten about Quixote. So had Chalmers and Malambroso. Now, without warning, the knight, armed and armored and astride his giant war steed, interposed himself between Chalmers and Malambroso.

"*Sir Chalmero does not accept your challenge!*" Quixote boomed. "*I am his champion—and I have sworn an oath against your body, vile fiend, malodorous wizard, by God and my Lady—and by God and the Lady Dulcinea del Toboso, and by all that is good and right, you shall issue your challenge to me.*"

This speech had an electric effect on Malambroso. He froze, and stared blankly at the knight, and his mouth began to move. His eyes widened, and it became apparent to Shea that he was fighting Quixote's spell—and losing. The sorcerer looked as if an invisible puppetmaster was pulling the words out of his mouth one at a time. "*I ... ch-challenge ... you, s-s-sir ... knight, ch-ch-champion ... of ... my enemy, ... R-r-reed Chalmers, to s-s-single combat.*" Sweat beaded on the sorcerer's face, and ran down his forehead and along his narrow, hooked nose.

Chalmers yelped. "I don't need the help of a crazy old man to beat Malambroso! I can take care of that second-rate charlatan by myself."

Shea made shushing motions. He ran to Chalmers' side. "Shut up, Doc," he whispered. "Let the knight handle it. Malambroso was right—you don't know how to use this system."

Sancho Panza, on Chalmers' other side, said, "Do not insult my master, Señor Chalmero. He's fighting for *you*."

Quixote, meanwhile, paid no mind to Chalmers. His attention remained fixed on Malambroso. In what Harold Shea had come to think of as the "bullhorn of God" voice, the knight said, "*By God's will and my might, your magic cannot harm me, vulgar conjurer.*" Quixote and his armor began to glow with pure pale blue light. Shea found the effect impressive.

Malambroso hissed and backed up a step. "*By the Devil in his Hell, and all his archangels, your sword* will rust between your fingertips and your lance fall to ashes, sir knight."

The knight held up his unblemished, blue-glowing sword, and watched as little flickers of red light beat uselessly against it. He laughed hollowly and advanced against Malambroso. "You battle the greatest knight in the world, wizard. You did not think to defeat *me* in such manner, did you?"

Malambroso cocked his arm back as if he were getting ready to throw a baseball, and there appeared between the magician's fingers a blazing ball of fire. The sorcerer threw the fireball—it shot straight at Quixote, hissing and squealing like arcane fireworks, trailing sparks behind it. The fireball picked up both speed and size as it went, so that as it neared the knight, it looked like a comet.

Quixote swung his sword in an easy arc and hit the thing—it vanished with a "pop" as if it had never existed. "Enough, knavish enchanter," the knight said. "You would hound me with your petty magics—so then will I harry you with the force of my arm."

Quixote's visor clanged down, and he spurred Rosinante forward. *"For Dulcinea!"* he shouted, and swung his sword down at the sorcerer.

Malambroso ducked. Even so, Quixote's sword slashed through his robe, and Shea saw blood start from a deep wound in the magician's shoulder. The magician screamed in pain, and waved his good arm, shrieking unintelligible words. Red flames leapt up around him, and Rosinante started and backed, whinnying.

"Forward," Quixote cried, bringing the beast under control. Knight and horse shot through the flames. Malambroso cowered. The Knight of the Long Face swung again. The sorcerer sidestepped and cried out, bleeding from a new wound.

Chalmers snorted in exasperation. *"Damn it all to*

hell, Harold," he growled, and his voice boomed around Shea's head, "*Quixote* can't *be beating Malambroso. He's nothing but a doddering old man on a nag too decrepit to use for dog food!*"

The smell of fire and brimstone overwhelmed Harold Shea. Lightning flashed, thunder cracked—and the knight on the horse changed. Where before two magnificent creatures had battled the evil Malambroso, now a scarecrow of a man with a washbasin tied to his head charged against the wizard on a horse so knock-kneed and splayfooted it could barely trot. The horse stumbled on the uneven ground and pitched the transfigured Quixote feet-over-head into the bleeding sorcerer.

Malambroso, bloodied and weak, crawled away from the knight. Freed by Quixote's transformation and the breaking of the spell that had bound him to fight, he growled, "There will be another time and another place, Chalmers. Beware!" Then he vanished into nothingness, leaving only stinking yellow smoke behind him.

Sancho Panza cried out: "My master!" Then he picked a short, gnarled stick off the ground and attacked Chalmers. "You were one of them all along, you monster!"

Chalmers yelled, "He's cured! Look, Harold. Now you see the true Don Quixote!" He ran behind Shea.

Sancho Panza got in a solid lick with his cudgel. "Give me back my master," he demanded.

"This is the break we've—been waiting for—Harold," Chalmers panted as he dodged behind Shea again to avoid Panza and the stick. "With Quixote rational, his—delusions won't affect the m-m-mathematics of magic any further. Keep this luna—tic off of me and I'll—spell us out of here." Panza doubled back, and landed another thwack on Chalmers' ribs.

Harold Shea stepped in and grabbed the squire's

wrists. He twisted both of them outward until the little
man dropped his stick. "Enough, sir squire," he said.
"I'll take care of this now." He looked at Chalmers,
who squatted, panting, at his side. "Go ahead, Doc."

Chalmers pulled Florimel's handkerchief out of the
little leather travel bag that hung at his waist, and with
it a feather Shea suspected of having chicken origins.
He drew two circles side by side in the dirt, with
an intersection between them like the set-and-subset
diagrams children used in grade school.

The older psychologist carefully placed his wife's
handkerchief, the feather, and a strand of his own hair
into the intersection formed by the two circles, then
asked Shea for a hair from his head. Shea complied.
Chalmers dropped that into his intersection, too.
Then he chanted:

> "We stand in the center of the circle comprised
> Of all the places we have ever been.
> So Florimel stands in the center of the circle
>   comprised.
> Of all the places *she* has ever been.
> I call upon the archangels and saints,
> And Lord of Heaven—hearken to my plea.
> With the speed of winged birds
> To the intersection of these circles take us
>   three."

Nothing happened. Chalmers waited. Shea waited.
Even Sancho Panza stopped struggling and watched
the circles in the dirt with keen interest.

When the silence stretched to uncomfortable lengths,
Chalmers muttered, "That should have worked." He
stood and turned to his associate and the still-captive
squire, brushed the dirt from the knees of his garment, and fixed both men with a withering glance.

"That should have worked. *Dammit,*" he muttered. "*It's just like the chicken.*"

Shea saw a minor puff of sulfurous smoke erupt behind his partner, and a small, furious ball of feathers materialized with a squawk. It could have been the chicken the villagers had given Shea the day before—except *that* bird, feet still firmly tied, was digging bugs out of the weeds not twenty feet away.

Chalmers jerked around and stared down at the chicken he had conjured. He squawked louder than it had.

Harold Shea shook his head and turned Sancho Panza loose. The little squire had lost interest in flattening Chalmers. With a bewildered expression on his face, he looked one final time at the mysterious chicken, then hurried to his master's side. Shea watched him.

Panza tapped Quixote on the shoulder, spoke to him, shook him lightly—and finally wrung his hands and stared at the ancient, scrawny man who had once been a knight.

Don Quixote did not seem to know that Sancho was even there. The one-time knight stood in frozen silence, staring down at himself. *He's in shock*, Harold Shea thought. The emaciated old man slowly reached up and lifted the dented washbasin off of his head, and held it in front of his face. In the first faint light of dawn, Shea could see the glimmering wetness of tears that etched their way down the furrows of the old man's cheeks. He watched as Quixote studied his decrepit steed, Rosinante, then turned his attention to his skinny arms and gnarled hands. He watched as the old man, head hanging, shoulders stooped, mounted the swaybacked horse with arthritic caution, and began to ride away from his squire and the two psychologists, further into the hills.

Harold Shea felt as if he had witnessed the vandalism

of a magnificent cathedral, and its replacement with a concrete block service station. Pity wrenched his heart. *"By God,"* he swore softly, *"I would not have you any other way than as the greatest knight in the world, on the greatest horse alive, whether Chalmers was right or not."*

Lightning flashed again, and thunder cracked. A sheet of light enveloped the old man, and inside, forms flickered—and out of the light rode none other than the great Don Quixote on his mighty warsteed.

The knight pulled his steed in and held out one gauntleted hand. He looked long and hard at the horse and its gleaming trappings. Then without warning, he leveled his lance at Chalmers and charged. "Traitorous enchanter!" he yelled. "Two-faced fiend, who would magick me even while I fought as your champion! Now you shall reap your just reward!" The point of the lance dipped lower, aimed for Chalmers' middle.

Sancho Panza was a statue, wide-eyed with amazement. Reed Chalmers froze, and his face drained of color. Quixote galloped across the uneven field before Shea could even cry out a protest. The point of the great knight's lance closed the space to its target, crashed with thunderous impact into Chalmers' belly—

—And shattered like glass into a thousand shards that rained shrapnel across the hillside. Rosinante flew backward onto his hindquarters from the force of the impact, and for the second time that morning, the knight Quixote was unhorsed.

Reed Chalmers looked down at his abdomen, ran his fingers over the unmarked surface, and whispered, "It didn't touch me." Then he fainted.

Now I'm in shock, Harold Shea thought bemusedly, while the world spun around him in fuzzy, loopy little circles. *What just happened?*

Quixote staggered to his feet and raised one mailed

fist to the heavens. "After what this scoundrel has done to me, God, you cannot keep me to my oath!"

"*OH, YES I CAN,*" a disembodied kettledrum voice thundered. "*I HAVE A PERSONAL INTEREST IN THIS CASE.*"

Yipes, Shea thought, *divine intervention comes home. And I wish it hadn't.* He found the thought of a personally interested deity who made housecalls unnerving. It made agnosticism a hard line to hold.

Shea hurried to Chalmers' side, and knelt next to the unconscious man. He checked for a pulse. Chalmers had one—it was a bit fast, but strong and regular. Shea sighed with relief, until a pair of armored legs moved into his field of vision. Shea looked up . . . and up, into the scowling face of the knight. "God will not permit me to break my oath by killing him," Quixote said, "but I will aid him no more. My squire packs our belongings, and we shall leave you when he is done."

Harold Shea bit his lip and nodded. Without Quixote, finding Florimel was going to be tougher. Still, he couldn't blame the knight for being upset. "I understand," he told the knight. "And I'm sorry."

"As indeed am I. You are a man of arms and action like myself, Geraldo de Shea, and I have heard you call upon the name of God, and seen God answer." Quixote clasped his gauntleted hands together. "In truth, it is only by your prayer that I am once again myself. You have my thanks."

Shea looked at the ground. "Don't mention it."

The knight nodded. "Nor shall I again. But if you ever leave this vile serpent, I would welcome your arm at my side in any great adventure."

Panza finished packing. "We can go now, your worship," he yelled from his place next to the horses.

Quixote glanced over his shoulder at his squire. Then he looked down the path the way the foursome had come the night before, shading his eyes against the sun. "Very well. It is time. Señor Geraldo, may God be with you and may your fair lady look upon you with favor." Without even waiting for a reply, he strode, clanking, to his horse.

He mounted with a grace Shea found hard to believe. Harold Shea had, at various times in his recent career, worn plate mail. He knew from experience the stuff weighed a ton—there were times when he had wished someone could have winched him onto the back of the horse, rather than making him climb on board. Yet Quixote vaulted, lithe and graceful as you please, into the saddle in defiance of all physical laws—which of course, Shea reflected, was the crux of the matter.

The knight waved a hand. Sancho Panza wheeled his Arab mare about, Quixote spurred Rosinante forward, and knight and squire broke into an easy canter—which made the crash as Quixote hit the invisible wall sound all the more like a dozen trash cans dropped from the top of a ten-story building.

"*God!*" Quixote bellowed, "*I didn't kill him! What more do you demand of me?*"

God thundered, "*ONLY THAT YOU MEET THE TERMS OF YOUR AGREEMENT, SIR KNIGHT.*"

I really wish God wouldn't keep butting in that way, Shea thought. The disembodied voice made his skin crawl. Wisely, he did not express his opinion out loud.

Quixote stood, admittedly with some difficulty this time, and crossed his arms over his chest. "Which terms?" he demanded. Quixote showed no fear in dealing with God—a fact Harold Shea noted with admiration. Shea was perfectly willing to admit that he was scared silly.

"*SEE IF THIS SOUNDS FAMILIAR—'HEAR ME, LORD IN HEAVEN,'*" God mimicked in a very Quixote-like voice. "*'I SWEAR I WILL GIVE MY*

*AID AND MY ARM TO ASSIST IN THIS JUST
CAUSE FOR THE GLORY OF MY OWN FAIR DUL-
CINEA, THOUGH IT COST ME MY LIFE, MY
ESTATES, AND EVEN MY OWN GOOD NAME.
NOR WILL I EAT, NOR SLEEP, NOR PARTAKE
OF WINE OR SONG OR OTHER BATTLE UNTIL
HIS LADY IS RECOVERED UNTO HIM—YOU
REMEMBER SAYING ANYTHING OF THAT SORT,
QUIXOTE?"* God stopped and waited.

Quixote said nothing.

*"WHEN YOU ASKED ME TO HEAR YOU, I
HEARD YOU,"* God pointed out. *"IF YOU'D PRE-
FER, I COULD QUIT LISTENING FROM NOW
ON."*

"Then you intend, Lord in Heaven, for me to continue to lend my might and my honor to that
enchanter?" Quixote pointed melodramatically at
Chalmers, who chose that moment to open his eyes.
"Even though he is a heretical miscreant and a back-
stabbing scoundrel as well?!"

"YOU'RE CATCHING ON," God thundered.

"Who was that?" Chalmers whispered groggily to
Shea.

"That was God," Shea said.

Chalmers gave the information an instant's thought.
Then he fainted again.

Quixote, meanwhile, did not intend to give in. "It
is your command, then, O God, that I must stay my
hand for worthier causes—a maiden in distress, or
perhaps a downtrodden servant—in favor of this fiend
who serves the Evil One?"

"MY WAYS ARE INSCRUTABLE," God snapped.
*"AND ABOVE THE QUESTIONING OF MORTALS.
BESIDES,"* He added, *"A DEAL IS A DEAL."*

When God's voice stopped booming around the
hills, Sancho Panza remarked to Quixote, quite loudly,

"If your worship will just hold him still for me, I'll kill him. I didn't promise God anything."

Shea thought for just an instant, from the expression on Quixote's face, that he was going to take Sancho Panza up on his offer. But then the Knight of the Sad Countenance sighed. "As God said, 'A deal is a deal.' I shall meet my obligations as a knight, no matter the unfairness of the burden God has placed on me." He stared long and hard at the unconscious form of Chalmers, and added, softly, "Nevertheless, my good squire, if he turns me into that doddering old man again, you may act as your heart leads you."

The atmosphere during the morning meal would have strained a sloth's composure. Chalmers and Sancho Panza exchanged murderous looks, Quixote was pointedly praying at Chalmers, and Harold Shea felt an incipient ulcer brewing.

The meal took place amid dead silence, broken only by the twin cluckings of the chickens—which served as an unfortunate reminder of all that had gone before. Harold spent the time desperately trying to remember exactly what it was he had promised God. He thought it was patently unfair, somehow, that God had a flawless memory, and he did not. Shea also felt it a bit unfair to find that God had not only been listening—but also paying attention. He sincerely hoped that in the heat of battle, he had not gone for a really gaudy oath.

On the other hand, he was not quite ready to up and ask God for the sort of instant replay the Almighty had given Quixote. Shea had a dark suspicion that if he did, he would not like what God would say.

After breakfast, while Reed Chalmers finished stuffing his few belongings into his pack, Shea gave some thought to the problem of transportation. Quixote had not offered them horses—and after the disastrous events of the morning, Shea didn't think he ever would. But Harold hated the idea of tromping on foot over half of Spain through the dust Quixote's and Panza's horses kicked up. Neither Chalmers nor Shea had any local currency—and he doubted that the peasants or the Church of Catholic Spain would look too kindly on men riding magic brooms.

He eyed the two chickens. He certainly did not want to eat them. Perhaps—seeing his magic was working well enough—he could turn them into usable mounts.

Surreptitiously he yanked a few hairs from the tail of Panza's horse. Then he grabbed both chickens—no great feat when their legs were bound—and trotted around the side of the hill and out of sight.

First he had to come up with a spell. Catholic saints ought to meet the requirements for the Law of Heroic Namedropping, he decided. He tried to think of a few who would be appropriate. George was the patron saint of Boy Scouts—and probably, Shea thought, of knights who fought dragons. Not awfully useful, but he was the first saint that came to mind. Shea pondered a bit longer. There was Francis of Assisi. He had something to do with beasts, didn't he? Or was Antony the patron saint of animals? Christopher was travel—or had he been disbarred? Probably not in Quixote's time, Shea finally decided.

Enough saints. He developed his incantation, deciding to incorporate the Laws of Contagion and Similarity into the spell as well as the Namedropping Law, on the theory that every little bit might help. Then he settled the trussed chickens in the dirt and draped a horse hair over the back of each. Around each bird he scratched the outline of a horse in the dirt. He winced as he studied his outlines—it was a pity he had never been better at art. Oh, well. He shrugged and took a deep breath.

He recited:

"By Francis of Assisi,
By George and Antony,
By Christopher of travel,
I conjure you to be,
Not birds but beasts of burden,
Fair steeds of noble clan,
By God and dearest Belphebe,
Now form you to my plan."

The air around the chickens blasted outward, fling-
ing dust into Shea's eyes. When he could open them
enough to see his results, he groaned. His reputation
as a conjurer of singular monsters was not going to be
hurt one bit by this pair. He looked the two of them
over from front to back, trying to figure out what they
were and where his spell had gone wrong. He decided
he had probably gone awry with his insistence that
they "form to his plan." He was going to have to learn
how to draw.

His prospective steeds still had feathers—and little,
lumpish wings. He supposed he could see how the
spot in the dirt where his stick had joggled would
suggest wings. Their faces were long and rather
anteater-ish. Their legs were horselike enough,
although covered with little slick feathers clear down
to the hooves. The tails were very horselike, too. They
didn't have manes, though—instead their head feathers draped in crests that, on closer inspection, proved
to mimic his drawings very closely.

He had sketched bridles onto the beasts in his pictures. The chicken-steeds wore bridles. He had forgotten to draw saddles, and there were no saddles
anywhere to be seen.

"This isn't what I had in mind," he muttered.

"IF YOU WANTED HORSES, WHY DIDN'T YOU SAY HORSES?" God asked.

If Harold Shea could have jumped out of his skin, he would have. "Don't do that!" he yelped. The—well, the whatever-they-were—stared placidly, as unaffected by the booming voice of God as they were by their sudden creation in the middle of the hot Spanish hills.

Harold took a long, slow breath and said, "Okay, God, can I have horses?"

"NOT NOW, YOU CAN'T." Harold noted that God sounded peeved. *"THAT'S NOT WHAT YOU ASKED FOR. I GAVE YOU WHAT YOU ASKED FOR."*

"Right," he said. He saw no sense in annoying God. The chicken-steeds were better than nothing. Instead, he grabbed both beasts' reins and led them back around the side of the hill.

Chalmers had Harold's gear packed as well as his own by the time Harold got back with the beasts. Sancho Panza hurriedly crossed himself when he saw the monstrosities, while Quixote pretended not to notice them at all.

Chalmers' eyebrows merely rose.

"What in the world, Harold?" the older psychologist asked.

"The end result of concision without precision," Shea growled and pressed the reins from one of the creatures into Chalmers' hand. "Take one—it will be better than walking, I suppose."

Chalmers harrumphed. "Yes, I suppose it will. What is this thing, anyway?"

"It's a shurdono."

"A shurdono?"

"Right. Because I sure don't know," Shea snapped. He picked up his pack, slipped it over his shoulders, and vaulted onto the middle of his steed's back, just behind the wings. The creature's spine jabbed him in the groin. Harold gasped and inched forward until he rested on the relative padding of the wing muscles. These creatures were not going to be comfortable for long bareback rides. He crouched on his animal in silence and discomfort, sulking. Why hadn't he mentioned the word "horse" somewhere in his spell? He should have been able to fit a one-syllable word like that into the poem. He was a far better poet than Chalmers—for all that his results were about as erratic.

Chalmers struggled onto his beast—the expression on his face told Shea his shurdono was not the only one with too many bones in bad places. "These will serve as long as we don't run into any monks of the Dominican Order," Chalmers remarked. "I'll remind you that the Spanish Inquisition is in full swing right now. I don't doubt they'd be fascinated by the heresy involved in riding—shurdonos."

Shea ran his fingers through the soft feathers at the nape of his beast's neck and sighed. How could anyone forget the Spanish Inquisition? He tapped his heels lightly into the beast's flank. It lurched into a tooth-rattling trot. Pain shot through parts of his body that, at that moment, Shea would just as soon have forgotten existed. The Spanish Inquisition couldn't be much worse, he concluded.

Quixote and Panza rode in front, Quixote carrying a fresh lance as if he wished he could run Chalmers through with it, and Panza equipped with the final spare. Chalmers and Shea kept well back. Neither party spoke to the other. They were well out of the high hills, and wending their way over rolling countryside dotted with small farms and the occasional village.

Chalmers was in a foul mood. He had stared at the spot between Quixote's shoulderblades so long Shea was surprised the back of the knight's armor did not melt and puddle. "That old lunatic doesn't need to hold such a grudge," Chalmers growled. "*I'm* not holding it against him that he tried to spit me on his lance."

"You turned him into a decrepit old man, Doc," Shea answered. "You stopped him from defeating Malambroso and humiliated him—and in spite of that, God won't let him out of the oath he swore to find Florimel for you." Shea wriggled into a new position for the umpteenth time, trying to find one place on his anatomy that was not terminally bruised by the shurdono's sharp spine. "You can't expect him to be happy with you."

Chalmers snorted. "*I'm* still not convinced that Quixote's change was my doing. I think in the heat of battle, he could have suddenly snapped out of his delusional state. Still, I suppose I can't expect him to look at it that way." Chalmers pulled some of the bread from the morning meal out of his pack and calmly chewed away at it. "On the other hand, I should be furious with you."

"With me?"

Chalmers took a long swig from the wineskin he had appropriated from Panza. He did not offer any to Shea. "Certainly. Quixote was cured. If my theory is correct, this universe reverted to its normal state when that happened. Given enough time, I'm sure I could have developed a workable spell for defeating Malambroso and rescuing Florimel. At least we could have made a syllogismobile to get us to more familiar territory. However, you returned Quixote to his delusional state before I had time to ascertain the precise rules of mathematics and magic in effect—and now we are back to your madman's chaotic magic of confusion."

Harold Shea frowned. "That would be true if your theory were correct—but I'm not convinced that it is, Reed." When the senior psychologist gave him a frosty glare, Shea swallowed and said, "I think we may be dealing with the complete separation of Quixote's universe from the universe Cervantes described—perhaps we are in the world to which Cervantes' Quixote, the madman Quixiana, was actually attuned."

Chalmers snort was derisive. "The universe is not a Chinese puzzlebox, Harold. Universes of fictions within fictions are improbable to the point of ludicrousness and—"

"Monstrous and diabolical crew!" Don Quixote bellowed. "Release immediately the noble princesses whom you are forcibly carrying off in that coach or prepare to receive instant death as the just punishment for your misdeeds."

Chalmers stopped lecturing, and Shea looked down the road to see what Quixote was making such a racket about. Two men in dark robes carrying sunshades, their faces covered by masks, rode ahead of a black carriage of immense proportions. "I remember this incident," Chalmers whispered. "They're the Benedictines. Harmless monks—in the book, they were just riding in front of the carriage—had nothing to do with it—"

One of the two masked men called out, "Sir Knight, we are but poor, harmless monks of St. Benedict, travelling about our business. We don't know a thing about princesses."

"See? Now he's going to charge and they're going to run," Chalmers predicted.

Sure enough, Quixote cried, "No fair speeches for me, for I know you, perfidious scoundrels!" Then he dropped his lance into position and charged.

The Benedictine monks, however, did not flee as Chalmers had guessed. Instead, one of the two drew patterns in the air with his hands, while the second chanted something and threw a handful of powder toward the charging knight. Instantly, a giant thicket that glittered with thorns grew across the road.

Quixote waved his lance and called out a promise to his lady Dulcinea in his ringing battle-voice, and the thicket smoked and burst into flames and cleared itself out of his way.

Behind the thicket lay a sea. The disguised enchanters and the giant coach had vanished. "Hah!" Quixote roared, and touched the water with his lance. It hissed and drew back, and Rosinante cantered across the path between the two towering walls of water. With every foot the knight won, the sea shrank, until knight and horse reached the other side—and nothing was left of the sea but a puddle, rapidly evaporating in the heat of the day.

The enchanters were busily at work, building yet another spell. Quixote galloped nearer.

"Freston, you carrion rot—I know your handiwork! *I'll have your head, by God and all that is fair!*" The knight waved his lance.

Sancho Panza kept back, behind the line where the magical thicket once blocked the road, crossing himself vigorously and praying loudly for deliverance from the evil wizards.

Shea slipped off his shurdono, grateful for the respite from the beast's hideously uncomfortable back. He watched the magical attacks and feints of the knight and the two enchanters, and as he did, the irksome insistence that he was missing something important began to grow on him.

"Say, Doc," he said, "didn't Quixote have some kind of clause in his agreement with God about not fighting for any other purpose until he won Florimel's freedom?"

Chalmers, watching Quixote, said, "Um-m-m—I think so."

Shea forced himself to get back on the shurdono. "Then if this were not a battle for Florimel, he wouldn't be able to fight it."

"He's fighting Freston, one of his delusions," Chalmers said. An expression of envy flickered across his face, though, as Quixote turned one of the two enchanters into a small green bird. "Why can't I do that?" he muttered.

The transformed enchanter turned himself back into a man, and stretched his hands, clawlike, at the knight. Something disgustingly slimy and sticky-looking shot from his fingertips and enmeshed Quixote.

"There are *two* enchanters over there, Doc. What if Freston and Malambroso have joined forces? Couldn't Florimel be in the carriage?"

Panza took a moment from his prayers to give the two of them an indignant glare. "Certainly the Lady Florimel is in the carriage—why else have we come this way to meet the enchanters? Why else does the great knight Don Quixote fight?"

Shea and Chalmers exchanged glances.

Chalmers grimaced. "Harold, I must register my protest toward your getting involved with this fight. I feel if you had not returned Quixote to his delusional state, Florimel would be with us and we would be home by now." The psychologist twisted his shurdono's reins between his fingers. "If you stay out of this, Quixote may once again snap back to rationality. If, however, you feed his delusions by participating in them, we will certainly loose any chance of that happening—and I may never find Florimel."

Harold Shea raised an eyebrow, then slowly shook his head. "Quixote didn't snap out of his delusional state. You *transformed* him into Señor Quixiana. *Think* about this, Reed. I postulate that this situation illustrates your theory of delusional states perfectly—except that we're in the universe Quixiana tapped into, and not in the universe he inhabited."

Chalmers' face reddened, and he asked, "But if we

are in a genuine magic-based universe, why doesn't my magic work?"

Shea's attention drifted to the battle between Quixote and the enchanters. Amazing things were happening. The booming of oaths and counter-oaths filled the air. Fires flickered and vanished, thunderheads formed and unformed. One of the enchanters conjured a cloud of giant bats, and Quixote quickly changed them into roses, which fell to the ground and littered the plain like the tribute of invisible maidens. Quixote sent a giant lizard at the wizards—it became a little yapping lap-dog.

"Sometimes your magic does work," Harold Shea said. "Just try to remember what you were doing when it did." He drew his saber and kicked his shurdono into action. He was jouncing painfully toward the fight when an idea occurred to him. *"By God and my lady,"* he yelled, *"if I can't have a horse, I want a saddle for this thing!"* A weirdly shaped, wonderfully comfortable saddle appeared between Shea and the shurdono's bony back. He sighed happily and urged the chicken-steed into a lumbering gallop.

Shea was always terrified at the beginning of a battle—but the terror wore off quickly, as the practical issue of survival pushed the fear from his mind. As he assessed the ongoing battle, he grew calmer.

Quixote's second lance had broken early on, and he was fighting close in and on horseback with a heavy, double-edged straight blade. Rosinante, Shea noted, was as much a weapon as Quixote's sword. The ineffable horse leapt and kicked with deadly accuracy; his schooled moves were as perfectly executed as any Shea had seen the famous Lippezan stallions perform in his own world.

Quixote saw Harold ride up and yelled, "I must

defeat Malambroso, on my oath and honor. Do you then take on that despoiler, Freston?"

Harold Shea, armed with his saber and riding the effable shurdono, was not sure how much help he was going to be. *Still,* he thought, *I made a difference with the giants.* "I will, sir knight!" he answered.

He raised his saber, keeping a close eye on Freston, who was trying to get behind Quixote to bespell him. *"By Belphebe and God, I'm going to pound you into the ground, Freston!"* Shea swore. He urged the shurdono forward. The shurdono, sensing danger, balked. Shea kicked, he pled, he smacked the shurdono's rump with the flat of his blade, and finally he snarled at the heavens, *"By God and the saints and Belphebe and the Cleveland Chamber of Commerce, I want a good fighting horse, and I want him NOW!"*

The sheet lightning that surrounded him left him seeing stars and smelling ozone—but the horse beneath him, huge as Rosinante, lunged at Freston with minimal urging.

Freston saw trouble coming. He waved his hand over his mule. *"By Satan's spawn, I'll ride a tiger to your doom, you spineless outlander."* Freston's mule became a mammoth orange Bengal tiger that roared and pounced.

"Aaagh!" Shea yelled, and then yelped, *"Flame, sword, by God!"* The tiger made for Shea's horse's throat, the horse made a fancy little dressage side step out of the tiger's way, and Shea, a good rider but certainly no master horseman, found that the horse had stepped completely out from under him, and he was riding air—with a blazing sword in his hand and a tiger coming directly at him.

His rump hit the dirt with a painful thump. Still, he brandished the sword, and the tiger laid its ears back and snarled. Freston, astride the tiger, was starting into another curse. Meanwhile, the wizard's big cat crouched, close enough that Shea could smell his breath, and the cat's tail twitched restlessly. His eyes never left Shea's throat. When Harold saw the tiger's rump wiggle in the same way housecats did just before they attacked, he panicked. "Yah!" he shouted, and straightened his arm and lunged. The flaming blade nicked the tiger's nose and singed his fur, and the giant cat leapt back and to one side; as quickly as that, Freston landed in the dirt. The tiger, with one backward snarl, padded toward the hills.

Meanwhile, Quixote, freed of the concerns of keeping watch on two enchanters at a time, began getting the better of Malambroso. The knight was still on horseback, while the evil enchanter had been unseated. Malambroso was sending magical beasts against Quixote, but the knight parried them with bursts of light and sound, and the attacks failed.

Malambroso tired visibly. The monsters he conjured became smaller and less frightening. He began backing, losing ground.

At the same time, Shea pressed his attack on Freston. The Spanish wizard's eyes darted from Shea to Malambroso and back to Shea. He kept retreating, and under his breath he muttered another curse. *"By hells dominion, swing a sword no more—but find you hold a snake in hand."*

Shea's saber melted under his fingers, and writhed. Shea found himself swinging a king cobra. *"Yaaagh!"* he howled, and then his eyes narrowed and he grinned maniacally. *"On my lady's honor, let's have some more snakes—snakes in Freston's cloak, snakes in Freston's hood, snakes up Freston's sleeves and down his boots and in his underwear—if he's wearing any—"*

Freston's clothing writhed horribly, and the enchanter paled and shrieked, *"Aaaie! Devil take me— but not the clothes! Not the clothes!"* Red puffs of smoke shot out of his clothing, and abruptly the empty monk's robes fell to the ground.

Almost empty, Shea amended, watching the clothing squirm on its own. *"No more snakes, O Lord in Heaven,"* he said. His cobra reverted to saber form, and he sheathed it gratefully. He whistled to his horse, and the warsteed trotted over. Shea mounted and looked to Don Quixote.

Quixote had Malambroso backed against the coach. The coachman on top cowered well out of the way of the knight and the wizard. "Surrender!" Quixote shouted. "You're done for, wretch!"

"By the legions of Hell, I'll never surrender—but for now, I and mine will take our leave—and what's not mine, I'll hide in Hell. Find it if you can!" Malambroso waved an arm, and puffs of red smoke appeared in his place—and from the top of the coach where the driver had crouched, and trailing in wisps from the coach's half-opened door.

When Shea charged down the road to help Quixote, Chalmers sat on his shurdono and watched, feeling miserable. He twitched under Sancho Panza's suspicious glare, and he longed to attack Malambroso and Freston with a few well-crafted, clever spells. He would bet they had never seen anything like the disembodied strangling hands with which he'd once bested the enchanters of Faerie. Now he could not successfully bespell a chicken. He felt useless, and worse yet, he felt especially useless in that one area where his talents usually shone—magic. It nettled him that Harold Shea, who had lost none of his ability at sword-fighting and other physical feats, seemed, in Quixote's world, to have acquired the magical ability that should rightfully have belonged to Chalmers.

For a man who was used to effecting events on a grand scale, it was a bitter, bitter pill to swallow.

Chalmers watched Shea fighting alongside Quixote, mixing feats of magic with strength of arms, and envy gnawed in his belly. Incompetence was misery. *Oh, Hell . . ."* he swore, softly.

He became aware, gradually, of a sense of general expectancy in the air. Around him, the light took on shimmer and weight, and hung electrically, sending shivers through his skin. He looked over his shoulder, trying to see what had changed, worrying that what he sensed was the phenomena of lightning preparing to strike—or something akin to that. However, he could see nothing that might be causing his skin to crawl and his hair to stand on end.

The silence stretched on, crackling, until his nerves quivered and sweat beaded in the palms of his hands.

A deep, throbbing voice finally shredded the silence. *"YES . . . ?"* it asked from the air around him. *"YOU CALLED?"*

The shurdono bucked, and Chalmers heart pounded itself into the back of his throat. "G-G-G-God?" he squeaked. He looked all around, hoping to catch sight of the speaker.

He could see nothing out of the ordinary. The invisible speaker sniffed indignantly. *"DON'T BE INSULTING."*

Reed Chalmers felt that voice vibrating in the base of his spine. "Th-th-th-then who?" he asked. He noticed that Sancho Panza crossed himself and muttered prayers. The squire never took his eyes off the psychologist who talked to empty air.

"FENWICK, THIRD DEMON IN COMMAND OF THE LEGIONS OF HELL, AT YOUR SERVICE. YOU DID CALL ON HELL. . . ."

Chalmers felt the universe begin to spin around him. Little white dots circled just within his peripheral vision, and he noted that everything was turning gray and fuzzy. He heard a sound closely related to the roar of the ocean—and recognized, just in time, the symptoms of fainting. He lowered his head to the shurdono's back, and took long, slow breaths that smelled strongly of musty chicken. *Fenwick,* he thought. *A devil—at my service.*

The world gradually stopped whirling, and Chalmers sat up again. He jutted his chin and squared his shoulders and made a conscious effort to control any quaver in his voice. "I've only called on God," he said primly. "Any reference to Hell was merely accidental profanity."

Fenwick, Third Demon in command of the Legions of Hell, digested this in long silence. Then, in stunned tones, he asked, *"YOU HONESTLY CALLED ON HEAVEN? WHATEVER FOR?"*

He sounded sincere. For some reason, Chalmers felt this was a bad sign. "Because," he answered, hoping to talk his way out of an increasingly uncomfortable situation, "the magic system in this universe appears to be based on spells that utilize oaths to God and promises to various saints and loved ones—"

The voice interrupted with a rude cackle. *"YOU MORON,"* it said, wheezing with laughter. *"THAT'S EXACTLY THE SYSTEM—IF YOU'RE A KNIGHT. BUT YOU AREN'T A KNIGHT. YOU'RE AN ENCHANTER. ALL ENCHANTERS DRAW THEIR POWERS FROM HELL."*

"I'm not an evil enchanter. I'm a good enchanter," Chalmers sniffed.

"HE-HE-HE!" Fenwick giggled. *"AND I'M A SAINT. HE-HE-HE! A GOOD ENCHANTER. BOY, JUST WAIT 'TIL I TELL THE GUYS IN MARKETING: SO, MR. GOOD ENCHANTER, DID YOU WANT SOMETHING OR DID YOU JUST CALL FOR THE HELL OF IT—HE-HE-HE-HE!"*

Reed Chalmers felt that he was reaching the end of his patience. "Did I want something? Let me tell you what I want. I want a horse instead of this razor-spined monstrosity. I want magic to work for me. I *want* my wife back and I *want* to go home."

"HM-M-M-M." Fenwick pondered, then said, "WELL, THE MOST APPROPRIATE FORM FOR THAT IS 'BY SATAN AND HIS MINIONS'—"

"Listen, *dammit*—" Chalmers interrupted.

"YEAH, THAT WILL DO TOO," Fenwick agreed, "BUT TECHNICALLY SPEAKING, IT'S PRETTY RUDE."

Without further warning, Chalmers found himself astride a very fine horse, appropriately saddled and bridled. He discovered, as well, that he abruptly understood the magical system of Quixote's universe. But Florimel was nowhere evident, and *he* most definitely wasn't home.

"What about Florimel?" he asked. He felt a bit better. He felt a sort of warm, tingly happiness toward the whole of creation. Magic had once again worked for him, irreproachably. He understood why it worked, and this gave him a comforting feeling of control. He also realized that with every second he was not sitting on that miserable shurdono's back, being gouged in the groin by the beast's nightmarish spine, his happiness increased by another degree.

"*I CAN'T GIVE YOU FLORIMEL*," Fenwick said. He sounded contrite. "AN ENCHANTER WITH A HIGHER RANKING HAS CLAIMED THE SERVICES OF THE SECOND DEMON IN COMMAND OF THE LEGIONS OF HELL, AND THE TWO OF THEM HAVE LEGAL POSSESSION OF HER. SORRY." He coughed once, diffidently. "AND YOU'RE GOING TO HAVE TO GET YOURSELF HOME. IT'S OUT OF MY TERRITORY."

"Malambroso again!" Chalmers clenched his fists and glared at the fight going on near the coach. "*Damn him!*"

Fenwick's voice became irrepressibly and annoyingly cheerful, as he said, *"OH, THAT WOULD BE REDUNDANT, REED CHALMERS. HE'S ALREADY AN ENCHANTER."*

The deeper implications of that statement sunk in, and Chalmers shivered in spite of the heat, as full realization hit him. Heaven and Hell in Quixote's universe were not only real, but picked their teams according to profession—at least where his profession was concerned. He thought about what he had come to know from Fenwick's infusion of magical understanding. A corrupt knight would still fight under God's banner—while the most benign magician—himself, for example—would automatically be consigned to the ranks of Hell. Thus Harold Shea, who functioned well as a man-at-arms in these backwater universes, had been able to open a magical account with God—metaphorically speaking—while he, Chalmers, a superb theoretician and first water magician, was stuck banking with the Devil.

What he withdrew from the Devil's bank, he'd have to pay back. He had, thanks to Fenwick, a sudden and appallingly clear grasp of the mathematics involved. When he concentrated, he could see, on a glowing screen in his mind's eye, the tab he had run up with the Devil. He had acquired one giant chicken on his account, and one regular one—and the transformation of a knight into a lunatic. Quixote, in this universe, really was the mighty hero he appeared to be. Chagrined, Chalmers studied that part of his account with Hell and tried to figure out how he was going to apologize. Last but not least, of course, there was the replacement of the shurdono with a very good horse. He checked the price on that, and groaned. He had not realized how good pain had been for his soul.

Down the road, Quixote and Shea combined on final attack, and the two magicians and the coachman vanished in a puff of garish red smoke. Shea gave Chalmers a thumbs-up sign. Then he and Quixote rode to the abandoned coach and opened the doors.

It's a good thing Shea's proving adept at magic in this world, Chalmers thought, *because now that I know what I have to pay to use magic, I don't think I'll dare.* He tapped his horse lightly with his heels and trotted down the road toward the coach.

Harold Shea reached out to pull the coach door open, then stopped. The coach hulked over him, huge and menacing, exuding danger, and his nerves tingled at the slightest idea of looking inside. It was ridiculous, but he found the big black coach with its four stamping, snorting black horses more terrifying than the tiger had been.

"I like this not at all," Quixote said out of the blue. He stood beside Shea, looking at the door which still hung partway open. "This unseemly coach stinks with the taint of enchanters."

Shea would have felt better if he had been the only one experiencing a bout of nerves. "Florimel," he called. "Are you in there?" He noted a higher-than-usual pitch of his voice and winced. Piano-wire nerves—ugh!

Only silence answered from inside the coach.

"Perforce, we must enter," Quixote said. "I shall essay the first advance." He drew his sword and tapped the door open with the point of it. A carrion stink roiled out, laced with the faintest whiff of sulfur.

Shea's eyes tried to adjust to the darkness inside the carriage, and could not. The inside admitted no light at all. Almost unconsciously, he drew his saber.

Shea heard Chalmers ride up behind him and dismount. "I don't think Florimel is going to be in there," the older psychologist said. "Malambroso's deal with the Devil here has apparently given him legal rights to her in this universe."

Shea kept staring into the unremitting blackness of the coach's interior. It seemed impossible to him that he could make out no detail inside the coach, despite the light from the brilliant Mediterranean sun that blazed down on everything.

"*Light, by God,*" Quixote demanded, and his sword glowed with pure silvery brilliance. He shoved the sword through the coach's doorway, and both he and Shea edged closer. Inside was still a featureless void—except for a narrow, crooked trail that began at the doorway and led downward, as far as the glow of the light could illuminate, and then, Shea thought gloomily, probably for an infinity or two further.

He sighed, and Don Quixote nodded. "Even so," the knight said softly. "Señor Geraldo, you have been a most brave and stalwart companion, yet I fear me this is a path only God's sworn knights dare take. Do you then pray for my soul whilst I descend—for I fear much that this is none other than the very road to Hell."

Shea's jaw jutted out in defiance of his screaming nerves and all common sense, and he heard himself saying, "Don Quixote, I was knighted once by Sir Campbell, and was a Companion of Gloriana's court in the land of Faerie"—common sense intruded, and he added, with a quick glance to his side—"as was Sir Chalmers here."

Quixote's eyes went round and his mouth fell open. "For two reasons, Geraldo, this cannot be. In the first instance, did you not tell me even after we fought those loathsome giants of Freston's that you were proof against the requirements of knights and gentlemen, because you were not one? I mind me you said it was for that reason you could strike the blackguards from behind."

Shea winced. "It was a technicality. I was knighted in Gloriana's universe, but nobody in this universe had ever knighted me. I was just guessing that there wouldn't be reciprocity."

Quixote frowned, and mouthed the word "reciprocity." "From what manner of world came you, Sir Geraldo, that you would think a knight in one world would not be such in any other?"

Shea sighed. "It's a long story—and you really couldn't understand unless you'd been to Cleveland."

"Perhaps not. These Clevelands are terrible things, no doubt, to make a brave knight such as yourself doubt his honor." Quixote's eyes narrowed, then, and he said, "But there is the second matter. How, if that one is a knight also"—and he pointed at Chalmers— "how can it be that he is in league with the Devil?"

"I'd hardly say he was in league with the Devil," Shea protested. "He's just having a little trouble getting his magic to work—"

"In fact, Harold—" Chalmers interrupted, "Don Quixote is quite correct. By the rules of this universe, I am indeed in league with the Devil—at least every time I utilize magic. You see," he added, turning to Quixote, "while I was knighted for my services to Gloriana's government, which consisted, coincidentally, of ridding the land of an enchanters' guild, I never served in the capacity of man-at-arms. I was and still am primarily an enchanter. Therefore, despite my good intentions, I find myself lumped in the same category as all other enchanters and most uncomfortably allied." Chalmers frowned and stared at the tops of his shoes.

"Thus the answer to the mystery of God's willingness to let one of his own serve a servant of the Devil. He was not such in his own world." Don Quixote steepled his fingers and stared over them at Chalmers.

"Well, then, fellow knights, let us to arms and assail the Devil in his summer home."

Chalmers started backing away, shaking his head, hands up. "I'm not going to Hell, Harold. My tab down there is too big right now—somebody might decide to collect."

"Florimel's down there, Doc," Shea said.

Chalmers stopped backing. "Why do you say that?"

"Malambroso, just before he vanished, said that whatever he had that wasn't his, he was going to hide in Hell. He told us to find it if we could. That had to mean Florimel." Shea magicked light onto his own blade and peeked back into the coach. The road to Hell did not look any better than it had a minute ago.

"Help us, someone," he heard a faint, feminine voice calling from down in the stygian gloom.

"Did you hear that?" Shea asked.

Quixote said, "I heard, Sir Geraldo—maidens in need of rescue, pleading for help. A knightly duty is that, and what an honor it will be to test my arm against the Devil himself. Sancho Panza will hold our horses. Sancho!" he yelled. "Wait for us here."

"It will be my pleasure," Sancho called back.

Quixote smiled. "He is ever a faithful and willing squire, who, out of obedience and love for me, abstains at all times from garnering glory for himself. Someday, for his obedience, I shall make him governor of an island." The Knight of the Woeful Countenance sighed. "If I live to give him that honor. But for now, it is of no matter. Let us go to Hell."

So saying, Quixote caused the light on his blade to burn even brighter. He leapt to the coach's threshold and made to step down onto the road to Hell. As he tried to cross the threshold, however, he was stopped fast—held in place by an invisible wall. "Ho, what magic is this?" he shouted, and slashed his sword against the unseen barrier. "*By God's own right hand, let me pass,*" he roared.

"*IT IS BY GOD'S OWN RIGHT HAND THAT YOU CANNOT, QUIXOTE,*" God said. "*YOUR OATH PREVENTS IT.*"

Quixote started and stared up at the heavens. "But I seek to fulfill my oath by rescuing the Lady Florimel from Hell."

Thunder rumbled and the ground shook as God spoke again. "*YOU CANNOT. SHE'S NOT THERE— AND YOU CANNOT INVOLVE YOURSELF WITH OTHER KNIGHTLY DUTIES UNTIL YOU ARE FREED OF YOUR OATH TO SIR CHALMERS.*"

"Who, then, cried out for help?" Quixote asked.

"*A LITTLE FLOCK OF PRINCESSES, ABDUCTED FROM A NEARBY CASTLE BY FRESTON AND KEPT IN THIS COACH UNTIL MALAMBROSO CONSIGNED THEM TEMPORARILY TO HELL.*"

Shea leaned over and spoke softly into Chalmers' ear. "Even if he can't help us, we can't just leave them down there, you know."

Chalmers looked green. He swallowed hard and tried to put his hands in the nonexistent pockets of the tunic. "Perhaps we could ride to the castle from which they were abducted and tell the inhabitants we know their whereabouts.

Shea raised one eyebrow, but said nothing.

Chalmers harrumphed. "Perhaps not. Well, I just hoped—" He fixed Shea with a sudden fierce glare, and Shea heard an unexpected urgency in his voice. "I wasn't kidding about owing Hell. If I go in, there isn't any way I'm going to get out. I have a fair amount of magic left on my balance before total disaster hits— but . . ."

"What do you have to do to pay on your balance?" Shea asked. "Any idea?"

Chalmers chewed on his upper lip and nodded.

"Hell in this universe apparently offers enchanters either a sort of cash-on delivery plan, or the installment plan. If the loan officer decides you're on the C.O.D. plan, a devil is sent to collect your soul as soon as you've used up the magical credit you were allotted." Chalmers peeked into the coach and stared gloomily down the long, dark road into Hell. "Fortunately for me, I apparently qualified for the installment plan—which may stave off the inevitable long enough for me to figure a way out of this mess. In the meantime . . ."

"Yes," Shea said. He crossed his arms over his chest and glared at Chalmers from under lowered brows. "In the meantime, what do you have to do to make your payments?"

"Well, I could sacrifice a virgin . . . ah, steal a few infants from their mothers . . ." Chalmers stared off into space, avoiding Shea's eyes. "Or make the village cows go dry, or start a plague—anything of that sort."

"I assume you're planning on defaulting on your payments."

Chalmers snorted. "No matter what I do, there's going to be hell to pay. I dare not enter Hell, Quixote cannot, and if you go alone, you won't have much chance of success. But the princesses must be rescued." He stood, thinking hard. Shea noticed a sly smile stealing across the other man's face. "Of course," he whispered, "I may have a few useful cards to play. *Fenwick! Get up here, by damn!*"

Fenwick's giggle echoed through the rolling hills. *"CHALMERS, I'M SO GLAD I WAS ASSIGNED TO YOUR ACCOUNT. I HAD THE GUYS IN MARKETING ROLLING IN THE AISLES WITH YOUR GOOD ENCHANTER LINE. A GOOD ENCHANTER! HE-HE-HE! BEST JOKE THEY EVER HEARD—SO WHAT YOU WANT, OH GOOD ENCHANTER? HE-HE-HE-HE!"*

Chalmers smiled cheerfully. "Oh, I thought we'd discuss my account. What would it cost me to give every peasant in this part of Spain a nice new milk cow?"

Fenwick's giggling took on a strained quality. "*CHALMERS, YOU ARE A VERY FUNNY MAN, BUT PLEASE—NO MORE—IT GIVES ME INDIGESTION.*"

"I really want to know," Chalmers insisted. "What would it cost."

Fenwick stopped laughing. "*HELL'S ENCHANTERS DO NOT GIVE PEASANTS MILK COWS,*" he said haughtily. "*UNLESS THE MILK WERE POISONOUS—*" He sounded hopeful. "*DID YOU MEAN POISONOUS MILK COWS, REED CHALMERS?*"

"Nope. Nice, normal, healthy milk cows."

"*THEN YOU'RE TALKING ABOUT BLESSINGS.*" Fenwick was clearly appalled. "*HELL'S MINIONS DON'T BLESS. WHY—HALF A MILLION COWS AT ONE BLESSING PER COW, AND ONE NEGATIVE CREDIT PER BLESSING—ACCOUNTING WOULD HAVE MY HORNS IF I LET YOU PUT THAT ON YOUR LEDGER.*"

Chalmers squatted in the dirt and began drawing out the set-and-subset diagram again, and chanting under his breath.

Quixote and Panza came over and looked over his shoulder. Quixote asked Shea, "What is Sir Chalmero doing?"

"Giving a cow to every campesino in Spain," Shea said.

"My wife would like a cow," Panza said, looking more interested in the dirt scratchings. "She would have liked the chicken, too," he added thoughtfully.

"*DON'T DO THIS,*" Fenwick pleaded. "*THE OTHER DEMONS SERVE ENCHANTERS WHO STEAL THE SOULS OF YOUNG CHILDREN, AND DRIVE KNIGHTS MAD, AND DRINK BABIES' BLOOD. IF YOU GO AROUND GIVING OUT COWS, WHAT AM I GOING TO TELL EVERYONE?*"

"Not my problem," Chalmers said, "but I'll tell you what. You have a couple of princesses down there that don't actually belong to you folks. If you accidentally misplace them back to their home, safe and sound and happy, I won't put half a million milk cows on my account."

"THAT WOULD BE A KINDNESS—YOU WANT ME TO DO A KINDNESS? WOULDN'T YOU RATHER CURSE SOMEONE? OR HAVE YOUR OWN CASTLE IN THE HILLS, FILLED WITH GOLD AND GUARDED BY DRAGONS?"

Chalmers raised both hands and, still squatting, began rocking back and forth. In a high-pitched, nasal voice, he started his incantation. *"I swear by Hell and all its minions, by hoof and horn, give every peasant—"*

Fenwick shrieked. *"NO! I'VE DONE IT! THE PRINCESSES ARE HOME! DON'T DO THE COW SPELL!*

Chalmers closed his eyes and called up his account sheet. There, with its amount in neither the debit column nor the credit column, but in a new third column, he read, "Rescued, three virgin princesses— from the bowels of Hell." The amount in the third column was almost as high as the collected amounts of all his other spells. He noticed how that entry seemed to glow and shift. Strange, he thought.

"Well, I suppose that means Teresa won't be getting a cow," Panza said. "I'm not surprised. The blessings of the rich are always the curse of the poor."

"We must go," Quixote said, suddenly.

"Why so, your worship?" Panza asked.

"I can once again feel the presence of the evil Malambroso, and Florimel with him. That way," he pointed, further down the road the four had been travelling.

* * *

The four travellers cantered up to a spot about a hundred yards from the moat and drawbridge of a massive castle and reined in. Chalmers rode over beside Shea and the two sat quietly for a moment, studying the huge edifice.

"Looks like Saracen design, probably twelfth century," Chalmers told Shea. The older psychologist rubbed his hands together and Shea noted the delight on his face. Chalmers pointed to some holes built into the arch of the gate. "See the machicolations up there? In a fight, the castle defenders can pour boiling oil through them onto the attackers."

Shea eyed the innocent-looking holes warily. "Lovely," he said.

Chalmers missed the irony. "Isn't it? Fine piece of architecture."

Shea found it hard to get excited by machicolations or Saracen architecture. A home that did not need to be defended by boiling oil and men-at-arms, where he and Belphebe and their future children could live in peace and quiet, seemed very alluring—and very far away. He felt a stab of homesickness.

Quixote led them up to the outer gate, where a mail-clad guard with a light helmet leaned against the wall. Music and the sounds of revelry emanated from inside. Gaudy pennants flew from the peak of every tower and banners decorated the gate and draped from the narrow windows high overhead. The guard wore a beaming expression and greeted the knight and his companions with boozy, cheery bonhomie. "Hi-i-i, Don Quixote de la Man-cha—and all your friends. Welcome to the castle of Don Tibon de Salazar. Wanna go in?"

"We would," Quixote said sternly. "But first I would know— what celebration leaves the watchman drunk at his post and the gates thrown wide open?"

"I'm not—drunk!" the guard protested. He became

confiding. "Well, maybe just a little—but our princesses came home today. An enchanter stole them from us, and we thought we would never see them again, but all of a—sudden, they appeared in a cloud of bright red smoke. So—" he concluded, smiling triumphantly, "we're having a party. Good one, too. Lots of food, lots of wine, an' even a talking ape and a puppet show later. G'wan in." He leaned back against the wall of the guardhouse and waved across the drawbridge. "I'll let'cha announce yourselves."

Shea, Chalmers, Panza, and Quixote rode across the drawbridge, through the barbican, and into the outer bailey. The grounds were filled with milling people who danced and shouted and drank healths to their Don and his returned daughters; with fiddlers and guitar players wailing away; with dark-eyed gypsy girls in bright skirts of red and yellow and blue who clattered their castanets and swirled and stamped. Along the inner wall, fat, middle-aged campesinas served slabs of meat from a roasted ox, and cheeses and bits of chicken and fish and goat. Liveried servants poured a mediocre red wine for the peasants and a better one for the nobility. Shea and Chalmers, introduced by Quixote as knights of a foreign land, got some of the good stuff.

The lord of the castle, Don Tibon de Salazar, got word Quixote had showed up for his party and made a personal appearance. He was short and obviously well-fed, and he had the same glow of alcohol about him Shea had seen on the guard.

"Noble knight," he yelled, hugging the armor-clad Quixote as best he could and kissing both his cheeks. "You heard about my daughters? How good of you to come! Please, come in out of the heat."

Quixote smiled. "We three, Sir Reed de Chalmero, Sir Geraldo de Shea, and I, Don Quixote de la Mancha, freed your daughters from Hell. Sir Shea is a knight, and Sir Chalmero," he indicated the psychologist, "is a good enchanter."

"How, then——?" The little Don looked wide-eyed at Chalmers. He smiled nervously and edged back a pace. "A *good* enchanter, heh, heh!" Then his eyes went trustingly toward Quixote. "But come, you saved my daughters? They knew not the method of their rescue—only that the devils who held them were suddenly lured away while the girls were spirited back here in the blinking of an eye." He smiled. "Come in, do come in, and tell us all your tale."

The party went on, and on, and on. Shea found himself recounting the rescue of the princesses to all manner of happy drunks, sometimes several times in a row. As the day progressed into night, and he continued to partake of his host's free food and wine, he began to feel a little warm and fuzzy inside himself. He noticed that the guests were getting wittier and the jokes were getting funnier. It was, he decided, a very good party—even better because he got to be one of the heroes.

When the evening entertainment began, he found himself seated front row and center with the lord of the castle, facing a makeshift stage. Chalmers and Quixote and the princesses—who were uniformly short and round and giggly—took up the rest of the first row.

A liveried servant walked out onto the stage, bowed, and announced, "Master Peter and his talking ape, who knows all the past and all the present."

The man who followed the servant onto the stage was ugly in the extreme. Master Peter's long, pointed nose drooped at the tip so that it looked as if it were trying to touch the wart in the center of his sharp chin. He had a hunchback and limp and greasy gray hair that trailed down to his shoulders. His ape shambled at his side, a big, raggedy chimpanzee with a silly grin on his face. The chimp waved to the crowd and everyone stamped and whistled.

Don Tibon de Salazar leaned over and whispered, "We must ask our questions to the ape, who will whisper the answers in his master's ear. It's a grand ape by all accounts. Master Peter is a rich man because of the puppet show and the ape."

Master Peter settled himself onto a low stool and rested one hand on his ape's shoulder. The man's beady-eyed gaze darted from one corner of the audience to the other, and settled with unnerving intensity on the princesses and their rescuers. "Greetings, good folk" he rasped. "Who would ask my ape a question?"

Sancho Panza called out, "Tell me what will happen tomorrow."

Master Peter answered for his ape. "He cannot tell the future, but only past and present."

Panza snorted. "I swear I wouldn't give a farthing to be told what happened to me in the past—I know that well enough myself. But tell me then, excellent ape, what is my wife Teresa Panza doing now?"

The ape grinned at Panza, then ran to Master Peter's side and stretched up and gibbered in its master's ear for an interminable time.

Suddenly, Master Peter gave the group in the front row a startled look, and flung himself prone on the floor. "Glorious reviver and flower of knight-errantry," he cried. "Don Quixote de la Mancha, and noble squire Sancho Panza, best of all possible squires to the best of all possible knights, I embrace you! Oh that I have lived to see this day!" He glanced up, added, "Your wife Señor Panza, is cooking dinner while she drinks wine out of a cracked blue pitcher."

Panza gasped. "That's what she does every night," he whispered.

Master Peter then stared at Chalmers and Shea,

and ground his face into plank floor of the stage again.
"Oh, mighty swordsman Geraldo de Shea, and knight-
enchanter Reed de Chalmero, heroes of far-off places,
I kiss the ground, so happy am I to find myself in
your presence."

Quixote was visibly flattered. Shea, still warm and
happy from the wine, thought Master Peter's homage
was a fair tribute to someone who had done all the
great things he had. He swelled with pride. He
ignored the rest of the questions and answers, instead
allowing himself to bask in the delicious warmth of
praise.

By the time the ape had been led offstage and the
puppetmaster's sets were in place, however, Harold
Shea became aware that Don Quixote was muttering
to Sancho Panza. He caught the tail end of the conversation. "—And thus, if he could not tell the future,
his prophecies had to come from the Devil, for while
God knows all the seasons of tomorrow, the Devil can
only guess at that which comes past today."

Shea had no interest in Quixote's philosophies. The
puppet show was beginning.

Trumpets blared, kettledrums beat, and a small boy
called out: "Now see the true tale of the lord Sir Galiferos who freed his wife Melisendra, who was captive
of the Moors."

The show started with the puppet of Sir Galiferos
playing backgammon in the square, until his father-in-
law, King Charlemagne, came and told his idle son-
in-law to go rescue his daughter. Shamed, Galiferos
got his horse and armor and charged off for the Moorish city, found his wife, and, in broad daylight, carried
off a daring rescue right under the nose of King
Marsilio.

Shea was enjoying the play greatly until he suddenly
realized that there was something wrong about the
puppets. He stared, watching the tiny characters move

about the stage, and it dawned on him that no matter how hard he looked, he could not see the strings that animated the marionettes. "Doc," he whispered. "Can you see the strings on the puppets?"

Chalmers leaned forward on the bench and squinted. "No," he said finally. "What's more, Melisendra looks just like Florimel, and Galiferos looks like Malambroso." Chalmers then tapped Quixote on the shoulder and whispered something to him, and Shea saw the knight lean forward and stare, too.

The play had just gotten to the part where the Moorish cavalcade, led by King Marsilio, streamed out of the city after Galiferos, when Quixote leapt to his feet. "I know you now, Freston," he shouted at Master Peter, "and you as well, knavish Malambroso." He stood and drew his sword and pointed it at the stage. "Hand over to us the Lady Florimel, or all will go ill for you!"

The stage seemed to grow, along with the characters in it, until horses, actors, and the Moorish city backdrop were all life-sized. Shea loosed his saber in its scabbard and charged to his feet. Chalmers ran beside him, while Sancho Panza dropped back and looked for a safe place to hide.

"Florimel!" Chalmers shouted.

Florimel, seated ahead of Malambroso on his horse, looked at her husband with dazed and uncomprehending eyes. "She can hear you, Chalmers, but she doesn't know you," Malambroso snarled. "All she can think of is me." The sorcerer bared his teeth in a hideous parody of a grin, and pressed his knife against the base of Florimel's neck. "If I slit her throat right now, she'd die loving me for it," he added.

Florimel turned her head enough that she could look at the sorcerer, and her rapt expression seemed to bear his brag out. Chalmers snarled, "I'll kill him. I swear I will."

Shea said, "Only if I don't do it first, Doc. He and Quixote charged the sorcerer with weapons drawn, and Chalmers ran behind, trying hard to come up with a spell to destroy the two evil enchanters.

But the Moors, who had been so vigorously pursuing Malambroso in his guise as Galiferos, arrived and surrounded Quixote, Shea, and Chalmers instead. Most of the horde aimed their weapons at their three captives. A few of the Moorish warriors dismounted and bound the captives' wrists. Quixote was separated from Shea and Chalmers by force, and made to mount a saddled ass backwards. Shea and Chalmers, apparently judged less of a threat, but also less worthy of humiliation, were chained together at the waist and marched at spear-point to face Malambroso. Quixote, backwards on the donkey, was brought beside them an instant later. And just minutes after that, the Moors dragged Sancho Panza, kicking and biting, from his hiding place, knocked on the head and draped over another donkey.

"Now I have you all. Bound, you cannot use weapons against me," Malambroso gloated. "And as for magic, *by all the demons of Hell and their servants on Earth, you shall cast no evil spell against Freston or against me.*" Malambroso waved to the Moorish warriors and bellowed, "Bring them back to the city, and tonight we shall feast on the livers of our enemies."

Their captors let out a cheer.

Freston, no longer in the guise of the puppeteer, cantered through the throng, straight up to Quixote. "I don't want your liver, sir knight. I intend to eat your heart."

Quixote smiled gently, and said, "A coward can derive no greatness from eating the heart of a great man. My heart will only poison you with envy, that you are puny and despicable and without honor."

Freston reddened and spat in the knight's face. "Brave words. You'll repent of them soon enough."

The Moors, with wild ululations, started their captives marching toward the nearby city. The prisoners, surrounded, marched helplessly.

Shea tried an easy spell against Malambroso, just to see if it would work. Nothing happened. He groaned and leaned back slightly to whisper to Chalmers, who was tied behind him, "We're doomed, Doc. I tried a spell to make Malambroso sneeze—and nothing happened."

"Don't worry. I have a spell I think will work," Chalmers said. He whispered a bit of doggerel to Shea, and grinned. "Well—?"

Shea shook his head. "That's sweet of you, Doc, but I don't see the point."

Chalmers chuckled softly. "Trust me. All you have to do is remember the words and repeat them with me."

Harold shrugged. "I guess it can't hurt."

"Precisely, my dear boy. Precisely." Chalmers laughed, and said, "Begin."

"By God and all the angels, and all that is good—" Shea intoned.

"And by Satan and all his minions, and all the dark powers of hell—" Chalmers seconded.

"Oh, base Freston and ignoble Malambroso,
You shall spread a little sunshine everywhere that
     you go.
A thousand blessings you shall give,
In every second that you live.
These blessings you will never know,
Yet, infinite, they'll spread and grow.
And every step that you now take,
Will leave sweet flowers in your wake."

"That's vile poetry, Reed," Shea said after they'd finished. "Pointless, too."

Chalmers snickered. "Hardly. Just watch."

Shea watched. Behind the two sorcerers, little clumps of flowers were springing up. Harold Shea rolled his eyes. "Aw, how sweet. Malambroso has posies trailing in his wake. I hate to say this, Doc, but I think you've gone round the bend."

"The flowers were just to let us know the spell was working. Give it a few minutes for the rest of it to fall into place," Chalmers insisted, but refused to say any more.

Shea looked around. Nothing seemed to be happening, except that the road started looking like the Moorish Ladies Home and Garden Club had gotten hold of it. And then he happened to rest his eyes on a Moorish warrior just as that warrior's clothes changed. They ceased to be threadbare and ragged, and became rather nice—well-cut and of good cloth. *Odd*, Shea thought. An instant later, that same warrior's horse became a considerably better horse of similar appearance. Startled, Shea looked around at the other warriors. All of them were becoming progressively better and better dressed, but always in tiny increments. He looked down at his own clothes, and found that they were of the finest linen, beautifully embroidered and quilted. As he watched, they changed again, and he caught the glimmer of jewels and gold in amongst the silk threads. The rope around his wrists suddenly untied itself and fell to the ground. He looked at Don Quixote, and saw that the knight was now riding face-forward, unbound, and on Rosinante. Prudently, he kept quiet.

"See," Chalmers whispered. "Isn't this nice?"

"Very," Harold agreed. "I think I see what you were aiming for."

"Not yet. You will very soon now, though. You must

realize that the effects of our little spell are being felt, not only here, but all over this planet—perhaps even all over this universe."

Harold Shea shrugged. "I'm sure everyone is thrilled."

Chalmers snickered again. "No, I don't imagine *everyone* is."

A supernatural wail split the air.

"Someone has just checked the books," Chalmers said. Shea looked puzzled.

"*FRESTON, YOU HAVE OVERDRAWN YOUR ACCOUNT BY MORE THAN A MILLION PERCENT!*" the demonic voice roared. "*ALL IN GOOD WORKS. YOU HAVE NO CHANCE OR HOPE OF REPAYING WHAT YOU OWE—THEREFORE, WE ARE COLLECTING YOUR SOUL NOW!*"

Freston abruptly ceased to exist.

"There's nothing deadlier than an angry accountant," Chalmers said with a bright laugh.

An instant later, the same demonic voice screamed, "*WHAT IS THIS? MALAMBROSO, YOU ALSO HAVE OVERDRAWN YOUR ACCOUNT BY MORE THAN A MILLION PERCENT, AND IN TOTALLY NON-TRANSFERABLE GOOD WORKS! AAAGH! HOW HAVE YOU DONE THIS?—NO MATTER, I'LL HAVE YOUR SOUL NOW—*" Malambroso did not vanish the way Freston had, however. There was a moment of silence, and then the voice returned. The invisible speaker was obviously in a snit. "*I'VE BEEN INFORMED THAT YOU ARE FROM A UNIVERSE OUTSIDE OF THIS ONE. APPARENTLY, BECAUSE OF THAT, I CAN'T CLAIM YOUR SOUL IN LIEU OF PAYMENT—BUT I CAN BANISH YOU AND EVERYTHING OF YOURS FROM THIS UNIVERSE FOR ALL OF ETERNITY. I DO SO NOW!*"

Malambroso vanished. Florimel went with him.

"NO!" Reed Chalmers screamed. *"Fenwick, dammit, bring her back here!*

Fenwick answered. *"REED CHALMERS—YOU WERE RESPONSIBLE FOR THAT PLAGUE OF GOODNESS. YOU HAVE TOTALLY RUINED MY REPUTATION, AND EVEN SATAN IS PISSED AT ME!"* The demon snarled. *"I'M REVOKING YOUR ACCOUNT AND BANISHING YOU."*

Chalmers grabbed Shea's arm and held on. Light began to swirl around them, howling assaulted their ears, and the world of Don Quixote dribbled away as if it had been buried in a deep fog. The last sound the two psychologists heard was Fenwick, squawking, *"I'M SENDING YOU WHERE WE SENT MALAMBROSO—AND I HOPE HE FINDS YOU!"*

"I hope so, too," Chalmers said.

ARMS AND THE ENCHANTER
John Maddox Roberts

...and Shea frowned. "That would be...
theory were correct—but I'm not convinced that it...
freed." When the senior psychologist gave him a hard
glare, Shea swallowed and said, "I think we may be

1

This time the millions of whirling spots of color underwent a color change during passage. They began a nice, restful blue, a sort of sky-blue reminiscent of a pleasant summer day. It did not last long. The blue shaded to a purple that seemed, somehow, ominous. The purple went to blood-red, then to a lurid yellow-orange. And it got *hot*. Then they were standing on a broad pavement and the yellow spots coalesced into flames that shot skyward for hundreds of feet. It got even hotter.

Even over the roaring of the flames they heard an unearthly screeching, wailing racket that could only be likened to banshees being fed into a buzzsaw. For a moment the screeching was drowned out by a thunder of crashing masonry. They were in a city, and the city was in flames.

Shea looked up. "I don't see any bombers." Surely nothing else could account for such wholesale destruction.

"I would think not," Chalmers said. "The technological

level would seem to preclude them. Look there." He
pointed to the far end of the huge plaza upon which
they stood. There, men waving long, bronze swords
and oversized spears were herding hundreds of
women and children into a sort of impromptu corral
made of stacked furniture, hangings, platters and cups
made of gold and silver, lamps and tripods of bronze,
chains, sculptures, wine jars, tables inlaid with ivory,
chests, in fact a whole department store of valuable
goods. This was the source of the horrid screeching,
which was set up by the women. They tore at their
hair, rent their garments and scratched their faces.
Mostly they wailed, in a demonstration of terror and
grief that seemed exaggerated even in the midst of
such a catastrophe.

"That's the worst acting I've seen since our sopho-
more production of *MacBeth*," Shea commented.

With a roar, a tower at least four hundred feet high
began to topple on some buildings that capped a low
hill just beyond the plaza. Its fall began in slow and
stately fashion, picking up velocity as it reached forty-
five degrees, flames shooting from its windows in a
dazzling display of pyrotechnics. It crashed down like
a bomb, hurling flames, stones, smoke, and dust over
a vast area. The men guarding the prisoners cheered
and waved their weapons.

"Somebody wants to take this city right off the
map!" Shea said.

"I think this is not a good place to be," Chalmers
observed. "Perhaps we should find a quiet corner to
think things out."

"Right. Maybe we can find a bar still open somewhere. Let's . . . who's that?"

They had turned to go down a side street and found
their way blocked by a large man who was speaking
to an even larger woman. The man was dressed in
bronze armor, with a lion skin thrown over his shoulders

and back. He was spattered from head to foot with blood. The woman stood more than a head taller, her height boosted even more by the fact that her feet were three or four inches off the ground.

The man wore a look of utter distress but the prevailing racket prevented Shea and Chalmers from hearing what he was saying. He reached up, as if to embrace the woman around the neck, but his arms passed right through her. He had another try, with the same result. Apparently he was slow to learn from experience, because he had another try at it. This time, the woman faded from view. He seemed on the verge of bursting into tears, but the appearance of Shea and Chalmers distracted him. His facial expression switched from grief to grim determination so quickly that it was like an optical illusion.

"You two slaves," he called. "Come here and pick these up." He pointed to a pile of weapons on the pavement by his feet.

"We aren't slaves!" Shea said indignantly.

"Foreigners, then. Pick these up and follow me, if you would leave this city alive. They are sparing only comely women and children fit for slavery."

"It might be the best idea," Chalmers said.

"I don't know," Shea said hesitantly. "It looks like joining the losing side to me."

"Jump to it!" the huge man roared. They jumped.

"You seem somewhat the sturdier," the man said to Shea. "You bear my shield. Your companion may be my spear-bearer for my last walk through my beloved city. Be ready to hand me a trusty, ashen spear at my call, and have my shield ready for my left hand's grasp." With that, the warrior strode down the street.

Shea stooped and pulled the shield upright. Grasping the straps on its inner surface, he struggled to lift it. The thing was astoundingly heavy, seventy or eighty pounds by his estimation. It was as tall as he was, a convex oval with small oval cutouts giving it a narrower "waist" section. It seemed to be made of multiple layers of hide faced with decorated bronze. He staggered along beneath this load, Chalmers beside him having similar difficulty with his armload of spears. Their polished shafts slithered around as if they were oiled.

They caught up with the man just as he strode out into another great square. This one was lined with lofty, templelike buildings, all of them spouting the now expected flames. Bodies lay everywhere; on the pavement, on the temple steps, hanging out of windows. The square was dominated by some sort of immense sculpture, an animal figure that towered over the rooftops. It was a sinister thing with its fierce, painted eyes and upstanding mane, despite the incongruous trapdoor hanging from its belly. Chalmers gasped.

"The wooden horse!"

"Aye," said their leader. "It was with this ruse that the Greeks took storied Ilium, not with valor. We were mad, for the gods made us so. We heeded not the warnings of Laocoön the priest, but dragged it through the gates and celebrated with drunken revelry. Thus are we punished for our impiety."

"We're in the *Iliad*!" Shea groaned.

"Harold," Chalmers chided, "surely you cannot be that ignorant."

"I don't see why not!"

Chalmers sighed. "I can see that the classics are no longer taught as they were in my day. The *Iliad* ends with the funeral of Hector. Troy still stands, the Horse is unbuilt, Achilles is alive."

"Well I was too busy with psychology to pay much attention to the classics. What is it, then, *The Odyssey*?"

"Difficult to say. That one has some flashback sequences about the Horse and the fall of . . ." Their leader had stopped, Shea stopped likewise, and Chalmers bumped into Shea with a clatter of ashen shafts. Three enemy soldiers came down the street toward them, shield to shield. They were even bloodier than the man Shea and Chalmers followed, white plumes nodding from their helmets, making them appear even taller than they were, which was a head taller than the Americans, although not quite so tall as the man in the lionskin.

"Shield!" barked that worthy. Gratefully, Shea shoved it toward him. The man slipped his left forearm through a strap and grasped the handle near one edge and lifted the massive contraption as easily as if it were made of wicker. He snapped his fingers and Chalmers laid a spearshaft in the upturned palm.

"Here's a Trojan dog still alive!" crowed the warrior in the middle. "Dibs on his armor!"

The Trojan raised his spear. "Eat bronze, Danaan!" He hurled the heavy spear from a distance of twenty feet. It struck the enemy shield dead center. A fifty-caliber machine-gun bullet could not have struck harder. It plowed through bronze and hide without losing velocity, slammed into the man's breastplate, plowed through his body and out through the backplate, knocking him back a dozen paces to fall clattering to the pavement.

"Spear!" Chalmers gave him another. Shea could only gape. The warrior on the right hurled his own spear but their guide batted it aside with his shield. It nicked Shea's ear in its whispering passage. The second spear crashed through that man and pinned him, shield and all, to the doorpost of a nearby house.

The third Greek heaved his spear almost simultaneously. The Trojan whipped out a long sword in a bronzen blur and hacked the head off the spear in flight. A second blow did the same for the Greek. The helmeted head, plumes spinning, disappeared over a rooftop as the body toppled, adding to the general mess.

Shea gave a low whistle. "This guy really knows his business!"

"A hero," Chalmers affirmed. "They usually did."

The Trojan set off again and they followed. They had to step lively to keep up with his long strides, but he really was not hurrying, considering he was fleeing from a city fallen to the foe. But then a warrior, especially a hero, Shea reflected, would never *run* from the enemy.

"There is something," Chalmers muttered, "decidedly familiar about that man."

"How is that possible?" Shea asked. "Nobody knows what Homeric heroes looked like, not in any detail."

"I don't know, it's just ..." He shrugged and trudged on. Chalmers only had three spears now, so they were much easier to handle. Relieved of the shield's weight, Shea was having an easier time of it as well.

"Ah, sir," he hazarded, "just where are we going?"

"To the inland gate. A little way beyond that gate lies an ancient funeral mound, and a shrine of Ceres the Bereft. There await some folk of my household, whom I must lead away from this place."

"Does that sound familiar?" Shea asked Chalmers.

"It does. Let me see ... it's been so long ..." Just then a couple more Greeks showed up and it was spear-handing time again.

By the time they reached the inland gate they were down to one spear, and the Trojan's sword was getting notched and dull. They were not alone going through the gate. A stream of people, mostly women, the elderly, children and downtrodden sorts who were probably slaves, were on their way as well. Many carried pathetic bundles of belongings, and they looked like war-stunned refugees of all times and locales.

When they were outside Shea scanned the surrounding plain with amazement.

"There's no detachment out here to bag the catch,"
he said. "No surrounding army at all!"

"The Greeks were too primitive for that," Chalmers
told him. "The so-called siege of Troy was really no
such thing. The Greeks just camped on the beach and
raided the countryside. They fought the Trojans when-
ever the Trojans felt like coming out to fight. They
didn't even try to starve the city out or cut it off from
the rest of the world. People pretty much came and
went as they pleased."

"That's no way to run a war," Shea protested.

"It may be just as well that they were so naïve about
organized warfare, considering the level of carnage
they could wreak without it."

The hero turned to gaze toward the towering wall
and the city that was now little but a pillar of flame
and smoke. Tears ran down his cheeks, plowing furrows in the blood, soot, and dirt and making a ghastly
mud on the gorget of his armor.

"Farewell, beloved Ilium! You are fallen at last, but
the gods have foretold that I shall raise a new Troy
upon the banks of a foreign river, where the race of
Priam shall flourish once more!" With that he turned
and trudged away. Shea and Chalmers, for lack of a
viable alternative, followed the broad, armored, lion-
skinned back.

"I think I've got it," Chalmers said, "but I want to
be sure. There were so many poems and legends from
the Trojan cycle. The *Iliad* and *Odyssey* were just the
most famous."

The walk was not a long one, but the sky was growing pale by the time they reached the mound. It was
no small household waiting there, but a crowd of several hundred people of all ages. Some wept on the
altar of the shrine, others sprawled exhausted on the

mound, but most gathered beneath a large, stately cypress tree. At the base of the tree sat an elderly man, cradling in his arms an object or objects wrapped in fine cloth. The hero made his way to the old man and bowed respectfully.

"Did you find your wife, my son?" asked the old man.

"I did, father, but death had already snatched my beloved Creusa from me. In despair, I was about to throw my life away in battle with the Achaeans, but her shade appeared to me, chiding my despair and assuring me that the immortal gods had other plans for the son of Anchises. Travel far from Ilium, she said, as the gods guide you by sea, and found a new Troy whose kings shall be your own descendants. And so I returned to you. Now, we must be away, for soon the Danaans will weary of their swinish rapine and plunder. They will harness their swift horses to their chariots and scour the countryside for us."

A small boy came up and took the hero's hand. "Father, who are these strangely-dressed people who came with you from the city?"

The hero, who seemed to have forgotten them, turned and took notice. "Oh, these fellows rendered me some small service as I made my way through the city. They have earned a place in our little band, which seems to have grown."

"Yes, a great many have arrived since you went back to the city to seek your beloved Creusa," the old man said. "I had thought them a great bother, but if you are to found a new city and a new royal line, then you must have followers."

"Very well. Father, you must carry the household gods a while longer. I cannot touch them until I have purified myself of blood in running water." With that he handed his shield to a brawny youth. To Shea's amazement, he bent and tenderly lifted the old man, shifting him to a piggyback carry on the lionskin. With the boy's hand in his he raised his trumpeting voice.

"All who would come with Lord Aeneas, follow me! We go to seek our fate upon the broad breast of father Neptune!" With that he began to walk away, closely followed by his household. By ones and twos, then in small groups, the others picked up their goods and went as well.

"That's it!" Chalmers said. "This is the *Aeneid*! Aeneas, the last of the great Trojan heroes, fled from the burning city, carrying his aged father, Anchises, and leading his son, Ascanius. In the flight he lost his wife, Creusa, and he returned to the city to find her."

"How did he lose her?" Shea asked.

"Nobody knows. That part of the poem is missing. Anyway, he went through the burning city and saw the bound prisoners and the piled plunder. The ghost of Creusa appeared to him, 'larger than life,' the poem says, that's why she looked so big, and told him what he just told his father."

"Well, I wish him all the best, but what do *we* do?"

"We go with him, of course!" Chalmers said.

"Why? I can't say that building a new Troy is on my list of things to do this week. I didn't see enough of the old one to conceive a real affection for it."

"Because this man is going to travel!" Chalmers said. "We are looking for Florimel, and if she's in this world, the only way to find her is to travel. Of course, we could always go back to the city and hope the Greeks don't kill us. Then we might hitch a ride with Odysseus; he's going to travel, too. Of course then we have to risk Scylla and Charybdis, the Sirens, the Laestrygonians, and so forth, get turned into pigs, eaten by a Cyclops, that sort of thing."

"On second thought," Shea said, "following our friend Aeneas sounds like a dandy idea." And so they went.

The day got hotter as they walked along, but at least there seemed to be no pursuit. There was little talk among the despondent refugees, so there was plenty of time to observe and ponder. It seemed odd to Shea that the people around them were all rather large. Not giants like Aeneas and the men of his household, but averaging bigger than typical twentieth-century Americans.

"I thought ancient people were much smaller," Shea noted. "But even the women here are bigger than I am."

"It's the age of heroes," Chalmers said. "Everything was bigger, better, handsomer. Men were stronger, women more beautiful and virtuous, or conversely more wicked. The heroes of Homer are always picking up stones 'such as three men could lift, as men are now.' "

"Kind of like the way we picture the Old West, eh? The good guys are better, the bad guys are badder, and everything is much cleaner than it actually was."

"Exactly. In all probability, the Earps were back-shooting cardsharps who wore filthy clothes that never got ironed and had rotten teeth, but legend has made them towering, heroic exemplars of good fighting evil. It was the same with the heroes of antiquity."

"But these don't even look like Mycenaeans," Shea complained. "Just a while ago, I saw an article in *National Geographic* . . ."

Chalmers shook his head. "Homer lived, if he lived at all, around four hundred years after the Trojan War. Virgil lived another eight hundred years after that. He had no idea what the people of the Mycenaean civilization looked like. What we see here," he swept an arm to take in the solemn procession, "is how Romans of the Augustan Age *pictured* the people of Homer. It's an amalgam of general Hellenistic fashions and old Greek paintings from walls and vases, sculptures and so forth. There's a prevalence of bronze, because Homer stressed that all the weapons and armor were bronze."

Before them, Aeneas walked tirelessly along, still carrying his father.

"Aeneas has lots of followers, even slaves," Shea said. "Why does he always carry the old guy?"

"That's Virgil again, rather than Homer. Virgil wanted to create a Roman national Epic, using Homeric models. But Roman heroes had to have Roman virtues, and to the Romans no virtue was greater than *pietas*. It was the scrupulous observance of duty toward one's parents, ancestors, hearth and gods. Those are the household gods Anchises is carrying wrapped up in that cloth. The image of the great hero carrying his aged father and the Penates on his back is the most vivid image of *pietas* in all of Roman legend."

"I see. So you know the poem pretty well?"

"It's coming back to me: 'Arma virumque cano,' it begins, 'Of arms and the man I sing.' "

"I thought George Bernard Shaw wrote that."

Chalmers sighed. "And to think I once thought you were an educated man."

2

"What about it, Doc? Do you think you can work us up a little magic?" Shea profoundly hoped so. The band of refugees had reached Antander near the foot of Mt. Ida and there had set about building a fleet to bear them westward. Their number included numerous

craftsmen, and even the noblemen did not seem
averse to working with their hands, as long as the
work involved weapons, horses, or ships. They cut and
hauled wood and the ribs and planks took shape
almost as if by magic, for the craftsmen worked the
same way the heroes fought, with inhuman swiftness
and certainty.

Even in the midst of all this legendary activity there
was scut work to be done by inferiors. Boiling pitch
and hauling it to the growing fleet was one of these.
It was the job to which Chalmers and Shea had been
set. Apparently, they were good only for such filthy,
unpleasant labor. Harold was anxious to raise their
status, especially if they were to gallivant around the
Mediterranean with this crew. And the crew was growing, as more refugees from the sack of Troy and its
nearby villages trickled in. Already, a dozen ships were
near completion and more keels had been laid.

"I think I can work something," Chalmers said. "It's
not simple. The people of this mythos don't go in
much for the mechanical sort of sorcery we've seen
elsewhere; the use of spells and rituals that are actually rather scientific, even if the rules seem arbitrary."

"Yes, but?" Shea said, impatiently.

Chalmers ignored the urging and laid aside the stick
with which he had been stirring a cauldron of boiling,
stinking pitch. He sat wearily on a convenient rock
and mopped his brow with a rag. Both of them had
swapped their sixteenth century garb for tunics of local
weave.

"Classical magic," Chalmers bore on, "characteristi-
cally involves bribing, flattering and manipulating the
gods, getting *them* to do what you want."

"That sounds bad. Are Greek gods as hard to deal
with as university department heads?"

"Oh, nothing that difficult. More like police or
small-time politicians. That's the good part, you see:

Greek gods work cheap. All they really want is modest sacrifices and *lots* of flattery. They respond readily to suggestion that other gods, who are invariably rivals, are trying to horn in on their glory. They are extremely childish and extremely powerful."

"But then don't you run the risk of falling afoul of those other gods?"

"Unfortunately, yes. And gods will frequently strike at a rival by attacking the rival's worshippers and favorites."

"Who are the favorites?" Shea asked, picking up the stick and giving the pitch a stir. It was almost hot enough.

"Their children, for one. Take Aeneas over there." Chalmers nodded toward the beach, where the hero was inspecting a rack of oars made of polished olive wood. Like everything else here, the oars were exquisitely designed and made. They could have hung in a first-rank art museum.

"What about him?"

"Well, you've seen his father. Do you know who his mother is?"

"Mrs. Anchises?"

"The goddess Aphrodite. Or, rather, Venus, this being a Roman story."

Shea gaped. "Venus? You mean Aeneas is a demigod?"

"A great many of the heroes were. Greek gods and goddesses spread themselves pretty thin."

"But Venus herself!" Shea shook his head in wonder. "But what did the goddess of love and beauty see in old Anchises?"

"I daresay he was younger then," Chalmers said drily. "Doubtless he was handsomer as well. It was a great help on the battlefield. Once, the Greek hero Diomedes wounded Aeneas but his mother spirited him away before Diomedes could deal the deathblow."

"And American soldiers complain that *their* officers get too many privileges!"

"Ah, yes, I suppose so. Anyway, there were smaller magics sometimes practiced in the classical world, and some of these used the principles with which we are familiar; affinity, sympathy, contagion and so forth. I may be able to accomplish something minor but impressive."

"Maybe you could whip up some soap," Shea said hopefully.

"I could do that without magic, I think. All you need is animal fat and wood ash, although I'm not truly certain of the process. My grandmother used to make soft soap on her farm. The magic would be in getting these people to use it."

"I guess so. The way they rub themselves with olive oil and scrape it off. . . . well, it gets the worst off, but it sure doesn't make them smell much better." It distressed Shea that even the most spectacularly beautiful noble ladies always trailed a scent of rancid oil.

At least he had that to salve his vanity. People of the heroic age could bruise the twentieth century ego. The nobles were gigantic and beautiful. The yeomen, craftsmen and other freemen were large and handsome. Even the slaves were bigger and better looking than the average modern American. Shea had never considered himself a vain man, but he had never thought of himself as both small and ugly. Activity near the shore caught his attention.

"There they go again," Shea said. "Sacrificing another bull, looking for omens." These people seemed to spend half their time on the lookout for omens. "They went over a calf's liver yesterday and the omens were fine. If that foretells a good voyage, why do it all over again?"

"That isn't how it works," Chalmers told him. "Omens, auguries, haruspices and the like don't foretell the future. That's a confusion with the sort of biblical prophecy that entered our culture after Virgil's time."

"If they aren't reading the future," Shea said, exasperated, "then what is all this rigamarole about?"

"The gods are fickle, even childish, remember?" Chalmers said, patiently. "They can change their minds. When the omens are taken regarding an enterprise, they indicate the will of the gods *at that time*. Things can always change. The idea is to keep testing the weather, find the prevailing trend of divine thought, and start out on the right note."

"That seems awfully uncertain."

Chalmers shrugged. "No more so than the stock market."

That evening there was a banquet. Somehow, refugees in this mythos seemed to live better than their twentieth-century counterparts. Due to the cunning of Prometheus, the gods got only the fat and bones of the sacrifice. The worshippers got everything else. Another good reason for so many sacrifices, Shea thought, his mouth watering at the smells wafting from the firepit. Some traveling entertainers had chanced by and were performing acrobatics and juggling for the feasters as they waited for the viands to cook. In the hospitable Trojan fashion, other travellers, going up or down the coastal road, had been invited to partake.

All took their seats on the beach in strict order of precedence, with Anchises and Aeneas at one end, Shea and Chalmers very near the other, just above the slaves.

"Got your magic ready?" Shea whispered.

"I believe so," Chalmers said, uncertainly. "If this were the genuine Homeric world I would be in despair, but Virgil lived after the great age of Greek logic. It was from this that our scientific method and symbolic logic were derived. Even though these people are the near-barbaric characters of Homer, this continuum should be infused with the rigor of Greek logic."

"That sounds logical. No pun intended, of course. When do we pull it?"

"After the banqueting, when everyone is jovial and well-disposed. That's when the serious drinking starts."

The slaves and children began to serve the sacrificial meat. Like the heroes of Norse myth, these people seemed to live on little else, although to Shea's relief they would set out bread, fruit and cheese for any who craved such common fare. The upper end got served first, and they tore into it without waiting for the rest.

A boy staggering under the weight of a wine jar filled Harold's wooden bowl, using a bronze ladle. He took a swig and made a face. It was thin, sour stuff, resinous from the pitch-caulked cask in which it had aged and salty from the seawater that had washed out the cask. It was also weak, since it had been cut with at least four parts of water.

"How do they ever manage to get drunk on this swill?" he asked Chalmers.

"The heroes get better wine," Chalmers said. "But even what they have is poor wine by our standards. It's drunk green, before it can go sour, at which time it's passed along to the lowborn."

"Here comes the grub!" said a shipwright who sat to Harold's left. A team of slaves walked down the line bearing a stretcherlike serving platter, from which a serving girl hooked slabs of meat with a fork. Before the Americans and the shipwright she laid a smoking rack of pork ribs. Shea's salivary glands went into overdrive at the smell. He tore a rib loose and ripped off chunks of stringy meat with his teeth. It had been sauced with something sweetly pungent. It was not quite barbecue, but it was close enough.

"Look at them nobles," groused the shipwright. "Eatin' all the best parts while we're left with the offal."

"They're getting the prime rib and sirloin, eh?" Shea looked toward the head of the "table" and saw, to his amazement, that Aeneas was carving on a smoking ox head. He sliced a gristly hunk of flesh from the jaw and ceremoniously presented it to his father. Anchises thanked him courteously, stuck the tough plug into his mouth and gnawed at it with teeth that were no longer what they had been.

"*That's* what they consider gourmet eating?" Shea said, incredulously.

"They have no way of knowing that spare ribs are a delicacy to us," Chalmers said. "After all, not so long ago in America, pork ribs were slave food. The masters ate the hams and chops, the slaves got the ribs and trotters. Barbecued spare ribs are one of those triumphs of culinary ingenuity, like oxtail soup."

"Let's not clue them in," Shea advised.

"Your pardon," said a man who sat across from them, "but did you gentlemen happen to witness the fall of the great city?" He was one of the invited travellers, a merchant of some sort, whose tunic and robe were of decent quality but stained with much travel.

"We saw the final night," Chalmers told him. "Have you just learned of it, sir?"

"That is so. I am Pierus, a traveller in fine cloths dyed with Tyrian purple."

"Another anachronism," Chalmers muttered to Shea. "Homer knew about Sidon, not about Tyre."

"Eh?" the merchant said.

Shea made a throat-clearing sound. "Ah, you asked about the fall of Troy. As it happens, we were in the city on its very last night." He went on to give a brief description of what they had seen and what they had learned from the refugees.

"How splendid!" the merchant said. "Heroes, gods, a long war ended by a subtle stratagem." He slapped his knee. "Wait until my customers hear about this! I'll bet we get a few good songs out of this one!"

"Undoubtedly," Chalmers said. "Do you travel widely?"

"Wherever there's a demand for Tyrian purple, which is to say everyplace. Can't have royalty without purple, and the world is crawling with royalty. The temples need it, too, robes for the gods and that sort of thing. Why, I was just at the sanctuary Ismaros . . ."

"Ismaros?" Shea asked.

"Yes. That's an island up near Ciconian territory, Thrace, you know. The sanctuary of Phoebus Apollo needed a full-length robe for the god, heavily embroidered with gold. Biggest sale I ever made."

"Ismaros!" Chalmers said.

"That's what I said: Ismaros."

"Does the priest there dwell in a sacred grove?" Chalmers had, Shea thought, an odd gleam in his eye.

"That's right. His name is Maron."

"And did he, by any chance, give you some of the fabled wine of that grove?"

"That he did. It was a signal honor. In gratitude for the robe, he gave me a cup no larger than a thimble, and it was no more than a drop of the wine, the rest was water, but it was like the nectar of the immortals. Spoiled me for wine ever since." He got a faraway, wistful look, like a man who once got a peek into heaven.

"Oh, look!" Chalmers said, pointing at something over the merchant's shoulder. The man turned to see what it was, and when he did Chalmers switched wine-cups with him. It was not done with quite the expertise of a sleight-of-hand artist, but it got the job done. Shea was mystified, but made no comment.

The merchant turned back. "What was it?"

"Oh, I thought I saw a falling star. An omen, you know. I guess it was just a firefly."

"Firefly? What's a firefly?"

"Oh, ah, um . . . well, it's something we have back home in the Orient. A sort of bug that carries a lamp."

The purple merchant looked as if he doubted Chalmers' sanity. He took a sudden interest in the carpenter who sat next to him and proceeded to ignore the two Americans.

"What the hell was that all about?" Shea asked.

"Had enough to eat, Harold?"

"I guess so." The rack of ribs was now a little pile of gleaming bones.

"Then let's go take a walk."

The two got up, Chalmers cradling his expropriated wine cup carefully. Perhaps a couple of tablespoons of vinegary dregs swirled in its bottom. They drew back to a tiny poplar grove situated near the beach and sat on flat stones.

"We've just been granted a golden opportunity!" Chalmers said.

"How?"

"Ismaros! Maron, the priest of Apollo on Ismaros, had . . . that is to say, *has*, in his house a store of the greatest wine in the world; a wine so powerful that it can be mixed with twenty parts of water without losing its strength. It's the wine that Odysseus . . . or rather Ulysses, since this is the *Aeneid*, will use to get the cyclops Polyphemus drunk . . . that is, if he hasn't already." Parallel poems caused Chalmers to tangle his tenses.

"Sounds like good stuff," Shea observed. "But as I understand it, Thrace is a ways north of here. What good does the wine do us up there?"

Chalmers held up the bowl. "You remember the magic principle of contagion, don't you? Things that have come into contact will always retain an affinity. The Catholic church of the Middle Ages built the whole trade in holy relics on the principle. Well, that man recently drank Maron's wine, and his lips touched this cup. I think my little demonstration this evening is going to be far more spectacular than we expected."

"Reed, if I didn't know what a dignified and self-possessed scholar you are, I'd swear you were chuckling with glee."

"One doesn't get an opportunity for a coup like this very often."

"Always assuming it works," Shea added.

"Well, yes, that is always a consideration. If it doesn't, they'll probably kill us for wasting their time."

By the time the moon was high, the overfed feasters were growing bored with the entertainment. All fell silent when the two strangers came forward to stand in front of Aeneas and Anchises. They bowed, low, and Shea launched into his prepared spiel.

"Noble Anchises, heroic Aeneas, with great generosity you have permitted us to join your band, to share in your adventures as you fare forth to found a new city, nay, a new kingdom! This night, you have feasted us royally and we wish, in our humble way, to repay your liberality."

This seemed to amuse Aeneas. "The Orientals, is it? To men of honor, generosity looks for no reward. But, if it is your desire to bring us some gift, my father and I accept with thanks."

"What might this gift be?" Anchises asked.

"We wish to bring you something a little different in the way of entertainment. My companion, the estimable Reed Chalmers, is a magician of some note. This evening, he will essay a feat of magic which shall strike you with wonderment, gladden your hearts, and provide a noble addition to this feast, so bounteously provided by our princely host and his semi-divine son." Shea had learned that the nobles loved flattery as much as the gods, and he laid it on thick.

"Not a rabbit out of a hat," Anchises said, peevishly. "I've seen that one."

"No, my lords," Chalmers said. "I intend something a bit more subtle. For this feat, I shall need an amphora of sour wine, one that has turned undrinkable."

"That seems reasonable enough," Aeneas said. "Half our store is vinegar by now, fit only for cooking and for cleaning jars. Fetch one."

A pair of slaves brought a forty-gallon jar by its thick handles. They jammed its pointed bottom into the sand and left it standing there.

"Now, a ladle, please," Chalmers said. One of the serving girls handed him one. He removed the stopper from the jar and dipped up a ladle full of the sour fluid. This he carried to Aeneas and Anchises. He passed it beneath their noses, which wrinkled in aristocratic disdain.

"Are you satisfied, my lords, that this wine has gone sour beyond hope of redemption?"

"Decidedly," Aeneas said.

"I shall improve it," Chalmers said. He raised his arms heavenward and cried out in a melodramatic voice: "I call upon you, Dionysus of the grape and Phoebus Apollo of the laurel! Behold, for the benefit of your favorite, I wreak a metamorphosis. Venus, aid me to provide a vinous crown for your son's festivities!" He looked down and waved his hands over the amphora, saying as an aside to Shea: "Here goes. Modern chemistry meets Aristotelean logic meets primitive shamanism. Keep the bowl handy."

All fell silent as he began to intone his spell.

"Let this be the proposition, that wine is wine, that

is to say; A is A. Let it further be postulated that vinegar is wine that has undergone a change, that is to say; AB. Let it be postulated yet further that this change is a consequence of alteration among molecules, which are made of atoms, which indivisible particles are asserted by Empedocles, Democritus and Leucippus.

"No logical reason exists forbidding the reversal of this process. Let us therefore rearrange these molecules, restoring them to their former chains." He turned to Shea. "The bowl," he whispered. Shea handed it to him. Chalmers swirled the dregs in the bottom and chanted in a high, quavering voice:

"Phoebus Apollo of the grove of Ismaros, let the example of your matchless vintage guide these errant molecules into the divine paths of your own creation!" Solemnly, he tipped the bowl and allowed the few drops of sour wine to drop within the great jar. Then he dipped the bowl into the jar, allowed it to fill, and released it to sink to the bottom. He replaced the stopper and stood with head bowed. He whispered to Shea. "Be ready to run if this doesn't work."

"All set," Shea said. He had already picked a direction.

Chalmers took a deep breath and ceremoniously raised the stopper. The pin-drop silence continued as something emerged from the jar. It was a fragrance, intensely sweet and so powerful that it seemed to have color. The crowd of feasters looked puzzled, then rapturous. There was a collective "Aaaaahhhhhhh!"

Hesitantly, Chalmers filled a ladle, raised it and let the contents cascade back within. The formerly reddish-yellow liquid had turned to something not merely red, but a maroon so deep that it was almost black.

With an expression of wonderment, Aeneas rose and came forward. He held a cup of hammered gold, with tiny doves perched on its handles. He held it over the amphora and Chalmers filled it. The fragrance was almost overpowering by now. Reverently, Aeneas took the cup to Anchises and offered it to him. The old man raised it to his nose and sniffed, going almost cross-eyed when the full bouquet hit his olfactories.

"Uh, m'lord," Shea hazarded, "it really ought to be mixed with water, twenty to one. This stuff will lay a Cyclops out flat." The two aristocrats paid him no heed. Anchises took a healthy belt. A moment later his eyes bugged half out of his head and his face turned scarlet. He gasped for a few seconds, then spoke.

"Whoooooooeeeee! That's some hooch!" Everybody cheered and clapped, already half-drunk from the fumes alone.

"Make up a bowl with twenty measures of water and one of the new wine," Aeneas yelled, "so that all may have some. First, though, fill me a cup of the straight goods!" Chalmers did so, and Aeneas knocked back a slug. When his eyes refocussed he clapped Chalmers on the shoulder.

"Boys," said the hero, "not only have you capped my banquet in rare style, but you've risen in my estimation as well. From now on, you're off pitch-boiling duty. I'm making you wine stewards for the fleet, with all the honors due that noble station."

Within minutes, the whole crowd was blissfully plastered. Amazingly, there was not a mean drunk in the lot. All were singing and romping around and carrying on, as if they had been robbed of all care and all rancor.

"Well, you did it," Shea said. "But let's lay off the stuff until they're all safely out."

"Agreed," said Chalmers. "And I think we had better content ourselves with the diluted wine. It's even more potent than advertised."

Within an hour, the whole company was on the sand, snoring in unison. Shea and Chalmers each dipped a bowl, clicked cups in toast, and took a drink.

It was like concentrated delight, what the gods would drink if the gods were committed winos. It made Chateau Mouton Rothschild taste like Dago Red.

"I can't believe Aeneas and his father could drink it straight and live," Shea said.

"Heroic appetites are notorious," Chalmers explained. They took another sip.

"Ah, Doc, is this stuff supposed to be hallucinogenic as well?"

"Not that I had heard. Why?"

"Because there's a guy made of gold and about twenty feet high standing over there by the ship we were caulking today."

"Uh-oh." Slowly, Chalmers turned to look. The man, if that was what he was, strode toward them. When he was near they came to just above his knee-caps and had to squint their eyes against his brightness. His beautiful, terrible face glared down at them. He was not happy.

"Mortal fools! Know you who I am?"

"We . . ." Chalmers began.

"I", the huge golden man said, cutting him off, "am Phoebus Apollo, Silverbow, Shootafar, Apollo of the Golden Locks, solar deity extraordinnaire!"

"Lord Apollo," Chalmers cried, "what have we, poor wretched mortals that we are, done to anger you?"

Apollo bent low and hissed. "What have you done? You don't know? You miserable, impious, blaspheming *bootlegger!*"

"I, ah, don't understand," Chalmers said.

"We intended no disrespect, sir," Shea assured him.

"You think that excuses you?" His expression grew thunderous. "You just came in here and usurped the sacred wine of Apollo, and you expect to get off easy? You should have known better than to invoke my name, mortal! That brought me all the way from Ethiopia to witness your sacrilege."

"Hey, we were just trying to keep the party going," Shea protested.

"Silence!" He gave them an evil grin. "You know what happens to mortals who mess with me? Ever hear of Niobe? My sister Diana and I killed her six sons and six daughters. Shot them dead! I guess you've heard of Marsyas, that satyr who said he was a better musician than Apollo?"

"I'm not sure," Shea said weakly while Chalmers just looked pale.

"I skinned that bastard alive!" He chuckled sadistically. "I'm going to have to think up something *really* bad for you two. I'll teach you to mess with Phoebus Apollo!"

"But, but we didn't . . ."

"Oh, shut up, you little worm. While I'm thinking this over, I want *you* to think it over. Anticipation is half the fun. I'll be seeing you, mortals, just when you least expect it!" There was a sudden, gusting whirlwind, and Apollo, to their unutterable relief, was gone.

"Now we're in for it," Shea groaned. "Just when things were looking up!"

"Well," Chalmers said weakly, "it might have been worse."

"How?"

"How? My dear Harold, Apollo is one of the *nicer* gods!"

3

The morning of the fleet's departure dawned clear and sparkling. Aeneas made his last-minute arrangements, assigning crews to the fleet that had now grown to twenty ships. He took Shea and Chalmers to a vessel that was wider and deeper-bellied than the others.

"This is the fleet's wine ship," Aeneas explained. "It is commanded by my friend, Achates. Ah, here is the master now."

By the stern of the vessel stood a man who was taller than most, but not so tall as Aeneas: about six foot five by Shea's estimation. This classed him as a noble warrior, but not quite of hero rank. There were a number of them with the fleet. Shea had dubbed them heroids.

"Brave Achates!" Aeneas called.

"Noble Lord Aeneas!" Achates said, grinning obsequiously and displaying a small gap between his front teeth. Next to him a plump lady sat on a bale of wool, doing needlework. "How may I serve my lord?"

"Achates, these men shall sail in your vessel. They will keep our wine from souring. It is an important duty, and they are to have no others during the voyage."

"Absolutely, my lord. I shall care for them as if they were my own children. A warm berth and a soft life, that's what it shall be, my lord. Anything else?" If he had a tail, Shea thought, it would be wagging.

"That suits me excellently. I place much trust in you, Achates. Half an army's or a fleet's morale lies in the quantity and quality of its wine."

"My lord does me too much honor." He grinned and bowed at the same time.

"My ship goes first," Aeneas said. "The others launch immediately after. A good voyage to you." He turned and strode away.

"I shall not fail you, Lord Aeneas."

Achates straightened up to his full height. Then he glared at the new additions to his crew.

"Oh, this is just what I need! Not bad enough I get the bloody wine ship, but I'm saddled with a couple of layabout foreigners with nothing to do but taste the wine from time to time! Well, I ought to be used to this sort of treatment by now, always 'Achates, fetch my spear' and 'Achates, see if the bulls to be sacrificed are without blemish' and 'Achates, take charge of the wine ship.' Now I ask you: Is that any way to treat a bloody hero? No, it is not!" His half-hysterical rant ceased abruptly and he looked down at the lady who sat next to him. "Isn't that right, dear?"

She paid him no attention, but set her embroidery hoop aside and smiled engagingly. "So you two will be sailing with us? How nice. I'm sure we'll get along famously. I'm Mrs. Achates, but just call me Harmonia."

"Charmed," Chalmers said, taking her hand and kissing it. Achates turned his face aside and made a disgusted sound.

"Where do you want us to stow our belongings?" Shea asked, pro forma since they had almost nothing to stow.

"Let's go find you berths," Harmonia said, standing. She was only a little taller than Shea and Chalmers.

"Listen, you lot," Achates said. "*I* am in charge of this ship!" He punched a forefinger against his bronze-sheathed sternum.

"Yes, love," Harmonia said, not glancing at him. "Now, come aboard, you two. I'm afraid it's going to be awfully crowded for a while." Achates wandered off to bark at some slaves toiling at last-minute sailing preparations. Shea and Chalmers followed the woman up the rickety gangplank.

"Let's see, now," she surveyed the little ship, "his lordship and I have the little hut at the stern, and the slaves will sleep among the amphorae, but nobody has that little decked area up at the bow. Will that suit you?"

"Admirably," Chalmers assured her. Most of the vessel was open, with two small stretches of deck fore and aft. Most of it was given over to cargo space, with an open, pitlike hold that was devoted to the amphorae. The ship was ballasted with sand and the wine jars were stuck by their pointed bottoms into the sand, where they were securely held.

"It won't be as comfortable as the town house in Troy, I'm afraid, but I hope you won't be too distressed." She smiled sunnily, revealing teeth slightly more gapped than her husband's.

"The destruction of your city must have been a terrible shock for you," Chalmers said solicitously.

"Oh, I didn't live there all that long. Dear Achates acquired me when he and his friends sacked my father's citadel. It was a great bother, but that's the way heroes are, you know."

"And what a lucky man he was," Shea said gallantly.

"I've always thought so. Now, dear Mr. Chalmers, will you be making more of that divine wine for us?"

"I fear I cannot," Chalmers said. "There are, let us say, diplomatic reasons that forbid it. But what is left in the amphora I transformed should last a long time, since it can be so heavily diluted."

"Oh, splendid! It was so nice to have the boys pleasantly drunk for a change. And not a trace of hangover afterward! Well, you two make yourselves comfortable. I must go now and undo whatever it is my husband's done."

Like the others, their ship was beautiful but of alarmingly light and flimsy construction. Since the ships were usually dragged up on shore at night, they could not be too heavy.

"It's hard to believe they propose to sail these things all over the Mediterranean," Shea said. "When Aeneas talked about building a fleet, I pictured something like those massive galleys in *Ben Hur*."

"Such ships probably never existed," Chalmers told him, "except perhaps as harbor defense vessels, or specially built craft for storming port defenses. The galleys of antiquity had to be built as light as racing sculls. Even the Roman triremes would look flimsy to modern eyes."

"If you say so."

Trumpets announced the time to sail. The sacrifices were done, the omens taken, and there was nothing left to do but haul the ships down to the water. This was accomplished with a great deal of grunting and groaning, and then the ships were afloat. They ran out oars and assembled a quarter mile offshore and the order was given to hoist sail. Halyards strained, yards rose up the masts, and the sails bellied out with the late-morning breeze. There was a great deal of weeping at this leavetaking, for the refugees knew they would never see their native land again. Slowly, majestically, the fleet began to sail north.

"Why north?" Shea asked. He stood in the bow of the wineship with Chalmers, Achates and Harmonia.

"Why north?" Achates said in a conversational tone. "Why north? Because that's the way the bloody wind's blowing!" By the last word, his voice reached its accustomed shriek. "Perhaps you want us to sail south when the wind's coming from that direction? You want us to defy the gods by sailing against the wind, is that it? That's the way the gods let you know where they want you to go, after all. You raise your sails and they blow you where they want you to go! Oh, I suppose we could be like bloody Agamemnon and sacrifice a princess or two for the wind of our choice, but as it happens we're fresh out of princesses. Lord Aeneas has just the one boy, and he's not about to sacrifice him so that some silly little twit of a foreigner can have a wind that blows from a less southerly direction!" He seemed on the point of collapsing from apoplexy, his face turning scarlet between the cheekplates of his helmet and his horsehair crest quivering with rage.

"Remind me not to ask again," Shea said.

"Lovely day, isn't it?" Harmonia commented.

"Yes, it is, dear, quite," said Achates, perfectly calm.

Their prow divided the water cleanly, sending up twin fans of spray. As they reached the deeper water the color of the sea grew strangely dark, with violet undertones. Shea commented on this phenomenon.

"A holdover from Homer," Chalmers told him. "This is the famous 'wine-dark sea.'" Dolphins frolicked alongside the ship, and occasionally they saw tritons, fishtailed and bearded with seaweed, rise to the surface. Aboard the flagship, they saw Aeneas leaning over the rail to confer with a triton. Apparently, he was asking directions.

That night they hauled their ships ashore, built fires and ate frugally before rolling into their blankets to sleep. The next day they made landfall on a stretch of rolling coastland. Aeneas announced that he would go ashore to test the omens. It looked, he said, like a promising place to found a city.

"Oh, I hope not," Harmonia said. "This is Thrace. The people here are *such* savages." She stayed aboard ship and tended to her embroidery, but Shea and Chalmers went ashore with the rest of the men.

"Thrace?" Shea said. "It didn't take very long to get here."

"This is an epic poem," Chalmers informed him. "It skips over the long, dull stretches."

Slaves manhandled a bull off one of the livestock ships and brought it, protesting, ashore. Aeneas was thumbing the edge of his knife. It was sacrifice time again. Men were piling rocks for an altar.

"You two," Aeneas said, beckoning to Shea and Chalmers. They came running. "We must have a bower for the altar. Today I sacrifice to my divine mother and other gods for their blessing upon a work begun. Go to yonder hillock," he pointed toward the intended terrain feature, "and bring me shoots of cornel and myrtle."

"Aye, aye, sir," Shea said. They tramped up the hillock and stood among the slender saplings.

"Do you know which are cornel and which are myrtle?" Shea asked.

"I doubt that anyone will notice," Chalmers said. "Let's just pull up a few of these and take them to the beach."

Shea stooped and grasped a sapling about a foot from the ground. With both feet braced, he hauled on it. There was a slight, strange give, then, shockingly, a loud groan sounded from beneath the ground.

"What the hell? Reed, what was that?" At that moment Chalmers tugged another sapling, and this brought an even louder groan.

"I think we are dealing with something very bad here," Chalmers said. "I suggest we pass this on to the authorities." They went back to the beach and found Aeneas conferring with his captains.

"My lord," Chalmers said, "we've run into difficulty getting you the wood for the bower."

"Difficulty?" Achates barked. "Is pulling up a few weeds beyond you? I mean, what's the problem? Granted you two are spindly as reeds, but you ought to be up to . . ." Aeneas signaled him to silence.

"These are my wine stewards, old friend. Let them speak."

"Absolutely, m'lord. Perfectly understood."

"When we tried to pull up some saplings," Shea said, "a loud groan came from beneath the ground. It sounded human."

"This is truly an omen," Aeneas said. "Let us go and investigate it." They tramped to the knoll and Aeneas selected a sapling. He pulled one-handed and the sapling came up reluctantly. The groan was alarmingly loud this time. The root tangle came free with a repulsive ripping, popping sound. He held it up for inspection. The root mass was covered with blackish goo and half-congealed blood dripped from it.

"Oooohh, gross!" said someone at the back of the crowd.

Aeneas tried another sapling: same groan, same blood. Being a man who always did things by threes, he tried again: groan, blood, and this time a sob. Then a voice sounded from deep below.

"Is that you, Aeneas?" said the sepulchral voice.

"I know that voice," Aeneas said. "Polydorus?"

"That is who I am, or at least, was. I'm dead now. Priam sent me north with a chest of gold to bribe the king of Thrace to come to Troy's aid. He killed me and took the gold instead. His men pinned me here with spears and the shafts took root."

"What a bastard!" Achates cried.

"That's what I said," Polydorus confirmed.

"That does it," Aeneas said. "You can't ask for a worse omen than this. No city here, by Jupiter. Polydorus, we'll perform all the rites for you and set your shade to rest."

"Much obliged," said the shade.

So the bull was sacrificed to the shade instead of to Venus, a mound was raised over the burial site, and the women were brought ashore for some of their extravagant mourning. When the last libation was poured out, they sailed away.

"Nothing like a good cry to make you feel better," Harmonia said. "Of course, Trojan women have done very little but cry for the last ten years, so I suppose we should be the happiest women in the world. We aren't, for some reason."

The winds took them to the island of Thymbra, where the king received them hospitably but let them know that the island was full up, with no room for new cities. Aeneas went to the local shrine and asked for a sign. There was a minor earthquake and a godly voice, suggesting that Crete might be a nice place to visit. A recent civil war had left plenty of land unoccupied.

So off they went, spreading their sails to whatever breeze the gods decreed. They passed islands that rose dreamlike from the dark sea. Strange creatures came to the shores to gaze on the fleet. Stranger ones glided in the sea beneath their keels.

As it turned out, there was plague in Crete. One night there, as Aeneas slept, his household gods appeared to him and told him that Italy was the place to be. So they packed up, made their sacrifices, and set sail for Italy.

"Italy!" Achates shouted as the mast creaked from an overfilled sail. "Italy! Where in the name of Mercury is bloody Italy? I never heard of the bloody place and that's where we have to head! I mean, why can't the gods just come out and say where they want us to go, instead of sending us all over the bleeding wine-dark sea like a bunch of bloody driftwood?" He began to beat his head against the mast, which did little except put a few new dents in his helmet.

"For once he's making sense," Shea said. "Why don't they just say what they want?"

"It wouldn't be an epic if things were easy," Chalmers assured him.

A few days after Crete they fetched up on an island where herds of cattle and flocks of sheep ran about near the shore unattended. They were out of fresh meat, so the men stormed ashore with bows and spears, whooping after prey. By nightfall, whole carcasses were turning on spits and all were preparing for a feast.

"This is going entirely too well," Shea said. Truer words were never spoken. They were scarcely out of his mouth when something perfectly hideous swooped in from the darkening sky, screeching like souls in purgatory.

"What the hell . . ." Shea ducked as scabby claws scraped his scalp.

A whole flock of winged monsters converged on the roasting meat. They had bodies like vultures but their faces were those of women. Long, forked tongues slashed from their mouths as they tore at the roasting flesh. A horrible smell of decay filled the air.

Achates snatched off his helmet and hurled it to the sand. "Harpies!" he screamed. "We're on the island of the bloody harpies! I give up! I just bloody well give up!"

Equally distraught but even more enraged, the men drew their weapons and flailed wildly at the disgusting creatures. They were unable to inflict a single wound. The harpies were as bulky as large turkeys and looked as ungainly, but they avoided the slashing bronze as easily as if they had been bats. Even the blindingly swift blows of Aeneas were to no avail. The creatures slithered around the blades without nicking a feather, as if they were playing a game. Then they flew away, all but one. The remaining harpy perched on a crag and glared balefully. Shea decided that absolutely nothing in the worlds could glare as balefully as a harpy. This one was even uglier than the others, with the hair and features of an ancient hag.

"Do you know me, mortals?" the thing croaked.

"I know you, Celaeno," Anchises said. "You are wide-famed."

"Know, then, that you have violated our land, slaughtered our beasts, and offered violence to those you have despoiled. For this you have earned my curse."

"Speak on, Celaeno," Aeneas said. As Shea had

come to expect, he offered no excuses. A hero would never do such a thing.

"You seek Italy? You shall find that land, but as punishment for your slaughter of our beasts, you shall not raise the walls of your city until you have suffered deadly famine, a famine that shall make you grind your tables with your teeth! Farewell, Aeneas!" With a parting screech, Celaeno flapped away into the shrouding dark.

"Well, isn't that just ducky?" Achates said, as the last ratty feathers drifted to the ground. "Look at that! I mean, just look!" He held out a hand, palm up, to draw everyone's attention to the roasting meat, as if the awful smell had not already done that for him. "It's honking! Pure rotten from the touch of those foul creatures!" The carcasses had turned a livid purple, and their stench was all but palpable.

"Peace, brave Achates," Aeneas said, sounding to Shea's ears just a touch weary for the first time. "We have more to concern us than some prematurely decayed flesh."

"Excuse me, my lord," Chalmers said. "But all may not be lost."

"Say you so, friend Chalmers?" Aeneas said, his eyebrows going up quizically. "Your prince would be most grateful were you able to temper the evils of this ill-starred evening."

"You recall how I mended the soured wine?" Chalmers said.

"Who could forget it?"

"I may be able to do the same for this decayed flesh."

"Truly?" Aeneas frowned. "But decay is a part of the god-decreed consequence of mortality. May you do this without attracting the disfavor of the gods? No feast is worth such a punishment, as I have just found out."

"I think so," Chalmers said. He held up a finger in pedantic fashion. "Natural decay, as my lord so perspicaciously points out, is a part of mortality. These beasts died for our benefit but a few hours ago. Should they be rotten now? Not so!" There were murmurs of agreement from the crowd. "No, they grew rotten with unnatural swiftness from the touch of unclean creatures. I think I can restore them to their natural condition without violating any divine rules."

"Then work your wonders," Aeneas said, "and earn the further gratitude of your prince."

"Ah, Doc," Shea said as Chalmers made his preparations. "Do you think you can really do this? We're talking about an irrevocable biological process here."

"No, Harold. You keep forgetting that we aren't on our own Earth. There, decay is caused by bacterial action. What those harpies just did to this meat would be utterly unnatural there. This world knows two sorts of decay, and perhaps more. This accelerated, not to say instantaneous, sort, is the type of petty magic that can be easily reversed."

"Easily?" Shea said, an eyebrow slightly raised.

"Well, I think so. First of all, we need a virgin."

"Doc! I'm shocked! They're crazy about sacrificing around here, but even they don't go in for human sacrifice. You don't propose to sacrifice a virgin just to salvage the banquet, do you?"

"Harold, sometimes I question your judgment. No, this is a mere application of sympathetic magic. Surely you remember the principle?"

"Voodoo dolls, right?"

"That is the most familiar example. Things that share certain things in common, characteristics or appearance, have a magical affinity. Believe me, Harold, the young lady will not suffer the slightest damage. And we'll need the local equivalent of extra-virgin olive oil, and some wine from the first pressing."

The oil and wine proved to be no problem, but the virgin was. Not because of a shortage, but because every mother seemed determined that her daughter should be the representative virgin. Shea rejected infants and immature girls. That, it seemed, would be cheating. The girl had to be nubile. The winner was a lovely girl of fourteen, with waist-length, black hair and enormous eyes.

"She'd have been wed by now," her mother said wistfully, "but that awful Diomedes hewed her betrothed asunder."

While the assembly maintained silence, Chalmers took the girl by the hand and led her to one of the carcasses, which still sizzled on its spit, a horrid sight and a worse smell. Shea stood by with the oil and wine. Chalmers raised his face to the skies and intoned:

"Oh, divine Hygeia, also known as Salus, daughter of the splendid Aesculapius and goddess of health, by these tokens of purity, I call upon you to restore this unnaturally corrupted flesh to wholesomeness, for which favor we will raise a shrine in your honor upon this spot, and our prince, the noble Aeneas, will establish your worship in far, barbaric Italy."

He nodded to Shea. Ceremoniously, Shea poured some of the oil onto the carcass, then some of the wine. Chalmers held the girl's hand out toward the carcass.

"Now, my dear, you must touch it."

The girl wrinkled her nose. "Oooohhh! It's nasty!"

"Nevertheless, it is necessary."

With great reluctance, the girl extended her hand, then brushed her fingertips against the flesh for an instant, snatching her hand back as quickly as she could. Little brown fingerprints appeared where her fingers had touched, and the brown swiftly spread over the carcass, eliminating the decayed flesh in less than a minute. Even the rips and gouges made by the harpies had disappeared.

"Aaaaahhhhhh!" went the crowd.

They went from one carcass to another, repeating the ritual. The girl had lost all her reluctance and delighted in all the attention she was getting. Her mother looked fit to burst with pride. Within minutes, all had been restored and the stench of decay had vanished as if it had never been.

There was great rejoicing and congratulation, Chalmers and Shea being on the receiving end of a large amount of back-slapping. This was a perilous thing when the back-slappers were heroes. The interrupted banquet resumed.

With a pleasantly full stomach, Harold took a walk along the beach. The night was graced with a full moon. A few Nereids splashed in the shallows, playing strange music on conch shells. He paused when he saw a bulky figure seated on a rock, chin in hand. Then he recognised Aeneas. The hero seemed uncharacteristically melancholy.

"Is everything all right, m'lord?" Shea asked.

Aeneas noticed him for the first time. "Ah, friend Shea. I cannot thank you enough for salvaging this night's feast. And perhaps my leadership as well."

"Surely the confidence of your followers in your leaderhip is unshaken, my lord!"

"Would that it were so." Aeneas sighed deeply. "But heroes are a fractious lot at the best of times. One can keep their esteem while the favor of the gods holds out, but let the immortals indicate disfavor, and the doubt sets in. Even now, they grumble in discontent, and each thinks himself a worthier leader than I. Why have the gods forsaken me, Harold Shea? Why do they lead me this weary chase instead of speaking forth plainly?"

It was unsettling to see the leader and foremost hero

subject to self-doubt. It was positively un-Homeric. He sought words to comfort a hero. What would such a man find bracing and reassuring in a time of trial? Then he hit upon the perfect formula. He put a hand on the leader's armored shoulder.

"Lord Aeneas," Shea said, "a man's gotta do what a man's gotta do."

Slowly, Aeneas turned his head and looked Shea in the eyes. Even sitting he had to look down slightly.

"A man's gotta . . . say, I like that. Priam himself never said anything wiser." He rose from his rock. "You have done me another great favor, Harold Shea. I shall not forget it." He walked back toward the campsite, whispering to himself. "A man's gotta do what a man's gotta do. A man's gotta . . ."

4

The storm blew for days. At first Shea and Chalmers were terrified that their fragile ship would sink, then they were too seasick to care. The voyage seemed to be lasting forever, and they were no nearer to finding Florimel than when they landed in the *Aeneid*.

From the island of the harpies they had sailed past a whole archipelago of Achaean islands where they dared not put in. Sailing past Ithaca, home of the detested Ulysses, they had jeered and thumbed their noses, but had kept their distance. In one land they visited with some fellow Trojan refugees. Considering the scale of the destruction, it seemed that an inordinate number of survivors had escaped. Chalmers explained that this was due to the Hellenistic fad for tracing every city-state's origins to a Homeric hero. Greece and the eastern Mediterranean were home to the Achaean heroes, so the west had to be settled by fleeing Trojans.

On Sicily they had sighted a whole tribe of cyclopes, including the now-blind Polyphemus himself. In Drepahum they had cremated and buried Anchises, amid much extravagant mourning and sacrifice. It seemed that the old boy was not fated to see his son's new city after all.

In the end, the storm abated and they were down to seven ships. One had been seen foundering but the others, it was hoped, might just be scattered. At last, they made landfall. They were not sure of their location, but it seemed to be somewhere in Libya.

They staggered ashore and hauled up the ships, stern-first, on the sand. Everything they had was drenched, so they emptied the holds and spread their belongings out to dry. Then they flopped wearily onto the beach.

"Achates," Aeneas called out, "start us a fire, will you? Then we must see about a sacrifice."

"You and you," Achates said, pointing in turn to Chalmers and Shea, "go fetch me some kindling." As they gathered twigs and dry grass, they heard him muttering to himself. "Give us a fire, Achates. Must be all I'm good for. Could've told any slave to do this, but no, we must have good old Achates to fix us up a fire, mustn't we? Just because his mother's a goddess . . ." and so on. The fact was, Achates had an uncanny knack with flint and steel (another advantage, Chalmers pointed out, of being in a Virgilian, rather than an Homeric, epic. You couldn't get a fire started with flint and bronze.) With the kindling gathered, Achates had a flame going quicker than the Americans could have accomplished with a Zippo.

"Achates," Aeneas called.

Achates muttered, "Now what the bloody hell does he want?" but aloud he said, "Yes, my lord?"

"Fetch my bow and arrows. We must find some food before these people starve. And send someone out to get us some sacrificial beasts. We need a white goat and a black one."

"At once, my lord." Achates smiled. "That's more like it. A bit of hunting, just dear Prince Aeneas and his beloved companion Achates. You noticed he didn't ask any of the others to go with him, didn't you, dear?"

"I noticed, love," Harmonia said, already at work on her damp embroidery.

"You two," Achates once again pointed to Shea and Chalmers, "have been lying about too long. Go find us a white goat and a black one."

"Goats?" Shea said, instantly regretting it.

"Oh, yes, goats. You know what goats are, don't you? Wooly things? Bad smell? Go 'bleat'? Two of them, eh? One white, one black? Is that difficult? I mean, IS THAT SO BLOODY DIFFICULT?" Achates' raging shriek caused pebbles to fall from a nearby bluff.

"Got you, boss," Shea said hastily.

"Now where are we going to find a white goat and a black one?" Shea asked when the two were gone.

"I suppose we could go searching in the hills," Chalmers said despondently. "Wild goats seem to thrive everywhere. I might be able to come up with a magical lure."

"Oh, sit down, you two," Harmonia said. "Just relax for a while. Look around you. This is inhabited country. You can see fields and vineyards from here. Sooner or later a goatherd will come along and we'll just buy a pair from him. Half a jar of wine will buy as fine a pair as you could ask for in the colors of your choice, with a couple of pounds of goat cheese thrown in."

"How eminently sensible," Chalmers said, collapsing cross-legged to the sand. Shea sat beside him.

"Now, dear Mr. Chalmers, tell me what has you so despondent. After all, things could be worse. You might have been on one of the ships that foundered or was lost. We might have fetched up on a hostile shore, or one inhabited by monsters. Really, things aren't so bad."

"I know," Chalmers said, "but we've been searching for Florimel for so long, and so far we've found no trace of her."

"Florimel?" Harmonia said. "Is that a woman?"

"The most beautiful woman in the world," Chalmers averred.

"Well, it's not a good idea to set your heart too keenly on one woman. That's what poor Prince Paris did, and look what happened to Troy because of that!"

"But Florimel is my wife," Chalmers said.

"Oh, that's different. It's all right to put yourself out a bit for a wife. How did you happen to misplace her? Did Achaean pirates carry her off?"

"Not exactly," Chalmers said.

"Well, don't lose heart. I'm sure you'll find her. We keep running into old friends from Troy, so there's no reason why you shouldn't find your wife."

They spent a couple of hours unsouring and desalinating wine that had gotten contaminated with seawater during the storm, and by the end of the job, Chalmers was restored to cheerfulness.

"You're looking better, Doc," Shea said.

"I think Harmonia is right. These epics always involve a great deal of coincidence, and people are always reencountering each other after long separations and in unlikely places. We may just have fallen into the odd logic of ancient storytelling."

A horn blew and they looked up to see the hunters returning with the makings for dinner. Achates carried three dead stags and Aeneas four, a stag for each ship. These they dumped on the beach to be dressed, skinned and cooked by the slaves. Then they came walking toward the wine ship.

"Heads up, Doc," Shea said. "Here comes the boss."

"My friends," Aeneas addressed them, "during our hunt we encountered an adventure that was passing strange." He was not winded, despite the half-ton or so of stag he had just been carrying.

"Strange adventures often fall the lot of heroes," Chalmers observed.

"That is so," Aeneas said. "For on our hunt we met with my mother."

"The goddess Venus?" Chalmers said.

"Exactly. She appeared to us in the guise of a huntress, with bow and high-laced boots. She told us that this land belongs to a new city called Carthage. Its ruler is the daughter of the king of Tyre, Dido by name."

"Dido," Achates snorted. "What sort of name is that? Dido! It isn't a name. It sounds like one of those indecent objects that pack of sleazy Phoenician merchants tried to sell to us!"

"Peace, Achates," Aeneas said.

"Sorry, my lord."

"Anyway, friend Chalmers, I would see this city and perhaps look upon its Queen. But I would prefer to accomplish this unseen. Have you a spell for this?"

"Hmmmmm," Chalmers pondered. "I haven't attempted a spell of invisibility in this world . . . that is to say, since coming from the Orient. However, if you will give me leave to think upon the problem, I believe I can come up with something!"

"Very good. We shall feast upon stag-flesh, then I shall call upon you again." He turned to go examine the altar his slaves had erected. As soon as Aeneas was away, Achates gave them a beady eye.

"Where are those goats?"

"Here they are, dear," came Harmonia's cheery voice. A group of local villagers had come to the shore to trade with the newcomers. Harmonia came from the impromptu market leading two goats, one white and one black. "A lovely pair of prime billies, ripe as ancient cheese." She handed the lead ropes to her husband. "Now run along and give these to Lord Aeneas, love. He has his knife out already."

"All right," Achates said stiffly. "If you want to do these lowborn rascals' work for them, you won't catch me complaining about it." He stalked off, tugging the reluctant goats behind him.

"Can you do it, Doc? Invisibility is a pretty subtle business."

"I believe so. Invisibility occurs a number of times in the Greek myths. The helmet of Mercury confers it, for instance. Harmonia, would you happen to have a mirror you can bear to part with? A cheap one would be adequate. Ideal, in fact."

"I'm sure I have." She threw open a chest and rummaged around in its contents. "Aha!" She withdrew a flat disk of bronze with a wooden handle. "It's gone all dingy, but I could polish it up."

"Perfect," Chalmers said. "I'm afraid I'll have to damage it a little, but it should be repairable."

"Not to worry, love. Dear Achates will find me a really good one next time he sacks a village."

The afternoon was given over to gorging on stag-meat washed down with watered wine. Then everyone stretched out and took a much-needed siesta. About three o'clock, had there only been clocks, Aeneas' son shook Shea and Chalmers awake.

"My father wants to know if you have your spell ready," he said.

"I have. Tell your father we shall join him momentarily, Ascanius."

"My father says I'm to be called Julus from now on," the boy informed them. He ran back to his father, who was donning his most splendid armor.

"Why would Aeneas change his son's name?" Shea asked.

"Names were frequently changed to acknowledge some crucial event, such as the founding of a new city. But the real reason is that Virgil was writing propaganda for his patron, Augustus."

"Propaganda?"

"Yes. After the civil wars, everyone wanted stable, settled government. Augustus, née Gaius Octavius, derived his legitimacy from his adoptive father, Julius Caesar. The Julian family traced its ancestry to Julus, the son of Aeneus, and thence to the goddess Venus. In Troy, the boy was called Ascanius. In Italy, he was, or rather will be, Julus." A look of enlightenment came over Chalmers' face. "That's it!"

"That's what?" Shea asked.

"Remember how I said that Aeneas looked familiar? Now I remember. He looks just like the portrait busts of Julius Caesar!"

"Whatever are you two babbling about?" Harmonia asked.

"Just sorcerer talk," Shea assured her. "Come on, Doc. The boss is getting impatient." They hurried over to where Aeneas and Achates stood.

"My lord," Chalmers said, "with a day or two to work on it, I could probably come up with a more efficient spell. As it is, my companion and I must go along with you to keep the spell working."

"I could not ask for doughtier or more loyal attendants," Aeneas said.

"Oh, bugger!" Achates murmured.

"What was that, Achates?"

"I said, 'oh, wonderful,' my lord."

"Excellent. Chalmers, work your enchantment."

Chalmers took the disk of thin bronze, now polished to reflective brilliance, in both hands. "Oh Helios, whose rays illuminate the world with incomparable beauty and glory, hear my supplication. As I bend this light-glancing mirror, so, I pray you, bend your rays around us four, so that they pass by us, never rebounding to strike the eyes of observers." Slowly, he bent the mirror until it formed a discoid half-circle. He then held it by the handle as it shimmered for a while, then became oddly opaque, as if it neither reflected nor absorbed light.

"Ready, my lord?" Chalmers said.

"Is that all?" Aeneas said. "I feel no different, and I see the three of you quite clearly."

"Yet we four," Chalmers told him, "who stand within the radius of my spell, are quite invisible to anyone outside the circle."

"Then let us go forth to look upon Carthage," Aeneas ordered.

The journey was not a long one. They passed through a brief stretch of fields and woods, then up to a rocky ridge line. From the top of the ridge, they looked down upon a spectacular scene: Below them, a great city was under construction. A girdling wall stood more than man-height, its defensive towers risen to twenty feet or more as wagons brought cut quarry blocks to raise them higher. Houses and temples stood already roofed, and men were digging away at a vast, semicircular foundation where soon a theater would rise. All around the new city, fields were under the plow and vineyards being laid out. It was a scene of beelike industry.

"Now *that's* how to build a city!" Aeneas said with awestruck admiration.

"Never be a match for dear Ilium," Achates said, wiping away a nostalgic tear.

They descended the ridgeline and entered the cultivated land. Everywhere, colonists were planting crops and orchards, but no one saw the strangers as they passed. Dogs sniffed the air and barked in bewilderment.

They walked through the wide gateway and into the city, where the sound of chisel on stone and hammer on nail assailed them from every direction. Huge ox-drawn carts rumbled and squealed by on ungreased axles, carrying building materials or hauling away excavated earth. In the center of the city a grove had been planted, and in the middle of the grove was a lofty temple, nearer than the other public buildings to completion. Its doors were of massive bronze. Through the doors they went, and into the vast, echoing interior.

The interior walls were completely carved with scenes in low relief, painted in realistic colors. Most of them appeared to be battle scenes.

"By Jupiter!" Aeneas said. "It's the Trojan War!"

"Word sure does get around," Shea commented. In accordance with the compressed time frame of epic verse, the whole story of the siege of Troy was depicted, from the judgment of Paris to the abduction of Helen, all the battles that followed, culminating with the wooden horse being dragged into the city.

"Here I am!" Aeneas cried. "I'm squaring off with Achilles. I was just about to chuck a rock at him when Father Poseidon of the sea-blue hair yanked me out of the fight."

"Just when you were about to squash him, too, m'lord!" Achates said.

"Yes, it was a pity. The old boy meant well, though." They continued to wander around admiring the decorations, like tourists in a museum.

"I don't see me anyplace," Achates said, disappointed.

From outside came a sound of music. Someone was playing harps and flutes, gently thumping on tambourines and rattling sistrums. Shea looked out through the doors and saw a gaily clad procession making its way up the broad ceremonial avenue through the grove toward the temple.

"Company, boss." Shea called out. Aeneas came to join him by the door.

"I think the queen comes, with her court," Aeneas said. "She may wish to sacrifice, or perhaps she will hold court here, since this stately temple befits royal majesty."

"And has a roof," Shea pointed out.

"Let us retire to yonder corner," Aeneas said, "and all invisible observe this queen, to see if she is wise and just, as well as beautiful."

Shea had not spotted Dido yet, but Aeneas seemed to be in no doubt that she would be beautiful. In the age of heroes, queens were always beautiful.

First up the steps and into the temple were the musicians. These were the sort of youths and maidens who always seemed to liven up the festivities at these affairs. You never saw a paunchy, middle-aged musician. After them came girls scattering flower petals. Then the Queen entered, followed by her court. She was almost as tall as Aeneas, with the sort of regal bearing that made crowns and regalia superfluous. Her hair was midnight black and her flawless complexion was tawny. This, Shea thought, must be how Virgil pictured Tyrian royalty. Behind her came her court, mostly dark men and women in vaguely eastern-looking robes. Chalmers gasped and gripped his arm.

"Yes, she's a looker, all right," murmured Shea.

"Look!" Chalmers strangled out, pointing. Amid the dusky pulchritude of Dido's ladies-in-waiting was a willowy fair brunette, spectacularly beautiful but tiny by comparison with the heroically scaled competition.

"Florimel!" Shea said.

"Be still!" Achates hissed.

"But that's my wife!" Chalmers protested.

"The queen?" Aeneas said.

"No, the pale one!"

"Ssshhhhhh!"

Some of the courtiers were looking around, trying to find out where the odd sounds were coming from. Slaves brought in a portable dais and a carved throne and set them up. The dais they draped with a huge, gold-embroidered purple cloth. The throne was covered with lynx and leopard skins. Dido mounted the dais and seated herself on the throne. Ranged near her were her advisers and courtiers. Just behind the throne stood the ladies of the court. A chamberlain thumped on the floor with his staff.

"The glorious, beauteous, and most sagacious Queen Dido of Carthage holds court! Let all who have business before Queen Dido come forward with humility, and you shall be heard." He thumped the staff three more times and stood aside.

Before any supplicants came forward, Dido reeled off a list of the next day's work assignments, both agricultural and construction-oriented, from mixing the mortar to sweeping up the refuse in the evening.

"She's not even using notes," Shea said. Chalmers was too agitated to care.

Next she dealt with the division of property among her nobles and freemen; then she assigned military duties and training schedules. Then she entertained supplications. First to come forward was a man of expensive clothing and pompous demeanor. Gold and jewels winked all over his hands and arms.

"Most gracious Queen Dido," the man intoned. "I come once more to press the suit of my royal master, King Iarbas, that splendid chieftain who was so smitten with your beauty and majesty that his generous heart was touched and he was more than anxious to part with this land upon which your nascent city now rises in glory." He bowed deeply.

"The esteem in which I hold King Iarbas," Dido said, "is so boundless that the immortal gods themselves could never set limits upon it. However, I have consulted closely with my augurs and they assure me that the time has not yet come for me to marry. Assure your royal master and my friend, fabulous King Iarbas, that, when I find that my time to wed has come, his suit shall be among the first to which I give serious consideration."

"Your majesty is too kind," the envoy said, bowing deeply and gritting his teeth. He backed his way out of the temple, bowing all the way.

"I'll cuddle up to a leper before I crawl into that old goat's bed!" Dido said. The court laughed heartily. "Who's next?" An official came forward.

"Your majesty, we have a little problem. Several shiploads of lost mariners have shown up on our coast. We tried to drive them back, but they keep swarming in. If they were raiding we'd just kill them, but they insist they just need a place to stay. Their own home has been destroyed, they claim."

"Refugees?" Dido said, exasperated. "I just get a kingdom off the ground, and now I'm supposed to take in *refugees*? Do they think I have land for all of them? Where will they find jobs?" She fumed for a few minutes, during which nobody said anything. Then: "Where do they come from?"

"Troy," the official said.

Dido slapped her forehead. "Wonderful! Just great! Not only do I get refugees, but the most gilt-edged wanderers in the whole Mediterranean show up on my doorstep. Now if I send them away, everybody will say that heartless Dido was cruel to poor, homeless

Trojans!" She fumed a while longer. "On, well, let's have a look at them."

The crowd parted and a large group of tattered, bedraggled men and women entered the temple. They clearly had not been eating well for some time, but they bore themselves with dignity. In the forefront were several men of the heroid class.

"Antheus!" Achates whispered. "And Sergestus!"

"And there are Cloanthus and brave Ilioneus!" said Aeneas. "Our lost ships are safe!"

Dido's heart seemed to melt at the sight of the stalwart supplicants, and the women who carried or led wide-eyed children.

"Speak, Trojans," Dido said.

One came forward. "Majesty, I am Ilioneus. Since Priam's peerless city fell to the stratagems of wily Ulysses, we have sailed Poseidon's watery domain, seeking a new home promised by the gods. The noble Aeneas was our leader, but we lost him in a great tempest. Whether he and the others dwell yet above ground, or below with the shades, we know not. We crave your favor, Queen Dido. If we cannot abide here, I beg you do not drive us forth untimely, but allow us a little while to repair and rebuild our ships. Allow us provisions sufficient to keep life in our bodies, so that we may sail to Italy, there to seek noble Aeneas. And if he be dead, perhaps king Acestis of Sicily, who is of Trojan blood, will allow us to become his subjects."

Dido sighed. "Fear not, Trojans. It is not in my heart to drive forth people who are both brave and bereft. If it is your wish to continue your voyage, I will give you all you need. If you would rather abide here, lands shall be found for you." There was wild applause from the court at this generosity.

"That's what I wanted to hear!" Aeneas said. "Chalmers, disinvisiblize us!"

Chalmers took the mirror between his hands and slowly straightened it. As he did, it lost its strange opacity until it reflected normally, although it had a slight ripple in the middle. Aeneas strode forward superbly, closely followed by Achates. Towering above the crowd, he went through the throng like a warship through an enemy battleline.

Dido noticed the commotion. "Now what?" Then she saw the man coming toward her. "Ooh, who's this?" She reached up and patted the hair at the nape of her neck.

"Hey, it's Aeneas!" shouted Antheus.

"Yes, Queen Dido. I am Aeneas Anchisiades, late a prince of far-famed Troy. The gods, ever mindful of the son of Venus, have cast me here, upon the shores of the beloved and most bounteous queen of Carthage."

"What a terrible time you must have had," Dido said. She smiled, a gleam in her eye, and patted the broad seat next to her. "You just come sit right here and tell me all about it."

Chalmers hurried over to the gaggle of court ladies, Shea close at his heels. He and Florimel embraced noisily amid the scandalized stares of the others.

"It's okay, they're married," Shea assured them. "Long separation, many hair-raising adventures before being reunited, that sort of thing."

"You're one of Lord Aeneas' men?" a lady asked.

"We've followed him since Troy," Harold said.

"He's a knockout!" the woman gushed.

"I just adore a man in shiny armor," said another one. "There's something about bronze that makes me go all quivery."

"Is he married?" asked a third.

"He's a widower," Shea informed them.

"Eligible!" they all cooed. Apparently, husbands of suitable bloodline were in short supply hereabout.

Chalmers and Florimel had not yet emerged from their clinch.

"So your Queen is unmarried as well?" Shea asked.

"She was. Her husband was Acerbas," said the lady with a thing about bronze. "But her brother, Pygmalion, murdered Acerbas, and that's why she had to flee. We went to Cyprus first, then we came here to Libya."

Shea was beginning to form a picture of the Mediterranean world in the heroic age as a sort of perpetual gang war combined with a mass migration of okies, everyone alternately murdering each other and looking for the promised land.

"How did Lady Florimel happen to be among you?" Shea asked.

"We were just getting the city started," said the first lady. "Queen Dido was about to consecrate the boundaries of the city and she'd just cut a bull's throat and asked Minerva for a sign, when Florimel popped out of thin air and plopped right down into the blood. You should have seen the look on her face! Well, her majesty took this as the best sort of omen. She's so cute and tiny and fair that Dido adopted her as a pet."

Shea tapped Chalmers on the shoulder. "Uh, Doc? Doc?" He gave up. "I won't be able to pry those two apart with a crowbar for a while."

He wandered around the temple until Dido announced an official court banquet to be prepared that evening. With her arm linked firmly into Aeneas', she led them to the sprawling palace complex, where she assigned quarters for all the better-born newcomers. Achates was dispatched, moaning and grumbling, to fetch the highborn refugees from the ships while abundant provisions were sent out for the rest of the crews.

The banquet was lavish, and Dido stuck to Aeneas like glue throughout, feeding him tidbits with her own royal fingers. Chalmers and Florimel had at last come up for air, and Shea was able to get some of her story at last.

"It does so embarrass me to own my foolish vaporings," she told him, "but in my silly vanity I thought I had mastered my dearest Reed's magical equations, and thought to try some small faring to test my new skill. Imagine my chagrin when I found myself in a world I knew not—and then in another, and then in another still until finally I discover myself sitting in a great mess of bull's blood and surrounded by . . ." Florimel gestured vaguely at those around her.

"Must've been a shock," Shea opined.

"Howbeit, I was most fortunate in my place of landing, for Queen Dido has been most gracious. She is a most capable Queen, but her land suffers from a shortage of heroes. A hero is something like a knight, but there is no ceremony to dub a hero. When people spoke of the war in Troy, I knew that my knowledge of this world was not utterly wanting, for who has not heard of Troy, of brave Hector and wrathful Achilles? But soon I knew that this was but one of the manyfold worlds, for all knew the name of Troilus, son of Priam, but none had heard of his ladylove, Criseyde."

"Yes, she was a medieval creation," Chalmers said, "well known by the time of the *Orlando*."

"Well, this is all very interesting," Shea said. "But now we're all reunited and it's time to make our way home. This is a fine party, but I'm really craving a decent salad, a scotch and soda, a hot fudge sundae and the company of my beloved Belphebe, not necessarily in that order. And what kind of story can I give her for why I'm so late?"

"If you tell her all that has happened since we left," Chalmers advised, "by the time you get to the end of it she shall have forgotten why she was angry in the first place."

"I so look forward to seeing her too," Florimel said, "and returning to a world which, although dull and full of unpleasant smells, has little of the savagery and uncertainty of this, and where animals are slaughtered decently, out of sight, instead of wherever people happen to be when they wish the favor of their heathen gods." She cast fond eyes toward the head of the table, where Dido was casting fond eyes toward Aeneas. "And my lady Dido will soon wed Lord Aeneas, and they shall dwell happily here, raising a dynasty to rule Carthage."

Chalmers looked much abashed. "Well, ah, my dear, you see, that isn't going to happen."

"And wherefore not? It seems written in the stars, for these two match one another marvelous well."

"I am afraid," Chalmers told her, "that there's a tradition in classical mythology of heroes treating women very shabbily. Theseus and Ariadne, Jason and Medea, these are typical. Sad to say, Aeneas and Dido follow the same pattern."

She looked at him darkly. "Pray what becomes of them?"

"They live happily here for a while, but it is the destiny of Aeneas to found Rome. His followers urge him to leave her and go on to Italy. Naturally the gods join in, and he abandons her."

Now Florimel was glowering. "And does she weep a while, then dry her tears, console herself that Aeneas was not a mete husband for her, and find one worthier?"

"No, no. . . ." Chalmers stammered, unable to look her in the eye. "Actually, she stabs herself and dies slowly from a sucking chest wound."

"Damn! I'd forgotten that," Shea said.

"I forbid it!" Florimel said. "She has been too kind to me. I shall not allow her to suffer so ignoble a fate!"

"Hey, don't blame Reed," Shea said. "This is Virgil's doing."

"I care not," Florimel said. "If there be a world where Troilus hath his Criseyde, and another where he hath her not, then there may be a world wherein Queen Dido does not slay herself over a vagabond with the face and form of a god and the brain of a dung-beetle."

"You know, Doc," Shea observed, "that sounds like one of your syllogisms."

"Why, yes, it does! And it may just be valid. If we effect an alteration in this continuum, allowing Dido to live and continue her reign in Carthage, then we shall merely have brought about an alternate *Aeneid*, among many possible *Aeneids*. And this one may have existed!"

"What do you mean?"

"Virgil is known to have torn up early drafts of his epic. This could be one of his earlier versions. In fact, as Virgil was dying, he dictated in his will that the *Aeneid*, and all other works he hadn't had a chance to polish, were to be destroyed. Fortunately, Augustus forbade any such thing and rescued it, along with lesser works."

"You mean," Shea said, "that it's possible Virgil wrote a version where a couple of weird Orientals showed up, saved the wine and the banquet contaminated by harpies, and concocted a spell of invisibility for Aeneas?"

"Even epic poems need comic relief," Chalmers assured him.

"And to think," Shea said, "we may have ended up in a first century, b.c., wastebasket."

"If we pull this off," Chalmers said, "we may even be doing a future Rome a favor."

"How's that?" Shea asked.

"As Dido dies, she curses the departing Trojans, calling upon her own descendants to savage the descendants of Aeneas. The ancient Romans believed Hannibal to be descended from Dido."

5

"It is a disaster," Florimel wailed. "I tried to tell the queen that this Trojan would be a poor choice for king of Carthage. I urged upon her that his mother is Venus, and the antipathy between Venus and her own goddess, Juno, is widely famed. She was vexed and waxed most wroth with me. She did call in her sister, the Princess Anna, and asked her advice. Anna did say that Carthage is surrounded by enemies and while rich in artisans and husbandmen, it is poor in warriors, while the martial valor of the Trojans is renowned throughout the world. Then Anna urged withal that Carthaginian industry wed to Trojan valor would make her both safe and great. Even now, the sisters go to every nearby shrine, sacrificing ewes and rams, heifers and flawless bullocks, seeking the favor and advice of the gods."

"Anna has the hots for Ilioneus. I've seen her mooning after him." Shea took a sip of the new vintage. "It doesn't look promising."

"These intemperate passions seldom last long," Chalmers said.

"The question is, which will run out first: the passion or the livestock?"

"And that is not all!" Florimel said. "The Queen no longer takes any interest in the building of her city, whereof before she was so diligent in care. No longer do the walls rise, no longer do the young men drill upon the common in warlike exercise. But rather have all caught their sovereign's strange lassitude, and while away their days like lovesick swains."

"I thought things seemed awfully quiet," Shea said. "I was getting used to all that hammering and sawing."

"She's like the queen bee in a hive," Chalmers said. "Everything centers upon her. When she is busy, they're busy. When she acts like an infatuated schoolgirl, so do they. This is more serious than I had thjought."

"Do you see divine intervention here?" Shea asked. "After all, Aeneas's mother is the goddess of love. Could this be her work?"

"I don't doubt it," Chalmers said. "Actually, Venus was a fertility goddess. Romantic love was the business of her son, Cupid. No doubt she put him up to this. It's been too long since I last studied the poem, I no longer remember the details, but as I recall it's all some sort of power play between the gods that favor Italy, and those who want Carthage to rule."

"You just can't get away from politics," Shea complained. "How shall we handle this?"

"We don't want to fall afoul of any more gods," Chalmers told him. Still . . ." He fingered his chin and took on an abstracted expression. " . . . this lovesickness is inflicted by Cupid's arrows, therefore it must in some way be analogous with a toxin. The very word toxin is derived from the Greek *toxicon* 'of the bow.' Therefore, an antitoxin may be efficacious."

"Love is not a poison!" Florimel protested. "it is the pure emotion of the knight, the troubador or the goodly clerk for the lady he worships."

"Preferably somebody else's wife," Chalmers said. "Anyway, this is a very specialized sort of love, deliberately inflicted by the gods and almost always for a bad purpose."

"Right," Shea said. "Considering what she's in for, Dido really needs to be cured of this passion."

The chamberlain appeared at the door of the suite the three now shared. He rapped importantly with his staff, even though they were less than ten feet away.

"Her Majesty, Queen Dido," he droned, "requires the attendance of the foreign sorcerers, Reed Chalmers and Harold Shea, at her sacrifice in the temple of Poseidon."

"She wants us *as sorcerers*," Chalmers muttered. "This sounds ominous."

"It's a chance to gain some leverage," Shea told him. "Let's make the best of it."

They brushed their sandals and Florimel fussed over their tunic seams, straightening them and picking off bits of lint. "Thou need'st a haircut, my love," she told Chalmers.

When they were presentable, they hurried to the temple of Neptune. This was an imposing structure near the harbor, its walls faced with polished marble and its bronze roof gilded, with sculpted Nereids and tritons tootling conch shells from every corner. They mounted the broad steps and entered.

Inside, the air was heavy with incense smoke that billowed from bronze tripods full of coals. Huge garlands of flowers draped the walls and heaps of petals all but obscured the floor. The queen stood before a massive altar carved from rich porphyry. Surrounding the altar were men in long, striped robes wearing pointed caps. They looked decidedly downcast. Dido and her sister, Anna, flanked a massive bull. The animal was covered with garlands and festal wreaths and was even chewing on one.

"Oh, no," Shea said. "I hate this!"

"Come you here, my guests," Dido said imperiously.

"What would you have of us, my lady?" Chalmers asked.

"These soothsayers of mine," she indicated the glowering men in striped robes, "can avail me nothing. They've gotten so they can't tell a liver from a spleen! I need to know that the gods favor my marriage to Aeneas, that noble prince of Troy. I need to know that he loves me and no other and will dwell here with me in Carthage forever!" Obviously, the Queen was going to entertain no doubts.

"Your majesty," Shea said, "in our land we have a special spell to determine this. You see, no bull is necessary. All you need is a daisy."

"A daisy?" the queen said.

"Yes. You pull off the petals in succession, reciting the formula: 'He loves me, he loves me not. He loves me, he loves me not. He . . .'"

"That," Dodo said coldly, "is not sufficient to attract the attention of the Olympian deities. Now attend me." She addressed Chalmers. "I want you to read the liver of this bull for me. Tell me what the great Neptune thinks of my destiny. I must know if he approves of my nuptial plans."

An attendant handed her a knife and she nodded to her sister. Anna raised a hammer suitable for pounding railroad spikes and brought it down on a spot midway between horns and eyes. Shea and Chalmers closed their eyes as the crunch echoed through the temple. They opened them in time to see Dido cut the unfortunate beast's throat, sending a foaming torrent of blood to splatter everyone near and puddle around their feet. Some of it swirled down the drain in front of the altar.

The bull collapsed, and attendants held up the legs on its upper side. With a single, practiced sweep of her knife, Dido opened it from throat to tail. A great mass of viscera came tumbling out onto the floor. Shea and Chalmers turned pale and tried not to gag too loudly.

"Brace up, Doc," Shea said when he was in control of his esophagus. "We always knew those steaks and hamburgers came from someplace really unpleasant."

Dido handed her knife to an attendant. Another stood by with a bronze model of a beef liver, its bumps and valleys labeled for convenience in taking the haruspices. It was a sort of religio-medical reference for soothsayers.

"Now get that liver and interpret it for me," Dido ordered.

Chalmers took a deep breath and waded into the quivering mass of hawserlike intestines and began sorting through the ghastly mess, pushing aside the still-gurgling stomach chambers, lifting the twitching heart out of his way, at last emerging with the slippery purple liver in both hands. An assistant priest deftly snipped a few tubes and membranes to free the organ from the body cavity, sending decorative arcs of blood, bile and gall in several directions. Chalmers seemed about to faint, but Shea grasped his elbow.

"Just keep breathing through your mouth and tell her what she wants to hear, Doc."

They stumbled their way clear of the disgusting tangle and found a spot of dry floor where they could examine their trophy. Slaves heaped more incense onto the braziers to help kill the smell. The queen and her sister stood unself-consciously dripping with gore as attendants plied mops around their feet.

Chalmers raised the weighty organ toward the altar. "O great Neptune of the Sea-blue hair, Earthshaker, god of horses, of seafaring Tyrians and horse-taming Trojans, hear the prayer of gracious Dido! How rests your mind upon the question of a royal marriage of Carthage and Troy? Shall Queen Dido wed noble

Aeneas, and abide with him here until dread death darkens the eyes of them both?"

There was stillness for a moment, then the liver in Chalmers' hands began to wobble, wriggle and writhe. A collective gasp of horror went up from the assembly as the gelid mass bulged and put out pseudopods, shaping itself into something that began to resemble a human head. Tendrils of liver sprouted all over it to form hair and beard. A beaklike nose divided the face and lids opened to reveal livery eyeballs. The stern mouth gave the expression "liverlips" new meaning. When complete, the glaring portrait bust was stern and intimidating.

"But that isn't Neptune!" gasped a priest. "That is his terrible brother, divine Pluto!"

Dido bowed and covered her head with a fold of her gown. "Dread lord of the nether world, we were expecting a sign from Neptune!"

"And what am I, chopped liver? You wanted a sign, didn't you? Of course, if you really don't want to hear what I have to say . . ."

"By no means, my lord!" Dido babbled out. "It is just that I was not prepared to speak with a chthonic deity! I haven't performed the proper rites and . . ."

"Think nothing of it. Now hear me! You are under no circumstances to wed this peripatetic Trojan. The gods have other plans for you both. Even as we speak, he follows the counsels of the Olympians, to sail for Italy, there to found a kingdom for his son, Julus. You must abide in Carthage, and begin a glorious dynasty of your own blood. Forget about him! I, Pluto of the underworld, brother to Neptune and Jupiter, have spoken!" The head collapsed into multilobed shapelessness and Chalmers dropped it to land on the mosaic floor with a resounding splat.

Dido collapsed on the floor, sobbing. Her sister put a comforting arm across her shoulders and priests helped her to her feet. Then a slave ran into the temple.

"Your Majesty! Bold Aeneas sets sail for Italy! He sends word that Mercury, messenger of the gods of Olympus, came to him and bade him fare forth without delay. He sends you his gratitude and affection, but he requests that you not seek to detain him here."

"That's a lot of gall!" Princess Anna said indignantly. "Does he really think the queen will beg him to stay?"

"Even now," the slave said, "his ships leave the harbor."

With a stricken expression, Dido strode toward the entrance of the temple, the rest hurrying behind her. Last of all came Shea and Chalmers.

"Doc," Shea said, "was that really Pluto? Or was it a trick of yours?"

"Honestly, Harold, even I am not certain. But I will never, *never* eat liver again!"

Outside, they found the queen weeping. In the harbor, the black ships were under oars, making for the open sea. Some had already hoisted their sails, for the gods had thoughtfully provided a favorable wind. Many of the women sniffled at the sight of so many prospective heroic husbands getting away.

Slowly, Dido turned and began to walk toward the palace. Her escort joined her in mourning. After a while, they tried to cheer her up.

"After all," said Anna, "we haven't sent out the invitations yet."

At the palace she dismissed them all except Chalmers and Shea. "Tarry here with me a while," she said. Then she took her seat on the purple throne.

"How may we serve you, Your Majesty?" Chalmers asked.

"You come from afar, and you may see the will of the gods without the fear and favoritism of my own priests. Tell me truly: Was this for the best?"

"Assuredly, Queen Dido," Chalmers said. "It is Aeneas' destiny to found a city that will one day be Rome."

"Rome?" she said.

"That's what they will call it. You are well rid of him."

She nodded sadly. "Aye. That may be so."

"Your Majesty," Shea said, hesitantly, "you won't do anything ... rash, will you? I know this has been a blow, but you'll get over it."

She looked up at him. "You mean I'm not to kill myself?"

"Well, uh, yes."

She sat back, her hands gripping the lion heads of the armrest. "Do you know how I happen to own this city?"

"Actually, I'm not really clear on that," Shea admitted.

She leaned forward. "When we arrived here, refugees like the Trojans, I went to King Iarbas and asked to buy land. He agreed to sell me as much land as could be encompassed by an ox hide. Then in his contempt he tossed me the hide. I swallowed my pride and agreed to his price, much to his surprise. His mistake was in using the word 'encompassed' rather than 'covered.' I spent days cutting that hide into a single, continuous string and with that string I marked the boundary of my new city."

"That was very sagacious, Your Majesty," Chalmers said.

"Many have thought so. King Iarbas has not ceased pestering me since with his suit of marriage. Now tell me," she looked from one of them to the other. "Do you think that I am the sort of queen who would kill herself and leave her beloved nation without a sovereign just because a footloose adventurer tossed her over for a country of his own?"

"Assuredly, you are far too wise for that," Chalmers said.

"So I am." She cupped her chin in a palm and pondered for a minute, then she rose and walked to a broad balcony that opened off the throne room.

"Everybody back to work!" yelled Queen Dido. Immediately, the sound of hammer, saw, and chisel resumed. She turned back to them. "You may go now." Shea and Chalmers bowed their way out of the throne room.

Florimel almost fainted when she saw them. "You look horrible!"

"We had a run-in with a god and a liver," Shea told her. "Aeneas is gone, Dido isn't going to kill herself, and we don't have time to take a bath. Let's get out of here. Just a second while I get my sword."

Chalmers took a parchment from a table. "This has the equations I've been working on. If I can recite them with perfect precision, I believe they will return us to our own world. Come on." He placed the parchment on the floor. They sat cross-legged around it, holding hands.

"By the harp of Homer and the stylus of Archimedes," Chalmers intoned, "by the shape-shifting magic of Proteus and the logic of Zeno; by the arts of the Muses and the mathematics of Pythagoras; I call upon you Olympians to witness that granting the existence of P and likewise that of Q, then P equals not-Q, even as Q equals not-P ..." As he spoke, someone entered the room.

"Are you leaving us?" It was a slave. In fact, it was the slave who had run into the temple to announce the departure of Aeneas. Chalmers, concentrating on his parchment, did not look up.

"Go away!" Shea hissed. It was imperative that Chalmers recite his equations precisely.

"My, my," the slave said. "And you're not even

going to say goodbye?" Something seemed familiar about the slave's lopsided grin. Then the man seemed to swell. He grew several feet in height, and he turned gold.

"Forgot about me, didn't you?" said Phoebus Apollo. "Well, I never forget a mortal who crosses me!" He pointed at the parchment and a beam of blinding light shot from his finger, incinerating the parchment in an instant. "Have a pleasant journey, mortals!"

The room wavered around them and it began to fade. So also faded the laughter of the vengeful god. Last of all, there was a rustling, crackling sound, as of a giant pair of hands crumpling a first draft to toss it into the wastebasket. Then they were off into the aether.

EPILOGUE

The kaleidoscope of colored spots whirled on, and on, and on for, it seemed, hours. Harold Shea, clutching Reed Chalmers' bony hand in his, said:

"Hey, Doc, where is this taking us? At this rate, my kid will be a grown-up young woman by the time we get back to our own space-time continuum!"

"I'm sure I had the formula correct," replied Reed Chalmers. "It included Florimel, and I double-checked it before starting the spell. But then that rascally deity Apollo wiped it out halfway through the formula. I finished as best I could from memory; but I may have misplaced an item or two. So, to answer your question, I simply do not know. We shall have to wait and see."

"Assuming we're going to land anywhere! What if the god's interference leaves us trapped between universes forever?"

"Then we shall have to compose ourselves and submit to fate with the best grace we can muster."

"Easy for you to say!" snorted Shea, never one to submit supinely to fate however overriding. "I can see myself coming home and having Belphebe say: 'Oh, darling, what a shame you weren't in time for our daughter's wedding yesterday!' ... But hey, I think we're about to land somewhere!"

The polychromatic whirl slowed, and beyond it a landscape was taking shape. As it formed up, however, it became increasingly evident that, whatever space-time continuum it formed a part of, it was not that of the neighborhood of Garaden, Ohio.

FOR COMPLETISTS: COMPLETE IN ONE VOLUME

Some concepts are too grand, too special to be confined to one book. The volumes listed below are examples of such, stories initially published in two or more volumes, collected together by Baen Books to form one unitary work.

The Fall of Atlantis
by Marion Zimmer Bradley

65615-5 • 512 pages • $5.99

The saga of an Atlantean prince. Combines *Web of Darkness* and *Web of Light*.

The Complete Compleat Enchanter
by L. Sprague de Camp & Fletcher Pratt

69809-5 • 544 pages • $5.99

Includes *all* the de Camp & Pratt Harold Shea *Unknown*-style stories of the Incompleat Enchanter and his intrepid adventures in lands of fable and story.

The Starchild Trilogy
by Frederik Pohl & Jack Williamson

65558-2 • 448 pages • $4.99

Epic, galaxy-spanning adventure, beginning with an Earth enslaved by the rigorously logical Plan of Man, and ending with the creation of a newborn intelligent star. . . .

The Compleat Bolo
by Keith Laumer

69879-6 • 320 pages • $4.99

Combines all the Laumer stories dealing with Bolos,

the ultimate weapon and the ultimate warrior in one.
Includes the Retief Bolo story.

The Devil's Day
by James Blish   *69860-5 • 320 pages • $3.95*
A bored multi-billionaire hires a master of black magic to
summon up *all* the demons in Hell and release them
upon the world for a night—but once released the infer-
nal legions have no intention of returning to Hell ...
Combines *Black Easter* and *The Day After Judgment* in
one of the scariest apocalypse stories ever written.

Wizard World
by Roger Zelazny   *72057-0 • 416 pages • $4.95*
Banished as a child from his universe of sorcery, Pol
Detson must return from Earth to defeat a master of
technology who is conquering his lost homeworld—but
will he return as a liberator or a new conqueror ...?
Combines *Changeling* and *Madwand*.

Falkenberg's Legion
by Jerry Pournelle   *72018-X • 448 pages • $4.99*
The governments of East and West have created a tyran-
nical world order that will not rule the stars— because of
John Christian Falkenberg, a military genius who will not
permit mankind to be cast into eternal bondage....
Combines *The Mercenary* and *West of Honor*, two of the
cornerstones of Pournelle's future history.

The Deed of Paksenarrion
by Elizabeth Moon   *72104-6 • 1,040 pages • $15.00*
The brilliant saga of grittily realistic fantasy. Combines
Sheepfarmer's Daughter, *Divided Allegiance*, and *Oath
of Gold* into one BIG trade paperback.

Across Realtime
by Vernor Vinge   *72098-8 • 560 pages • $5.99*

The ultimate defense against *all* weapons leads to the
ultimate tyranny—but also leads to a way to escape into
the future, where the Earth is inexplicably deserted....
Combines *The Peace War, Marooned in Realtime* and
"The Ungoverned."

FALLEN ANGELS

Two refugees from one of the last remaining orbital space stations are trapped on the North American icecap, and only science fiction fans can rescue them! Here's an excerpt from *Fallen Angels*, the bestselling new novel by Larry Niven, Jerry Pournelle, and Michael Flynn.

*   *   *

She opened the door on the first knock and stood out of the way. The wind was whipping the ground snow in swirling circles. Some of it blew in the door as Bob entered. She slammed the door behind him. The snow on the floor decided to wait a while before melting. "Okay. You're here," she snapped. "There's no fire and no place to sit. The bed's the only warm place and you know it. I didn't know you were this hard up. And, by the way, I don't have any company, thanks for asking." If Bob couldn't figure out from that speech that she was pissed, he'd never win the prize as Mr. Perception.

"I am that hard up," he said, moving closer. "Let's get it on."

"Say what?" Bob had never been one for subtle technique, but this was pushing it. She tried to step back but his hands gripped her arms. They were cold as ice, even through the housecoat. "Bob!" He pulled her to him and buried his face in her hair.

"It's not what you think," he whispered. "We don't have time for this, worse luck."

"Bob!"

"No, just bear with me. Let's go to your bedroom. I don't want you to freeze."

He led her to the back of the house and she slid under the covers without inviting him in. He lay on top, still wearing his thick leather coat. Whatever he had in mind, she realized, it wasn't sex. Not with her housecoat, the comforter and his greatcoat playing chaperone.

He kissed her hard and was whispering hoarsely in her ear before she had a chance to react. "Angels down. A scoopship. It crashed."

"Angels?" Was he crazy?

He kissed her neck. "Not so loud. I don't think the 'danes are listening, but why take chances? Angels. Spacemen. *Peace* and *Freedom*."

She'd been away too long. She'd never heard spacemen called *Angels*. And— "Crashed?" She kept it to a whisper. "Where?"

"Just over the border in North Dakota. Near Mapleton."

"Great Ghu, Bob. That's on the Ice!"

He whispered, "Yeah. But they're not too far in."

"How do you know about it?"

He snuggled closer and kissed her on the neck again. Maybe sex made a great cover for his visit, but she didn't think he had to lay it on so thick. "We know."

"We?"

"The Worldcon's in Minneapolis-St. Paul this year—"

The World Science Fiction Convention. "I got the invitation, but I didn't dare go. If anyone saw me—"

"—And it was just getting started when the call came down from *Freedom*. Sherrine, they couldn't have picked a better time or place to crash their scoopship. That's why I came to you. Your grandparents live near the crash site."

She wondered if there was a good time for crashing scoopships. "So?"

"We're going to rescue them."

"We? Who's we?"

"The Con Committee, some of the fans—"

"But why tell me, Bob? I'm fafiated. It's been years since I've dared associate with fen."

Too many years, she thought. She had discovered science fiction in childhood, at her neighborhood branch library. She still remembered that first book: *Star Man's Son*, by Andre Norton. Fors had been persecuted because he was different; but he nurtured a secret, a mutant power. Just the sort of hero to appeal to an ugly-duckling little girl who would not act like other little girls.

SF had opened a whole new world to her. A galaxy, a

universe of new worlds. While the other little girls had played with Barbie dolls, Sherrine played with Lummox and Poddy and Arkady and Susan Calvin. While they went to the malls, she went to Trantor and the Witch World. While they wondered what Look was In, she wondered about resource depletion and nuclear war and genetic engineering. Escape literature, they called it. She missed it terribly.

"There is always one moment in childhood," Graham Greene had written in *The Power and the Glory*, "when the door opens and lets the future in." For some people, that door never closed. She thought that Peter Pan had had the right idea all along.

"Why tell *you*? Sherrine, we want you with us. Your grandparents live near the crash site. They've got all sorts of gear we can borrow for the rescue."

"Me?" A tiny trickle of electric current ran up her spine. But . . . *Nah.* "Bob, I don't dare. If my bosses thought I was associating with fen, I'd lose my job."

He grinned. "Yeah. Me, too." And she saw that he had never considered that she might not go.

'Tis a Proud and Lonely Thing to Be a Fan, they used to say, laughing. It had become a *very* lonely thing. The Establishment had always been hard on science fiction. The government-funded Arts Councils would pass out tax money to write obscure poetry for "little" magazines, but not to write speculative fiction. "Sci-fi isn't literature." *That* wasn't censorship.

Perversely, people went on buying science fiction without grants. Writers even got rich without government funding. *They couldn't kill us that way!*

Then the Luddites and the Greens had come to power. She had watched science fiction books slowly disappear from the library shelves, beginning with the children's departments. (That wasn't censorship either. Libraries couldn't buy *every* book, now could they? So they bought "realistic" children's books funded by the National Endowment for the Arts, books about death and divorce, and really important things like being overweight or fitting in with the right school crowd.)

Then came paper shortages, and paper allocations. The science fiction sections in the chain stores grew smaller. ("You can't expect us to stock books that aren't selling." And they can't sell if you don't stock them.)

Fantasy wasn't hurt so bad. Fantasy was about wizards

and elves, and being kind to the Earth, and harmony with nature, all things the Greens loved. But science fiction was about science.

Science fiction wasn't exactly outlawed. There was still Freedom of Speech; still a Bill of Rights, even if it wasn't taught much in the schools—even if most kids graduated unable to read well enough to understand it. But a person could get into a lot of unofficial trouble for reading SF or for associating with known fen. She could lose her job, say. Not through government persecution—of course not—but because of "reduction in work force" or "poor job performance" or "uncooperative attitude" or "politically incorrect" or a hundred other phrases. And if the neighbors shunned her, and tradesmen wouldn't deal with her, and stores wouldn't give her credit, who could blame them? Science fiction involved science; and science was a conspiracy to pollute the environment, "to bring back technology."

Damn right! she thought savagely. We do conspire to bring back technology. Some of us are crazy enough to think that there are alternatives to freezing in the dark. *And some of us are even crazy enough to try to rescue marooned spacemen before they freeze, or disappear into protective custody.*

Which could be dangerous. The government might declare you mentally ill, and help you.

She shuddered at that thought. She pushed and rolled Bob aside. She sat up and pulled the comforter up tight around herself. "Do you know what it was that attracted me to science fiction?"

He raised himself on one elbow, blinked at her change of subject, and looked quickly around the room, as if suspecting bugs. "No, what?"

"Not Fandom. I was reading the true quill long before I knew about Fandom and cons and such. No, it was the feeling of hope."

"Hope?"

"Even in the most depressing dystopia, there's still the notion that the future is something we build. It doesn't just happen. You can't predict the future, but you can invent it. Build it. That is a hopeful idea, even when the building collapses."

Bob was silent for a moment. Then he nodded. "Yeah. Nobody's building the future anymore. 'We live in an Age of Limited Choices.'" He quoted the government line without cracking a smile. "Hell, you don't *take* choices off a list. You *make* choices and *add* them to the list. Speaking of which, have you made your choice?"

That electric tickle . . . "Are they even alive?"

"So far. I understand it was some kind of miracle that they landed at all. They're unconscious, but not hurt bad. They're hooked up to some sort of magical medical widgets and the Angels overhead are monitoring. But if we don't get them out soon, they'll freeze to death."

She bit her lip. "And you think we can reach them in time?"

Bob shrugged.

"You want me to risk my life on the Ice, defy the government and probably lose my job in a crazy, amateur effort to rescue two spacemen who might easily be dead by the time we reach them."

He scratched his beard. "Is that quixotic, or what?"

"Quixotic. Give me four minutes."

PRAISE FOR
LOIS MCMASTER BUJOLD

What the critics say:

The Warrior's Apprentice: "Now here's a fun romp through the spaceways—not so much a space opera as space ballet.... it has all the 'right stuff.' A lot of thought and thoughtfulness stand behind the all-too-human characters. Enjoy this one, and look forward to the next."   —Dean Lambe, *SF Reviews*

"The pace is breathless, the characterization thoughtful and emotionally powerful, and the author's narrative technique and command of language compelling. Highly recommended."   —*Booklist*

Brothers in Arms: "... she gives it a geniune depth of character, while reveling in the wild turnings of her tale.... Bujold is as audacious as her favorite hero, and as brilliantly (if sneakily) successful."   —*Locus*

"Miles Vorkosigan is such a great character that I'll read anything Lois wants to write about him.... a book to re-read on cold rainy days." —Robert Coulson, *Comics Buyer's Guide*

Borders of Infinity: "Bujold's series hero Miles Vorkosigan may be a lord by birth and an admiral by rank, but a bone disease that has left him hobbled and in frequent pain has sensitized him to the suffering of outcasts in his very hierarchical era.... Playing off Miles's reserve and cleverness, Bujold draws outrageous and outlandish foils to color her high-minded adventures."   —*Publishers Weekly*

Falling Free: "In *Falling Free* Lois McMaster Bujold has written her fourth straight superb novel.... How to break down a talent like Bujold's into analyzable components? Best not to try. Best to say 'Read, or you will be missing something extraordinary.' " —Roland Green, *Chicago Sun-Times*

The Vor Game: "The chronicles of Miles Vorkosigan are far too witty to be literary junk food, but they rouse the kind of craving that makes popcorn magically vanish during a double feature."   —Faren Miller, *Locus*

MORE PRAISE FOR
LOIS MCMASTER BUJOLD

What the readers say:

"My copy of *Shards of Honor* is falling apart I've reread it so often.... I'll read whatever you write. You've certainly proved yourself a grand storyteller."
—Liesl Kolbe, Colorado Springs, CO

"I experience the stories of Miles Vorkosigan as almost viscerally uplifting.... But certainly, even the weightiest theme would have less impact than a cinder on snow were it not for a rousing good story, and good storytelling with it. This is the second thing I want to thank you for.... I suppose if you boiled down all I've said to its simplest expression, it would be that I immensely enjoy and admire your work. I submit that, as literature, your work raises the overall level of the science fiction genre, and spiritually, your work cannot avoid positively influencing all who read it."
—Glen Stonebraker, Gaithersburg, MD

" 'The Mountains of Mourning' [in *Borders of Infinity*] was one of the best-crafted, and simply best, works I'd ever read. When I finished it, I immediately turned back to the beginning and read it again, and I can't remember the last time I did that."   —Betsy Bizot, Lisle, IL

"I can only hope that you will continue to write, so that I can continue to read (and of course buy) your books, for they make me laugh and cry and think ... rare indeed."   —Steven Knott, Major, USAF

What do you say?

Send me these books!

Shards of Honor • 72087-2 • $4.99 _____
The Warrior's Apprentice • 72066-X • $4.50 _____
Ethan of Athos • 65604-X • $4.99 _____
Falling Free • 65398-9 • $4.99 _____
Brothers in Arms • 69799-4 • $3.95 _____
Borders of Infinity • 69841-9 • $4.99 _____
The Vor Game • 72014-7 • $4.99 _____
Barrayar • 72083-X • $4.99 _____

Lois McMaster Bujold:
Only from Baen Books

If these books are not available at your local bookstore, just check your choices above, fill out this coupon and send a check or money order for the cover price to Baen Books, Dept. BA, P.O. Box 1403, Riverdale, NY 10471.

NAME: _____

ADDRESS: _____

_____

I have enclosed a check or money order in the amount of $ _____.